The Seven Beauties of Sci

○ ○ ○ ○ ○ ○ ○

THE
SEVEN BEAUTIES
OF
SCIENCE FICTION

Istvan Csicsery-Ronay, Jr.

WESLEYAN UNIVERSITY PRESS

Middletown, Connecticut

Published by
WESLEYAN UNIVERSITY PRESS
Middletown, CT 06459
www.wesleyan.edu/wespress

Printed in United States of America
ISBN for the paperback edition: 978-0-8195-7092-5

Library of Congress
Cataloging-in-Publication Data
Csicsery-Ronay, Istvan, Jr.
The seven beauties of science fiction /
Istvan Csicsery-Ronay, Jr.
p.   cm.
Includes bibliographical references and index.
ISBN 978-0-8195-6889-2 (cloth: alk. paper)
1. Science fiction—History and criticism.
2. Science fiction—Philosophy. I. Title.
PN3433.5.C75   2008
809.3'8762—dc22   2008029054

For ETTI *&* SACHA

Amor est plusquam cognitiva quam cognitio.

○

CONTENTS

PREFACE

I wanted to have a bird's eye view;
I ended up in outer space.

○

This book began with a pedagogical purpose. I had hoped to map out some ideas about the historical and philosophical aspects of science fiction (sf), and through these ideas to outline the concepts I felt were most useful for studying sf as a distinctive genre. I had hoped to do it in language that would be accessible not only to specialists, but to readers outside the academy as well. In time I understood that I was also writing it for my own small, dispersed community of literary comparatists. The great literary theorists of the twentieth century from whom I learned the most — Georg Lukács, Erich Auerbach, M. M. Bakhtin, Northrop Frye, and Edward Said — had little or nothing to say about the genre to which I had devoted most of my professional life. Thus I aspired to establish a place for sf in the historical continuum of literature and art. Consequently, my approach is somewhat Old School. In the constantly accelerating transformations of our technoscientific culture, many of my vehicles are probably already receding in the rearview mirror. Consider *Seven Beauties* then a work of steampunk criticism. I have not tried to be systematic or complete. Neither have I tried to debate, or to anticipate criticism. The main purpose of this book is to inspire better ones, not to have the last word.

My greatest challenge has been to design arguments that will account for both refined artistic examples of sf and the popular commodity forms of "sci-fi." Theories concerned with the former tend to treat popular forms with contempt. Populist theories tend to ignore or discount the most artistically and intellectually interesting works: sf's contributions to elite culture. I have tried to formulate categories that will account for sf in all its manifestations. My goal is to understand *science fictionality* as a way of thinking about the world, made concrete in many different media and styles, rather than as a particular market niche or genre category. This book is only the first step in that project, which still requires close study of sf in film, television, visual art, music, and new digital media. Although the Seven Beauties appear in many different forms, they are attractors of all forms of science fiction.

My title alludes to a revered medieval Persian poem. The *Haft Paykar* (Seven beauties), a mystical epic by the twelfth-century Azeri poet, Nizami, tells of the legendary King Bahram Gur's discovery of a secret room in his palace, in which he finds the portraits of seven beautiful princesses. He falls in love with each of them, sets out to find them in the seven main regions of the known earth, marries them, and builds a palace with seven domes for them, ensconcing each in her own hall. Each of the princesses represents a different cosmic principle. He visits each of them for a night, during which they tell him a rich allegorical tale of mystical love and moral enlightenment.

So is my title meant to evoke the image of a fantastic edifice with seven halls. Each is rich and intriguing in its own right, and each contains the others. I am not entirely sure how my "beauties" should be understood in rationalistic terms. They are perhaps *cognitive attractions,* intellectual gravitational fields that draw our attention. They are perhaps *mental schemes,* through which we organize our thinking. They are perhaps *tools for thought,* so well made that we admire their design at the very moment we are using them. Whatever else they are, they compose a constellation of thoughts that sf helps us to become conscious of. Some readers will find seven an arbitrary number; others, a full set.

This book emerged out of dialogues with hundreds of students and most especially with colleagues and friends, who alerted me again and again that science fiction is more than a literary genre or a social passion. It is a way of organizing the mind to include the contemporary world. There is much to criticize in a genre that is dominated by entertainment industries and popular tastes. But there is also much to care about. SF is an art that delights in vision, intelligence, and the infinite possibilities of change. It calls into question all verities, except curiosity and play.

o o o o o o o

Many friends and colleagues inspired and supported this work. I thank especially David Porush, Katherine Hayles, Scott Bukatman, Brooks Landon, David Seed, Robert Philmus, and my colleagues in the English department of DePauw University. My coeditors at *Science Fiction Studies*— Arthur Evans, Joan Gordon, Veronica Hollinger, Rob Latham, and Carol McGuirk — taught me that sf is not only an object of study, but an occasion for love, care, and inspiration. Most of all, I am grateful to my wife, Etti, and my son, Sacha, for understanding what this book was truly all about.

PREFACE

I also thank DePauw University and the National Endowment for the Humanities for fellowships to pursue this work. The chapter "Fifth Beauty" was originally published in somewhat different form in *Science Fiction Studies* 29, no. 3 (March 2002); a shorter version of the chapter "Sixth Beauty" appeared in *métal et chair/flesh and metal* 4 (February 2002).

INTRODUCTION

Science Fiction and This Moment

○ ○ ○ ○ ○ ○ ○

"These are the days of lasers in the jungle."[1] SF has emerged as a pervasive genre of literature — and of film, video, comics, computer graphics and games — in the postindustrial North. Indeed, it elicits intense interest in the rest of the world. It is not so much that sf has grown into this position, as the reverse: the world has grown into sf. Gertrude Stein once pronounced the United States the oldest country on earth, because it was the first to enter the twentieth century. By the same token, sf is one of the most venerable of living genres: it was the first to devote its imagination to the future and to the ceaseless revolutions of knowledge and desire that attend the application of scientific and technical knowledge to social life.

From its roots, whether we trace them to Lucian, Swift, Voltaire, Mary Shelley, or Hugo Gernsback, sf has been a genre of fantastic entertainment. It has produced many works of intellectual and political sophistication, side by side with countless ephemeral confections. Unlike most popular genres, it has also been critically self-aware. The fiction has inspired a steady production of commentary about what distinguishes it from other modes of expression. This body of critical work is rich in social diversity, and unparalleled in its allegiance to reimagining the world with a passion that has at times resembled the commitment to a political movement.[2]

The once-regnant view that sf can't help but be vulgar and artistically shallow is fading. As the world undergoes daily transformations via the development of technoscience in every imaginable aspect of life, (and, more important, as people become aware of these transformations) sf has come to be seen as an essential mode of imagining the horizons of possibility. However much sf texts vary in artistic quality, intellectual sophistication, and their capacity to give pleasure, they share a mass social energy, a desire to imagine a collective future for the human species and the world.

In the past forty years, not only have sf artists produced more artistically ambitious works than in the previous hundred, but works of criticism have

1

established the foundations for definition and self-examination characteristic of mature artistic movements. Major critical works — from Darko Suvin's *Metamorphoses of Science Fiction* (1979) to Scott Bukatman's *Terminal Identity* (1993), journals of academic scholarship and criticism (*Foundation, Extrapolation, Science Fiction Studies, The New York Review of Science Fiction*), and the *Encyclopedia of Science Fiction*'s second edition, which gave the first comprehensive overview of the history of the genre for scholars — have provided tools for thinking about the genre and its implications in sophisticated philosophical and historical terms.

At this moment, a strikingly high proportion of films, commercial art, popular music, video and computer games, and nongenre fiction are overtly sf or contain elements of it. This widespread normalization of what is essentially a style of estrangement and dislocation has stimulated the development of science-fictional habits of mind, so that we no longer treat sf as purely a genre-engine producing formulaic effects, but rather as a kind of awareness we might call *science-fictionality*, a mode of response that frames and tests experiences as if they were aspects of a work of science fiction. It is one mode of response among many others, and it influences people's actions to different degrees. Some are inspired to create, as H. G. Wells's novel *The World Set Free* inspired Leo Szilárd to imagine nuclear fission,[3] or as William Gibson's depiction of the cyberspace matrix and virtual reality in *Neuromancer* stimulated countless computer programmers.[4] Some are drawn, in games and in life, to playing out roles they identify with in sf texts. Most people merely bracket difficult-to-process, incongruous moments of technology's intersection with everyday life as science-fictional moments.

Increasingly, this sense of technosocial aspiration meshing with the limits and desires of concrete social life, often involving violent collisions of hard techniques with human and natural complexity, is the appropriate response to contemporary reality. Consider the daily news: the postmodern hecatomb of the World Trade Center; Chernobyl's lost villages and mutant flora; CGI pop stars; genocide under surveillance satellites; the cloning of farm animals; Internet pornography raining down in microwaves; helicopter gunships deployed against stone-throwing crowds; GM pollen drifting toward the calyces of natural plants; Artificial Life; global social movements (and even nations) without territories; the ability to alter one's physical gender; the evaporation of the North Pole. It is sf that has most assiduously imagined and explored such collisions and transitions. It is from sf's thesaurus of images that we draw many of our metaphors and models for understanding our technologized world, and it is as sf that many of our impressions of technology-aided desire and technology-riven anxiety are processed back into works of the imagination. It is impossible to map the extent to which the perception of contemporary reality requires and encourages science-fictional orientations.

The Gaps of Science Fiction

The genre of sf has been notoriously difficult to define; how much more so a mode of thought like science-fictionality, which is neither a belief nor a model, but rather a mood or attitude, a way of entertaining incongruous experiences, in which judgment is suspended, as if we were witnessing the transformations happening to, and occurring in, us. Nonetheless, let us make a tentative approach. The attitude of science-fictionality is characterized by two linked forms of hesitation, a pair of gaps. One gap extends between the belief that certain ideas and images of technoscientific transformations of the world can be entertained, and the rational recognition that they may be *realized,* with ramifications for social life. This gap lies between the conceivability of future transformations and the possibility of their actualization. The other gap lies between belief in the immanent possibility (perhaps even the inexorability) of those transformations, and reflection about their possible ethical, social, and spiritual consequences. This gap stretches between conceiving of the plausibility of historically unforeseeable innovations in human experience (*novums*)[5] and their broader ethical and social-cultural implications and resonances. SF thus involves two forms of hesitation: a historical-logical one (how plausible is the conceivable novum?) and an ethical one (how good/bad/ altogether alien are the transformations that would issue from the novum?). These gaps compose the black box in which technoscientific conceptions, ostensibly unmediated by social and ethical contingencies, are transformed into a rational recognition of their possible realization and implications. The resulting fictions may be credible projections of present trends or fantastic images of imagined impossibilities. Usually, they are amalgams of both.

SF embeds scientific-technical concepts in the broad sphere of human interests and actions, explaining them, mythologizing them, and explicitly attributing social value to them. This embedding may take many literary forms, from the exhumation of dead mythologies, pseudomimetic extrapolation, and satirical subversion, to utopian transformation and secularized apocalypse. It is an inherently, and radically, future-oriented process. Imaginary worlds of sf are pretended resolutions of dilemmas insoluble and often barely perceived in the present. The exact ontological status of sf worlds is suspended in anticipation. Unlike historical fiction (of which sf is a direct heir), where a less intense suspense operates because the outcome of the past is still in the process of being completed in the present's partisan conflicts, sf is suspended because all the relevant information about the future is never available. Because future developments influence revisions of the past, sf's black box also involves the past, in the hesitation that comes in anticipating the complete revision of origins. A past that is not yet known is a form of the future. So too is a present unanticipated by the past. Further, because sf is concerned mainly with the role of science and technology in defining human cultural value, there can be as many kinds of sf as there are theories of technoscientific culture. This conception of sf concerns not just the actual historical production of the commercial genre known as Science Fiction, but the range of possible science fictions, many of which have not been realized.

This range is why sf is not a genre of aesthetic entertainment only, but a complex hesitation about the relationship between imaginary conceptions and historical reality unfolding into the future. SF orients itself within a concept of history that holds that science and technology actively participate in the creation of reality, implanting human uncertainty into the natural/nonhuman world. At the same time, sf's hesitations also involve a sense of fatality about instrumental rationality's power to transform or to undermine the conditions of thought that gave rise to it. The same freedom that detaches nature from a mythology of natural necessity restores that fatality, ironically, in the irrepressible drive of human beings to transform nature continually and without transcendental limits.

SF has become a form of discourse that directly engages contemporary language and culture, and that has, in this moment, a generic interest in the intersections of technology, scientific theory, and social practice. Since the late 1960s, when it became the chosen vehicle for both technocratic and critical utopian writing, sf has experienced a steady growth in popularity, critical interest, and theoretical sophistication. It reflects and engages the technological culture that pervades modernized cultures. The irresistible expansion of communications technologies has drawn the traditional spheres of power into an ever-tightening web of instrumental rationalization. Simultaneously, the culture of information has rewritten the notions of nature and transcendence that have dominated Western societies for the past few centuries, replacing them with an as yet inchoate worldview of *artificial immanence,* in which every value that previous cultures considered transcendental or naturally given is at least theoretically capable of artificial replication or simulation, and eventual transmutation. In this sense, sf has established its own domain, linking literary, philosophical, and scientific imaginations, and subverting the cultural boundaries between them. In its narratives it produces and hyperbolizes the new sense of immanence. SF regularly employs radically new scientific concepts of material and social relations; these relations, in turn, influence our conceptions of what is imaginable or plausible. Indeed, sf is ingrained within the quotidian consciousness of people living in the postindustrial world; each day they witness the transformations of their values and material conditions in the wake of technical acceleration beyond their conceptual threshold.

So it is that, encountering problems issuing from the social implications of science, and viewing dramatic technohistorical scenes in real life, we displace them into a virtual imaginary space, an alternate present or future that we can reflect on, where we can test our delight, anxiety, or grief, or simply play, without having to renounce our momentary sense of identity, social place, and the world. We transform our experience into sf, if only for a moment.

The Seven Beauties

I believe that sf can be treated as a particular, recognizable mode of thought and art. But rather than a programlike set of exclusive rules and required devices, this mode is a constellation of diverse intellectual and emotional interests and responses that are particularly active in an age of restless technological transformation. I consider seven such categories to be the most attractive and formative of science-fictionality. These are the "seven beauties" of my title: *fictive neology, fictive novums, future history, imaginary science, the science-fictional sublime, the science-fictional grotesque,* and the *Technologiade.* Each is an aspect of sf that audiences desire from the genre.

1. *Fictive neology.* Readers of sf expect to encounter new words and other signs that indicate worlds changed from their own, just as viewers of visual sf expect special visual effects, and listeners expect special sonic effects representing new sense-perceptions and aesthetic designs. Our culture treats sf as the primary source for such symbolic indications of radical newness. The fictive neologies of sf are variations and combinations based on the actual process of lexicogenesis experienced in social life. They can appear in a great variety of forms, in diverse registers, from the prophetic to the comic. In every case, they imply linguistic-symbolic models of technological transformation, playfully suspended and seriously displaced. They engage audiences to use them as clues and triggers to construct the logic of science-fictional worlds.

2. *Fictive novums.* Similarly, sf is expected to provide imaginary models of radical transformations of human history initiated by fictive *novums.* The concept of the novum, introduced in sf studies by Darko Suvin, refers to a historically unprecedented and unpredicted "new thing" that intervenes in the routine course of social life and changes the

trajectory of history. The novum is usually a rationally explicable material phenomenon, the result of an invention or discovery, whose unexpected appearance elicits a wholesale change in the perception of reality. The very concept of history requires the notion of innovation to distinguish it from myth. Every sf text supplies fictive novums and responses to them, and thus engages the sense of real inhabitants of technorevolutionary societies that they are bombarded with real-world novums to an unprecedented degree.

3. *Future history.* Although sf need not always be set in the future, the genre is inherently future-oriented. The discovery of an alternative history, a parallel universe, or a concealed past changes the horizon of the future and the meaning of human history just as much as does an explicitly futuristic setting. SF audiences expect the genre to provide futures that are relevant to their own times. The genre consequently relies on the techniques of realism: not only the detailed decor of circumstantial realism, but cause-and-effect logic, commonsense motivation, and familiar perceptions of the object world that are the characteristic qualities of naturalistic narrative. By maintaining a sense of the integral connection between the present and the future, sf constructs micromyths of the historical process, establishing the audience's present as the future-oriented "prehistory of the future." SF is treated as the culture's main repository and generator of imaginable (albeit often extravagantly playful) future horizons.

4. *Imaginary science.* SF is the main artistic means for introducing technoscientific ideas and events among the value-bearing stories and metaphors of social life. And yet, precisely because a gap exists between the fundamentally rationalistic, logocentric universe of scientific discourse and the diffuse culture of social myths and alternative rationalities, sf texts are expected to involve playful deviations from known scientific thought. The scientific content of sf, even though generally based on the scientifically plausible knowledge of its day, is always fabulous. SF's science is transformed to fit the parameters of cultural myth and aesthetic play. In sf we "take some persistent fiction in contemporary human life, and we turn it into science."[6] We make science of our metaphors.

5. *Science-fictional sublime.* Of all contemporary genres, sf is the one most expected to evoke the experience of the sublime. The subject matter of sf necessarily involves the elements of the classical Kantian sublime: the sense of temporal and spatial infinitude of the *mathematical*, and the sense of overwhelming physical power of the *dynamic sub-*

lime. Beyond this, it also invokes the historical mutation that David E. Nye has named the *American technological sublime:* the sense of access to, and control of, the powers of nature that typified the American populace's responses to the monumental engineering projects of the nineteenth century.[7] The sense of the sublime most characteristic of post–World War II sf is the *technoscientific sublime,* which entails a sense of awe and dread in response to human technological projects that exceed the power of their human creators.

6. *Science-fictional grotesque.* The technoscientific grotesque is the inversion, and frequent concomitant, of the technosublime. It represents the collapse of ontological categories that reason has considered essentially distinct, creating a spectacle of impossible fusions. This is the domain of monstrous aliens, interstitial beings, and anomalous physical phenomena. Where the technosublime is extensive, inducing sentiments of awe and dread in response to phenomena either created or revealed by human techniques, the grotesque is implosive, accompanied by fascination and horror at the prospect of intimate category-violating phenomena discovered by human science. Because technoscience is the guardian of the rational categorization of matter, the grotesque attacks the very rationality that made its apprehension possible. This facet, one of the most powerfully attractive of the genre, draws its reason-based irrationality increasingly from actual scientific innovations that combine phenomena previously held to be naturally distinct (such as, for example, genetic engineering, molecular computing, and Artificial Life) and the constant weakening of category boundaries that seems to menace the sense of personal identity.

7. *The Technologiade.* Although sf does not generate story-structures of its own, it transforms popular cultural materials by reorienting their concerns toward its characteristic horizon: the transformation of human societies as a result of innovations attending technoscientific projects. Audiences expect sf (a) to tell stories that will make sense of their contemporary historical experiences of technomodernization, and (b) ultimately to moralize them by drawing them back into the axiological structures of their familiar cultures or subcultures. These miniature myth-structures simultaneously dislocate the audience's orientation toward its familiar reality, and link the fictive predicament — radically new in its objective conditions — to conventional story-structures that recontain the radical newness. They act as historically ambivalent and complex fables of technohistory.

Although any story-form can be adapted to science-fictional uses, certain literary tale-structures are especially favored by the genre: the space opera, the modern adventure tale, the Gothic, and the utopia. These tale-forms reveal a profound kinship; each gives shape to certain historical and philosophical attitudes toward human control over nature. Each kind of tale has a distinct genealogy of its own, and each produces a rich variety of ironic inversions and formal deformations. To sf, they have offered established narrative forms for articulating dramatic relationship between technology and social life. In sf their shared qualities converge.

The narratives of the modern adventure cluster were closely allied with the popular discourse of colonial expansion and imperialism, a discourse they drew from and influenced in their turn. SF's characteristic mutations of the adventure forms reflect the discourse of a transnational global regime of technoscientific rationalization that followed the collapse of the European imperialist project. SF narrative accordingly has become the leading mediating institution for the utopian construction of technoscientific Empire. And for resistance to it.

The Seven Beauties are not classically aesthetic qualities that inspire contemplation and admiration for their harmony and balance. They are not pure. They are riven, indecisive, chaotic, sometimes corrupt, always ludic. They are beauties of a mind incapable of making itself up. Although their themes are the central ones of our age — the relationships between knowledge and ethics, technology and identity, material reality and the imagination — very few sf writers have taxed their spirits to create arresting, self-risking fables for their worlds. SF is primarily an art of the marketplace, willing to fold sublime moments into cheap, received formulas that are proven sellers. SF almost always asks its readers to be both more expansive and more limited than they already are. As its name implies, science fiction is an oxymoron. It invokes and delivers dichotomies, insoluble dilemmas, deceptive solutions. It makes manifest worlds upon worlds that are too contradictory to exist.

Within sf's generic universe of discourse, each of the beauties implies all the others. New signs signify new things. New things change the direction of history, and lead to new science. New discoveries and inventions inspire sublime and grotesque responses. And all these movements coalesce in fables of imaginary resolution. The sequence and hierarchy of these domains may be imagined in any order. New technoscience may invent new things, which require new names, and initiate new historical conditions. New things and the transformed knowledge that attends them require new perceptions and world-hypotheses; these perceptions may be sublime or grotesque, or each in turn. Finally, these moves must be comprehended, and narrated, intelligibly, without violating their energy. Many of the most memorable works of the genre display all these qualities working in impressive balance. But not all sf manifests all of them to the same degree. It is doubtless my literary bias to believe it is much more common for all the beauties to complement one another in literary sf than in film or other spectacular forms. Indeed, the power of visual representations of the sublime and the grotesque, and of neological objects, is so great that it can easily eclipse matters that demand intellectual reflection, such as fictive history and imaginary science.

Individual texts and styles can be distinguished by the beauties they emphasize and underplay, especially in the interesting borderlands of the genre. The works of J. G. Ballard and David Cronenberg, for example, eschew fictive neology, history, and science, while emphasizing the novum, the grotesque, and the sublime. In Kim Stanley Robinson's work, fictive history and science play central roles, while neology and the technoscientific sublime and grotesque play minor ones. Beyond the genre, narrowly defined, sf-inflected texts may be characterized by any combination. In life, the social experiences upon which these matters are based tend to be articulated, and to emerge into awareness, discreetly. It is one of the cultural tasks of sf to draw them into an aesthetic constellation. This is also its primary pleasure.

On Method

This book is not intended to be a systematic exposition of a theory of sf, even less a history. I have been able to work outside a specific theoretical model of criticism mainly because important work has already been done to establish a rich critical discourse about the genre. Darko Suvin, Fredric Jameson, Peter Fitting, Marc Angenot, and Carl Freedman, among others have established a major body of Marxist sf criticism connecting sf with ideology-critique and utopian theory. Samuel R. Delany and Damien Broderick have written fundamental texts for semiological and postmodernist approaches. Joanna Russ, Veronica Hollinger, Jenny Wolmark, Brian Attebery, Wendy Pearson, and others have constructed a formidable apparatus for feminist and queer sf criticism; DeWitt Douglas Kilgore, Daniel Bernardi, Greg Tate, and Kodwe Eshun have done the same for Afrofuturism. Mark Rose's study of the genre in terms of archetypes and romance, *Alien Encounters;* Carl Malmgren's structuralist criticism, *Worlds Apart;* and Gary K. Wolfe's study of sf's iconography, *The Known and the Unknown,* have established terms for studying the genre's narrative psychology. Scott Bukatman's, Vivian Sobchack's and Brooks Landon's work on sf film has established the lines of a rich and varied scholarship about sf in spectacular media. And many of the most original categories have appeared in the critical reviews of Gary Wolfe and John Clute, and the meditations of writer-theorists, such as Stanisław Lem, Joanna Russ, Ursula K. Le Guin, and Bruce Sterling.[8]

In this book, I shall approach sf on the one hand as a product of the convergence of social-historical forces that has led to the current global hegemony of technoscience, and consequently as an institution of ideological expression; on the other, as a ludic framework, a wide-ranging culture of game and play, in which that hegemony is entertained, absorbed, and resisted. SF is both an institution of mediation for a real historical moment, and also a free space for deconstructing those values. As a free space, it invites many different constituencies with varied interests, and inspires a great variety of styles. It imagines a universe of discourse held together by its constantly expanding megatext of neologies, speculations, and counterfactuals. In this book, I have tried to accommodate this identity and variety through a method of constellation, by linking and meditating on ideas from different disciplines and national traditions, without attempting to define a single underlying mechanism of production. I hope that most readers will take *The Seven Beauties of Science Fiction* as I intended it: a map of suggestions, made necessarily from a great distance, of possible paths that are still open to travel.

Texts and Media

Sf criticism and ancillary sf culture has reached a point where they have many film and literary texts that they consider canonical, either for the genre as a whole or for a particular current of culture and theory. As a result, much has been written about certain texts, styles, artists, and themes — *Alien, Blade Runner, Star Trek, Neuromancer, Solaris,* H. G. Wells, Jules Verne, Philip K. Dick, Ursula K. Le Guin, Octavia Butler, cyberpunk, anime, race, and gender, for example — while very little, indeed in some cases nothing, has been published on other important works and writers. I have had to decide whether to remain with texts that are familiar to most readers of sf, or to address other texts that deserve a wider audience. The first approach could easily lead to banality; the second, to obscurity. I had hoped originally to create a balance, but I now know that it is most difficult to make unfamiliar theoretical claims using unfamiliar texts as illustrative supports. So I too shall gather the usual suspects, and many of the discussions will revisit works that are justifiably regarded as canonical.

This dilemma I felt especially with regard to non–Anglo-Saxon sf. Very rarely have sf works produced in languages other than English attained popularity among the global sf audience, and received proper critical commentary.

For every such work as the Strugatsky brothers' *Roadside Picnic*, Stanisław Lem's *Solaris*, and Mamoru Oshii's *The Ghost in the Shell*, there are dozens, if not hundreds, of non-Anglo works of sf that deserve attention—both for their intrinsic merits, and as examples of national styles that could modify our dominant views about the genre. And yet, in this respect as well I have chosen to emphasize the familiar over the unfamiliar, and consequently the Anglo-Saxon tradition over others. SF is undeniably a predominantly Anglo-American genre, and its current influence reflects the cultural power of U.S. hyper-modernism and the technoscientific ideology that undergirds its cultural hegemony. Other national traditions of scientific fantasy have existed parallel to the Anglo-Saxon mainline, and they should be included in an overview of the genre, not as evolutionary exceptions or atavisms, but as legitimate cultural expressions and, indeed, as possible alternate lines along which the genre may develop in the future. However, that must wait for another book.

Finally, a study of science-fictionality should not restrict itself to one medium only. Most sf criticism has emphasized written sf. This emphasis is understandable; until recently the most significant works of the genre were in literary form, and the critical apparatus for studying literature has been refined over centuries. Nonetheless, it is clear that the same critical approaches cannot be used unreflectively to study other media, such as film. The technical ways with which film conveys its meanings, and the cognitive and aesthetic engagements that inexorably attend cinematic perception, require that sf theory accommodate sf film's overwhelming emphasis on perception at the expense of reflection. Such accommodation is vital, considering the increasing weight of sf film and television in establishing the dominant cultural conceptions of what sf is.[9] And this re-visioning will certainly hold true for computer games, as well. Although that medium is only emerging, and there has been as yet little reflection on the aesthetic and cognitive aspects of constructing sf in it, it is abundantly clear that the genre is a privileged source of its narratives and effects. Computer games are already having a profound influence on the ideas of literary and cinematic sf artists, and computer-generated sf film associated with game design and aesthetics will certainly become a major art form in the near future.

Perhaps the most orphaned of all sf media is music. Little has appeared in print discussing the relationship between music and sf, a connection that is much richer than may at first appear. Rock and electronic music, film soundtracks, even operas have established a vocabulary of sounds that establish a range of conventional—and sometimes innovative—emotional responses characteristic of sf *sensations* parallel to the explicitly narrative and spectacular media. Music is central to digital culture. New interpretations of its history, theories of its apparatus, critical reflection on its response to and effects on social life have generated poetic and sophisticated reflections that are clearly shaped by science-fictional figures.[10] These reflections, too, should eventually be factored into a comprehensive idea of what makes sf a distinctive mode of art and thought.

The SEVEN BEAUTIES *of* SCIENCE FICTION

FIRST BEAUTY

Fictive Neology

○ ○ ○ ○ ○ ○ ○

Signa Novi. Readers of sf anticipate words and sentences that refer to changed or alien worlds. All fantastic genres make some use of fictive neology. Heroic fantasy invents words to evoke the archaic origins of its worlds. Phantasmagoric satire delights in wordplay that simultaneously masks and insinuates the objects of its derision. Gothic and supernatural tales invoke esoteric and folkloric terms to create the sense of a concealed or forgotten past. SF is distinct, in that its fictive neologies connote newness and innovation vis-à-vis the historical present of the reader's culture. They are fictive *signa novi*, signs of the new. In the real world, any design or fashion motif whose purpose is to refer to a "New Thing," whose meaning depends on its newness, is a sign of newness — from the girder-skeleton of the Eiffel Tower to the fins of a 1956 Eldorado, from a new slang phrase to a new electronic timbre. The *signum novi* does not signify any particular objective historical content. It is a dialectical trope that implies a conception, at once aesthetic and cognitive, of the difference between the historically familiar and the as-yet imaginary designs and social relations that are supposedly just emerging.

Fictive neologies have a paradoxical function. They conjure up a sense of the inevitability of a new thing, or of a new discourse in which the neologism is embedded. If there is a word for it, it must already exist. And so the future must also already exist. The more convincing it is in creating an illusion of projected historical reality, the more successful the neology. Yet fictive neology also displays that it is fiction. Because the future cannot exist yet, we know that the neology is a playful, poetic conjuring device, suggesting that any imaginable future is always a poetic construction.

Every future inevitably becomes obsolete. A fictive date set in the reader's future, the simplest of all imaginary neosemes, is always superseded by the real historical experience of the calendar: 1984 becomes 1985; 2001 becomes 2002. Every such superannuation reinforces readers' suspension of disbelief about the prospective reality of any futuristic date. SF readers know that different stories depict different conditions for identical time-space niches of the future. Writers sometimes try to link their concepts with those of other works, but even readers of such "shared-universe" tales expect each artist to create at least a few signs that indicate a future never seen outside those works before.

Neology in the Real World

In everyday language, neologies have many functions. They may name phenomena that until recently had no names — things and practices that have been newly discovered, invented, or imagined by a community. Or, they may be less denotative than rhetorical and poetic, drawing attention to a group's style of discourse.

The coining of new words is both an aesthetic and a practical matter. Each new word disrupts the previous flow of language. Roman Jakobson proposed a model for distinguishing the discourse of functional communication from language that is aesthetically charged. In the former, words evaporate as soon as a message is understood; in the latter, the words remain in play in memory and consciousness, even after the practical message has ceased to be pertinent.[1] Neologies call attention to themselves; they are artful. They also call attention to the linguistic power of their users. A new word is a new source of power, which may originate from artistic invention, technical gnosis, or from the user's privileged access to new things at the leading edge of history.

Neologogenesis, the production of new words, is a vital process in all living languages. Grammars tolerate few changes over time, so languages usually accommodate social and cultural changes through new vocabulary and usage. This accommodation is especially true when communities establish connections with foreign cultures or undergo technoscientific transformations. Neology is consequently of central importance for modernizing societies, whose languages must be dynamic and flexible enough to permit new customs, concepts, and objects to become part of collective experience. If they are not so by tradition, they are made to be so.[2]

Scientific-technological development in particular creates its own neologistic momentum. Before the nineteenth century, the provinciality of German and other Central European languages, for example, forced their scientists and philosophers to write most of their works in French and Latin. Eventually, reforms were instituted for bringing them "up to date," and capable of articulating whatever a modern scientific Englishman or Frenchman might know. These reforms were emulated throughout Europe and Asia, wherever the nationalist intelligentsia wished to join the Club of Modern Nations.[3] Much of this renovation was devoted to the translation of foreign terms, the accommodation of loan words within native morphemic structures, and the invention of new words from native roots. This last goal was a particular ambition of modernizing nationalists, for whom a national language enriched with new words could become a vehicle for political consciousness-raising.

Languages have an inherent potential for development through their interaction with the discourses of other cultures and their own internal elaboration. Whether the potential is realized or not is largely a matter of the politics of culture. If a community of speakers cannot agree that the language should be capable of modern intercultural expression, then that role will be filled by another language.[4] The dominant cultures of scientific modernity — Britain, France, Germany, the United States, Japan, and Russia — are endowed with languages that employ many different kinds of lexicogenesis concurrently, from lists generated by Academies to spontaneous informal neology and the easy assimilation of loanwords. It is not an accident that theirs have also been the main languages of sf. Chinese, Spanish, Portuguese, Turkish, and other languages of ascending technopolitical influence, are endowed with a similar flexibility for the development of popular technoscientific discourse, and consequently of sf. Others, like Arabic and Persian, may be constrained by a conservative cultural loyalty to their classical stratum; such loyalty limits the possibilities of sf.[5]

Technolects, Social Exchange, and Slang

In social life, most neologisms are invented and introduced in three areas of discourse: scientific technolects, the language of institutions and markets, and slang. Technical neologisms name concepts and objects brought under careful, systematic organization. Like all languages that emulate legal discourse, technical terminology strives to minimize ambiguity by constructing words that have restricted usage and convey a sense of purified reference. Its technical terms are attempts to construct words sufficiently redundant (by virtue of their likeness to similar terms, their Greek and Latin roots, their conventional system of affixes, and so forth) to be quickly understood by all competent users of scientific language, while also sufficiently narrow to name a single class of referents. They may be intended to denote something so precisely that there is no ambiguity about the referent; yet, until the word is made familiar, it carries with it a connotation of newness that may have nothing immediately to do with the qualities of the reference itself. A new scientific term often calls attention to its linguistic newness independent of the newness of the referent. Perhaps for only a very short while, and perhaps only faintly, it reorganizes discourse around itself. In short, it must be *learned,* and this terminological learning may be independent from learning about the new phenomenon it names. In its most highly developed form, such learning is the basis for nomenclature and taxonomy, where the system of terms ultimately suggests the rules for the development of further new terms. The theoretical and ideological presuppositions of taxonomic systems are usually evident for anyone who cares to examine them. (Linnaeus constructed his botanical nomenclature on the model of the patriarchal bourgeois family. Some recent emulators have proposed botanical taxonomies based on neoliberal economics.)[6]

The second major domain of neology is social exchange, especially markets and institutions, where new objects and practices are introduced into, and classified for, social life. Here, words for commodities, customs, procedures, and social innovations are generated in a variety of ways. They might be loanwords, if they are of foreign origin; they might be transposed or metaphorical terms from other practices; they might be outright inventions. Their purpose is simultaneously to make the new referent seem fresh and interesting, yet also easy to employ in everyday exchanges. While scientific neologisms connote the power of esoteric language to contain new knowledge, neologisms of exchange promise to enrich the status quo. In our age, the main sources of such neologisms are advertising and commercial discourse, whose language of newness conjures up solutions to existential problems via the commodity-names of putatively new objects.

Another important source of social-exchange neology is the language of social science. Terminology in the social sciences differs from that in the natural sciences, in that it discourages the invention of esoteric words, appropriating instead terms already in widespread use for focused, context-specific meanings.[7] Psychologists, sociologists, economists, and anthropologists often reject the monosemic ideal of natural-science terminology, in favor of terms that are concrete, familiar, and vague. Because their dominant context is general usage, such social scientific terms are easily reappropriated by usage. Ego, incentive, aggression, culture, ethnicity, behavior, attitude, role, tribe, minority — all have been important concepts in the social sciences, and have returned to general usage with new connotations gained from their terminological use. Such technical terms are particularly sensitive to changes in social-political attitudes that produce semantic shifts.

The third domain of neologogenesis is subcultural appropriation, the restless invention of new terms for objects and practices that already have familiar, normal names. Through metaphorical transfer, apocope, combination, and similar tactics, these referents are converted into slang or creolized terms that signify the countercultural power of *détournement,* wresting control of normal language and using it for a group's own purposes — the linguistic equivalent of William Gibson's famous phrase in *Neuromancer:* "the street finds its own uses for things." Such terms imply a code, accessible only to initiates, that subverts the accepted meaning of things. This street-level lexicogenesis is the shadow of technoscientific discourse, whose esotericism it imitates while substituting the quite unscientific values of constant creative shape-shifting and the restless self-disguise of liminal speakers.

None of these domains is isolated from the others. At different times, they draw on one another's resources, in tune with different social alignments. All scientific naming, for example, strives to be systematic, but the basis of the system is sensitive to social-cultural power. Planetary naming for our solar system, to take one example, continues to be based on classical mythology and literature. The moons of Neptune are, by convention, named after nymphs and deities taken from Greek and Roman mythology. The moons of Saturn are named for Titans; the moons of Jupiter for Jovian amours. A most peculiar convention has developed around Uranus, whose satellites are all, with one exception, named for Shakespearean characters, a practice begun by William Herschel in 1787 with Titania and Oberon. The names of the so-called *icy moons* are drawn almost exclusively from *The Tempest;* they now include Miranda, Ariel, and the recently discovered Caliban, Sycorax, Prospero, and Setebos. (The one exception, Umbriel, is taken from Pope's *Dunciad,* making it our system's sole satirical moon.)[8] This literary sourcing continues in physics with modern twists, as in the naming of the *quark* from *Finnegan's Wake,* and the even more whimsical *boojum.*[9]

As scientific work became increasingly democratic in the twentieth century, some scientific neology became emphatically playful and antielitist, borrowing its terms from popular rather than elite culture. This greater latitude has been particularly apparent in some areas of molecular biology, many of whose objects are too new to be covered by earlier conventions. Molecules are named after anything the discoverer wishes. Dozens of them are named for places (*americanin, yemenimyciin*), persons (*buckminsterfullerene, mirasorvine*) and shapes (*birdcage, dogcollarane*). The most extravagant populist nomenclature can be found in drosophila genetics. Because most of the many genes discovered in the fruit fly are identified for their phenotypic behavior, their names are treated as temporary until the discovery of deeper structural relationships mandates more systematic naming. In this way, a formidable subculture of joking taxonomy has arisen in fruit-fly biology. The naming of a *hedgehog protein* (after the spiky appearance of the particular mutation it engenders) has led to the further elaboration of the *Indian hedgehog,* the *desert hedgehog,* and inevitably, the *Sonic hedgehog* protein. (It's not over; there's also a *Tiggy-*

Winkle hedgehog.) The massive list found at Flybase, a database of fruit-fly genes maintained by a consortium of research institutions, includes *lunatic fringe, radical fringe, Tinman, ZapA* (after Frank Zappa), *Snafu, Hamlet, amontillado, sevenless, bride of sevenless, crossbronx, Deadpan, fuzzy onions, genghis khan, Godzilla, jekyll and hyde, ken and barbie, Malvolio, king tubby, klingon, out at first, pacman, roadkill, rolling stone, singles bar, vibrator, viking,* and the heroic *I'm-Not-Dead-Yet.*[10] Paleozoologists have sometimes concealed eccentric names for their dinosaurs in Latin formulas, but even this custom has become unusually slangy, as with the *Masiakasaurus knopflerensis,* named by its discoverers after guitarist Mark Knopfler, whose music accompanied them in their excavations.[11]

In a linguistically dynamic culture, where language is constantly being invented and recast in tandem with social-technological changes and cultural contacts, people become accustomed to learning new terms quickly. Such rapid acquisition has complex and varied social effects. A culture of speakers skilled in learning new words and concepts learns to anticipate linguistic newness; indeed, it may be difficult for them to distinguish between the expectation of new discourse and the expectation of material changes. This indeterminate balance is a spur to different kinds of creativity and play. Subcultures strive to keep pace with transformations in society at large by absorbing them into their alternative universes of discourse, and revaluing them. These subcultures themselves mutate under the pressures of larger social transformations, and the terms that might once have been used to establish playful and distinctive shibboleths of particular groups may attain currency across dissolving subcultural boundaries. With each transformation, political power is redistributed, dissipated, and reconsolidated. The creation of language is a source of power.

Imaginary Neosemes and Neologisms

The etymology of a science-fictional neologism reflects imaginary laws of social evolution. Some writers, like J. G. Ballard, may insist on the zero-degree plausibility of untransformed language to evoke a frozen reality. Others may use satirical, symbolizing, uncanny, or prophetic registers. In all cases, science-fictional neologisms will represent the social-evolutionary powers that dominate that fictive world's history.

Artists must consider whether their audiences will be willing to process their aesthetic information in the ways they wish, and whether audiences will be willing (or even able) to break away from routine interpretations to construct new designs that will accommodate the new techniques. These new de-

The SEVEN BEAUTIES *of* SCIENCE FICTION

signs may make many demands: historical familiarity with artistic expression, generic competence, openness to new information, and a willingness to reflect. Beyond these personal tasks is the encompassing social question of what forms and mutations of discourse are intelligible to a given interpretive community. A coterie of scientists or hipsters might find it fun to decode an array of imaginary terms, but the majority of even educated readers may have a consensual limit to how many new words and neosemes they can entertain, beyond which the experience seems empty, pretentious, or mad. It is rare to find many early sf works in which imaginary neologisms are common currency, while in post–World War II — especially post-1960s — sf the saturation of real social discourse with neologisms licenses writers to increase their density in their fiction.

If sf is a quintessentially estranging genre,[12] it is in imaginary neologies that this estrangement is most economically condensed. Imaginary neologies stand out from other words as knots of estrangement, drawing together the threads of imaginary reference with those of known language. Science-fictional neologies are double-coded. They are prospectively anachronistic and, more than most anachronisms, they are chronoclastic. They embody cultural collisions between the usage of words familiar in the present (a neologism's "prehistory") and the imaginary, altered linguistic future asserted by the neology. All neologies seem to offer some new knowledge about the world. To get on with the sentence and the story, the reader must imagine what tacit knowledge went before to make the particular new meanings possible. It is implicit that this knowledge must have been important and widespread enough within the fictive community of the characters to have generated its own words. Fictive neologies pretend to represent syntheses of different social domains. They imply either that something previously ineffable and mysterious has been synthesized with the familiar, or that two kinds of ideas previously isolated from each other have been linked in language.

Science-fictional neology operates between two termini. At the first are neosemes, semantic shifts of words and sentences that remain familiar in structure and appearance, but have been appropriated by imaginary new social conditions to mean something new.[13] The pleasure of reading them lies in inferring surprising, and often humorous, pseudo-evolutionary connections between the familiar and the imaginary new meanings. Science-fictional neosemes correspond to sf-extrapolation; they are imaginative extensions of historical and current linguistic practice. At the other terminus is neologism in the strong sense, the invention of new words that have no histories. The intelligibility of such words does not depend on social changes in usage, but in their ability to evoke imaginary differences of culture and consciousness. SF neologisms are constructed on analogy with strange words in natural languages, on the model of normal speakers encountering the language of newly discovered foreign cultures.

Semantic shifts occur, quintessentially, on Jakobson's syntagmatic/metonymic axis of discourse.[14] They mark the effect of changes in historical time acting on relatively unchanging material components of language. To the extent that they signify that there is no need to invent new words from whole cloth, semantic shifts affirm the continuity and solidity of language, whose material elements remain stable over time even when their social environments change. Neosemes also privilege readers' familiar discourse. Along with the inevitability of mutations, they evoke a certain containment of change. They keep language "in the family," as if to say that the reader's language is capable of accommodating the novums to come. (Their satirical and comic possibilities are manifold, too, as this accommodation of the future may be pure delusion — nothing shows communicative chaos better than when the same word means different things for different people.)

Newly formed words appear on the metaphoric/paradigmatic axis. They are drawn less from the obligatory structures of familiar language, than from a thesaurus of sounds and connotations, which often supplies surplus, sometimes serendipitous, meanings. Radically new words, in contrast with neosemes, give a sense of distance and otherness; the reader does not participate in generating linguistic innovation. In practice, sf writers exploit both strategies together. A characteristic style has much to do with how an author combines these two aspects of imaginary neology. Most sf neologies are playful combinations of arbitrary poetic connotations and established techniques of making new words out of old ones.

Neology without Neologisms

Semantic shifts show sf's kinship with other literary modes that also depend on placing untransformed language into transformed contexts, such as parable, comedy, and satire. Parable, for example, prefers common, straightforward diction that appears to be semantically transparent. Once the reader acknowledges the overarching figurative character of the parable text, the ostensibly unassuming terms acquire new meanings. Satire in particular thrives on the appropriation of conventional discourse for meanings it does not intend. Stipulating to the hegemony of established language, satire mocks as absurd what normality considers common sense. Satirical readers, like readers of sf, detect the just noticeable insinuations implied in deviations from familiar usage, and actively infer an ironic counterdiscourse — one reason why sf writers have, in all national traditions, used the genre for satirical purposes.

Robert Heinlein illustrates the principle in "All You Zombies" (1958):

Vocabulary shift is the worst hurdle in time jumps — did you know that "service station" once meant a dispensary for petroleum fractions? Once on an assignment in the Churchill Era, a woman said to me, "Meet me at the service station next door" — which is not what it sounds; a "service station" (then) would not have had a bed in it.[15]

SF writers customarily slip such neosemes into their narratives, sometimes to intimate a microcosmic social history through a verbal jump cut, sometimes to disrupt the reader's attempt to construct just such a history. The narrator of Pat Cadigan's *Synners* (1991) repeatedly mentions ubiquitous *pickle-stands* at rock concerts; only well into the action does it become clear that these involve not pickles, but getting pickled. In a passage from "Burning Chrome" (1981), William Gibson's narrator describes a virtuoso viral hack of a corporate asset program, "disguised as an audit and three subpoenas":

[But] her defenses are specifically geared to cope with that kind of official intrusion. Her most sophisticated ice is structured to fend off warrants, writs, subpoenas. When we breached the first gate, the bulk of her data vanished behind core-command ice, these walls we see as leagues of corridor, mazes of shadow. Five separate landlines spurted Mayday signals to law firms, but the virus had already taken over the parameter ice. The glitch systems gobble the distress calls as our mimetic subprograms scan anything that hasn't been blanked by core command.[16]

While Cadigan's neoseme evokes a science-fictional reality effect, Gibson's opens into an extended image of the electronic viscera of the future world, demonstrating the novel's design in action. Damien Broderick notes that "[e]xposition in such a generic regime becomes implicated in the innovative language itself. New signifieds are constructed within our apprehension that these oddly aggregated signifiers must reflect and not construct *ab initio* some unprecedented collective core meaning: namely, Gibson's 'lived-in future.'"[17]

Philip K. Dick often pursues this implication of an imaginary "collective core meaning" far beyond the hyperrealistic effect favored by most sf writers. Dick is partial to the neosemic sf trope of the literalization of metaphor resulting from a technoscientific contextual shift, a discovery or invention that converts an imaginative figure into a deadpan denotation. In *Ubik* (1969), for example, readers are introduced to *half-life* and *cold pac:* technologies that keep deceased humans in suspension for up to two years in a cold state, during which they can muster sufficient consciousness to have remote conversations with living interlocutors. The meaning of cold-pac is transferred from a consumer commodity to a fatal technology, while half-life completely ignores its grotesque metaphorical linking of life with radioactive decay in real usage, asserting instead a more logical, material, and entirely fanciful, link with cryogenics. The practice of technogenetic literalization is the source of much of the satire in sf. In Charles Stross's *Accelerando* (2005), *identity theft* is the crime of stealing the portable external drive storing someone's downloaded consciousness. In Jeff Noon's *Vurt* (1993), an *illegal alien* is an extraterrestrial creature from the Vurt (the consensual hallucination that synthesizes mythology, psychedelia, and game), whose presence on our plane of existence is a police matter.

In most sf, semantic shifts are subtle and unmarked. They invite readers to supply the missing links themselves. Samuel R. Delany proposes that it is precisely this challenge to readers to infer a given sf milieu from specific semantic implications that distinguishes the genre from what he calls "mundane fiction." SF readers expect to construct a world by supplying motivation and rationales for unfamiliar signs. Readers understand realistic stories of everyday terrestrial life by recognizing references to known experience. SF readers, by contrast, actively supply imaginary new referents that will give rational meaning to the implied science-fictional neosemes:

> Because in the discourse of mundane fiction the world is a given, we use each sentence in a mundane fiction text as part of a sort of hunt-and-peck game: All right, what part of the world must I summon up in my imagination to pay attention to (and, equally, what other parts— especially as the sentences build up — had I best not pay attention to at all) if I want this story to hang together? In sf the world of the story is not a given, but rather a construct that changes from story to story. To read an SF text, we have to indulge in a much more fluid and speculative kind of game. With each sentence we have to ask what in the world of the tale would have to be different from our world for such a sentence to be uttered — and thus, as the sentences build up, we build up a world in specific dialogue, in specific tension with our present concept of the real.[18]

Possible-worlds theorists maintain that most readers tend to follow the principle of "least effort" or "minimal departure," treating new sentences as if they were similar to ones they are already familiar with.[19] When a narrative treats as familiar references that the audience finds unfamiliar, the reader is invited to imagine them as if they were real. The more normal the prose, the more normative the reality. This technique favors sentences with familiar syntax, reinforcing continuity with readers' familiar experience and culture, in which new meanings can be implied through subtle, often barely noticeable semantic differences.

Most early Anglophone sf writers used neology sparingly. As if to defend the conservative religious ethics underlying literary culture, the first generations of writers and audiences affected by Marx and Darwin worked hard to restrain the disruptive energies of novums and neologisms. Potentially revolutionary innovations went unnamed, or were given discreet epithets that seemed continuous with familiar discourse. In *The Strange Case of Dr. Jekyll and Mr. Hyde* (1886), Jekyll's chemical compound is treated with profound discretion. Describing his experiment, Jekyll reveals to his confidante, Lanyon:

> [I] not only recognised my natural body for the mere aura and effulgence of certain of the powers that made up my spirit, but managed to compound a drug by which these powers should be dethroned from their supremacy, and a second form and countenance substituted none the less natural to me because they were the expressions, and bore the stamp, of lower elements in my soul.[20]

Jekyll does not give a name to his compound or the process of transmutation by which the higher elements of his nature are suppressed. The drug never passes beyond the threshold of Jekyll's person. It is not revealed, exchanged, or distributed. The narrative doesn't permit it to act independently of its protagonist. By refusing to give his novum a scientific name Stevenson kept his tale from engaging with the discourse of science. Most early writers of sf approached imaginary neologism with similar discretion. The normative pull of common discourse was sufficiently strong in Victorian England for even a few unfamiliar scientific words to create a powerful sense of estrangement. In a milieu where eternal verities are suddenly called into question, small novums loom large.

H. G. Wells was also chary of neologisms, by and large. In his early, foundational romances, new words are relatively rare. For Wells, the world-shaking novum was effective precisely in proportion to the familiarity of the routine it disturbed. Where Verne covered the globe, both in diegetic travel-action and in the scope of his science, Wells based his scenes in the ostensible stability of the late Victorian suburbs, bringing his momentous changes into relief against a familiar background. By presenting the setting in unestranged and realistic manner, he could make every new word have powerful effect. In "The Land Ironclads" (1903), an early story, the only new term at variance with the pragmatic narrative prose is *land ironclad* itself—a term that gives the new war-machine a simultaneous aura of quiet naturalness and grotesque momentousness, evoking the evolutionary move of the lungfish onto the original beach, of which this weapon is the demonic inversion. This chaste British attitude toward quasi-scientific neology continues well into the twentieth century. In the United States, by contrast, the general trend, beginning with the Gernsback era, has been toward the use of more and more fictive neology.

The New Neology

For the most part, extrapolative sf stays close to the norm of pseudorealistic plausibility. It usually introduces neosemes discreetly in order to maintain the sense of familiar discourse. In a survey of extrapolatory word coinages in Anglophone sf, Gary Westfahl finds that the overwhelming majority of futuristic sf neologisms are nouns, which he classifies in terms of morphemic transformations: *bound-morpheme constructions,* containing at least one affix or root that is not itself a word; *free-morphemic constructions,* that is, "either existing words given a notable new meaning . . . or two or more words combined to form a self-evident compound"; *reduced morpheme constructions,* "words containing at least one morpheme which has been shortened in some way—clipped words . . . , abbreviations used as words . . . , acronyms . . . , and blended or portmanteau words"; and finally, other constructions, such as echoic words, imitations of baby talk, and mysterious "possible root constructions." The first three groups of neologisms each have distinct class origins. Bound morpheme constructions originate with scientists, scholars, and intellectuals; free-morpheme constructions from the "simple expressions of common people"; and reduced morpheme constructions from underclass slang. In Westfahl's view, the historical movement of technology from the laboratory to everyday life, and finally to the street, is reflected in the shift in dominance from bound-morpheme constructions in the early periods of sf, to the increasing centrality of common speech and freer morphemic moves:

> As inventions move from the laboratory to become familiar and finally overly familiar objects, one often sees a progression of terminology down through these three categories: thus, "cinematograph" becomes "motion picture" or the "big screen," which becomes "movie" or "flick"; and "television" becomes the "small screen," which becomes "TV" or the "telly."[21]

Early sf favored scientists or intellectuals for its heroes, and its coinages tended toward the bound-morphemic. As the protagonists increasingly became scientific commoners, so did the prevailing neologisms. For Westfahl, this trend also indicates the dominant influence of the Gernsbackian audience of "everyday men and women."

The kinds of discourse on which the neologisms are modeled, and to which they refer, also changed in the course of sf's career. In the Gernsbackian phase, neologisms referred primarily to physical-scientific and technological ideas. This period was followed fairly quickly by the Campbellian "Golden Age," in which sf neologies referred more and more to biology, the social sciences, and social-political behavior. In the New Wave of the 1960s and 1970s, the new words refer to personality, with a striking emphasis on consumer styles and fashions. In cyberpunk, finally, Westfahl detects a synthesis of previous phases, and a recurring focus on intimate technologies and communication.

This periodization marks how neological invention in sf reflects changes in the public language of technoscience in the Untied States and Britain. Scientific-technical terms drawn primarily from physics and the cult of the inventor reinforced the heroic phase of the individualist scientist-superman, whose ability to manipulate scientific terminology reflects his control over the forces of nature.[22] Later, as scientific and technological vocabulary was increasingly applied to human behavior (especially biological terminology to social and political life), the vocabulary of twentieth-century science was introduced into social routines. Advertisers learned to legitimate their influence by using sophisticated psychological and sociological research to design their delivery techniques, and to give power to their suggestions by investing them with the aura of scientific authority. Political propaganda developed in tandem.

This widespread application of technoscientific vocabularies to social life reached a saturation point during the cold war, when the competing superpowers justified their moral superiority with their scientific and technological achievements. (In the United States, for example, nuclear power was to bring energy "too cheap to meter"; in the USSR, the so-called Scientific-Technological Revolution was to initiate the transition to a Communist society.)[23] In rebellion against this instrumentalization of human life, the countercultural movements of the 1960s turned away from rationalistic models, and attempted to reinvent both science and politics in more personal terms. The dominant discourses of this period provided metaphors for sf from experimentation with psychotropic drugs, the social psychology of identity formation (gender, race, intelligence, personality), concepts of normality and deviance, and, above all, communications technology and media.

As the interests of the consumer-and-service economy supplanted those of the state at the end of the cold war, scientific energies turned away from large public projects toward the production and distribution of commodities. This diffusion of technology through everyday life, and the saturation of everyday behavior with mechanical prostheses, has stimulated many subcultural groups to style their language and object-relations on those of advertising that functions as political-economic propaganda. The assimilation of the language of advertising and technology in everyday use leads to the proliferation of technical metaphors for living systems and vital metaphors for machines. Informally, spontaneously social existence is modeled and remodeled at the speed of, and with the interests of, marketing. In tandem, sf has become less concerned with the agency of scientists as special individuals who understand the universe better than others, or with the power of large institutions vis-à-vis social groups—or even, as in the counterculture, with the problems of authentic personal identity and consciousness vis-à-vis autonomous technology. Instead, sf now interrogates the ways people might use complex and barely governable processes that are neither immanent (because they are the products of technoscience), nor transcendent (because they are manifestations of material processes, even if "forced" by human technoscience to evolve in certain ways). Rather, these processes are *artificially immanent.*

Millennial hypercapitalist culture favors images of radical individualists capable of appropriating emergent technologies for private ends. These range from technologically savvy youth (like cyberpunks and their friends) to technoutopian posthumanists who envision speculative technologies supplying terminal supplements for the body's various fatal lacks. With this new focus on individual bodies, the complementary notion that globally mutagenic technologies—from hyperconnected networks to genetic engineering and nanotechnology—are necessarily out of control is often seen as liberating.[24] Surfing the bioinformatic flow with skill substitutes for ethics, and provides a mobile refuge in a restless world. This style now pervades the language of everyday discourse and sf to an unprecedented degree, as human-machine interactions, advertising, personal psychology, and biological theory provide metaphors for the most intimate personal interactions. This diffusion often generates wit, comedy, and imaginative revisions of reality, as well as a drastic reduction of the range of reference, and a willed ignorance about the imaginative life of thousands of earlier generations.

Responding to a parallel explosion of neologistic creativity in the sciences and computer engineering, cyberpunk cultivated the futuristic extension of contemporary discourse to a greater degree than any previous style of sf. The speed with which new scientific objects and concepts were produced and disseminated in popular media in the 1980s and 1990s created a feverish linguistic atmosphere surrounding the exchange of physical and virtual goods. New technoscientific terms, many of them whimsical and slangy, represented more than their proper referents/objects. They stood also for the culture of hyperactive exchange, the creativity of the personal commodity market, and the anti-authoritarian energy of subcultures that conceived of themselves as liberated from tradition, government, and collective rituals. The weakness of participatory institutions guaranteed the superheated production of language in commercial exchange — each word of which promised gains in power, enjoyment, and creative energy. With the saturation of society by technoscience, sf and social reality were finally recognized as inextricably entwined. Words rapidly crossed the science/fiction boundary, with heavy traffic in both directions: cyberspace, wetware, bots, gene hacking, nanofog, memes, firewalls, virus programs, and so on. Riding the tiger of technical and linguistic creativity, cyberpunk writers simultaneously critiqued the anarchy of postmodern politics and harnessed its language. Where earlier near-future sf writers restrained the use of new scientific concepts within a discourse of social discipline (or satirical permutations of it), cyberpunk and postpunk writers justifiably delight in the stream of neologogenetic language. It is already the discourse of reality on the ground, a romantic language of streaming technological creativity — not utopian, but *mutopian,* reveling in the constant, ever more rapid overcoming of ever more ephemeral limits.[25] The esotericism of this technolyricism has been based on a new conception of counterculture, in which the traditional postures of knowledge control have been countered by an edgy elite capable of synthesizing the actually existing gnosis of exotic popular culture; that is, the marginalized, out-of-control hipsters lately in charge of the American dream.

The language of cyberpunk and its successors reflects the postmodern penetration of technoscience into everyday life through a number of dynamic global transformations:

1. interfaces between commodities and individual human bodies;
2. interconnections via networks and flows experiencing continual upgrades and obsolescence, hacking, sabotage, and promises of a near-infinite extension and density of information and sensation;
3. cellular- and microcellular-level manipulation of matter, promising healthful mutation (*and* global disease and dysfunction), the end of scarcity, and the monocultural destruction of nature's replenishing powers;
4. the conflation and synthesis of every human domain via information's infinite flexibility and potential for invention and repair, and the breakdown of standards and discipline by which any particular domain might be judged;
5. the transformation of social life into a culture of technointerfaces mediating human connections, extending them to an unprecedented de-

gree, and increasing the potentials for disruption and exploitation proportionally.

All of these are reflected in cyberpunk discourse shot through with metaphors and portmanteau words from technoscience. Much of contemporary discourse about society imitates and mocks the model of a complex material system — hyperdynamic, perhaps chaotic, without clear ethical or political termini, replacing value-terms with operational ones.

Beyond the mimesis of hypermodernism, cyberpunk (like many previous styles of sf) can also capture the transmutation of instrumentality that all lyrical language, including that of technoscience, aspires to:

A gray disk, the color of Chiba sky.
Now—
Disk beginning to rotate, faster, becoming a sphere of paler gray, expanding — And flowed, flowered for him, fluid neon origami trick, the unfolding of his distanceless home, his country, transparent 3D chessboard extending to infinity. Inner eye opening to the stepped scarlet pyramid of the Eastern Seaboard Fission Authority burning beyond the green cubes of Mitsubishi Bank of America, and high and very far away he saw the spiral arms of military systems, forever beyond his reach.[26]

Damien Broderick provides the gloss:

Beyond . . . customary analytic moves, common to the anatomising of conventional prose and poetry in all its manifold variety, we are obliged to take a further step: to see in this verbal display the creation of something new under the sun. The logic of the passage is this: a computer is a simulation of certain mental processes, as an electric motor simulates adenosine triphosphate energy sources in muscles. Hence, its inner workings are in some sense homologous to our own, or will be when technology has developed to the generation of self-aware computers and beyond; hence we can imagine accessing this inner life by something like the procedure we use to access the consciousness of others. We do *that* by semiotic (iconic and less transparently motivated) forms of imaginative construction of the viewpoint/s of others. Gibson simply takes this recognition and builds a story from it. And while on some level that story is merely an adventure in an entertainment medium derived from the hard-boiled thriller, on the other it is a genuine contribution to the armamentarium of art in its ability to confront aspects of an *episteme* which in many important respects, while we lack the iconic registration to signify it, evades our authority.[27]

Mutant Extrapolation

Rapid increases in the quantity of new words leads to qualitative differences. New technoscientific words can be expected from any domain of social life. They inspire a general sense of metaphoric exuberance and connectivity, even in non-technoscientific discourse. In a climate such as this, the science-fictional world-constructor's task goes beyond creating words that signify the inevitable continuity of the present with the future. The present, after all, is cluttered with familiar words that had in the recent past connoted futurity. The evocation of future difference from the present requires another kind of neological difference, as well: disjunctive neologisms, which signify extrapolative discontinuity, the qualitative mutation of language into something different when it is submerged by unfamiliar referents; that is, the transformation of common discourse into a foreign language.

In the first significant analysis of linguistics in sf, *Aliens and Linguists*, Walter E. Meyers argued that the depiction of mutant and alien languages in sf should meet the same standards of plausibility as any other scientifically understood social phenomenon. The strictest version of this rule, the regime of *strong plausibility*, demands that imaginary future languages should adhere to what is held to be true by linguists, at least of the time in which the text was written.[28] Meyers criticized sf writers for paying much less attention to what linguists know about language change, than they do to accepted ideas of natural science, whereas literary sf should provide a much friendlier environment for exploring language change, even more than for exploring changes in nature, given that its medium is itself language. For the most part, sf evades this self-reflexivity. The only work that Meyers believes fits the criteria of strong plausibility in linguistics is *The Lord of the Rings* (1954–55). Tolkien's rigorous use of linguistic knowledge in constructing the Elvish language gives the fantastic epic a scientific foundation that more obvious linguistics-invoking sf texts — such as Delany's *Babel-17* (1966) and Jack Vance's *Languages of Pao* (1958) — do not.

It is certainly true that strong plausibility in linguistics has held no great attraction for sf writers. At the same time, most readers of sf would probably disagree that *The Lord of the Rings*'s linguistic rigor makes it a work of sf. The attraction of neology in sf is not that it imitates the laws of language, but that it plays with them. Stanisław Lem provides a better lesson than Tolkien. In *The Futurological Congress* (1971), Lem's Gulliver, Ijon Tichy, is given a demonstration of *futurolinguistics* by Professor Trottelreiner, his guide in the tale's "cryptopsychemocratic" utopia of the future:

> "A man can control only what he comprehends, and comprehend only what he is able to put into words. The inexpressible therefore is unknowable. By examining future stages in the evolution of language we come to learn what discoveries, changes, and social revolutions the language will be capable, some day, of reflecting.
> "Give me a word, any word."
> "Myself."
> "Myself? . . . My, self, mine, mind. Mynd. Thy mind — thynd. Like ego, theego. And we makes wego. . . . We're speaking first of the possibility of the merging of the mynd with the thynd, in other words the fusion of two psychic entities. Secondly, the wego. Most interesting. A collective consciousness. Produced perhaps by the multiple dissociation of personality, a mygraine."[29]

From the mundane word "foot," Professor Trottelreiner pre-derives *defeetism* and *twofootalitarianism,* the conflict between people engineered without feet (as "walking has become a vestigial activity") and fundamentalist pedestrians. When Tichy protests that the words have no meaning, the Professor retorts, "At the moment, no, but they will. Or rather, they *may* eventually. . . . The word 'robot' meant nothing in the fifteenth century, and yet if they had had futurolinguistics then, they could have easily envisioned automata"(110). Like the sentence-generating machine in Swift's Academy of Lagado, futurolinguistics caricatures the idea that the future can be known through the mechanical invention of words. But Professsor Trottelreiner's science is more eerie than the Academy's. There is a certain grotesque realism in the notion that linguistic invention can predict — and by predicting, generate — an infinite proliferation of material possibilities. It is realistic, because it is the secret serious incentive behind the neological play of extrapolatory sf.

Futuristic mutations in sf reflect imaginary social-evolutionary changes. Although today's sf writers place language mutation in the foreground of their styles more often than before, it is still rare for sf texts to narrate their estranged worlds primarily through radically estranged discourse. In most cases, disjunctive neologisms appear as spice for fairly stable narrative language. Like the *jaunting* (the ability of bodies to make telekinetic jumps) of Alfred Bester's *The Stars My Destination* (1956), a logically discontinuous etymology is proposed (the process was discovered by a scientist named *Jaunte*), a pun on a familiar word is evoked (*jaunt*), and the word is set loose in otherwise barely transformed discourse. Inspired parodists such as Bruce Sterling, Neal Stephenson, Charles Stross, and Cory Doctorow rely heavily on saturating narrative with playful neologisms derived from the already familiar or emerging vocabulary of computer science and geek culture, comically combined with common speech. Such word-worlds, teeming with neosemes, appear disjunctive because of the volume of new words in imaginary circulation:

> Somewhere there is the Earth, the meatspace from whence the Cloud-mind has ascended. His point of view inverts and now the Earth is enveloped in him, a messy gobstopper dissolving in a probabilistic mind-mouth. It's like looking down at a hatched-out egg, knowing that once upon a time you fit inside that shell, but now you're well shut of it. Meat, meat, meat. Imperfect and ephemeral and needlessly baroque and kludgey, but it calls to the Cloud with a gravatic tug of racial memory.
>
> And then the sensoria recedes and he's eased back into his skin, singing to the Kleinmonster and its uplink to the Cloud. He knows he's x-mitting his own sensoria, the meat and the unreasoning demands of dopamine and endorphin.[30]

SF writers sometimes undertake to simulate a full-fledged mutant discourse in which the rules of syntax and word construction reflect radical social change at the level of language. The most likely places for such transformations are utopias and anti-utopias; in utopias the transformation of signifiers is almost as necessary as the change in their referents. Moreover, in utopias the gap between signifier and signified must be dramatically reduced, lest misunderstanding at the level of concepts lead to discord at the level of social arrangements. Antiutopias, by the same token, often depict the tyranny of an excessive rationality that attempts to control the range of imaginable possibilities by reducing the number and range of signifiers it will permit.

With Newspeak in *Nineteen Eighty-Four* (1949), Orwell modeled the process of changing word forms and usage in bureaucracy and mass communication in order to change consensus reality. Newspeak exaggerates both bureaucratic clipping and the hyperrationalizing application of social scientific principles of language. Even so, for the most part Orwell's narrative remains in lucid, familiar prose, only rarely allowing the materiality of neologogenesis to take over ("dayorder doubleplusungood refs unpersons rewrite fullwise upsub antefiling").[31] Orwell does not permit the fiendish poetic delirium of Newspeak to dominate even a fraction of his storytelling.

In Burgess's *A Clockwork Orange* (1962) the delirium is much more prominent and powerful, in the form of Nadsat; the future argot of English thugs, who have mixed imaginary English slang with Russian loanwords and calques, which they bend to new and creative uses:

Now as I got up from the floor among all the crarking kots and koshkas what should I slooshy but the shoom of the old police-auto siren in the distance, and it dawned on me skorry that the old forella of the pusscats had been on the phone to the millicents when I thought she'd been govoreeting to the mewlers and mowlers, her having got her suspicions skorry on the boil when I'd rung the old zvonock pretending for help. So now, slooshying this fearsome shoom of the rozz-van, I belted for the front door and had a rabbiting time undoing all the locks and chains and bolts and other protective vesches.[32]

There are many real-world precedents for the extensive use of foreign words in urban slang. These are almost invariably bound up with colonial or dias-poric language (Creoles, Spanglish, Turkdeutsch, and so forth). Yet there is no sign of a Russian diaspora or cultural occupation of Britain in *A Clockwork Orange*. The text's offered motivation is that Russian words have infiltrated youth discourse subliminally, through media and pop culture. But that's a red herring. The polyglot Burgess, who had a deep affection for Russian and based his droogs on Leningrad youth gangs, does not displace real language muta-tions. Rather, he uses massive linguistic loaning to construct a fantasy of the convergence of the political and social subversion of authority. The use of lyri-cally mongrelized Russian by bullyboys subverts the Orwellian associations of Russia of the time, while also undermining the purity of English speech for National Front–style thug chauvinism. Nadsat reverses the expected clichés of anti-Russian feeling by showing that the Russian language can be used pre-cisely to facilitate freedom. The logic of Nadsat's estrangement is not cogni-tive, but poetic. Like the novel's action, *Clockwork Orange*'s discourse requires a sense of beauty in the violently strange — violent precisely because of its re-fusal to find a place in the evolutionary continuity of intellectually manage-able change. Burgess's neological trope constructs a world in which the power and attraction of Russian (at the time the great adversary of the bourgeois West) is so great that it becomes a counterdiscourse. But this ex post facto logic of reconstruction is not the point, as it was for Orwell. Rather, the reader is asked to practice poetic estrangement in the middle of a hyperrational universe.

Perhaps the most persistent attempt to embody science fiction through mutant discourse is Russell Hoban's *Riddley Walker* (1980). The story tells of the inhabitants of Kentish country three thousand years in the future, after a nuclear holocaust has sent humanity back into primitive conditions of social evolution. They are just beginning to move again from nomadic hunting-gathering to settled farming. The novel is written in an imaginary English dia-lect that has ostensibly degraded, on analogy with the genetic deterioration caused by radioactive fallout. Mutations of the English language determine every aspect of the fiction. There is no getting past them to some underlying layer that they can be translated or paraphrased into. The *material* of the story is the mutation of language and myth:

> Counting counting they wer all the time. They had iron then and big fire they had towns of parpety. They had machines et numbers up. They fed them numbers and they fractiont out the Power of things. They had the Nos. of the rain bow and the Power of the air all workit out with counting which is how they got boats in the air and picters on the wind. Counting cleverness is what it wer.[33]

Riddley Walker constructs an alternative world based on mutation at the level of the signifier. It demonstrates degeneration, in that it seems to return the language to its folk forms, via folk etymologies and transpositions. But it also demonstrates the richness of linguistic creativity of the archaic collective, embodied in Hoban's ludic imaginary tongue. Moving in a direction different from *Nineteen Eighty-Four* (which depicts the threat of rationalized language narrowing until it prevents imagination), *Riddley Walker* depicts the chaotic dispersion of language toward creative disorder. Readers have to work as hard to construct Hoban's narrative language as to read poetic figures. They have to bear in mind knowledge of nuclear history, the geography of east England, Punch and Judy, and the Myth of the Fall, to supply the contexts that will solve the puzzles posed by mutant words. Nothing in the text inspires readers with the feeling that Riddley's language of the putatively decayed future is less rich than that of the present. The effect is to draw readers into a fully languaged alternative world, whose words gain materiality, musicality, playfulness, and even some recovered innocence. [34]

Xenoglossia

At its "thinking" pole, extrapolative sf strives to create impressions of maximum plausibility and naturalness by using the rhetoric of common sense, plain style, scientific universality, and the megatext of ideological commonplaces. The opposite, metaphoric "dreaming pole" constructs radically alien words.[35] This *xenoglossia* relies on the knowledge that languages and cultures take diverse evolutionary routes, not only in terms of reference, but of the material means of making signs. In dreaming sf, the gap between the alien words of extraterrestrial/mutant cultures and the reader's mundane present is arced by intuitive, often overtly lyrical, leaps.

In many sf plots (transspecies wars, alien contacts, interplanetary romances, animal-human exchanges, and galactic anthropology) communication is a central theme. Sometimes the desired partner lacks language altogether, forcing messages to be exchanged at the level of actions. In Lem's *Solaris*, for example, the Solarists generate a library's worth of scientific neologisms, each one taxonomically well formed, but capable only of signifying their distance from their incomprehensible referents. In less skeptical kinds of romantic sf, new and different language often determines a project's success or failure. The ability to interpret the language of an alien or mutant group is often the key to power. The near-godlike technology of the Krell civilization in *Forbidden Planet* (1956) is accessible only through the unlikely mediation of a human philologist, Morbius. Imperial adventure heroes are traditionally good linguists, in any case. H. Rider Haggard's Alan Quatermain speaks Zulu and other Bantu tongues, while Tarzan becomes fluent in all the major European languages, several Arabic and African dialects, and a number of the Great Apes' tongues — including Mangani, the origin of human speech.[36]

Most sf shows relatively little concern for personal and cultural languages, relying instead on the supposedly universal qualities of scientific reason for communicating with other beings. Interlinguistic communication is usually achieved with marvelous technologies, like *Star Trek*'s Universal Translator and the *Hitchhiker's Guide*'s Babel fish. These gizmos of consecutive interpretation are not just narrative conveniences. They reflect the assumption that (verbalized) languages are all reducible to a basic stratum, a pure code capable of infinite varieties of incarnation with no loss of essential information, on the principle that all minds must share certain universal principles transcending biological and cultural difference. If universal translators exist, all linguistic beings must be able to understand each other. These assumptions inevitably hide the ethnocentric worldviews of national languages, when they are represented unreflectively as the natural ones shared by text and reader.[37] It is unreflective control over language, as over nature, that gives legitimacy to hard sf projects.

Contact sf recounts adventures of enlightenment through the awareness of difference, limitations, and the richness of what is not known. Its hierarchy of values is reflected in the dominance of those who are able to communicate new ideas and self-reflection, versus low monsters incapable of communicating, or unwilling to. Cultural anthropology and travel writing, with their long traditions of carefully noting foreign terms for foreign behavior, and introducing words for referents that do not exist in the mother tongue (potlatch, taboo, totem), have been two of the most influential models for such alien-contact sf. From its first exemplars, adventure fiction has relied on proto-anthropological fascination with the languages of exotic peoples.

The early forebears of contact sf generated fictive neologisms by combining the formulaic traditions of the classical journey with those of contemporary discovery literature. Both traditions were mainly interested in classifying human groups, as standards of civil society were shifting in their own cultures. More's *Utopia* (1516), for example, relies on the genre of explorers' journeys to alien lands for its rationalistic frame, but the names of officials, places, and neighboring nations (not to mention "Utopia" itself) are poetic transformations of Greek words that probably would have been familiar to a learned reader in 1516.[38] For More, neology was as ironic as the whole *Utopia* project. His exotic words evoked classical models, and were obviously inventions. *Utopia* only pretended to be a discovery of a new world. Its words indicated that it was as old as Plato. The terms of *Gulliver's Travels* (1726) go further. Beyond the traditional Greek and Latin, Swift also used contemporary foreign languages: French, Italian, Portuguese, German, Dutch, and Irish. He used several techniques for creating plausible new words from newly encountered languages, including Rabelaisian loans and calques, macaronic anagrams, and his own private cryptographs.[39] Swift worked to produce truly alien-sounding words in order to ratchet up the plausibility of his utterly implausible referents.

Romantic fiction often attributed supernatural knowledge and power to archaic peoples (such as gypsies, American Indians, Highlanders, Irish clansmen, Siberian shamans) that alternately threatened and redeemed the deracinated consciousness of modern European protagonists. With the full-fledged rollout of European imperialism in the nineteenth century, this ambivalence was extended to African, Asian, and Oceanic subjects, whose fictive powers were augmented by their distance from the metropoles. It took form in historical and adventure novels, in which European protagonists learned new words that named either newly found cultures or ancient ones lost through imperial violence. Walter Scott's model of the historical novel, emulated throughout the nineteenth century, routinely features diminished heroes who are required to learn the language of the political other, such as Highland Scots in Scott himself, or the Iroquois tongues of Cooper's *Leatherstocking Tales*.

Much of this fascination was shadowed by the intimation that alien tongues of the earth, and their unique worlds of reference, were endangered by the success of technological and cultural-political rationalization. This modernizing mourning led to two dialectically antagonistic xenoglossic projects at the cusp of the nineteenth and twentieth centuries in Europe. One was the attempt to complete the consolidation of European culture in a utopian shared language that would prevent the destructive competition of modernizing nationalism from destroying Europe itself. Thus began the movement for artificially constructed international languages like Volapük, Esperanto, and Interlingua. The other was the effort to communicate with more cognitively and spiritually evolved beings on other worlds through mental traveling. The former grew out of the Enlightenment project of universal civilization; the latter, from the hermetic tradition's belief in the distribution of consciousness throughout creation. Constructed languages were not particularly hospitable for depicting changed worlds, as their job was to rationalize and control communication, minimizing cultural differences. Communication with aliens, on the other hand, was proof positive of the rich diversity of culture, extended to the universe. As in the legendary case of Hélène Smith that fascinated Théodore Flournoy and Fernand de Saussure, mediums would travel on the astral plane to other planets in dream visions and séances, to speak with their alien inhabitants, and to return to Earth with memories of their extraterrestrial vocabularies.[40] These esoteric séances profoundly influenced early sf's mental travel to other planets, such as Edgar Rice Burroughs's *Princess of Mars* (1912) series, David Lindsay's *Voyage to Arcturus* (1920), and Stapledon's *Star Maker* (1937).

Twentieth-century anthropological writing has provided a rich store of models and texts for sf. As field researchers grew more and more self-conscious about their own influence as observers on the cultures they were studying, they introduced questions about narrative style, point of view, the relative positionality of subjects' perceptions, and the political implications of their methods.[41] These questions affected not only their ongoing research projects, they also inspired a wholesale reevaluation of the history of the anthropological enterprise. Their skepticism led to (1) a radical challenging of the ideas of cultural imperialism and the possibility of translating divergent experiences into a universal language of science; (2) entertaining the idea that there are varieties of reason; and (3) a political sympathy with nonmodern cultures who were now perceived to be endangered not only by the political-technological exploitation of the Great Powers, but by cultural investigators themselves.[42]

The 1960s in particular witnessed an explosion of interest in romantic conceptions of cultural anthropology. These conceptions, associated with Margaret Mead, Claude Lévi-Strauss, Edward Sapir, Benjamin Whorf, and Colin Turnbull, used the putatively unalienated consciousness of primitive people as a standard from which to critique postindustrial anomie and consumerism. Anthropological critiques were extended to sociology, and all social groups began to look like alien cultures studied by anthropologists. Eventually, science itself was reconceived as a particular professional culture with many subcultures, depending on scientists' fields of study and institutions. Science became an object of anthropological scrutiny, a process that soon contributed to a popular questioning of the universality of Western technoscientific ideas.[43]

The Absence of Alien Verbs

Decisions about how to construct words in an alien language are limited by two overarching constraints. One is the inherent *material* resistance of a culture's language to representing truly alien terms within its system of intelligibility. The other is the often unconscious set of *cultural* conventions about what can pass as alien. The first has to do with what a language can represent at all; the second, with the prejudices about what represents linguistic foreignness.

In his essay "A Lack of Alien Verbs: Coinage in Science Fiction," William C. Spruiell approaches sf as a way to study neology in a relatively pure form, unaffected by the number and structure of morphemes in actual use that dominate a speaker's sense of available combinations.[44] Words in imaginary alien languages might provide insights about what happens when speakers creatively try to "get outside their own language" (441). Spruiell calculates that 89 percent of the total inventory of his sample of neologisms are nouns, most of which denote objects or official titles, with few words for imaginary emotional states or nuances (445).[45] Most neologistic adjectives are honorifics; the sf reader does not need to know what they mean, only how they function synonymously with English honorifics. They are "phonetic neologisms," whose only new aspect is their sound (448). Verbs are rare, and they too mainly act as phonic neologisms, often as euphemisms for well-known concepts. (Of course, if alien words for *fucking, foreigner, slave,* and *master* were removed from the megatext, the number of alien words in sf would probably drop by three-quarters.)

Spruiell believes that this lack of alien verbs may mean that sf authors recapitulate, consciously or unconsciously, a "contact-borrowing" paradigm. In the real world, most borrowed words are nominals, and in this sense at least the preponderance of neological nouns imitates usage. Another reason might be that less cognitive effort is required from the author to make up nouns (447). Nouns also enjoy an early advantage in child development. Further, Spruiell notes, the discrimination of objects from their environment and the attendant formation of object-concepts may be hardwired in the human brain. Ease of learning may be related to ease of literary creation. Finally, novel nouns may disrupt the reading process less than novel verbs. If readers follow the principle of least effort in their reading, assuming the familiarity of the fictional world until they are forced out of it by the need to make sense of new information, neological nouns allow the narrative syntax to remain familiar, while creating the impression of exotic detail.

This last point is especially interesting. Familiar verbs allow unfamiliar objects and concepts to be handled in familiar ways, but a novel verb presents the nearly physical challenge of having to imagine new ways of actively experiencing and manipulating a world: "even the homeliest and simplest verbs, though they refer to events perceivable, encode also the unobservable present interests, purposes, beliefs, and perspectives of the speaker."[46] Proper nouns are easily fitted into the syntax of reality as it is spoken and practiced. Just as the results of scientific experiments, even if they are strange or negative, always reinforce scientific method (that is, even if experimental results are falsifiable, science itself is not), by themselves odd nouns reinforce the rules of plausible, cogent discourse. The appearance of an alien noun forces readers to rely on the familiar syntax in which it is embedded. The familiar syntactical manipulation of nouns stands in for the familiar manipulation of objects and concepts. In this way conventional syntax becomes a fictive ground of social being, the surrogate for experienced reality.

In everyday English discourse, neological verbs are common. Folks can *google* each other, they may expect to be *raptured,* to be *upgraded,* to be *texted.* In each case, the new verbs reflect either frequent use of a new object or frequent public reference to a term that was once esoteric, a practice made especially easy if the verbed noun has metaphorical qualities. In each case, the new verb is anchored in a familiar neosemic nominal whose prior usage licenses the new action. Fictive verbs on this model are easily imaginable, as long as the anchoring neological noun is well established in the narrative. But fictive verbs without noun-anchors are rare, because they require an intimately estranged orientation to the real. Imagining an action or experience that is unfamiliar to the reader changes his or her relationship to the world. New verbs signify more than a difference in condition; every new kind of action presupposes a world changed to make it possible. Neological verbs require an actively different consciousness from the reader, a different will, a different sense of what can be done, desired, or acted upon. Spruiell cites as a striking exception to the lack of alien verbs in sf Heinlein's *grok* in *Stranger in a Strange Land* (1961): "Heinlein's *Stranger* is unique in a number of ways and in fact devotes a great deal of prose to defining *grok;* in some ways, the book's major theme can be seen as an extended definition of the term" (447). To *grok* means to know through empathic mind-melding; thus it escapes the syntactical ground of Indo-European cognition by breaking down the subject-object relationships encoded in the grammar. The appeal of having a word for this act of I-Thou cognition was great enough to have given the word a widespread career in the Anglophone counterculture of the 1960s and 1970s.

Specifically cultural constraints loom just as large. Alien words, like aliens in general, are based on analogies with what a milieu considers quintessentially unfamiliar. Distinct strategies reflecting such assumptions are evident in two of the most ambitious works of anthropological sf, Frank Hebert's *Dune* (1964) and Ursula K. Le Guin's *The Left Hand of Darkness* (1969).

When *Dune* appeared, it had a revolutionary effect on the genre. It displayed a new sense of the organic unity of sf setting and action by showing the interactions of the elaborately detailed environment of the desert planet Arrakis and the cultural practices of its native inhabitants. But *Dune* is actually a deeply riven text, quite at odds with its reputation for holism. Much of the novel depends on the arbitrary importation of linguistic and literary devices unrelated either to eco-holism or to the Fremen plot. This disjunction is shown nowhere better than in the many imaginary neologisms of the novel that appear in the foregrounded action and continually challenge the reader's ability to construct a comfortable, unified imaginary world.

Dune takes place in a human cosmos of terrestrial origin, but so distant from it as to be in effect an alien alternative universe. Its world-construction involves several different kinds of discourse, each marked with its own kind of neology. These discourses are not actually neosemic, as neither biological nor technological differences are linked to earlier terrestrial usage. Each domain has its specific terms, pastiched from certain human languages. They break down roughly into three classes: (a) names and terms referring to the politics and culture of the Galactic Empire; (b) the names and terms characteristic of the mystic sodality of the Bene Gesserit; and (c) the barely displaced Arabic terms of the Fremen language.

Words associated with the Fremen and their names for Arrakean phenomena (Fremen, stillsuits, sandworms, the Shadout Mapes, crysknife, sietch, wormsign, sipwells) are imaginary in the uncomplicated sense that the reader is expected to imagine that they are not English words, but are derived by the Fremen from the lingua franca of the Empire. Herbert has his Fremen use a completely different vocabulary when they refer to the messianic religion implanted in their culture by the Bene Gesserit. These terms are all taken from the Arabic of our own history, and most are familiar to students of Islam (Muad'Dib, Usul, Shari-a, Lian al-Gaib, tahaddi al-bushan, ayat, Kitab al-Ibar, Shaitan, taqwa, djihad, Sayaddin, dar al-hikman, jinn, Azhar, and so forth).[47]

Because these terms are nowhere rationalized in the novel, the reader is left with a number of disorienting puzzles. Are these Arabic words tied to the history of the reader's Earth, which long ago ceased to exist in the fiction's chronology? If so, are we to read *Dune* as a resurrection of Earth's centrality, a version of Asimov's *Foundation*? Were the terms exported into the Fremen language by the Bene Gesserit (as they all relate to the coming of the messiah and the ensuing Holy War)? As the Bene Gesserit have their own terms for such things, this exportation is plausibly their tactic for localizing the myth and concealing its alien origin. Do these words indicate that the Fremen speak Arabic all the time, and that the narrative merely emphasizes the religious terms? (We are informed that they also have an archaic language, Chakobsa, that they use while hunting; *Dune* gives no instances of it, although we are told about it in the sequels.)[48] Or is Arabic merely a stand-in for a wholly fictional language, used only to connote "desert culture"? How far is the obvious analogy between the Fremen and Bedouin Arabs supposed to extend? Should we view the Fremen as allegorical Muslims? Did Herbert double-code the terms, evoking imaginary orientalism for those not in the know, and terrestrial history for those who are? Because neither the narrative itself nor the glossary appended to *Dune* addresses these questions, the reader looks for context to see how these foreign words — which hover between science-fictional neologisms (*as if* they were Fremen words) and concrete historical reference — are to be understood, and how the Fremen religion is to be judged in the novel's scheme of values.

That larger context, the language of the Empire, offers little assistance. The imperial neologisms are as motley as the Arabic-Fremen religious vocabulary is consistent. Herbert's imperial language is a pastiche of English transpositions (lasguns, filmbooks, chryskphife) or derivations from other dominant Indo-European languages: from Latin and occasionally Greek (Bene Gesserit, Galacia, Salusa Secundus, chemavit, ornithopter, Missionaria Protectiva, Mentat), from Sanskrit (prana, bindu), German (Landsraad) and French (melange). Herbert motivates this in his appendix by defining Galach, the language of the Galactic Empire, as specifically "Indo-Slavic," which implies that the Galaxy was settled by a terrestrial diaspora that included only Europeans and Arabs, and that did not encounter any other significantly powerful civilized species in its expansion. For the most part, the neologisms wear their origins on their sleeves. That Herbert intended the pastiche to be obvious is evident in his macaronic names, such as the Bene Gesserit priestess, Reverend Mother Gaius Helen Mohiam, or the full name of the cosmos-dominating CHOAM company, Combine Honnete Ober Advancer Mercantiles.

Whatever the intention of this mélange of tongues may be, it is clear that Herbert constructed two domains of loan-based neologisms: the Fremen's, derived literally from Arabic, and the Galactic, derived from the power languages of Europe. Read allegorically, this separation reinforces a reading of *Dune* based on the terrestrial historical opposition of the Arabs and the Ottomans, emblematic of tough messianic desert tribes fighting corrupt multinational empires. Left unclear, to a degree that it radically disorients how we interpret the novel, is whether these terms drawn from earthly languages, histories, and institutions are intended to be allusions, or placeholders whose historical contexts are unimportant compared with their connotations.

Space opera, of which *Dune* is an important example, often employs such foreign neologisms to create exotic effects. The genre depends on travel among diverse worlds, using the familiar historical human relations between familiar and exotic cultures as a model. Many space operas conceal the model. Herbert's does not. The source languages are so obvious that Herbert surely knew that they—at least the European ones—would be recognized. The Arabic was less familiar, especially at the time of *Dune*'s publication.[49] Still, it is hard to imagine that Herbert believed no one would notice that his humans of the far future in the Canopean system repeat the Muslim holy war, using exactly the same terms as on earth. Indeed, this war would be a revised version of *jihad,* wholly manipulated and cynically cultivated in a large-scale political power play. Very few Arab readers would be indifferent to the implications of such a device, yet it is primarily these readers who recognize the neologistic allusions. Further, judging by the commentary on the novel, few of the sf fans who have made *Dune* a success have reflected on the origins of its alien words. Hence, at the very least, Herbert enjoyed the benefits of the ignorance and ethnocentrism of his American audience.

Dune's indeterminacy is unusual in sf. Readers are not provided with enough grounding to decide whether the neological languages are historically descended from familiar terrestrial languages (hence genetically and historically connected), or whether they are arbitrarily familiar. There is not sufficient evidence for readers to decide whether they are reading (1) a cynical and original ripoff of Islamic history; (2) an artful and artificial oriental fable of the connections among charisma, the environment, and the course of religion; or (3) a postmodern experiment of writing *en abyme,* constantly dislodging the reader's center of reference by appearing to represent an imagined world systematically, complete with its own neological language, only to disrupt it with anachronistic and arbitrary invocations of historical allegory. The reader simply cannot know whether the neologisms of *Dune* are truly *signa novi,* or signs of allegorical stasis.

THE LEFT HAND OF DARKNESS

Herbert's use of neologisms in *Dune* is an example of the borrowing from non-Anglo cultures that typifies a good deal of sci-fi orientalism. Popular forms of sf characteristically mask their ethnocentrism from their audience (though it is blatant for non-Anglophones) by selecting and eroticizing stereo-typical cultural signs and concepts from others, and presenting them as indicators of the alienness that should fascinate the ethnic center.

Ursula Le Guin takes a different approach to alien-contact neology in *Left Hand of Darkness*, published five years after *Dune*. The daughter of two anthropologists, A. L. and Theodora Kroeber, Le Guin was influenced by the rigorous genre requirements of anthropological reportage. She evidently was also influenced by the dilemmas posed by cultural relativism and the status of the "anthropologist-as-hero."[50] What sort of knowledge does an anthropologist really bring back from the field? A higher understanding that transcends the partial knowledge of parochial cultures (including his or her own)? Or merely ignorance of everything but one's own ignorance?

Le Guin had bracketed out the problem of the anthropologist as culture-destroyer early in her career by introducing the Hainish, a transgalactic civilization so highly evolved that it has achieved a quasi-Buddhist, noninterventionist wisdom, while also overseeing the construction of the Ekumen, a society of worlds held together by mutual interest and tolerance, ultimately regulated by Hainish enlightenment. In *LHD*, Le Guin's anthropologist-surrogate, Genly Ai, travels as an envoy to the planet Gethen, bearing an invitation for it to join the Ekumen. Genly is a trained observer, and he scrupulously records the strange social institutions, practices, and biology of the Gethenians — especially those of the clan-based, traditionalist inhabitants of the country of Karhide. Open-minded by training and temperament, Genly finds his tolerance stressed by the Gethenians' sexuality. Although they are identical to human beings in other ways, Gethenians are sexless, except for short periods when they undergo *kemmer*, a process in which they develop sexual parts, the gender of which cannot be predicted. Because their gender is both transitory and arbitrary, Gethenians do not have institutionalized gender roles, and view those fixed in gender as perverts. Genly provides a running account of his observations in the field, acting as a guide to the even less knowledgeable reader. This narrative is interspersed with another, one of a native clan chief and royal minister, Lord Estraven, who becomes Genly's most important mediator and, ultimately, his rescuer. Estraven's narrative is that of an insider who would not have to spell out the civilization's exotic practices (they are not exotic to him, of course), if he did not have to guide Genly both physically and culturally across a forbidding arctic landscape saturated with mythical and religious lore.

LHD has quite as much information about alien cultures to convey as *Dune*. Le Guin's method, in contrast to Herbert's postmodern transposition of a historical Terran culture's language to the far future and another solar system, is to combine known aspects of studied human societies in unexpected ways, and to simulate both simple neologisms and foreign languages. Like Herbert, Le Guin employs two kinds of neologisms: the Gethenians' own names for people and things, and new, non-Gethenian terms that we must assume have been in use in the future long enough to be treated by the characters as part of a lingua franca. Unlike the macaronics of *Dune*, Le Guin's Gethenian languages are invented, and fashioned to resemble no terrestrial language group.[51]

Genly has to learn new referents. He identifies several new objects (gossiwor, kniffur, hieb, kardik, dothe, kyoremmi, and so forth), as if merely for the record, as most of these things play no role and need not be learned by the reader. This persistent communication of the names of objects that have no central significance functions as Barthes described the reality-effect: the inclusion of dramatically inert signs to help create a realistic field for much more important words (such as "shifgrethor" and "kemmer"), whose meaning does indeed have to be held in the reader's memory. "Shifgrethor" refers to a concept of honor equivalent to personal prestige or "face." The concept is so foreign to Genly that he requires an explanation, which he receives all the way into its etymology, revealing the deeply poetic and spiritual character of the Gethenians. "Kemmer" is another matter. The word has been learned by many readers as a real word for a striking and memorable imaginary biological process: the Gethenians' equivalent of estrus, when they enter their reproductive phase and temporarily manifest gender.

Kemmer's role in the novel is central and established as a theme. While shifgrethor may be an unfamiliar concept for Genly, he is a sufficiently social being to understand it. But kemmer is alien in a different way. The process of transient gender-manifestation over which conscious will has little control makes fluid one of the stable elements of Genly's understanding of humanoid beings — including himself. He cannot understand what the implications of such a new process might be, but it intrudes on his own intimate gender identity. Gethenians are humanoid enough to be able to have sex with humans like Genly, and this ability causes him great anticipatory anxiety. But as kemmer is a natural state for Gethenians, they cannot imagine why — or even *that* — Genly is disturbed by it. After all, *he's* the pervert. Thus kemmer is the occasion for several pivotal misunderstandings. Le Guin goes further, constructing Gethenian culture on dialectical principles natural for beings whose reproductive identity is not constant. Kemmer is thus also a heuristic device, posed to inspire real human people to think about their own gender qualities, and to imagine how much gender influences every aspect of culture and consciousness.

Le Guin distributes her neologisms among irreduceable Gethenian words and English terms standing in for new practices, either Gethenian or Ekumenical: Ansible, First Mobile, Prime World Weaver, Foreteller, Yomeshta,

Handarra, Sarf, Pervert, Clanhearth, Celibates, Indweller, Kemmerhouses, Voluntary Farms, hyperfood, gichy-michy. These are neologisms that require some elaboration, but can easily be interpreted by the English reader, as they seem to occupy psychological and ritual niches familiar to anyone who studies premodern cultures and religions. The neologisms of the last group in *LHD,* interestingly enough, are terms referring to advances in psychology and communication that could easily work as governing novums in other sf tales, yet are introduced relatively late in the narrative, emphasizing that they are not the decisive innovations. In the last chapters Genly introduces *mindspeaking, sensitives,* and *bespeaking*—phenomena that astonish Estraven as much as kemmer surprised Genly. But these novums, unlike kemmer, have established places in the sf megatext. Consequently, they have less of a neologistic effect than Gethenian biology does; they keep the focus on Genly's understanding of Gethenian culture rather than the reverse.

Klingon

Given the constraints, producing a text entirely in an alien language should be considerably more difficult than one in the mutant English of *Riddley Walker* or *A Clockwork Orange.* The alien cultural ground would have to be conveyed at the same time as the language itself; the linguistic iceberg's visible one-tenth would have to be supplemented by the implicit nine-tenths of the cultural knowledge submerged under it. Such a project has in fact been undertaken, with the construction and elaboration of the Klingon language.

This alien tongue was invented for *Star Trek* by Marc Okrand, a linguist trained in Amerindian languages, to provide the series with plausible science-fictional cultural effects. *Star Trek: The Motion Picture,* the first movie offshoot from the series, had included some risible dialogue in "Vulcan." (The syllable counts of the subtitled English matched the uttered syllables of the alien speakers so neatly, they might just as well have included a sing-along bouncing ball.)[52] *Star Trek's* producers decided to commission a more carefully constructed Klingon language, and Okrand was hired to develop its basic grammar, pronunciation, and vocabulary. That language, as taught by the online Klingon Language Institute, is a sophisticated artificial tongue. Okrand did not originally intend it to be used in conversation; rather, it was an elaborate game, and the properties he devised for it far exceeded the need to have a way of speaking that sounds plausible and systematic onscreen. Though there are apparently recognizable elements from Native American languages in Klingon, it is sufficiently eclectic and idiosyncratic not to be considered merely a displacement of Apache into space.[53] Okrand took seriously the mandate to create a language that was not derivable from a terrestrial social evolution. This mandate should make the language difficult to learn. It is quite regular in many important ways, but it is agglutinative, with an obligatory word order alien to Indo-European (and indeed most other languages).[54] Still, it cannot be too forbidding, as many thousands of people have acquired some conversational knowledge of it.

The language-construction project has since grown, almost entirely through fan demand, into a full-fledged correspondence school, complete with newsletters, dictionaries, and course plans in Klingon.[55] *Hamlet* has been "translated" into Klingon, and a project to render the Bible is also ongoing, although it appears to have been mired, less by sectarian disputes than the linguistic conundrums of an artificial monoculture. This project nonetheless raises interesting anthropological questions about the simulation of missionary religious practice in alien cultures — a drive apparently so strong that it penetrates into virtual reality. It will be interesting to observe how translators arrive at Klingon equivalents for some New Testament attitudes that have no Klingon cultural counterparts, especially words for mercy, loving-kindness, and meekness.[56] A debate about the rules for plausibility of an imaginary culture is an exemplary case of science-fictional thinking. In the absence of real historical forces, any side can draw on historical analogies to supplement its imaginary artifact.

The appeal of Klingon is undeniably complex. It speaks to the desire for a sort of Warrior Esperanto, the esotericism of cult behavior, the ludic pleasure of role-playing, an alternative community of outsiders, and an intimate symbiosis with the dominant legitimating institutions of post modern culture: the entertainment media. Although it shares some of the characteristics of International Auxiliary Languages (such as Esperanto), the inescapable idiosyncrasy of Klingon is that it is a consciously artificial collection of stories, rituals, and language derived from a commercial television series. The challenge for anthropologists is to account for the sincere emotional commitment and reward of pseudoethnic cultural masquerades deriving from an entertainment commodity intended for mass consumption. It is, as the poet says, "a real toad in an imaginary garden."

There have been less successful attempts to construct imaginary languages for other *Star Trek* aliens, notably Vulcans and Romulans.[57] Why have they been utterly eclipsed by Klingon? And why are so many Americans, otherwise notoriously reluctant to learn others' languages, enthusiastic about an imaginary tongue with no history or social context other than fan conventions and a set of revered, though often contradictory, mass-media texts? The most interesting puzzle remains why this play-acting project has turned into a serious commitment and tool for identity-construction. Klingon raises fascinating questions about the performance of culture in contemporary life. The language itself is only one aspect of a project to create a full-fledged *artificial culture,* in which every act and gesture is part of a total imaginary symbolic system. Elaborately codified rituals—funerals, initiations of adolescents, betrothals, and so forth—appear to function for committed performers of Klingon quite similarly to traditional rituals performed in historical, "organic" communities.[58] The fact that its practicing group is entirely self-selecting, and that the customs are neological, eclectic, and artificially patterned on organic traditions Klingon shares with cults and new religions. It is *aestheticized cult-behavior,* participation in an emotional community based in noncoercive structures, literal masquerade, and pleasurable stories—in short, a *ludic cult.* Few are committed to its mythology, in contrast with the believers in similarly science-fictional, but coercive sf myth-belief systems such as Scientology, Heaven's Gate, the Raelian Mothership, and even the Nation of Islam.[59]

It is not impossible to imagine a media-saturated world in which certain programs will have the effect of myths and rituals, the costumes and settings of virtually sacred masks and venues, and the alien language of a quasi-sacred metaspeech. The Klingon language and role-playing, however, will probably not outlast the broadcasts of *Star Trek* episodes. Ephemerality is of the essence in both the entertainment media and capitalism. The Klingon project of constructing a hermetic symbolic environment must surely decline under the strain of science-fictionality itself. SF's ludic conception of imaginary neology does not easily tolerate obligatory rules and academies.

SECOND BEAUTY

Fictive Novums

o o o o o o o

The Novum and the novum. Few critical concepts have had greater influence on sf theory than the *novum,* introduced by Darko Suvin in *Metamorphoses of Science Fiction* as the defining trope of the genre. For Suvin the novum is the central imaginary novelty in an sf text, the source of the most important distinctions between the world of the tale and the world of the reader. To be "authentic," in Suvin's view, a novum must be immanent, scientifically apprehendable, and *"validated by cognitive logic."*[1] It must produce effects in the diegetic material world that can be reasonably derived from the novum's causes, and these effects cannot contradict the logic of real social and natural history. In practice, sf novums are the radically new inventions, discoveries, or social relations around which otherwise familiar fictional elements are reorganized in a cogent, historically plausible way.

Suvin adopts the term from the visionary Marxist philosopher Ernst Bloch, but with significant differences. For Bloch, a Novum (note that Bloch's term is capitalized in approved English translations, while Suvin's English term is not) is a moment of newness in lived history that refreshes human collective consciousness, awakening it from the trancelike sense of history as fated and empty, into awareness that it can be changed. The Blochian Novum is "the unexpectedly new, which pushes humanity out of its present toward the not yet realized,"[2] toward "a blankness of horizon of consciousness . . . formed not by the past but by the future: what Bloch calls a not yet conscious ontological pull of the future, of a tidal influence exerted upon us by that which lies out of sight below the horizon, an unconscious of what is yet to come."[3]

Conceived in the atmosphere of revolutionary messianism that dominated Central European Jewish philosophical thought in the first third of the twentieth century, Bloch's theory of history attempted to alloy a materialist dialectic with a nearly religious eschatology.[4] For Bloch, the core story of history is the human species' striving for union and redemption against the forces of

47

greed, repression, and alienation. The powerless are inspired with hope for deliverance into a humanized, secularized Kingdom of God on Earth, which Bloch identified with *utopia*. Bloch believed that throughout history humanity has been inspired to fulfill the task of constructing utopia in art and action that continually reawaken hopeful consciousness. These wake-up calls manifest themselves as Novums.

Bloch's Novum does not lend itself to precise definition, nor are specific Novums always precisely locatable. They are embodied in an enormous range of material events and artifacts, but their significance derives from their effects on human consciousness. They are thus both historically immanent and situationally transcendent. Each Novum is unique, yet each reactivates the same hopeful expectation derived from the same "advent consciousness."[5] Each instance of the Novum is a hypostatized moment of apocalyptic cognition; and each such moment of cognition is a *recognition*.

Translated literally, Novum means The New or The New Thing, but its historical connotations and its capitalized, hypostatized form work against any sense we might have that it refers to radical newness. Its historical precedents — *Novum Saeculum, Novum Testamentum,* Erasmus's *Novum Instrumentum,* Bacon's *Novum Organum* — all refer to renewals of old promises; they are refreshments, not ruptures. The word's orthography is that of a typological noun referring to a class of events that happen transhistorically, inspired by designs more powerful than empirical reality. Indeed, Bloch's *The Principle of Hope* is a treatise against rupture and radical historical breaks; the new for Bloch is the most authentic and dependable of traditions, an ever-renewed covenant. And yet, whatever historical logic might be applied ex post facto to explain the source of an emergent Novum, the Novum itself is conditioned not by the past, but the future. Its historical-material logic is not derived from empirical experience, but from a higher, mystical-ethical rationality inherent in the world. The Novum is an intermediary, dialectical moment that brings renewed energy into history with each appearance. Eschatology, to which this future-oriented vision bears a superficial resemblance, is by contrast fixated on a mythical past, viewing "even the most progressive historical product solely as a re-membering or restoration of something once possessed, primally lost" (204). Instead of a primal moment of the past that is to be fulfilled by the Omega of the future, in the Novum the past is significant because of its role in constructing the future of the heart's desire, the consummate Novum, the "highest newness," which Bloch calls the *Ultimum* (201).

Bloch insists that the Ultimum can never be a closed, dogmatic Omega point; it is necessarily open-ended, leaving each preliminary future-oriented Novum open as well: "Where the prospective horizon is continually included in the reckoning, the real appears as what it is *in concreto:* as the path-network of dialectical processes which occur in the unfinished world, in a world which would not be in the least changeable without the enormous future: real possibility in that world" (223).

Throughout his career, Bloch devoted himself to identifying examples of the Novum in human institutions, above all law, religion, and art. He was especially drawn by literary texts for their inherent utopian content, even if only for the bare utopian minimum of the detective tale.[6] Like most of his contemporaries, however, Bloch did not consider sf worthy of notice.

The Rational Novum

Suvin's novum differs from Bloch's in important ways. Most significant is that Suvin's novum, uncapitalized, no longer connotes a hypostasis. Suvin downplays Bloch's messianic framework, bracketing out the apocalyptic shell after extracting the pearl of the utopian urge — which is the last enduring inspiration for Neo-Hegelian Marxism after the evaporation of revolution and the industrial proletariat. Suvin's sf novum acts within the confines of specific texts the way Bloch's Novum acts in history as a whole. The sf novum is a narratological mega trope, a figural device that so "dominates" (Suvin's term) its fiction, that every significant aspect of the narrative's meaning can be derived from it: the estranged conditions caused by a radically new thing, the thematic unity of the work, and even changes in readers' attitudes toward their own world, after reading. An sf text's novum is "'totalizing' in the sense that it entails a change of the whole universe of the tale, or at least of crucially important aspects of it (and is therefore a means by which the whole tale can be analytically grasped)" (*Metamorphoses* 64). This analytic transparency is crucial; it is what connects the novum to the reader's understanding of scientific rationality. A novum is "postulated on and validated by Cartesian and post-Baconian scientific method" (64–65). The reader interprets it through a process analogous to "scientifically methodical cognition" (66), as a thought-experiment systematically developed against the background of what is known about how the material universe works. Hard sf — in which the technical details of science play a heightened role in representation and theme — is expected to conform closely to generally accepted scientific knowledge. But most sf, Suvin allows, should be held to a looser standard of "ideal possibility," with the requirement only that the "premises and consequences . . . are not internally contradictory" (66).

Like Bloch, Suvin treats the science-fictional novum as both an indicator and a mediator of horizons of possibility. But for Suvin these horizons are strictly limited to science — the expansion of human knowledge of, and power in, the manipulable material world. The sf novum injects the principles of scientific thinking into the reading of fiction. Like Bloch's Novum, the originality and newness implied by its name paradoxically involves the renewal of established, indeed archetypal principles. With the sf novum, these are the historically immanent and situationally transcendent principles of rationalistic, materialist (Suvin's Cartesian and post-Baconian) science: "the necessity and possibility of explicit, coherent, and immanent or nonsupernatural explanations of realities; Occam's razor; methodical doubt; hypothesis-construction; falsifiable physical or imaginary (thought) experiment; dialectical causality and statistical probability; progressively more embracing cognitive paradigms" (68).

Even when it seems to violate consensus norms, Suvin's novum has plausible effects. Its quality depends on the degree to which it can be explained "in terms of the specific time, place, agents, and cosmic and social totality of each tale" (80), and the richness and density of the relationships it generates. Because these narrative elements must be modeled on analogies in the reader's experience, sf's settings and actants must be realistically plausible. Otherwise, the novum will provide no cognitive gain: "[T]he particular essential novum of any SF tale must . . . be judged by how much new insight into imaginary but coherent and this-worldly, that is *historical,* relationships it affords and could afford" (81). Without cognitive insight regarding historicity, it is no longer, for Suvin, sf at all.

The novum provides a "narrative kernel" from which the sf artist constructs a detailed imaginary alternative reality. This alternative world is a model that readers make sense of by constantly, though not always consciously, comparing it with the familiar world. All fiction works in this way, to some degree. In sf the process is heightened; in Suvin's frame, because the alternative reality's relationships are "cognitively validated" in the same way the reader's empirical world would be, if it were subjected to critical analysis. The novum establishes a distance from which reality can be seen with fresh eyes, a distance that the regime enforcing the reader's consensus reality strives to suppress. The sf reader shuttles back and forth over this gap, comparing the imaginary model with the ideological one, the process of feedback oscillation that Suvin calls *cognitive estrangement.*[7]

Novums at the Front Line

Suvin's sf novum is simultaneously a formal and a critical concept, both descriptive and normative. Every novum calls attention to the historical inertia

The SEVEN BEAUTIES *of* SCIENCE FICTION

of the reader's actual present. It includes in itself an evaluation of the inade-quacies of history and of the potentials offered by critical reflection. Its pri-mary purpose is to make critical recognition of the ideological mythology of one's own time possible. Its primary aesthetic pleasure is seeing the "transla-tion of historical cognition and ethics into form" (80). The true novum thus fuses aesthetic effect with ethical and historical relevance. The worthy novum stands in for, and also stimulates, the rational disillusionment that is a precon-dition for affirming utopian-socialist humanistic collectivism, the "historical destiny of man" (75). Accordingly, a true sf novum represents a decisive change, a change in the "front-line of history": "a novum is a fake unless it in some ways participates in and partakes of what Bloch called the 'front-line of historical progress'" (81–82). The metaphor of a "front-line" conjures up im-ages of an army moving forward toward a pivotal historical collision, led by a courageous, far-seeing vanguard of fighters.[8] To have its obligatory cognitively beneficial effect, the novum must, for Suvin, lead the reader away from ideol-ogy and toward the critical awareness that real history is a violent conflict.

Suvin's strict conception of scientific rationality makes no accommodation for irrational forms of the Blochian utopian unconscious. Thus an ostensibly descriptive difference turns out to be a massively normative one. The standard for determining whether a text is "authentic" sf and worthy of consideration in literary history lies ultimately in its power to demystify. Suvin insists that the novum's implications must be open-ended, but this openness is rigorously bound to a conception of science as rational but falsifiable, and of a morality based on that theoretically grounded rationality. Like most Neo-Hegelian Marxists, Suvin shares in the *Bilderverbot* (taboo against depiction) extended to actual representations of utopia,[9] as the desire for immature utopian solu-tions has led to Soviet and Nazi tyranny and genocide, and the global plunder of neoliberalism. The novum becomes even more important in this light: in it, scientific-rationalistic aspirations for a rational world and social visions of a just order intersect in a prefigurative knot.

By recasting the novum in lower-case as a concrete literary device, Suvin offers a way to link Bloch's hypostatic utopian archetype with its concrete traces in the details of artistic texts and experiences. But Suvin does not go there. He consistently resists the transcendental tug implied by the term. The unstated, but significant, differences between Suvin's concept of novum and Bloch's should now be clear. Suvin rigorously eschews religious and idealist connotations. One need not even assume the existence of actual Novums in real history to employ his novum for analyzing literary texts. (Suvin makes no reference, for example, to the Ultimum.) More important for this context is that Suvin disdains most of the popular genres of fiction in which Bloch detected a persistent utopian minimum. While Bloch's project was to establish the ubiquity of the utopian impulse, for Suvin there is only one useful manifestation of this impulse: materialist rationality. While utopia remains the essential concept, it is cognate for him with critical reason. It represents the element of hope in critical thought, rather than the messianic entelechy of earthly existence. Suvin retains the novum's essential utopian quality, but no longer as a source of political-historical consolation.

Novums Worthy and Unworthy

Still, how does the novum—a mere literary trope, after all, in Suvin's usage—command such critical force? How does its "hegemony" extend beyond the ludic context of fiction to correct reality? How does it act on the reader's consciousness to spur utopian awareness? Is it a trigger, a wake-up call for the Enlightenment project? A reminder of the species' original destiny? Or is it a reenactment of an original quest-vision, which takes new form at every historical moment to express the concrete social existence in which people are embedded at the time? Are novums moments of the promise of freedom remembered, flashes of daylight to dreaming cave dwellers?

For Suvin, the novum is the generating seed of a given sf text's possible world. This possible world is, in the best cases, a carefully elaborated, but tacitly suggested, "absent paradigm" that differs from the equally tacit paradigm of the reader's empirical reality.[10] The reader of an optimal sf text crafts a large-scale, multipoint metaphor, aligning the possible world and the real world to create a third, even more tacit paradigm of parabolic, critical freedom. "In optimal sf, the interaction of the vehicle (relations in the fictional universe) and the tenor (relations in the empirical universe) makes therefore for the reader's parabolic freedom: *this freedom is rehearsed, traced out and inscribed in the very act of reading, before and parallel to forming a conceptual system.*"[11]

The novum-event and its ripples can incite readers to believe in the possibility of something truly different coming about, but only if the novum is able to prompt them to imagine true difference. Although Suvin does not discuss the quality of novums per se, we can infer them from his evaluation of sf's narrative strategies:[12] "Pessimal" novums are banal, incoherent, dogmatic and invalidated ones. *Banal novums* are too tired to generate interesting and original effects. They lead to narratives with supplementary effects that are either clichés or pastiches from other popular genres. *Incoherent novums* are poorly conceived, lacking a clearly focused conception of the range of their likely effects. *Dogmatic novums* are essentially allegorical tokens intended to demonstrate a point, rather than to explore possible effects. *Invalidated novums* are those that cannot be unambiguously validated by (fictive) science. Their ontology is unclear, and readers cannot determine whether the imaginary universe they occur in is rational and material, supernatural, oneiric, or hallucinatory. Such novums are "inauthentic," because they cannot generate narratives that make readers imagine possible worlds sufficiently consistent, coherent, and original to stand up to models of their empirical worlds.

A bad novum may have all of these qualities at the same time — as does, I would argue, the green comet of Wells's *In the Days of the Comet* (1906). Although the tale begins in a particularly realistic mood, depicting class relations in a small town in late Victorian England more sharply than in Wells's other romances, the physics of the comet and its effects are not explored. A contemporary reader of apocalyptic fantasy might recognize it as a cliché derived from Camille Flammarion's spiritual comet in his *La Fin du Monde* (1893). Like Flammarion, Wells uses the comet as a pretext for a tale of social and moral redemption. The result is an incoherent narrative trying to find its way through fuzzy scientific romance, fuzzy moral fantasy, and fuzzy political parable. Wells's comet is a banal commonplace, a pretext for an extended sermon, leaving the reader unsure whether the tale should be read as a quasi-realistic vision or a fable.

For Bloch, Utopia is a barely secularized quest-goal and source of faith. The utopian drive is primal, inscribed even in the substance of the world, in nature. (This aspect of Bloch's mysticism brings it close to Engels's claim that the dialectic can be detected in the workings of raw matter.)[13] One cannot really distinguish between the human and the nonhuman — social and natural — Novum. As long as the Novum/novum is embedded in a determining myth-narrative, where it acts as the primary, recurring catalyst for change, it may represent newness, but it is never new. Suvin's novum can be used to estrange social conditions and ideology, but not the conditions of its own operation. In this, it resembles Wells's Time Machine, which is not subject to the changes of the time through which it transits. But what prevents the novum from altering its own mechanism?

Novums Normative and Ludic

Suvin's novum is much more modest than Bloch's Novum, and this modesty opens a way for its use in a less normative way. By making it textual and concrete, Suvin removes the novum from a mythic/religious context and brings it down to earth. In the same move, he decouples it from teleological destiny-discourse, leaving any particular novum's outcome indeterminate. And if the fictive novums of sf, which are imitations of the real novums of history, are not truly determined by a Master Narrative of Utopian Liberation, perhaps neither are those actually existing Novums of which the textual ones are imitations. Real novums might be viewed instead as undecidable events, capable of progressive, regressive, and even lateral or chaotic consequences, depending on their contexts of interpretation and their pragmatic issues. The sf novum does not need to be viewed within a Marxist weak-messianic framework. It can imply an open question, a problem to be solved: what does newness mean for human existence? More concrete, what is the meaning of *a given moment of newness?* In practice, sf artists are just as likely to treat the novum as a bringer of destruction or chaos, which may be "creative" without being friendly to the human species. Or it may neutralize human hopes and consciousness by depicting their unsurpassable limits. The sf novum does not need to be read as eschatology, or to be taken as a token of progress. Its newness is indeterminate. It does not require our commitment.

Critics sometimes employ the term to describe the premises of a given science fiction's alternative reality, without being sure where to draw its formal or thematic boundaries.[14] For example, is the Time Machine of Wells's Time Traveller the tale's dominant novum? Or merely a conventional narrative device enabling the story to get to its true novum, the evolution of the Eloi and Morlocks?[15] What should we consider the hegemonic novum of *Star Trek:* the Federation's intergalactic governance, the utopian humanism of its social makeup, or perhaps the dilithium technology of faster-than-light travel that provides the physical preconditions for the Federal imperium? Others are skeptical about the critical utopianism that Suvin believes is implicit in all novums. In my view, novums are among sf's most powerful attractions for readers, but their precise contours in a text are variable, and not always so totalizing as Suvin claims. Nor does the novum's evocation of global newness have any specifically differentiating connection to Utopia. A sense of utopian desire may indeed be inherent in sf, but for Bloch it is inherent in *all* art.[16] For sf as a historical phenomenon, utopian "humanist collectivism" is merely one of many entertainable goals of the radical open-endedness suggested by the imaginary novum. If open-endedness is a core value of sf, it does not help to close down its possibilities prematurely, and to dissolve it into an undifferentiated sea of social desire.

At first glance, one would think that the more rationalistic the design of the alternative reality in question, the more useful Suvin's notion of the novum would be. This notion would favor its application to hard sf texts, whose authors take special pride in scientific invention and engineering. But Suvin's rationalism is intensely humanistic; for him, the logic of the novum's cause and effect must extend beyond the physical world to the ethical and social. Most hard sf texts are in fact only superficially rational from this point of view, as they usually depict human social relationships and emotions conventionally and ahistorically. The ideal object for the Suvinian novum is a text that treats social life — including even the institutions of science — anthropologically. It is also a text highly unified aesthetically, whose images, tropes, and style all reflect one another with tight coherence.[17] Such rich works reward being read as high literature. But this standard also excludes the vast majority of works that readers treat as sf, along with the reasons why they do so. The Suvinian novum does not help us to think about sf that does not aspire to high-cultural sublimation. And by reducing the novum to critique, it seeks to discipline and control the imaginative pleasure of most readers.

Most of sf's audiences do not demand, nor are they inclined to process, semantically demanding tests. Still, they do demand as a minimum a powerful illusion of perceiving and understanding newness. For me, the underlying satisfaction of the novum is not primarily critical analysis or utopian longing, but a vertiginous pleasure, more ludic than cognitive, more ecstatic than disciplinary, in accommodating new relationships under controlled and friendly conditions. Of course, this ludic consciousness has its cognitive dimension; thinking craves stimulation and novelty, and learning thrives on intellectual pleasure. In this sense, I also employ Suvin's model of the novum as a tool for cognitive estrangement, with the caveat that estrangement is not always and necessarily theoretical and critical. The novum may well inspire readers to view their ideological embeddedness with fresh eyes; but a precondition for this is the ecstatic sense of being freed from predetermined relations, the opening up of a familiar, fully mapped, and hence seemingly enclosed world, out from the authoritarianism of the current version of techoscientifically defined reality. It is this sense of liberation from constraints through the New and the Other that Blochians feel is transcendentally satisfied by utopia.

The novum — in fact, the very concept of newness — necessarily implies some teleology. To recognize something as being new (as opposed, say, to a miracle or a religious epiphany) already requires a full-scale model of historical time, involving pasts, presents, and futures. The concept depends on the seeming paradox that recognizing the new involves placing it in the past, after it has been recast in a new containing paradigm. The new is a disjunctive analogy, not only to the "old," but to a past that has experienced its share of now-obsolete newness. Moreover, the future's horizons are contrasted not with the past, whose openness the novum has already closed down, but with *variant futures of the past*. I approach the novum in the spirit of *fictive history* (which I shall take up in the next chapter), in terms of the possible paths that a given generation felt were open to them as a consequence of major changes. The novum in this sense evokes the playful consciousness of facing a number of possible evolutions emanating from a given change, each of which can be more or less cogent in terms of the rules of the fiction's game. Thinking historically about one's present is always partially science-fictional. The meaning of events is always suspended and provisional. Room must be left for major alterations, revolutions, and new knowledge about what was once thought to be fully known.

Novums Material and Ethical

Each sf novum is a compound of at least two different kinds of radical change. The change usually first appears as a physical-material novelty: change in the material organization of existence. This form is complemented by an ethical novelty: a change in values and mores. The genre does not dictate how the two dimensions will be related in a given text, only that they will be. Ethical themes may constrain the material novum, overdetermining it with symbolic qualities (as in moralizing texts like *The Time Machine* [1894–95], where the Eloi and Morlocks are constructed not only out of zoological, but also political, technohistorical, and aesthetic metaphors). Or, vice versa, the material novum may set the conditions for the ethical, determining the possibilities of judgment (as the submersion of the Japanese archipelago does in Sakyo Komatsu's *Japan Sinks* [1973]).

Many variations are possible. In sf, the physical-material and the ethical are distinct realms, but they rub shoulders at the molecular level. At any point, an aspect of the physical substrate may mutate textually into the ethical: a gas cloud or a nano-assemblage can turn into the Other. Alternatively, the Other might be matter itself: in Arthur C. Clarke's "The Nine Billion Names of God," a computer programmed to accelerate a Tibetan meditation on divine names — which will end the universe with its ultimate iteration — succeeds in its task. In this respect, sf has greater affinity with fantasy and romance than with realism. Realism's reality effect requires an object world that, by being inert, can establish the material limits of ethics. In sf, however, the material universe is clearly in active dialogue with cultural axioms. Although in formulaic commercial art the possibilities for elaboration are restricted by popular taste and entertainment industries, in theory the permutations are infinite: *any* model of the dialectic between the novum and the paradigm in human history is raw material for sf analogues.

Still, it is important not to elide the two entirely. SF relies on the autonomy of the material universe. A physical novum is absolutely required, not only to reflect people's experience of consensus reality in the modern world, but as a critical lever for resistance to folk platitudes and traditionalism. Anything can, in theory, produce a physical novum, as long as it is independent at some level of culturally determined ethical control.

In the remainder of this chapter I shall refer to the novum as a device that creates a playful vertigo of free possibility in response to radical imaginary changes in readers' consensus physical and ethical worlds. The novum represents a critical intersection of natural and social reality. It reveals and brings into relief (that is, it dis-covers) a shared rational basis for ethical and physical existence. But that rationality is not necessarily guided by a default horizon. The fiction provides an imaginary *functional* rationality, a logic based on analogy with historical confrontations with radical innovations.

Novums in the Real World

If sf's language emphasizes neology, the sf novum emphasizes its *neo-logos,* the desire by readers to experience novelty not merely as entertaining ideas and techniques, but as an essential quality of fiction. Through the novum, the genre of sf is an engine for providing new concepts. But as with the neologogenesis discussed in the previous chapter, the process is also mimetic of empirical responses to real novums, concrete historical ruptures recollected in tranquillity.

A novum is a negative apocalypse. Its meaning lies first, before it is capitalized and hypostatized, in the sense that an event has separated the significant time of human species life into a past and a future. Whatever came before the novum is the past; all that lies in the future has been altered. Where the apocalypse of eschatology invokes an Omega-truth to demonstrate history's ultimate purpose, the novum reveals history's contingency: that, at any point, history can change direction, and consequently, its meaning. As the Russian proverb has it, "The past is unpredictable."

In premodern cultures, actual novums are rare. Newness there is viewed as a heteronomic intrusion from a noumenal zone into myth-cycles that have lost their power. They are the new dispensations, new testaments, new orders, new cargo—intimations of messianic or catastrophic transformations of Everything. Modernity, by contrast, is predicated on perceiving the incessant and ubiquitous emergence of newness. Mutations occur constantly; paradigms shift; adaptations follow. Modern historical consciousness is shaped by belief in novums. It is only the possibility of radically new things emerging in the course of time that distinguishes history from myth, whose events gain significance as repetitions, recursions. Western historiography, in particular, depends on identifying radical changes in human social and cultural life, and revaluations of what was held to be certain, ante-novum. For some, these innovations are introjections, and overwhelmingly ethical: the Fall, the Incarnation, Napoleon, the Revolution, the Rapture. Alternatively, the success of empirical science transforms history into an encyclopedia of material novums emerging from the immanence of social existence. The wheel, the longbow, the Venetian banking system, the Inquisition, the steam engine, the Pill, the Bomb — any perceived innovation is a potential node for tracing decisive historical change.

This model works for local and intimate life, as well. The more modernized a culture, the more its people are educated to expect and adapt to changes. Art itself becomes one of the main mediating agencies to accustom populations to change. Through fiction, cinema, video, and new digital media, people absorb models for moving from customary routines to new regimes of behavior. Early modern cultures retained some of their fidelity to mythic narratives by endowing certain agents and events with special powers, thereby containing the new in the casing of the extraordinary. But with industrialization and capitalist rationalization, the new becomes the norm, and there's a novum around every corner. The dominant cultural consciousness of the twentieth century perceived the nonstop emergence and production of novums in a myriad of technological and social relations. New perspectives brought estrangement: colonialist Europe seen from ex-colonies, the capitalist West from the Communist East, the earth from the moon, traditional gender politics viewed from transsexuality, the natural from the digital, technoscience from Gaia. And, of course, vice versa. The emergence of novums has accelerated to the point that they matter not only to academic philosophers and futurologists, but to people pursuing their everyday tasks. Populations are seduced to adapt to changing technological environments, and to learn to learn. Rather than relying on traditional axiomatic judgments and patterns, folks are taught to become adaptable to mass changes.

The novum is consequently no longer felt to be the enabling event of an overarching historical design, but an autonomous, somewhat chaotic process, whereby many distinct lines of development in technoscience and social life condense into world-transforming events — catastrophes. As the transformations reach a certain pitch, the very idea of transformation changes from mysterious to statistical, from transcendence to a selection among alternatives. Thus, as each technical and conceptual breakthrough separates the pre- from the post- in historical time, novums flash like paparazzi's flashbulbs. If future shock refers to the difficulty of adapting to technoscientific innovations for which populations are not prepared, and which have made their deepest ethical and philosophical commitments seem obsolete, then the postmodern era has become habituated to catastrophe, fascinated with the flood of historical innovations that seems to transform irreversibly and beyond recognition the very historical forces that made them possible. Under these conditions, social imagination becomes science-fictional, and the novum, far from being at the front line of humanistic history, becomes an ironic model of quotidian reality.

The concept of the novum thus conceals a paradox, and not just one. As the novum becomes customary, it becomes a type of historical event. In order to be framed in an intelligible way, the novum is recontained as an ironic archetype: the *archetype of the new*, apocalypse as a continually occurring, distributed process. The novum in fiction is based on analogy with the known. To be articulated in language and image, changes and discontinuity are always based on the known. In any given historical moment, people are aware that great transformations have occurred, and yet they rely on familiar cognitive structures to supplement and contain what they do not know about them.

Negative Apocalypse

The sf novum is a stone thrown into the pool of social existence, and the ripples that ensue. The stone may come from another world, like a meteorite, or it may rise from the pool itself, belched into the air by hidden historical forces and returning with the force of gravity. Even if it is shown emerging from human life, its impact on the world is as if it were of alien origin. The sf novum is most often a newly discovered or invented object/process that changes the course of history. Because sf's novums are fictions, their meanings are constructed by the fictive world's diegetic responses to them, and by readers' parallel reconstructions. For an alien intrusion to be intelligible, it must be incorporated into a prior system of intelligibility. At the same time, that system can only be revealed to be the nest of assumptions and selections it is when something not a part of it forces it to show itself.

The sf novum is the material condensation of a conceptual breakthrough, which Peter Nicholls in the *Encyclopedia of Science Fiction* defines as a moment of a global paradigm shift.[18] Such breakthroughs are not empty successions of new world models, but dialectical transformations of earlier models that are understood to be incomplete or illusory. The art of the sf novum lies in constructing imaginary objects of plausible material concreteness appropriate for abstract world models. The novum represents not only the new thing, but also the absences inherent in the old. A new object/process gives form to questions and lacks in a given conceptual paradigm. In "Tlön, Uqbar, and Orbis Tertius," Borges tells of the invention of an ideal world, operating according to laws that invert, and thereby "correct," the laws of material reality.[19] In the epilogue, Borges gives the process a characteristic twist, when a cone of unimaginable density and perfect solidity appears in material reality. That is what the sf novum is like. Its concreteness and rational materiality is the product of idealist imagining. For all its similarity to objects studied by science and produced in the real universe, its structure is established by the lacks inferred about the intellectual construction of reality.

These lacks-made-solid appear in the form of mysterious objects and processes. By trying to understand them, human faculties of comprehension are disturbed and dislodged. Often they are then restructured, revived and, in extreme cases, redeemed or renounced altogether. The more concretely material the novum, the less its effects can be evaded, and the more a redefinition of paradigm is required. Such shifts are usually represented on a cosmic scale, as in the discovery of extraterrestrial intelligence, pocket universes, minds-in-boxes, or the extension of humanity beyond Earth. But they may also appear in the intimate sphere, in the self-regulation of thought's brain chemistry, gender variety, consensual hallucinations, and sentient washing machines.

Discovery and Invention

SF's novums generally appear in two types of stories: (1) the introjection of an unknown phenomenon, or (2) the emergence of new things through evolutionary mutations and leaps from the familiar world. These correspond to the two vectors of scientific cognition: *discovery* and *invention*. Discovery assumes the reorientation of human knowledge in response to a reality putatively extrinsic to the human social one. Invention is the active intervention in nature by human beings. Discoveries have a wide range: from uncharted islands to scientific principles, onrushing asteroids to slab-monoliths from outer space. (They may even be negative discoveries, as in Kim Stanley Robinson's "Vinland the Dream," where the Vikings' landing in North America is revealed to be a recent hoax.)[20] Inventions have an equally wide range: a solitary scientist's superweapon and time machine, a whole society's technology, or the coming-to-awareness of the world's interfused computers. Pressed further, the difference between the two vectors evaporates; they work together in representation dialectically, as the Latin *invenire* (to find) implies. In sf, the discovered novum almost always produces technical inventions that lead to applying the new knowledge, acquiring the discovered reality for human purposes, reserving it as a future resource, or isolating it to prevent it from destroying society. Similarly, a technical innovation in sf usually leads to conceptual discoveries. Even a dramatic physical transformation of society by technology in sf acquires its meaning through the new knowledge it brings into view.

The dialectic of negative apocalypses implies that human history is a matter of the dynamic expansion of wavefronts, conceptual breakthroughs, scientific and cognitive advances. This expansion is not a simple matter. The new requires the old by necessity, as the vast implicit background against which newness is brought into explicit relief. As long as history is conceived in terms of breakthroughs and innovations, the archaic idols of the past paradoxically retain power. As the new has not established its values, already established values continue to exert strong attraction, because they are easier to imagine.

SF's novums tend to fall into certain classes that we might as well call archetypes. These archetypes are not irrational, ideological hypostases; they are dramatic abstractions of philosophical problems raised historically by theorists and practical inventors alike. They include the classic motifs of sf: extraterrestrial aliens; space travel (especially when enhanced by faster-than-light travel and cryonics); cyborgs and robots; artificial intelligence and A-life; rapid evolution/devolution; mutants; genetic modification and eugenics; prosthetic self-mastery and mastery over others; time travel; multiple realities; parallel and alternative universes; world catastrophe; telepathy; teleportation; precognition; utopia and dystopia. These archetypes fall into two main classes: plausible extensions of what is known, and fantastic extensions that would require new concepts of both scientific understanding and material laws to be taken seriously. Genetics, space travel, robotics and prosthetics, Artificial Life and artificial intelligence, global culture, gender mutability, and technologies of surveillance — all promise to develop new complexity and scope out of currently experienced trends. Other ideas (time travel, teleportation, parallel universes, telepathy, and precognition) are much more difficult to conceive realistically, based on current knowledge. However, all of the latter have been, at one time or another, thought to have some rational basis. Some may even be mathematically demonstrable and unassailably rational in formal terms: for instance, by using tachyons as a basis for time travel, or entanglement theory for teleportation.[21] Even so, these imaginary novums in the real world cannot as yet be plausibly transposed from the microcosm of quantum physics to the mesocosmic physics of gross human bodies. The character of a novum is determined not only by the tradition of sf archetypes, or the author's abstract conception of history and science. It reflects, and intrudes on, the public's conception of the powers and role of innovation in real life.

One Novum

Suvin contends that each work of sf depends on a single dominant novum, an attractor, as it were, forming the intellectual and aesthetic coordinates of the work. The claim that a given work is "dominated" by a "hegemonic" novum suggests that the narrative elements are constrained by a powerful and simple regime of top-down cause and effect. Even if the tale is only weakly plausible, the novum should produce a logical unity that should be paralleled by aesthetic elegance and coherence. In this view, the novum's effects should be as easy to isolate and paraphrase as the caption of a picture. The causes, of which the narrative events are the effects, should be transparent. At the same time, Suvin also considers the novum-cause's potential to create rich and varied effects to be essential for judging the aesthetic worth of a work of sf.

The model of a single novum is useful for reading narratively simple fictions, such as short stories and novels with relatively simple narrative arcs. The model applies also for many works on the novel's scale, especially in Central European and Russian sf, which are often patterned on the satirical tale and comic grotesque. Even mimetic and densely layered works, like Connie Willis's *The Doomsday Book* (1992) or Margaret Atwood's *The Handmaid's Tale* (1985), adhere to a single paraphrasable governing novum-premise that organizes all the other narrative elements.

However, once fictions cross a certain threshold of complexity it becomes more difficult to pin down exactly what the novum-premise is. And it is precisely such literary complexity that Suvin seems to demand from sf. Once a science fiction has several interlayered narrative arcs, novums can become complex, ambiguous, and multiple. The strain between the physical and ethical dimensions of the novum may lead them in different directions. (This diverging is especially true of sf film, where the competing pulls of the spectacle and the moral-of-the-story can be great.) What exactly is the governing novum of Dick's *Do Androids Dream of Electric Sheep?* (1968): the near-indistinguishability of androids and humans, or "World War Terminus?" What is the governing novum of Joanna Russ's *The Female Man* (1975): time travel, the multiplicity of identity, or utopian gender freedom? SF writers increasingly affect the carnivalesque, a mode in which many different novums seem to operate simultaneously, as if in a pluralistic society of innovations. In fact, many novel-scale sf works are of this kind. The most obvious novum of *The Left Hand of Darkness* is the Gethenians' kemmer, but the ethical issue of the story depends just as much on the ansible (a device for transgalactic communication) and Genly's mindspeaking. Even *The Time Machine* can be read as having two novums: the machine itself and the evolution of classes into Morlocks and Eloi. It is tempting to choose one (social evolution) and relegate the machine to the status of literary device; but it is the unfettered movement through time that allows the Time Traveller to have the freedom that he manifests. In fact, the two novums model two opposing notions of time: great (if not absolute) technological control, and sheer naturalistic determinism. To subject one to the other is to erect a hegemony where one does not exist. This modeling is independent of the fact that in complex narratives that are ruled by an overarching novum, a second antagonistic novum usually emerges as a dialectical change in the initial changed conditions. Most sf novels, like most adventure romances, build their narratives around two distinct phases of narrative, each with at least one phase-specific novum. In the first, readers are slowly made familiar with a changed world; in the second, this changed world is itself changed by an antagonistic novum.[22]

The difference between single and multiple sf novums was addressed by the Soviet Wells scholar, Julius Kagarlitsky, when he examined *fantastic premises* upon which sf tales are constructed.[23] The word *premise* (a term Kagarlitsky adopted from Wells) implies that an sf text is like an argument, its aesthetic construction following logically from prior stipulated conditions. This notion of sf as a logical transaction based on fantastic premises also acknowledges the genre's gamelike qualities.

Kagarlitsky distinguished the realistic-critical fantastic from the romantic fantastic by whether they are based on single or multiple changes in the projected world of the fiction. Realistic fantasy is almost always derived from a single premise:

> In such a work, the foundation of the plot usually consists of a single fantastic assumption, "the truth" of which is established in its elaboration by every possible means. This fantastic assumption makes it possible to develop a chain of events and thoughts, and the latter in their turn, insofar as they follow the logic of their basic premise, "train" the reader to use the premise, and by the same token, provide its justification. (43)

This was Wells's own position:

> Anyone can think up inside out people, antigravity, or worlds in the shape of dumbbells. Interest arises when all of this is conveyed in everyday language and all the other marvels are simply swept away. . . . Where anything can happen nothing is interesting. The reader must accept the rules of the game, and the author, insofar as tact permits, must exert every effort so that the reader can "feel at home" with his fantastic hypothesis. With the help of a probable supposition he must compel in the reader a wholehearted concession and continue the story as long as the illusion is maintained. . . . He must take the details from everyday reality . . . in order to preserve the strict truth of the initial fantastic premise, for any superfluous invention going beyond its boundaries gives the whole work an aura of senseless contrivance.[24]

The single premise is the characteristic move of the Enlightenment rationalist to reduce the multiplicity of impressions and conflicting opinions to a single proof. Romantic fantasy develops as a reaction to this rationalistic reductionism, and delights in the chaos of colliding impressions:

> The need of many premises of fantasy was a reaction to the Enlightenment. Realistic fantasy explains the diversity of forms of life which it exhibits with such pleasure in terms of the boundless riches of nature alone; romantic fantasy—by the fact that there are in operation many conflicting laws and that the world lacks unity. This universe knows only one general law—lawlessness. (45)

The single premise is the technique that has historically dominated most sf, and corresponds in most respects to Suvin's novum. It usually establishes a default social milieu that is disrupted by the new invention or discovery. Verne and Wells produced the dominant paradigms of the technique: the expedition and the experiment.

In Verne, the surface of the world is highly active. His scientists, inventors, and expedition leaders are forever percolating, projecting, traveling. Revolutionaries and governments relentlessly intrude on each others' territories or enforce their hegemony. Nations and tribes nervously act out their customs and cultural idiosyncrasies. And most of all, Nature unceasingly displays its fecundity and variety. Reflecting the romanticism and revolutionary nostalgia of post-1848 Europe, Verne's novums seem to fit easily into the reality picture; his world is already exuberantly active. Verne viewed history and nature much as Nemo did his ocean in *20,000 Leagues Under the Sea* (1869–70), as so deep that novums—the *Nautilus,* Robur's airship *The Albatross,* Lidenbrot's discovery of the hollow core of the earth—cannot affect it drastically. Verne's inventions were so plausible that they were either quickly invented in actuality, or were already in existence in rudimentary forms. His action rarely moves into the future. For him, time travel is unnecessary, as there is real travel into zones where the primeval survives and current practices are being transformed. Most important, however, is that Verne's novums produce very little controlled experiment. For him, science was exploration and discovery, as a naturalist perceives them. Travel and expedition, always accompanied by the field guides of positive scientific knowledge, give his work its characteristically exuberant pantography, and the sense that nothing new is being created. Verne's characters and readers inhabit a world that, although it may be dangerous for mortals, is predictable to the scientific intellect. As the Nautilus is a nineteenth-century drawing room, so Verne's world is a map replete with legends.[25]

Wells modeled his worlds less on exploration narratives than on analogy with experimentation. His protagonists usually do not have any idea what they are getting into, and have few skills for dealing with the novum-generated situations. The Time Traveller lands in 802,701 by chance, and it takes a good deal of failed hypothesizing for him finally to arrive at a plausible theory of the evolution of the Morlocks and Eloi. In *First Men on the Moon* (1901), Bedford and Cavor arrive where they have no useful knowledge, while in *The Island of Dr. Moreau* (1896), Prendrick lands somewhere he would love to learn less about. Their most reliable skills ultimately prove to be brute force (one of the interesting antirational motifs in Wells's work) and the quick intelligence of the scientific observer on new ground, intervening strategically. Wells's tales build on the logic of the classical experiment backed by violence.

Novum and Experiment

The classical experiment is essentially a juridical process, a trial extended to nature. One of its preconditions is a stable environment cleansed of, and protected from, extraneous sources of input. Only in such a controlled environment can the experimenter be sure that the phenomena being observed are specific to the trial at hand. The usual rules of observation and evidence, of repeatability and falsifiability, are predicated on the absence of noise in the final data. If the environment is changed at any point in the process, it has been "corrupted." Similarly, for a legal trial to be adjudicated fairly, the conditions must be ideally cleansed of political or personal interests, as if every similar trial were conducted in a chaste zone of dispassion and impartiality. For Wells, this model was important. The experimental environment of the setting had to be realistic, familiar, even domestic. The power of the intrusion from the Martians, Darwinian social evolution, or travel to the moon is brought home through contrasts with the familiar world of the middle-class late Victorian reader.

The single novum is congenial to critical sf for several reasons. It provides for a focal narrative, so that the selection of concrete details will always be guided by a principle of immediate relevance. The plots of critical-realist fiction are less about the representation of life as experienced, than about life as if it were the subject of a material experiment: the critical principle acts as the hypothetical explanation, the novum acts as the catalyst, and the fictional world as the medium. The style — both of the prose and the design — is governed by the same chaste rigor as scientific writing, or better yet, the displaced calculation and mathematical precision of detective fiction. (Hence the attraction of the detective form for many sf writers — and the shared provenance of detective fiction and SF in Poe and Conan Doyle.) The single premise/novum also creates a particular intensity of design: "Having freely made some fantastic assumption, the writer is no longer in command of his own novel. The more fantastic the premise (and it must be as fantastic as possible, for it is this which determines its suitability in a fantastic novel), the more difficult it is to provide a basis for it, the more every aspect of the novel serves this aim."[26] The attractions are evident: intellectual intensity, elegance, and a sense of dynamic rigor that may be treated as fatality or comedy. In more artistically ambitious works, these qualities may be manifest in the mutual reflection of rational argument and literary myth-forms.

For the scientistic mentality, experiment represents a form of secularized ritual, as significant for reinforcing the integrity and discursive conditions of the scientific method and worldview as for producing useful knowledge about the world. Experiments' power to produce such knowledge can distract us from recognizing that they rehearse a form privileged in Western thought: dramatic testing, which links drama, law, science, and alchemy within a logic of ritual ordeal. The repetition of questions asked of the universe, concretized by the strict adherence to defined procedures and discourses by elites trained to construct a purified ritual scene set off for the purpose (stage, court, laboratory, temple) and to conduct the questioning in the proper sequence, in order to create a link between the world under human control and the greater world that is not — all indicate the shared structure of rational ritual. In this sense, the universal application of technology to all aspects of human action and interpretation (even if consciously inspired by the Baconian ideals of comfort, efficiency and security) is a feedback process reinforcing the sense that experimental science is not just "magic that works," but the *only* magic that works, because it is the only visible one. Recently, critical science studies have taken this relation as a basis for critiquing scientific claims to universal rationality.[27] SF has often, also usually unconsciously, treated this relationship, which exists in mythoideological form in the social unconscious of technoscientific culture, in playful, imaginative forms.

A Limit Case of the Single Novum: *Solaris* (1961)

The domination of the single premise/ novum in sf parallels the dominance of the short-story form in the genre for much of its career. The classical construction of the short story invites the focus on intensive, single-minded problem solving that, repeated again and again, creates a horizon of expectations from readers: simultaneously of delight in successful "proofs," and a sense of distance from the messy, nonritualized engagements of concrete social life. Single-premise sf, as Kagarlitsky pointed out, tends to remove agency from characters as they become ritualized actors.

More specifically, a single novum encourages the view that its transforming effect is ultimately comprehensible, and even usable — at least by the elites and freethinkers most adept at conceptualizing the regular recurrence of dramatic change in history. This regularity gives them insight into the profound concrete differences that lie beneath ritual's repetitions (and hence flexibility in the face of change). Usually, they are scientists, but they can just as well be street mystics of flow, experienced diplomats, or oracle-programs. When it organizes narrative design, the single novum permits an aesthetic and intellectual economy that can develop its premise, under fictive experimental conditions, to extreme, revelatory conclusions.

One of the most rigorously extended examples of the single sf novum is Stanisław Lem's *Solaris*. The discovery of a planet that regulates its orbit around a binary star sufficiently to foster life, and that consequently appears to change our understanding of the objective conditions of the universe, is an addition to experience that cannot be ignored. Solaris is unexploitable. It is not a manageable colonial site. It offers no strategic or economic benefits. It seems unable or unwilling to expand much beyond its own atmosphere, and so it is not a physical threat to humanity. It is simply there, an anomaly refuting what the history of science has told us about the universe. The mere fact of its existence — which is all we really know of it — has fallen into human history. For every branch of science, its implications are momentous. It raises the possibility that there is another kind of life, with different principles of organization, than any we have imagined. It may embody a unique autopoetic evolution, occurring in isolation from all other factors of life. Its scene of eco-evolutionary interactions is on a scale several orders of magnitude greater than terrestrial life's. It refutes astronomy's "Gamow-Shapley hypothesis" that life cannot develop on a planet orbiting a binary star. And it calls into question the notions of embodiment and repression on which human psychology is based. In every domain, the Solarists studying the planet are unable to distinguish whether the planet is acting intentionally or automatically. This inability makes it impossible to tell whether the ocean-planet's behavior is the result of anomalous, possibly inexplicable natural causes that are probably consistent with the workings of the material universe, but that make those workings mysterious for human beings; or the anomalous, possibly inexplicable behavior of mind, on such a scale, with such power, and such means of control that they fall out of the paradigm.

The question is exacerbated by the Solarists' connection with the Phi-creatures, the humanlike Visitors who appear on Solaris Station without explanation. They are neutrino-based structures, and so indicate a technology or shaping force far beyond anything humans have imagined. It seems reasonable to assume that they originate with the ocean. But they are also the embodiments of the rational Solarists' irrational fixations, the fantasies of erotic bodies that they have repressed in order to pursue their work of abstraction and detached technoscientific conquest. The Phi-creatures take the Solaris-novum's disruption of the paradigm from the overliteral level of scientific thought to the domain of the psyche, where the paradigms are seen as possible fantastic projections of scientists' refusal to examine their own beings.

Solaris is a pure novum. It has no significant qualities other than its newness and difference. Yet, precisely because it cannot be assimilated into human history (because it does not signify any new path of historical development), it represents a void into which all human hypotheses fall. Its discovery is a pure negative apocalypse. It separates the history of human meanings, ideologies, projects, and successful experiments with existence, from the blank novum that signifies only that these things do not apply. The new thing is no longer new; it antedates difference. And in historical terms, this antedating means a pure difference in time, in history. Whereas Alpha and Omega complete each other, Solaris depletes the human cognitive project.

If there is a future in studying Solaris, Lem leads us to believe, it cannot come from human projection. The dream-connections with the planet that are intimately linked with the generation of the protagonist Kris Kelvin's Phi-Visitor Rheya may indicate that it is only through receptive passivity of experience that the unknown can be made known. But we should not be hasty. The dreams are somehow linked to an X-ray bombardment of the planet by the Solarists that was ethically proscribed. For all we know, there is a parallel for the ocean between X-rays and Phi-creatures. Similarly, the love affair between Rheya and Kelvin offers no salvation. The Phi-creatures are aptly named; they are empty vessels, composed of massless neutrinos. Their content and form are projected from the minds of their hosts. Even Rheya's autonomization, and her apparent heroism, may be literary reenactments of Kelvin's romantic conceptions. (He is a psychologist of emotions, after all). Rheya's gradual growth toward self-government ultimately issues in an archetypal sacrifice of "Woman" preventing her beloved man from becoming limited by her.[28]

Solaris forces humanity to deal with its own limitedness. It dislodges anthropocentrism without providing any means to recoup the loss. By not responding, by being arelational, the planet illuminates humanity's need to be in relation to some other intelligence. And in its indifference to relationship, it removes hope from the novum, leaving only the reinforcement of the negative historical processes of humanity.

Many Novums

Most sf has been single-novum based, if only because most of sf has appeared in short stories and tales. However, a sizable body of work, with distinct aesthetic styles and divergent worldviews, employs multiple novums. Multinovum sf is predicated on the multiplicity of historical lines of force. Unlike frontline conceptions of history, the multinovum universe posits a history in which many independent and branching lines of development unfold at the same moment. Especially since the 1960s, more and more sf has been designed around multiple historical lines intersecting in riven novums that have ambiguous implications for future developments. In these works, more than one potentially world-transforming innovation occurs simultaneously, representing distinct logics and histories. Cyberpunk, for one,

> realized that the old SF stricture of "alter only one thing and see what happens" was hopelessly outdated, a doctrine rendered irrelevant by the furious pace of late 20th century technological change. The future isn't "just one damn thing after another," it's every damn thing all at the same time. Cyberpunk not only realized this truth, but embraced it.[29]

In the twentieth century, science and mathematics dispersed into many specialized fields, whose languages and methods are notoriously barely comprehensible to outsiders. Specialists formulate the objects and possibilities of their models in ways that are hermetic to practitioners even in related fields. Any historian of science has to accommodate complexity, not only as an object of study, but as an institutional aspect of contemporary science.[30] This dramatic increase in cognitive boundaries also creates many opportunities for boundary-crossing. Scientific novums proliferate, both in theory and in new technological objects, and it is impossible to predict the frequency and the location of their emergence. In fact, a good many new models are themselves borderline cases between grounded scientific hypothesis and science-fictional speculation expressed in equations. The classical worldview of "Cartesian and post-Baconian" science, with its ideal fusion of observation and cosmic order, has been replaced by a scientific culture dominated by the proliferation of models and the volatile politics of technology.

The political aspect of technoscience is even more important in this context than in the internal refinement and dissemination of scientific work. Modern national politics has relied for its legitimacy on large-scale uncontrolled experiments with populations and the natural world — on a range from nuclear power and genetic engineering to the mass distribution of drugs, prosthetics, and mass hypnosis. Every large-scale technology is such an experiment. Every technology introduced on a mass scale is an engine creating certain effects on complex systems, but without means of controlling the experiment, neither in terms of the purity of the experimental space, nor of the containment of the effects. As a result, the twentieth century increasingly displayed many unpredicted consequences of scientific practices intended for deliberate ends, but producing quite different ones. These large-scale real-world novums are interconnected and inextricable; there is no way to isolate them because the world is the laboratory. For some sf artists, the chaotic interplay of these uncontrolled global experiments is a model for fictional worlds in which the only comprehensive novum is the indeterminate and volatile relationship among several autonomous novums.

In more prosaic compartments of the knowledge-culture, competition for project funding, the popularity of social science in universities, and the scientific trappings of economics and politics accustom researchers to competition among explanations. Popular notions of "separate realities," variant world-descriptions, and interest in virtuality intersect with the increased liberalization of social attitudes and assimilation of previously marginalized cultures. As technoscience produces increasingly varied and divergent world-models at the levels of experience and theory, an ontological imagination takes hold in the arts. Brian McHale contends that this change in cultural dominance, from epistemological questioning of the true nature of reality to the entertainment of ontological varieties of reality, favors sf.[31] In this climate, sf revels in the speedup of the many-faceted production of its basic resource, historical novums.

In times when publics are fascinated with cultural variety, the notion of historical experiment changes. It is no longer viewed as the ritual demonstration that history speaks the language of science, but that different rational groups will get different answers as they ask different questions.[32] This change opens the door to alternative rationalities that were once considered simply irrational, and to the admission of pseudo- or quasi-scientific elements.[33] It scatters rationality on a spectrum, from childlike magical thinking all the way to metascientific and metacritical assumptions that technoscientific work constructs its own legitimating mythology.

Many Novums: Philip K. Dick

No major writer of sf employed multiple novums to greater effect than Philip K. Dick. Early in his career, Dick wrote mainly short stories that, for all their originality, adhered to the classical form of sf narrative, the elaboration of a single premise/novum in each work. In the years between 1963 and 1969,

The SEVEN BEAUTIES *of* SCIENCE FICTION

when he produced most of his best sf, Dick turned seriously to novels. Their plots usually hinge on the materialized equivalent of delirium, unstable reality-continuums over which the protagonists have little control. The destabilized settings are populated by a rich cast of characters, many of whom possess unusual powers, and some of whom are not actually human beings, but androids, homeostatic taxicabs, incarnate gods, alien slime molds, intelligent refrigerators, musical mutant rats, and the like. In some of the stories, a group of metaphysical misfits struggle against one another to stabilize their world, while they are also compelled to cooperate against more powerful minds competing for dominance over the reality-continuum.

The mere presence of several characters with different extraordinary capabilities, or a variety of catastrophes, does not necessarily indicate multiple novums. Though Stapledon's *Last and First Men* (1930), for example, depicts several phases of human evolution, each markedly different from earlier ones, and each coming to a qualitatively different tragic end, the epic is unified by an overarching design that coordinates each rise and fall under the rubric of humanity's heroic persistence. With Dick, however, not only the characters carry their subjective world-burdens: the fictive timespace is irrecuperably riven as well. The rifts are sometimes caused by characters' own desires and powers, but just as often the cause of the reality breakdown cannot be fixed down. Even when the reader is clearly told who has engineered the breakdown of the consensus world (as, for example, Palmer Eldritch's self-pervasion of reality in *The Three Stigmata of Palmer Eldritch* [1964]), that knowledge does not reveal much about the underlying conditions of the world—or indeed, whether there are any. One of Dick's most widely read works, *Do Androids Dream of Electric Sheep?* also employs multiple autonomous novums. Most commentaries on the novel focus on the depiction of the android-human relationship, especially in comparison with its adaptation in *Blade Runner.* But an equally powerful novum is the religion of Mercerism, which has a different provenance than that of the android novum and which, via the virtual reality construct known as the Mercer box, can bleed into reality in inexplicable ways, opening into a different ontology. There is also the overarching fact that the action's setting is after "World War Terminus," a bizarre armageddon the novel says little about. We know only that its radioactive fallout killed most of the animals in the world.

Each of these zones is a novum. That artificial humans can pass as natural ones determines Rick Deckard's labyrinthine adventures as a bounty hunter. That human beings can share in a collective mystical experience of universal suffering and compassion through a mechanical box determines Deckard's pilgrim's progress toward quasi-Buddhist, nonreciprocal respect for all being.

And World War Terminus determines the global conditions of degeneration, "kippleization" (the tendency of being to turn to debris), and scarcity of life. Although these zones are closely related in the action, at no point does any of them dominate the others in Suvin's classical sense of the novum. Deckard's and his wife's concluding acceptance of a mechanical toad as if it were a living one does not help to resolve the ethical problem human beings have facing killer androids. The androids remain antagonists, with no hope of Mercerian redemption, even though they are not to blame for their own condition. And above all, World War Terminus runs the world down, dimming the character J. R. Isidore from a "chickenhead" into an "anthead," and may leave the earth populated by inorganic creatures with no empathy of their own. In fact, given the symbolic resonances of "Terminus," the reader has every right to wonder whether the world of *Do Androids Dream of Electric Sheep?* is truly a "real" quasi-material world in which material novums can appear. The dreamlike quality of the action, in which the Mercer zone can emerge into the real world, and the real world can project a false San Francisco, may suggest an afterlife, a *bardo.* In *Do Androids Dream of Electric Sheep?* the "hegemonic" novum may be the trivial fact that there is no single reality that can be subordinated to rational analysis. It is not the fact that a unified reality has broken down that governs the reader's response (though several of Dick's fictional works do, in fact, make this breakdown a central novum), but the great variety of new things, each with its own spacelike dreamtime.

Such Dickian proliferations of novums have become models for recent carnivalesque science fictions, such as Neal Stephenson's *The Diamond Age* (1996) and Paul McAuley's *Fairyland* (1995). Multiple novums are also the core devices of science-fictional phantasmagoria, the dominant narrative tropes of such influential authors Angela Carter, Jeff Noon, and China Miéville, who write at the boundaries of sf and other forms of fantastic fiction.

Must the Novum Be "Rational"?
The Novum Effects of Sci-fi

One of the essential qualities of the novum for Suvin is its rationality. The logical coherence and consistency of the novum is for him the single greatest (and perhaps sole) source of its aesthetic and ethical power. It ensures that every important aspect of sf will be salubriously rational: the development of the narrative, the construction of the fictive world, the mediated image of the empirical world, and the consciousness of the reader, who engages in a high-level fusion of aesthetic pleasure and critical awareness. This rationality is not merely a matter of how the response to the novum unfolds in the fiction, but a property of the novum itself. A well-constructed work of fantasy, for example, might develop its magical premises with compelling narrative logic. In strictly formal terms, it might not matter whether the novum is an alien artifact or a magic ring, if the magical system is depicted as having strict rules and limits that the narrative respects. But for Suvin, the novum is an analogy with scientific cognition per se, not "quasi-" or "pseudo-" scientific cognition. The novum must then imitate the sorts of things that stimulate science in the real world.

This stricture makes a great deal of sense, yet much of what is read and admired as sf is not very strict about its rationality. Many of sf's most typical novums are only ostensibly scientifically rational. Two-way time travel, telepathy, precognition, and communicating alternate universes are very difficult to formulate scientifically in the mesocosm of human existence. Yet they can be elaborated with consistency and coherence as if they were really possible. Suvin makes room for a form of weak rationality, allowing for whatever metaphorical and narrative logic is necessary for the consistency of the tale. Many marvelous things, however, can be explained *as if* they were rational, by converting the universe into a fictional game in which anything can be posited to be a material process (for example, in which even gods may be only infinitely long-lived higher intelligences), and any material process can be explained, using the proven rhetoric of scientific explanation. How do we distinguish this from an uncanny, fantastic, or even magical quasi-novum? A ghost or a vampire can be made to behave rationally, according to certain rules, even if it is not a mere human being suffering from spectritis or vampirism. A logically coherent and consistent vampire fiction might be considered a form of sf, and the vampire condition might be considered sufficiently materialist to be admitted as a novum.[34]

Some major texts of the sf canon flirt with this presentation of supernatural phenomena in materialist language. Arthur C. Clarke's *Childhood's End* (1953), Stapledon's *Star Maker,* and Ian Watson's *The Embedding* (1973) all construct quasi-mythic/religious novums that seem to violate the strict definition of a rational novum. In *Star Maker,* for example, neither the protagonists' astral traveling, nor the vision of the ultimate creator, are material in any meaningful sense, as what we consider matter is in the end the stuff of cosmic dreams. A more vexed question concerns the role of the novum in the most popular forms of sf, the *sci-fi* or scientific fantasies that purist critics repudiate, and yet that form the prototype of sf for the vast majority of the genre's audience.[35] In visual sf especially, the rational novum seems to have a more subordinate or repressed role than in literature. This subordination raises issues about the relative force of ideas and images in sf of different media that I must defer for another occasion. But some comment on them is in order.

The science-fictional ideas typical of sci-fi all fit nicely into Suvin's list of *pessimums*. The ruling styles of pastiche and spectacle, which have dominated popular sf from the beginning, treat those aspects that the classical style treats as core elements of the genre as detachable, semiautonomous, and freely combinable motifs. In sci-fi, sf is primarily a style of ludic performance, rather than a medium of contemplation. Where classical-literary sf treats the genre as a zone of playful game-rules that constrain the imaginary world-construction in sophisticated ways, sci-fi treats it as a stage for spectacular and colorful gestures, where rationality is not particularly prized. The spectacle has its own dictates, inspired by the rhythm and distribution of intensities and effects. As one television sci-fi director puts it, "anything can happen in space."[36] This sf is an imaginative zone where almost anything can exist if it is made to appear to interact with setting and protagonists. The rhetorical structures of argument and experiment are only as useful as the spectacle allows; they may be used to ground the action or as mere decor.

Sci-fi novums are often howlingly absurd. The credibility of giant ants and instant evolutionary mutations, tractor beams, and chronoclastic manipulation, depends less on persuasive rationalization than on narrative and design that keep an audience's attention focused elsewhere. In Suvin's framework, these are counterfeit novums and they are decidedly harmful. It is all too easy to link absurd ideas such as alien chariots of the gods establishing ancient Egypt as a base for their evil (the film *Stargate* [1994]) or for their redemption of humanity (as in *The Fifth Element* [1997]) to the destructive origin myths of nations and religions, catastrophic myths of magical nature, and paranoid world-pictures that take root in real cultures and real leaders. Hence the anxious discipline that Suvinian critical theory demands of sf writers and readers. We should, however, also keep in mind that sf has always invited satirical, parodistic, and extravagantly whimsical thought. Every sf text plays with cognitive dissonance, and most sf texts are tacitly aware of the enormous range of styles of incongruity-management used in the history of the genre, from outright satire and parody, comedy, pornography, and allusion, to near-surrealistic arbitrariness of imagery. As we shall see in the chapter "Fourth Beauty," with regard to the rational impossibility — and hence irrationality — of giant creatures, instant evolution, and superheroes of sci-fi movies, science often functions for sf as a contemporary package for archaic dreams and myths. The rationality of such novums, such as it is, lies not in the texts themselves, but in the often impossible effort to make them fit into a consistent and coherent world-picture.

In this sense, the popular quasi-novums of sci-fi are both less and more than rational. They are arbitrary devices constructed for spectacular effects that use the images and jargon from the archive of conventional science-fictional performances of the past. They are intended to create the feeling that novums are intrusions from the *anima mundi* or supernature that have been forced to adapt to contemporary conditions. They also exceed scientific rationality by claiming that scientific discourse can comprehend and penetrate the supernatural and the surreal. In this sense, they merely exaggerate the inherent rationalization at the heart of sf's novum-construction, calling attention to the fact that novums in sf are *novum effects,* just as sf's putative provision of rational cognition is itself actually a *cognition effect.*[37]

THIRD BEAUTY

Future History

o o o o o o o

Representing the future. SF writers sometimes place their stories in imaginary pasts and presents, but most science fictions are futuristic. They are set in a future time vis-à-vis the author's present, or they include an event — an invention, a discovery, a seed — that will prove to be a history-transforming novum. SF readers expect illusions of prophecy. This expectation may miss the point of some artists' symbolic and aesthetic ambitions, but it is completely consonant with the genre's attachment to realistic verisimilitude. SF's main narrative strategy has been to create convincing images of life in the future, through precise details and historical cause-and-effect relationships, recounted in the familiar voices of bourgeois subjects. It strives for the illusion of empirical clairvoyance; that is, a clear vision of other worlds (or the fate of this one), as if they were being empirically experienced.

Unlike real prophecies, sf's are narrated in the past tense. They don't pretend to predict a future, but to explain a *future past.* Peter Stockwell assigns the following thought-experiment: imagine that English possesses a true future tense, and use it to tell an sf story. Noting that French sf writers employ the narrative past, even though French *does* possess such a true future tense, Stockwell asks:

> [W]ould futuristic fiction written in the future tense retain the concrete sense of accomplished realism that the past tense gives current science fiction? Or would science fiction be more philosophically analytical and lyrically descriptive than it is? Would science fiction be a non-narrative genre? . . . Might science fiction not exist at all in this speculative universe? If not, does this mean that the past tense is not only central to narrative but is especially important for science fiction?[1]

I'll try it. Early in C. J. Cherryh's *Downbelow Station,* there's a spacious summary of the prehistory of the Alliance/Union epic in which the novel is set.

The following paragraph is transcribed verbatim, except for the verb tenses, which I have bumped one future forward.

And the star stations *will cling* to the memory of that lively, diverse world which *will have* sent them, Mother Earth in a new and emotion-fraught connotation, she who *will send* out precious stuffs to comfort them; comforts which in a desert universe *will remind* them that there is at least one living mote. The earth company ships *will be* the lifeline . . . and the Earth Company probes *will be* the romance of their existence, the light, swift exploration ships which *will let* them grow more selective about the next steps. It *will be* the age of the Great Circle, no circle at all, but the course which the Earth Company freighters *will run* in constant travel, the beginning and the end of which *will be* Mother Earth.[2]

The differences are subtler than I had expected. Cherryh's already elevated language gains some additional visionary weight from this new voice of an authoritative tragic seer. This witness is no longer modest, and the story no longer a fictive history that we can imagine is widely known in succeeding ages. The language of literal prophecy endows the narrator with an extraordinary, implausible clairvoyance. Cherryh's novel can support that disposition for a while, because its original tone is already cool and distant. (Unlike, say, Gibson's. "The sky *will be* the color of a television tuned to a dead channel" instantly turns the narrator into a café poet.) But sustained for hundreds of pages, readers will surely lose patience with this obsessive-compulsive precog who knows everything, down to the fine details. Worse, the story itself will cease to be compelling. Because it has not happened yet, we will stop thinking about the tale and begin having doubts about the trustworthiness of the narrator. Our main concern will be to check her prophecies against experience — and as we haven't had those yet, our resistance stiffens. Things that have already happened, by contrast, can be entertained as proved, or provable, even if they have occurred in the future, and we can relax our empiricist checking-behavior.

SF relies on the historical past tense, both because narrative requires it, and because sf's particular construction of the future does. It is the illusion of a completed future that allows science fictions to be told, and for a parable-space to be formed, through which readers can shuttle back and forth between the fictive world and consensus reality.[3] Even lyrical and performative sf texts that reject the epic conventions of the genre depend on the vast megatextual background of completed futures established in sf's archive of constructed worlds.[4]

No one believes that sf's completed futures close down the horizon of the future by depicting it. The future is not a wave front that can be collapsed simply by imagining it. Except for the rare world-end such as that of *The Time*

Machine, there's always another future waiting to exist after each imaginary cataclysm. There may be new protagonists who supplant the human species — an Omega-goo, a Black Cloud, AIs or aliens — but most sf does not terminate time altogether. There is at least another universe in line, waiting to be born. SF's completed futures *mediate* the relationship between the human present and the future. The genre interposes virtual futures that serve both as tools for organizing thought, and as illusions to defer awareness of immediate being. These projections are images of the collective human species's projects. They playfully represent the colonization of the future by the present, through the forceful extension of contemporary trends, and, at the same time, the returning feedback-colonization of the present by the future, the reified anticipations, anxieties, and projects of our technoscientific problem-solving.[5]

But why must sf's parabolic object worlds be in the future? Couldn't they just as easily be in another part of the universe or a variant past (as is actually the case in the subgenres of uchronia and parallel worlds)? Because the future does not exist to be concretely described, it is arguably only an empty elsewhere in story space, using futuristic details as poetic devices for exoticizing the present. Writers occasionally defend the genre's honor with the claim that it is not truly *about* the future at all. Le Guin has made the claim: "Sf is not predictive; it is descriptive."[6] Suvin maintains that the *extrapolations* of sf — the logical extensions of strategically isolated current trends into the future— are much less important than its *analogies,* where aspects of the reader's culture are systematically defamiliarized, their hidden significance revealed by parabolic indirection.[7] Delany proposes:

> Sf is not about the future; it uses the future as a narrative convention to present distortions of the present. And both the significance of the distortion and the appropriateness of the convention lies precisely in that what we know of present science does not *deny* the possibility of these distortions eventually coming to pass. Science fiction is about the current world — the given world shared by the writer and reader. But it is not a metaphor for the given world, nor does the catch-all term metonymy exhaust the relation between the given and science fiction's distortion of the given. Science fiction poises in a tense, dialogic, agonistic relation to the given, but there is very little critical vocabulary to deal with this relation of contestatory difference the SF figure establishes, maintains, expends, exploits, subverts, and even — occasionally, temporarily — grandly destroys.[8]

Such protests are oversubtle, however. Future-orientation is central to sf's project, and to science-fictional awareness. SF is *imaginary prediction,* draw-

The SEVEN BEAUTIES *of* SCIENCE FICTION

ing on the same sort of historical-projective suspension of disbelief as the real thing, if only to explore, to problematize, and to play with it. There is no denying that novums and projections displace aspects of the present. Paraphrasing Nietzsche, we can explain the future only by what is most powerful in the present. At the same time, the sense of the present in this present/future dichotomy is saturated with future-orientation: anticipations, anxieties, hopes, promises, and plans, in individual minds and in the audience's collective consciousness. It is the gradual crystallization and respect for this faculty of forward-looking in the dialectic of experience that enabled sf to emerge in the first place. To be aware of future possibilities means looking backward at the imaginary unfolding of the present's lines of force.

In this sense, there is a virtual aspect in all history writing. For the great French historian Marc Bloch, assessing the historical plausibility of an event (that is, the probability of its occurrence) requires historians to imagine what past generations were expecting to happen in the future:

> When a historian asks himself about the probability of a past event, he actually attempts to transpose himself, by a bold exercise of the mind, to the time before the event itself, in order to gauge its chances, as they appeared upon the eve of its realization. Hence, probability remains properly in the future. But since the line of the present has somehow been moved back in the imagination, it is a future of bygone times built upon a fragment which, for us, is actually the past.[9]

This is the rational source of futuristic history. History cannot be imagined without a conception of the past having a future. Historians go into the past before the events they want to study, and then approach them as if they were beginning to unfold into the future, still full of probabilities and desires. Then they write them down in the voice of what Schlegel called a *rückwarts gekehrten Prophet* — a prophet looking backward.

Initiating the Future

In *Origins of Futuristic Fiction*, Paul Alkon describes the difficult birth of the future as an autonomous chronotope. Until the European eighteenth century, the past and the present were granted "higher ontological status," while the future was merely an open space for the continuation of the present or for the consummation of the past.[10] The general view, according to Bakhtin, was that

> the present and even more the past are enriched at the expense of the future. The force and persuasiveness of reality, of real life, belong to the

present and the past alone — to the "is" and the "was" — and to the future belongs a reality of a different sort, one that is more ephemeral, a reality that when placed in the future is deprived of the material and density, that real-life weightiness that is essential to the "is" and "was." The future is not homogeneous with the present and the past, and no matter how much time it occupies it is denied a basic concreteness, it is somehow empty and fragmented — since everything affirmative, ideal, obligatory, desired has been shifted into the past. (Quoted in Alkon, *Origins* 14–15)

The past was separated from the present by its immutable gravity of memory and aura. The future had meaning only as entelechy, as the moment when developments originating in the past would be completed. Apocalypses occurring in the future would, by definition, abolish time itself, turning it, in retrospect, into the emptiness of mere expectation of its own annihilation.

Several shocks had to occur for writers and publics to conceive of the future as sufficiently habitable, autonomous, and real for mimetic representation to be useful in depicting it. They had to feel the effects of technoscientific transformations in their daily lives, and they had to hear predictions of more changes to come. They had to witness the interplay between prophecies about material development and the actual trends of transformation. (In some cases, these converged; in others, they did not.) They had to sense that their modes of life were in flux, that they might benefit from changes, that they might be compensated for their material and ethical losses. They had to feel it was possible to attain a critical distance from events. As long as the source of the value of human existence lay outside of time in an alien sacred space, history was basically a set of figures, its true meaning latent behind the masks of time. As sacred history became secular, the fate of the world came to depend on the outcome of its obscure, immanent story. Worldly events and explanations gained a social *weight*.

SF emerged as a genre and a mode of awareness when people felt that they had successfully constructed what Marx, following Hegel, called *second nature*, the creation by human labor and technology of a humanly constructed world.[11] This second nature, like the walls around ancient cities intended to keep wild things out, built havens in the human image. The cost was having to deal with the unforeseen struggles of species self-construction. Things thought to be eternal had to die. Desires that had been gods' prerogatives had to be fulfilled by mortals. The future had to be imaginable as a time when conditions might be completely different from those of the present, let alone the past. Human time had to be unmoored from the promises and curses of an original past.

The necessary concepts came from natural history and revolutionary politics. Much of the intellectual energy of nineteenth-century Europe went into imagining universal improvement and the need to contain the chaos that attends leaving the safety of mythic history. A central project of Western modernism was to invent the future as an autonomous time that could give purpose to the present, supplanting the myth of divine providence that itself had supplanted myths of eternal recurrence. The great scientific and philosophical systems of Darwin, Marx, Spencer, and positivism contributed to the sense of a future in which ideas of progress inherited from Christian humanism were dialectically combined with expectations of unimaginable material improvement, transformed worlds of greater freedom and power, whose very axioms would be constructed by New Men. More practically, the concept of the future gave people imaginary breathing room to conceptualize, and then to manage, the accelerating, intimate changes of modern social life.

As a mode of awareness, modernity is conditioned by this overdetermined dialectic in which historical continuity is fractured by new knowledge and technique, which then make possible the reconstruction of civilization in a projected, secular future time. European modernist high art strove to preserve the bourgeois humanist elite's ethical-cultural imperatives in the increasingly insulated domain of aestheticized experience. Aesthetic culture defended itself against the catastrophic succession of real social-historical shocks with the inoculations of metaphorical "experiments" and "revolutions." SF, for its part, engaged in close dialogue with the technosocial experiments and revolutions themselves, offering romantic, playful, and monitory stories of their consequences, and attempting to manage cognitive dissonance in images of the future of the entire human species. From the outset, sf addressed audiences who felt they had an immediate stake in the technosocial disruptions that were remaking a world. Doing so, it also jettisoned many of the aesthetic and historical axioms of elite Western culture.

The Future as History

The sf novum trails its future behind it, transforming the reader's present from just another moment continuous with the past into the prehistory of the future.[12] In that move it also initiates a new past. As the novum breaks up an old history it founds a new one, back-propagated to be continuous with the future implied by the novum's potentials. New things reverse the flow of historical time. They create the past from the perspective of the future.[13] Each sf tale embeds its action in a history told from the future, sometimes explicitly explained, more often artfully implied. This perspective is true even when the tale's action occurs in an alternative past or a parallel universe. Knowledge of these worlds' existence is in the reader's imaginary future.

Because truly new conditions differ radically from consensus reality, they are usually embedded in familiar narrative frames in order to be intelligible. Some artistically ambitious works (Delany's *Dhalgren* [1975], Zoline's "Heat Death of the Universe" [1967], Aldiss's *Barefoot in the Head* [1969], Ballard's *The Atrocity Exhibition* [1970], Russ's *The Female Man,* the stories of Cord-wainer Smith, Wolfe's *The Book of the New Sun* [1980–83], to name a few well-known examples) stretch the frames to make storytelling technique embody the novum's disruptions. But most sf writers abide by the convention that the strangeness of one narrative element — character, setting, point of view, voice — requires others to be familiar, in order to have a stable ground against which the strange can come into relief. In terms of narrative framing, sf is a conservative genre, in two respects. Its writers generally adhere to the conventions of epic world-building, and to the conventions of circumstantial realism, both of which depict the world as a relationship among objects and events externalized with respect to their agents.

SF world-construction is an intensely *epic* activity. Readers expect images of vividly detailed imaginary discourses, objects, and institutions — what Hegel called the *totality of objects* of the epic worldview.[14] In contrast with drama's *totality of movement,* in which all elements are caught up in a drive toward a collision of values, or lyric's *totality of consciousness,* in which a world is constructed from personal responses, epic places most value on the social world of tools, languages, and customs that mediate the protagonists' experiences. These things determine the relationships in the narrative, even when the action is full of dramatic movement. The protagonists' subjective experiences and ideas are reactions to the prior conditions of the world, while these imaginary material things and institutions are, at a deeper level, the emanations and repositories of the imaginary world's conflicting and contradictory ethical values.

SF writers usually construct these vivid object-worlds with two interlocking kinds of historical narrative: megahistories of the human species as a single great collective actor, and the personal histories of protagonists in a critical moment of that covering megahistory. A work of near-future sf might not explicitly tell a transgenerational story, but the dramatic collision it depicts implicitly determines or defines the rest of human species-history. In more expansive forms, the megastory is an imaginary *long durée,* an overarching, transgenerational epic that tells the story of the great forces at work over individual protagonists' and groups' lives, as in the future histories of Stapledon, Asimov, Heinlein, Le Guin, Cherryh, and the Strugatskys.[15]

Literary sf follows in the stylistic tradition of the realistic novel, despite its many quasi-marvelous elements. Northrop Frye identified sf with the archetype of romance,[16] but its romance elements are overwhelmingly *rationalized;* its parable spaces, plausible and prosaic. Just as the realistic novel, in Ortega y Gasset's phrase, replaced the ancient epic's "absolute gap between the mythical *yesterday* and the real today" with images of "*our* past [which] is thinkable as having been the present once,"[17] sf represents futures that are imaginatively continuous with the audience's present, not cut off by an "absolute gap" between ages. Futuristic history uses the proven devices of historical realism to create the illusion that the setting is in a real concrete time, whose texture of experience is familiar enough for readers to imagine their own reactions to the novum's disruptions. Most sf writers construct these prosaic, rationalized worlds in stories about typical characters navigating a futuristic object-world. As in realistic fiction, concretely represented intimate relationships, the familiar domestic territory of bourgeois realism, are constrained by the public sphere of historical forces. Like realistic historical fiction, which projects a seamless continuum of familiar private and public spheres into the past, literary sf relies on its readership's desire to see those divisions of experience continuing into the future.

History Free and Experimental

SF lacks the gravity of history, because it lacks the gravity of lived experience. It is *weightless.* Its represented futures incur no obligations. Ballard has observed that sf cannot produce a sense of grounded experience because its setting, typified by space fiction, is fundamentally fantastic: "Once it gets 'off the ground' into space all science fiction is fantasy, and the more serious it tries to be, the more naturalistic, the greater its failure, as it completely lacks the moral authority and conviction of a literature won from experience."[18]

The point is just as valid when we change the terms from space to future time. As John Clute puts it, sf is "free history."[19] It may be persuasive, but it is always poetic and figural. The concreteness of the represented future (that is, the sense of personal consciousness mediated by real things) is borrowed from documents and fictions, and there is no way for readers to test it against the reality of experience. There is, consequently, no reason for it to be believed in or committed to. What it provides is a free imaginative space for play, where it is always already given that the representation is ludic, that whatever responsibility one may be inspired to feel for the imaginary phenomena and the real feelings they incite will be a *chosen* responsibility based on fantasy and desire. SF's free history overtly represents fictive models that have acquired fatal weight in real social life. Works of sf *play out* myths of history, without competing models or recalcitrant facts, in stories into which events are intentionally and aesthetically constructed to fit. In every case, the cause-and-effect chain of human and natural events is emptied of the fatality of fact and experience. Like its beloved flying islands and space stations, sf levitates history, holding it in Earth-orbit.

So the question is not (or not only) how "cognitively valid" or "valuable" a given sf's adaptation of a historical model is, but what its ludic implications are. It is not difficult to show that Asimov's template of the Roman Empire in the *Foundation* novels, Herbert's jihad in *Dune,* Blish's and Van Vogt's Spenglerian cycles, and so on, distort the nuanced and complex understanding of real history that historians strive for. Dislodging and dispersing historical paradigms is one of sf's jobs. Here (as in all the aspects under discussion, from language to science) we must take sf's generic history seriously, as a constitutive part of every story. More than in any other genre of modern literature, sf writers expect their publics to know how other exponents of the genre have imagined things. SF texts are not autonomous; they depend on each other for comparison, dialogue, the grounding and elaboration of ideas, and for the sense that science fictions depict imaginary prophecies, their fictive ontology reinforced and supplemented by the existence of all other imagined futures. The future history of any given sf text is generally understood by authors and readers alike to be part of the megatext of all other fictive futures.

Hayden White has catalogued ways that nineteenth-century European historians cast their narratives in classical literary modes, or *mythoi,* that invite *metahistorical* analysis.[20] SF's future histories — which are constructed as literary plot structures *ab ovo* — return the favor, adapting the dominant models of modern historians, employing metahistories as their raw materials. SF writers have levitated toward three main models, all predicated on collective adaptations to novum-ruptures: (1) utopian social revolution (radical changes effected by human collectives' conscious activity); (2) evolution (adaptations to world-changing mutations that occur without conscious human agency); and (3) "dispersion," the uncontrolled stochastic distribution of virtual futures, with no central, unitary line of development (*Virtual History* 39–40).

THE TECHNOREVOLUTIONARY MODEL

The first to develop was the utopian/revolutionary model. In this paradigm, the central narrative is about civilization's control over nature. Utopian/revolutionary sf assumes that the main problems of the human species have to do with gaining autonomy from the impersonal forces of the universe. Rele-

The SEVEN BEAUTIES *of* SCIENCE FICTION

vant stories span the fate of human communities in the struggle against natural forces (the oncoming meteorite, the heat death of the universe), to contests within communities once physical nature has been tamed or distanced. In both utopian and revolutionary models of history, human beings engineer reality to meet their felt social needs against antagonistic forces — forces that appear just as often in the irrationality of human nature as in the nonhuman world. The construction of second nature is both a *technē* and an art for utopians and revolutionaries, and is justified by the liberation of humanity's higher, rational nature from the shackles of its Mr. Hyde–like bestiality. The technoscientific tropes naturally associated with this conception of history are *invention* (the creation of new material realities by human consciousness), and *engineering* (the global application of inventions to solve the problems of civilized life, and in the process converting as many human problems as possible into matters of material lack).

Utopia was the point of origin for this history. Utopias are distinguished from idylls by being not only good places, but fully *rational* ones that exist by virtue of their rational laws, institutions and customs. The great trenches and walls that separate utopias from the social mainland embody the imaginary gap between humanity's capacities in first and second nature.[21] The nearly impassable spatial schisms represent the space between utopian ideals and reality, and even more between the rationally conceivable impossibility of the former, and the inconceivable presence of the latter.

It was Louis-Sébastien Mercier, according to Alkon, who first introduced the notion of connecting utopian relations to the lives of a contemporary audience in a futuristic euchronia.[22] In *L'an 2440* (1771), Mercier placed what had previously been a genre of parallel reality, with an autonomous story disconnected from known history, on the same line of development as his own society. By structuring into the narrative a continuity from his present's Enlightenment ideals to future transformations, Mercier bridged the gap between the nascent struggles of 1771 and the fully rational world of enlightened human fulfillment. The bridge was future history. The year 2440's concrete feats of engineering and city planning were displayed as the consummation of the present's labors. In this sense, Mercier was the first to invent the imaginary revolution as a necessary step in the course of progress. The full history of the events leading from the present to utopia (which Mercier's narrative hides in a dream) requires a radical transformation of values to achieve its already envisioned goal. We know this cannot come about because of divine intervention, the will of the king, or the unperturbed course of everyday life. In the dream lies concealed the rupture of the novum (which the reader can infer as vividly as he or she wishes), implicit in the vision of the City of Reason at the end of the line.

Mercier's vision had a profound influence on futuristic fiction and sf, in nineteenth-century France especially. It contributed to the utopian polemics of Proudhon, Fourier, and the Saint-Simonians (and through them to Marx), and to Félix Bodin's theoretical definition of the *roman de l'avenir*. A rich tradition of parodies of the City of Reason developed in direct response to this model, as writers from Souvestre to Robida explored the unintended consequences of replacing first nature with second. (Verne's role is complex and original in this regard. Except for the disputed *Paris in the 20th Century* [1863] — written in a Souvestrian tone — the *Voyages extraordinaires* evade the problem both of revolution and utopia, by perpetually sending the protagonists away from the European center stage to an adventure space where their relationship is primarily to physical, not social, nature. It is also a *voluntary* relationship. Nemo's need to live under the sea is a private political decision. No compelling social-historical necessity drives Lidenbrock to the center of the earth, or the Gun Club to the moon. Nor do their inventions and discoveries change the political character of their worlds.)

This paradigmatic tradition inspired works of overt utopian-technoscientific sf in the Russian revolutionary period and immediately after (Bogdanov's *Red Star* [1908] and *Engineer Menni* [1913], Alexey Tolstoy's *Aelita* [1923]), along with equally overt antiutopias (Zamyatin's *We* [1921], Bulgakov's *The Fatal Eggs* [1925] and *Heart of a Dog* [1925]). The great antiutopian texts on which the respectability of sf (such as it is) is based — *Brave New World* (1932), *Nineteen Eighty-Four*, *A Clockwork Orange* — emerge from this tradition. So do the canonical critical utopias of the 1960s counterculture:[23] Delany's *Triton* (1976), Le Guin's *The Dispossessed* (1974), Piercy's *Woman on the Edge of Time* (1976), Russ's *The Female Man*. In this paradigm, the novum and its consequences — the inventions, technologies, and complex social responses to natural challenges, through which the future is constructed in the human image — are almost entirely of social origin. Aliens, too, exist only to be social catalysts in this paradigm. Their novum-role is to incite social responses, rather than to call attention to different physical evolutionary paths that extraterrestrial creatures might take. The borderline robotic dispassion of Klaatu in *The Day the Earth Stood Still* (1951) tells us nothing about xenobiology; only that we must take seriously his challenge to human civilization to transcend its parlous state and emulate the galactic revolution that has placed in Gort and his fellow police-robots the power to render Earth a "burned out cinder."

Perhaps the most ambitious contemporary example of the model is Kim Stanley Robinson's trilogy: *Red Mars* (1992), *Green Mars* (1993), and *Blue Mars* (1996). Robinson constructs a Mars free of monsters and subterranean aboriginals. It is a domain devoid of consciousness, intentions, or natural forces that might directly transform the raw materials of humanity. For some of its explorers, Mars is a blank slate to be inscribed with terrestrial desires, the project of *Areoforming* the planet that leads from Red Mars to Blue. For others, it is an autonomous world, with its own sovereign (in this case purely natural) history worthy of respect. Robinson employs many techniques of utopian/revolutionary sf, consciously gesturing to the tradition, establishing distance, and minimizing changes that do not originate in human transforming activity.[24]

THE EVOLUTIONARY MODEL

The main alternative to utopian/revolutionary history in sf has been the evolutionary paradigm, which uses elements from the monumental cognitive-mythic project of nineteenth-century Western thought to reconnect first and second natures, science and politics, in a theory of universal development. This project inspired an enormous variety of quasi-scientific myths, among them the approaching entropic "devolution" of the human species, its ascent to godlike consciousness, and the emergence of an autonomous technosphere.

A great advantage of the evolutionary model is its sublime scale. Its story is necessarily epic. Instead of the one-time novum provided by revolution, novums are evolution's dramatis personae, supplied by the archive of mutations, adaptations, and selections in natural and human history, from the origins of life to the most distant transmutations of sentience. First and second natures, so cleanly divided by Enlightenment materialism, were reentangled by the idea of universally immanent evolution. From its perspective, natural history and human history belong together because they are both aspects of History.

Darwinism has room for stories of evolution about any niche in the natural world, and along any vector. Its impact, nonetheless, has been felt overwhelmingly in narratives of the fate of humanity. Though Darwin repudiated the idea that selection favored the ascent of the human species toward global dominance, his ideas were popularly conflated with earlier concepts of social evolution in order to express precisely this idea. The most influential early scientific popularizers of evolution were, in one form or another, either eugenicists, devoted to the autoevolution of the human species through conscious selection, or polemicists for the inherent, quasi-transcendental superiority of human consciousness over the rest of nature. In the writings of Ernst Haeckel, Alfred Russell Wallace, and Herbert Spencer, among others, evolution became the story of the emergence of human beings as a "cosmic preference."[25]

As an empirical science, orthodox evolutionary biology rejects the idea that natural processes are guided by any sort of purpose, other than the survival of populations. But this hard-scientific commitment to a dynamic of mindless change and nonhierarchical differentiation did not become a significant story source for sf. Random disturbances (that is, novums that are not only the products of chance, but that teach that the processes responsible for human consciousness are also governed by chance) do not make for heroic or romantic entertainments. (The possibilities for satire, on the other hand, are countless.) For sf, science has been the pretext for romances and satires of the fate of intelligence. Evolution is the spacetime dialectic in which humanity's superior complexity and technology emerge or decay. In this respect, sf is always playing with its cultures' consensual boundaries between the social and the physical, hacking the firewalls between the cultural and the natural. It draws on the dominant cultural interpretations of evolution, which seek to make the global biological theory relevant to human societies. Most important publicists of evolutionary theory in the pre–World War II period particularly emphasized "evolution above the species level," the putative emergence of higher-level complexity, increased rationalization of organs, and greater versatility of response to environmental stimuli — all thought to characterize higher animals.[26] In his influential *Evolution: The Modern Synthesis* (1943), Julian Huxley (T. H. Huxley's grandson and Aldous's brother) argued that progress in evolution was evident in organisms' increasing control over, and independence from, their environments.[27] This view, widely shared by the European scientific intelligentsia of the time, and supported by scrupulous scientific investigation, envisioned that, with the consolidation of human consciousness and technology, the period of mindless natural selection had come to an end, and a new period of anagenetic, autotelic evolution had begun:

> Man, we can be certain, is not within any near future destined to break into separate radiating lines. For the first time in evolution, a major new step will produce but a single species. The genetic variety achieved elsewhere by radiating divergence will with us depend primarily upon crossing and recombination. (572)

Eugenic refinement might yield new mental powers, such as telepathy, by organizing previously latent and unused mental capacities:

> If this were so, it would be in a sense only a continuation of a process that has already been at work — the utilization by man for his own ends of hitherto useless by-products of his mental constitution. The earlier members of the Hominidae can have had little use for the higher ranges of aesthetic creation or appreciation for mathematics or pure intellectual construction. . . . The development of telepathic knowledge or feeling, if

The SEVEN BEAUTIES *of* SCIENCE FICTION

it really exists, would have equally important consequences, practical as well as intrinsic. (574)

Because every evolutionary step means giving up something from the past, as scales were replaced by hair, humanity may have to give up some very familiar qualities to gain its new powers: "The evolutionary biologist is tempted to ask whether the aim should not be to let the mammal die within us, so as more effectually to permit the man to live" (575).

Many of the most powerful prototypes of science-fictional evolutionary theory shared these premises. Particularly influential was J. D. Bernal's extraordinary vision in *The World, the Flesh, and the Devil* (1929) of a communist humanity in space, totally mechanized and modular, with a collective consciousness integrated by the literal telepathy of hyperrefined radio communications, and the perfectly shared labor of immensely powerful faculties transcending organic human capacities.[28] Equally powerful was Teilhard de Chardin's Neo-Christian apotheosis of the Noösphere, the next evolutionary zone after the consummation of the Biosphere, in which humanity's spiritual faculties would emerge to fuse the human organism with the transcendent terminal, Christ, at Omega, the consummation of the evolutionary process of existence.[29] Models of "transhuman" progress thrive today, in versions of extropian and posthuman technoevolution that envision the benevolent interfusion of human beings with artificial intelligence engines and perpetually self-upgrading nanomachines. As Ray Kurzweil puts it: "Evolution has been seen as a billion-year drama that led inexorably to its grandest creation: human intelligence. The emergence in the early 21st century of a new form of intelligence on Earth that can compete with, and ultimately significantly exceed, human intelligence will be a development of greater import than any of the events that have shaped human history."[30] Recasting the concept of spiritual transcendence in purely material/informational terms, Kurzweil and his cohort envision the autoconstruction of a this-worldly Omega: "When we can determine the neurological correlates of the variety of spiritual experiences that our species is capable of, we are likely to be able to enhance these experiences in the same way that will enhance other human experiences" (153).

THE UNIFIED EVOLUTIONARY FIELD

Wells, who was a student of T. H. Huxley, transformed sf by basing his stories on metaphorical extensions of evolutionary problems into humanity's future.[31] In "The Land Ironclads," the appearance of an amphibious battle-tank on second nature's steel beach recapitulates the emergence of the lungfish on the primal shore. *The Time Machine* fits out models of retrogression and parasitism in the degenerated descendants of human social classes, the Morlocks and Eloi. *The War of the Worlds* (1898) places humanity in a struggle for resources with invading aliens, who are made especially disturbing by the hypothesis that they are grotesque projections of our own evolution as hypertrophic tool users. Only our established adaptation to local terrestrial conditions gives us an edge against the Martians, an oblique judgment also on European invaders' illusion of technological superior fitness over that of "aboriginals."[32] With *The Island of Doctor Moreau,* Wells was explicit: human technical hubris glares in the project of transforming the animal into the human, the science-fictional inversion of Stevenson's *Dr. Jekyll and Mr. Hyde.*

Looking at the corpus of sf in the twentieth century, we see veritable schoolbook applications of evolutionary ideas. Cosmic dramas are based on motifs from the evolutionary process: mutations (the museum of mutants from *The Invisible Man* [1897] to *The Village of the Damned* [1960], all the way to the *Teenage Mutant Ninja Turtles* [1987–89]); selection (contests between humanity and dangerous rivals for resources — Martians, giant ants, pods from outer space, killer cyborgs); adaptation (postnuclear communities, colonies on distant planets, generation starships, life on neutron stars); dispersion (the migrations of species through the universe, notably in space opera, with its Hejiras, Cultures, and Diasporas); and even cross-species cooperation in dramas of cosmic sympathy (from Stanley Weinbaum's "A Martian Odyssey" [1934] and Stapledon's *Star Maker* to Eleanor Arnason's *Ring of Swords* [1993]). Space opera's history, in particular, is one of gradual development from crude displacements of competition between nations and races projected into spectacle-space, to epic dream-visions of the dialectics of cosmic evolution. Space opera is almost always an episode in an epic of cosmic selection: the competition for niche-dominance and hegemony among the technocivilizations of sophonts (Flash Gordon versus Ming the Merciless, the Federation versus the Klingon Empire), between beings on different evolutionary paths (carbon versus silicon, hive versus monad), or among the autoevolved variations within the species (Mechanics and Shapers, flying men and great brains).[33] Evolution provides an extremely rich repertoire of transformational plot mechanisms for mediating social contradictions.

In all this, the history of sf parallels that of scientific culture itself. In the twentieth century, biology gradually supplanted physics as the dominant science, and its paradigm increasingly extends to previously autonomous fields. The leading role of physics at the beginning of the century is reflected in early sf. Revolutionary breakthroughs in relativity and quantum mechanics inspired the imaginary breakthrough inventions of travel in outer space and time. Early heroes' mastery was manifest in the manipulation of spaceships, superweapons, and matter transmission. Yet, in the post–World War II period, the enormous shadow cast on everyday life by nuclear fission was, perhaps paradoxically, imagined less in terms of physics than biology. The prospects of mass annihilation that gave rise to technothrillers and nuclear fiction proved to be less compelling overall for sf than those of mass mutation from radiation, and adaptation to postnuclear wastelands. As the threat of atomic war became familiar, and even receded after the 1960s, sf writers turned again and again to the horrific, and yet encouraging, possibility that the hopeful monsters created by nuclear or chemical teratogenesis might trigger new, more complex and powerful variations on humanity. In marked contrast with the rather naive utopian sf of the Soviet thaw, in which anagenetic leaps into a world of New Men could only be imagined as a result of peaceful technoscience, Euro-American and Japanese sf writers became enamored with "the imagination of disaster,"[34] and the interconnections of mass destruction and beneficial transmutations. As horror/sf writer Robert Bloch complained to his colleagues, it seemed as if his fellow sf writers believed "every mushroom cloud has a silver lining."[35] With peacetime breakthroughs in cybernetics, biochemistry, and gene research, socially managed mutation has become a dream of autopoeisis, the transcendence of humanity's limits and scarcities through collective self-evolution. In our time, the model of evolution has been extended to every aspect of science: from psychology (evolutionary epistemology) and cybernetics (AI, A-Life), all the way to the notion of natural selection among the multiple universes posed by quantum cosmology. While physicists searched for a Grand Unified Field Theory, biology arrived at its own tacit GUT of Evolution, subjecting every object, including the cosmos and mathematics, to the dynamics of variation and selection.[36] In the evolutionary worldview, anything that can be brought under the rubric of human concern must be reducible ultimately to questions of progress and decay—from the construction of the body to the construction of axioms.

TECHNO-EVOLUTION

A significant branch development within sf has been the application of the evolutionary paradigm to the technosphere. Via evolution, technology has gained its own history analogous to nature's. Beginning with the sociology of Lewis Henry Morgan, who categorized the evolutionary stages of civilization in terms of their levels of technological development, technology has come to be viewed not only as an expression of social progress, but one of its prime agents.[37] This deep connection has expanded into a vast analogy of biological evolution to technological innovation that has become a widely accepted modernist conception of civilization. The generating core of these similarities is that they both can be described as open dynamic systems:

> Both are material processes with nearly the same degree of freedom; even their dynamic regularities are similar. These processes take place in the self-organizing systems formed by the totality of the Earth's biosphere and humanity's technological activities, and this sort of system as a whole is characterized by the "progress," that is, the improvement of their effectiveness, of homeostasis, and their direct goal is the striving for a condition of ultrastable equilibrium.[38]

In the *Summa Technologiae* Lem semiseriously identifies a number of morphological parallels between biological and technoevolution: a tendency toward imitation of earlier forms, adaptations to crises of resources and competition through gigantism and miniaturization, and ostensibly nonfunctional traits aimed at sexual selection. Lem treats his elaborately extended analogy of natural and human creativity with some irony; for others, however, the analogy has become the basis for a serious field of sociological research: cultural evolution, which draws on diverse fields with similar assumptions, such as sociobiology, memetics, cultural ecology, and evolutionary psychology.[39] John Ziman, a leading proponent of the model, elaborates:

> This analogy can be developed in considerable detail. First of all: what are the structural analogies between biological and cultural processes? It is easy to think of situations where material artefacts — indeed, also, less tangible cultural entities, such as scientific theories, social customs, laws, commercial firms and so on — undergo variation by mutation and recombination of characteristic traits. These traits can be associated with "memes" — elementary concepts that replicate themselves and shape the artefacts, rather like genes. The entities that survive are differentially replicated and diffuse through the population. Mutualistic relationships are very common, as between pens and inks, or bombers and radar systems. Isolated sub-populations — "demes" — may separate for long periods before recombining. And so on.[40]

Ziman provides a list of episodes in the development of technology that are structurally similar to aspects of bio-evolution: evolutionary drift, adaptation to environmental change, developmental lock vestiges, niche competition, diversification, speciation, convergence, punctuated stasis, emergence, extinction, co-evolutionary stable strategies, arms races, ecological interdependence, increasing complexity, self-organization, unpredictability, path-dependence, irreversibility, and progress (4–5). Mapping evolutionary theory onto the technosphere necessarily predicates that humanity has been the beneficiary of progressive biological development. Technology in this frame is the *next step beyond natural evolution,* implying that the emergence of humanity was just such a next step vis-à-vis the rest of the biosphere. Human evolution provides technology's historical foundation and mediation; technoevolution signifies a Second Evolution, out of second nature, instigated and constructed by human civilization.

SF is the repository of most of the historically elaborated myths of techno-evolution, above all the struggle of human beings to manage the course of their own autoconstruction. The emergence of machines helping humanity to achieve its maximum comfort, security, and efficiency has come to be viewed as a historical force in its own right, propelling not just the odd inventor and explorer, but the whole species into new zones previously concealed by human beings' physical and intellectual limits. With synthetic chemistry, nuclear physics, molecular biology, and information theory, technology arrives at a point where it no longer merely imitates nature — as a screwdriver mimics the wrist, and an airplane mimics birdflight — but actually transforms the material world, using scientific knowledge to make its physical substrate operate in ways that Nature "will not." Second nature extends itself in this way into the core of matter. This move — a revolution within evolution, at least in the eyes of the technoscientific culture making it — I refer to as *artificial immanence,* the use by human agents of immanent physical processes to transform elemental conditions. With artificial immanence, human beings act as de facto transcendental transformers of nature in potentially irreversible ways.

Evolution itself has become at least locally manipulable through mutagenic technoscience — and this has become a driving enthusiasm of hypermodernity. Extropianism and transhumanism envision the human species's autoevolutionary upgrading of its physical makeup, including consciousness itself. This upgrading is to be effected through radical prosthetic substitution of organic processes that will grant vastly greater physical and mental power than the crude mechanisms of natural physicality.[41] Current genetic technologies that promise to transform the human germ-plasm have inspired a mood of technoscientific Lamarckism at the level of culture; ultimately, the application of genetic engineering and cloning is a cultural-political decision about whether, and how, to alter the future conditions of corporeal existence. Just as plausible (at least for the science-fictional imagination) is that human beings will synthesize creatures — robots, Artificial Intelligence systems, bionic agents, and so forth — that will take the baton of evolutionary progress from them, applying knowledge of autotelic technologies in ways unimaginable by limited human intelligence (except perhaps through sf's hypothetical prophecies). This technoscientific intervention into evolutionary processes fuses revolution and evolution into a horizon at which, in Donna Haraway's words, the difference between reality and sf is an "optical illusion."[42] But this revolution-in-evolution differs from other revolutions in that it can envision the transformation of physical conditions only, leaving all other values to be determined by beings yet to emerge. Whether those future creatures' values will include gratitude for their conditions of existence cannot be known.

Dispersive Futures

Dispersive models of future history are gradually gaining equal consideration with the established revolutionary and evolutionary models. In this paradigm, history is not the propagation of effects in a unitary and coherent field of events; instead, diverse historical formations branch or scatter in time. The differences among envisioned futures are not synthesized into a single evolutionary zone, a great macrospacetime in which all development takes place *sub specie evolutionis*. Rather than a tightly bound cause-and-effect process linking a given present (all aspects of which supposedly constitute a single *total* world) with a single future world, history becomes a variety of paths that disperse into disjunct alternatives: parallel worlds, infinite immanent splittings of world-lines, or futures separated from the present by cataclysmic ruptures. These might be motivated purely by physics (by quantum indeterminacy on a macrocosmic scale, for example), or the imaginary property of information to create physicomathematical singularities, such as the *Alephs* of William Gibson's *Mona Lisa Overdrive* (1988). More commonly, because sf cannot excise the ethical charge of even the most formal scientific concepts when it employs them for stories, alternative futures are built from the metaphorical ascription of epistemological, ontothetic, and social-ideological values to world models. Alternative realities embody alternative values, from the omnipotence of *Star Trek's* Q continuum, where quasi-humans have achieved amoral mastery over indeterminacy, to world-systems extrapolated from counterfactual historical victories by Napoleon, the Confederacy, Nazi Germany, the Counter-Reformation, and similarly failed aspirants to global power.[43]

The notion that human existence unfolds in different realms walled off from each other, yet accessible through extraordinary techniques, is one of the oldest in literature. Its pedigree extends to the ancient heroes' descent into the underworld and prophetic dream-visions. One of scientific rationality's main projects has been to unify all imaginable aspects of existence into a single coherent continuum of causes and effects — to turn apparent differences into one cosmos: a *universe*. Scientific enlighteners measure their progress by how well they absorb pockets of experience previously thought to be heteronomic into a single, overarching, rational-material set of explanations. SF has evolved in this cultural context. But because it is fiction, not science, sf is less concerned with validating the scientific-materialist worldview than in playfully problematizing it — prodding it, prying open its contradictions, and exploring its inconclusions. Of course, it isn't only scientific rationalism that comes in for such provocations. Using scientific rationality as its baseline, sf plays with all totalizing worldviews that purport to explain everything. As in all games, the goal is to encompass those baselines from outside them, not to dwell inside.

Time-travel stories and alternative realities/histories have long been popular romantic subgenres. In romantic fantasy, they dramatize timeless love; in heroic fantasy, they establish mythic time outside time. In sf, however, the rules of logic, time, and space may not be sidestepped altogether. They can be exceeded and refashioned through artificial immanence, or they can be parodied, but they must be acknowledged. The conundrums of relativistic space-time and quantum physics gave a footing for science-fictional treatments of time travel and alternative worlds. By the 1930s and early 1940s, writers like Fredric Brown, Robert Heinlein, and Lester Del Rey were experimenting with the counterintuitive paradoxes of time dilation, the curvature of space, and the limits of light speed. The exploitation of these ideas followed an arc familiar in most areas of sf, described here by Lem:

> At first, authors and readers are satisfied by the joy of discerning the effects of innovations still virginal as far as their inherent contradictions are concerned. Then, an intense search begins for initial conditions that allow for the most effective exploitation of consequences that are potentially present in a given structure. Thus, the devices of chronomotion begin supporting, e.g., theories of history and philosophy.... Then, grotesque and humorous stories like Fredric Brown's "The Yehudi Principle" (1944) appear: this short story is itself a causal circle (it ends with the words that it began with: it describes the test of a device for fulfilling wishes; one of the wishes expressed is that a story "write itself," which is just what happened). Finally, the premise of time travel serves frequently as a simple pretext for weaving tales of sensational, criminal, or melodramatic intrigue; this usually involves the revival and slight refurbishment of petrified plots. [44]

In Lem's view, new scientific ideas are worked to exhaustion by the field, and only inflows from new models or applications can refresh these ideas. The increasing popularity of variant futures since 1945, and especially after the 1960s, indicates that such a refreshment was ongoing. The new ideas came from physics itself: from the extension of quantum mechanics to macrocosmic scale (as in Hugh Everett's enormously influential many-worlds model, which poses that the collapse of the wave function issues in the propagation of distinct universes to accommodate each possible outcome); from the hypothesis of superluminal particles such as tachyons and superbradyons; and from speculation that universes might be contained within physical singularities. They came also from analogous models in informatics, such as Artificial Life in virtual environments, the prospect of de facto sentience within a computer simulation, and the universe-on-the-table (the cosmic version of the brain-in-a-beaker so beloved by early sf). Chaos and emergence theories provided the essential notions that the character of complex systems is profoundly sensitive to changes in initial conditions, and that their existence depends on a virtually incalculable number of contingent factors.[45]

SF writers would be professionally interested in such speculative scientific models in any case, but these models have been dramatically reinforced by cultural currents independent of physical science. Cultural anthropology and anticolonial liberation movements gave militant currency to the idea that different cultures inhabit different conceptual universes, and construct their histories accordingly. The gradual erosion of faith in revolution and the politicization of Darwinism weakened the popular cultural authority of both paradigms. The evolving hegemonic system of hypercapitalism fueled the fragmentation of social relationships on a global scale, a process that has led to ever more complex and intense "pluralization" of experience. The model of a situationally transcendent individual self has been challenged by the alternative model: that personal identity is a combination of chosen or solicited roles. Mass media has adapted to prick and sate this desire for variety in consumers, and to supply marketers with a sophisticated apparatus of mass psychological stimulation. In Brain McHale's phrase, television and its successor digital media act as "ontological pluralizers."[46] For Fredric Jameson, post-Fordist capitalism has led to a global psychic deracination, the evaporation of historical consciousness for populations no longer bound by any form of social obligation that has not been commodified.[47] From another angle, the temporary autonomous zone of the Internet has encouraged people to imagine the future of psychological and social identity entirely as a matter of freely chosen associations. The multiple, contradictory interpellations of global cultural flows are plain to see on the streets of great world cities and in mass media and cyber-communities. They have been accommodated with a *Star Trek*–like avowal of "infinite diversity in infinite combination," or by reactionary withdrawals into fundamentalist singularities. Modernism's aesthetic ideal of authenticity has been superseded by that of performance. In postmodern culture, every claim is a gesture, every thesis a script, each identity a mask, every world a theater.

The profession of history has also been influenced, as evidenced by the rise of nonhistoricist, "stochastic" historiography. As Niall Ferguson explains it, many new historians strive to excise all traces of determinism from their explanations, other than of entropy and quasi-scientific conceptions of evolutionary selection and quantum-uncertainty applied to historical evidence:

> The world is not divinely ordered, nor governed by Reason, the class struggle, or any other deterministic "law." All we can say for sure is that it is condemned to increasing disorder by entropy. Historians who study its past must be doubly uncertain: because the artifacts they treat as evidence have often survived only by chance, and because in identifying an artifact as a piece of historical evidence the historian immediately distorts its significance. The events they try to infer from these sources were originally "stochastic"—in other words, apparently chaotic—because the behavior of the material world is governed by non-linear as well as linear equations. The fact of human consciousness (which cannot be expressed in terms of equations) only adds to the impression of chaos. Under these circumstances, the search for universal laws of history is futile. The most historians can do is to make tentative statements about causation with reference to plausible counterfactuals, constructed on the basis of judgments about probability. Finally, the probability of alternative scenarios can be inferred only from such statements by contemporaries about the future as have survived. These points could be held up as the manifesto for a "chaostory"—a chaotic approach to history.[48]

The most important factor in the rising popularity of dispersive futures in sf, however, probably lies in the inner history of the genre itself. As more and more works of sf have been produced, so too have imaginary futures. These have been by and large superseded by reality. Inventions of the thirtieth millennium had to be backdated to the early twenty-first century; 1984 came and went, as did 2001. The Gernsback Continuum veered away. Yet such works of imaginary prophecy are still valued. It is sometimes said that any prophesied future that does not come to pass becomes a divergent reality. The coexistence of so many different imaginary futures becoming autonomous in time as fantasy worlds leads to a fictive temporal multiverse, densely populated with different models. The more of these a public is exposed to, the less naive they become about projections, and the more comfortable with alternate histories that lack causal connections with the familiar present. Quantity turns to quality: so many predictions have been made, so many fictive prophecies have become uchronias and "fantastic philosophy," that they rival the number of sincere predictions. Reading sf now incorporates the discounting process of already viewing it as an alternative timeline or a retrofuture.

Modernizing societies require the future as a horizon toward which to orient their collective projects, and as a zone to which they can defer the resolution of current contradictions. As more and more of these political-cultural prophecies are made obsolete by real trends, they join the great documentary archive of cultures' and classes' deepest fantasies and tactics. Just as a philosophy that is not accepted by its culture is indistinguishable from science fiction, prognoses that are disproved by events — even if they were once widely believed — join all other fantastic cultural expressions. In postmodern techno-scientific societies the archive of obsolete futures is growing to match the archive of remembered pasts.

By disrupting the temporal logic of continuity with the present, alternative histories and parallel worlds appear to renounce the ethical seriousness of the revolutionary and evolutionary paradigms. If there is no connection, how can there be responsibility? On the surface, such dispersed worlds lack even the minimal gravity of other kinds of future history. It makes sense to view this scattering as an example of the flattening of historical consciousness that Jameson considers a defining quality of postmodernism. The sense of the continuity of unidirectional time lived toward death and succeeding generations, which links the experience of individual life with collective history, is replaced by an infinite array. World and time lines can come into being and pass away as a result of factors whose variety defies comprehension, leading to the cloning or deletion of human agents in any particular reality, and ultimately to only formal relationships among the worlds. The abstract dispersal of realities frees them not only from the burden of an inexorable past, but from the resistance of nature and embodiment altogether. Like flying islands, alternative histories are figures of our inability to imagine the future as something inevitable, fated.

Time Travel: History Permeable and Discontinuous

Time travel brings the question of whether there can be only one future into the foreground, as a philosophical and ethical puzzle to be explicitly contemplated. It also displaces the future outside of historical futurism by substituting temporal disjunction for continuity. Time-travel narratives take the basic science-fictional pretense of empirical clairvoyance a step further. They pose the possibility, not only of imagining how the future will come into being, but of intervening in events that have already happened, in order to change their future, our present. Time ceases—for a moment or forever—to be the absolute, inexorable current of fate, the one-way traffic of human existence toward personal death. It becomes an architecture that can be redesigned, a plasma that can be shaped, or a machine that can be manipulated by human intentions.

The distinctive aspect of time travel in sf is that this intentional power over time is mediated by inventions: time *machines*. They might be the clockwork vehicles of Wells, the Proust-serums of Marker's *La Jetée* (1962), or time bombs that literally blow time apart. In whatever form they take, time machines demonstrate the power of technological rationality to take control over the part of nature we can least control. Inversely, "chronomotion" may not be the result of an invention, but a discovery of passageways between the phases of flow, corridors between the compartments of time. In such cases, one doesn't need a machine, only the schematics of the machine that is Time itself, a manifest of its parameters, tolerances, and stress points.

Travel to the future is not especially problematic in the context of sf. The future-directed time machine is usually a vehicle for rationalizing sf's obligatory futurism. It is in travel to the past that the latent turbulence of time comes into relief. The looming paradoxes and loops are the same in both domains but, as the future has only virtual existence, the contradictions have no consequences. Travel to the past, on the other hand, threatens the present's conditions of existence. I shall not dwell on the main loop-paradoxes, which are well known. (I'll just mention some of the main ones: the *grandfather paradox:* "I am my own progenitor" and its catastrophic variant, the *autopatricide:* "I go back into the past and cause the death of my own progenitors, thereby preventing my own future existence, and the time journey that created the situation in the first place"; the *retroendurance paradox:* "I exist as my future self in the past"; *the lost change paradox:* "if my past is my present, where does/did time pass?"; the *bitemporal present paradox:* "I exist in the future and the past at the same time." And there's the technical problem of round-trip time travel: how can a time machine avoid an instantaneous head-on collision with itself as it moves backward and forward in time on its journeys, passing through the same spacetime in different directions?)[49] These questions all come down to a single overarching interrogation: how can a conscious mortal being return to its origins, when it is fated to travel down a one-way road to death?

Wells designed his Time Machine only to illustrate a problem of social-political evolution. He did not experiment with the possible historical consequences of a Victorian Englishman negotiating spacetime traffic in his ride. These would be obsessively parsed in later incarnations. Constance Penley has linked retrochronal travel (especially in film) with witnessing the primal scene.[50] The recognition can be repressed for a while, but we keep going back to it (*La Jetée, Back to the Future* [1985]), or it comes after us (*The Terminator* [1984]). And, being paradox, both take place at once: the agent who travels through time to make things right is apt to be caught in its fatality (as in Harlan Ellison's *Outer Limits* episode, "The Demon with the Glass Hand" [1964] and *Terminator 2: Judgment Day* [1991]). Time travel to the past may have one ultimate purpose: to find a way to prevent our own deaths: "The clandestine social psychological goal of virtual time travel is to exterminate the radical otherness of history and other cultures, to short-circuit the difficult course of mourning, to meet up with none other than myself."[51]

Mortality is not an abstract problem. The presence of the body in the oxymoronically immutable medium of mutability throws a spanner in the works. The time traveler's body carries its own ticking bomb with it through all discontinuities. It may explode comically, as in Heinlein's "By His Bootstraps" (1941) and "All You Zombies." Or, it may implode horrifically, as in Dick's "A Little Something for Us Tempunauts" (1975). The comedy and pathos of time travel comes out of characters' attempts to use it to serve their mutable bodily desires. Bodies occupy space and situation. They articulate the flows of human relationships and time itself. Time travelers can influence things simply by taking up space in a given time. Their power may be unconscious and involuntary, yet still decide the fate of the world.

One precondition for sf time travel is the imaginary permeability of history. A time traveler moves through time as one might move through space, and adds an element of will and control to a domain in which we cannot but always be acted upon. The journey is nearly always extremely rapid or instantaneous, without a mediating experience of passage and duration. Bracketing out problems of duration can turn the relation of the future to the past into one purely of logic, the geometrization of time.[52] That is of course precisely the import of the Time Traveller's exquisite pre-Bergsonian folderol:

> "Scientific people," proceeded the Time Traveller, after the pause required for the proper assimilation of this, "know very well that Time is only a kind of Space. Here is a popular scientific diagram, a weather record. This line I trace with my finger shows the movement of the barometer. Yesterday it was so high, yesterday night it fell, then this morning it rose again, and so gently upward to here. Surely the mercury did not trace this line in any of the dimensions of Space generally recognized? But certainly it traced such a line, and that line, therefore, we must conclude was along the Time-Dimension."[53]

A permeable history allows bodies to move through historical time discontinuously, maintaining some of its own suprahistorical integrity while everything else is mutable. The implications are many. What was once dead can come to life again (as in the gothic and the Freudian return-of-the-repressed). The later can "infect" the earlier, and colonize it. Time can be ideologically controlled. Time that can be manipulated by power is paradoxically linked to the felt need, shared by many writers and scientists, to believe that the physical universe must not permit the alteration of the past to cause different future outcomes. Even physicists who argue that time travel is theoretically possible tend not to believe there can be return trips. The grandfather paradox is so powerful a threat that writers have posited "time cops," or a universal defense of progressive timelines. Stephen Hawking has proposed a "chronology protection conjecture" according to which the universe has safeguards against causal loops.[54]

This hard-encasing of distinct timelines that are nonetheless accessible to outsiders is the source of comic and parodic play as well. The incongruity between individuals' free movement and the rigid structure of time usually plays out in two ways. In one, the characters' mobility interferes with the strict structure of historical cause and effect, creating time loops. (I gather that, pace Everett, for most sf writers a temporal causal chain in its default mode strives for maximum simplicity, and will try to reassert itself after any disturbance.) In the other, with the rule that there must be special transfer points or nexuses and techniques, the structural rigidity of time reasserts itself over time travelers' freedom by requiring them to be at a certain place at a certain moment in order to overcome their own spacetime structures. They may need to use specific technologies to make use of the achronic corridors between spacetime continua (Bill and Ted have their phone booth; Connie Willis's Department of History has its drop sites). These constraints indicate that spacetime itself is either a gigantic machine, whose parts come into alignment at certain points in their operation, or an edifice that can be navigated through appropriate portals.

The fact that characters suffer no duration while negotiating these alignments may be necessary for narrative simplicity. Otherwise, they would have to experience several time-lines simultaneously. Unless some lines are obliterated by the changes encoded in new timelines (as they apparently are in Ray Bradbury's "The Sound of Thunder" [1952] and Ward Moore's *Bring the Jubilee* [1953]), an infinite number of clones might live in infinite respective alternative universes. This proliferation of timelines is a superb source of farce, as in Ijon Tichy's "Seventh Voyage" (1971), in which the spaceship of Lem's space Gulliver is damaged passing through a magnetic storm, and the ship becomes crowded with versions of past and future Tichys brawling with each other, and eventually helping each other to repair the craft. It can just as easily produce uncanny effects. In Shane Carruth's *Primer* (2004) two young engineers who accidentally invent a time machine begin to live distinct lives in two barely displaced time-lines, creating loops of increasing amplitude as they plan and remember ways of enabling the conditions of each one in its other.

In serious form, the nexus point can become a focus of intense anxiety, as in Connie Willis's *Doomsday Book* (1992), where slight miscalculations in measuring temporal drifts take the heroine from a future Oxford into the midst of the Black Death, and create suspense about her chances of being rescued. Even more suspenseful is the possibility that the past might literally infect the future by accidentally passing through the juncture-points in the form of plague germs. In Willis's *To Say Nothing of the Dog* (1997), the same calibration problems reproduce the algebra of farce, so dependent on timing and coincidence, in the material medium of time and chance itself. In Ward Moore's *Bring the Jubilee,* the nexus point is the Battle of Gettysburg, chosen by the historian protagonist as the critical moment in the Civil War. By simply taking up a position to observe it, he changes the course of history, leading to a more enlightened outcome (that is, our own world), but destroying his own past and the possibility of time travel with it. The mechanism of time appears to be extremely sensitive to observation.

For the paranoid imagination, this permeability of spacetime implies that the flow of historical consciousness can be controlled, not necessarily by benevolent forces. This control is the basis of much of Philip K. Dick's later fiction. In the *VALIS* trilogy Dick imagines that human history has been frozen at the year 49 A.D. All that has passed since then has been a hallucination imposed by a dark demiurgic force. Adapting gnostic theology, Dick posits that the agents in control of history are jailers, and that humanity has been for centuries trapped in a "Black Iron Prison" of its own deluded consciousness.[55] Thus with Dick, the premises of time travel are reversed; it is no longer the individual subject that moves discontinuously through time; rather, it is time itself that is manipulated to create the delusion of a free human subject.

Alternative Histories

Alternative histories fit uncomfortably in the category of future history, as the one time in which an alternative history cannot occur is the future. Nothing can be alternative when nothing is yet the case. But some discussion of the complex relationship between "allohistory" and sf is appropriate here, as the

The SEVEN BEAUTIES *of* SCIENCE FICTION

genres overlap in certain ways. Classical allohistory—such as Trevelyan's "What if Napoleon had won the battle of Waterloo?" and Churchill's "If Lee had not won the Battle of Gettysburg"—is a rigorously consistent thought-experiment in historical causality. Even if history has no agreed-upon laws, the alternative historian can persuasively illustrate hypothetical laws by constructing imaginary events and institutions issuing out of well-established familiar ones. But as a writer de-emphasizes counterfactuality per se, making the imaginary past into a reasonable, habitable world connected materially and emotionally with the readers' present, alternative history satisfies the generic expectations of sf. If sf is free history, nothing can be freer of the facts than alternative history; and yet, so bound is it to the logic of historical plausibility and the rhetoric of historiography that sf is what offers it imaginative freedom.

The status of the novum in dispersed histories is, as one might expect, paradoxical: the new thing is the change of world lines, undetectable to anyone in the given world. In order for the text's world to be a history, and not a collective delusion, its inhabitants must accept it as unambiguously real. The novum in this case is not the intrusion of the new, but the simple existence of the different. Alternative History stands in sharp contrast to sf's dynamic of depicting causal adaptations to ruptures. Many alternative histories are constructed by voiding a break that occurred in real history, using the conceit of removing a real novum, and modeling what happens when extrapolation continues without having to adapt to particular impediments of experience. A novum that is not detectable may no longer be a novum, but a point of alternative linear origin, with no trace-memory of its obliterated past. The only reliable witness to the novum then is the reader, who watches imaginary events dischronically, as if from time outside of time.

Alternative histories pretend to mediate intractable social contradictions by placing them in an ideal space *to the side* of consensus reality, where they can be manipulated without the sense of urgency and implication that comes when the future is felt to be at stake. Suvin's definition emphasizes this mediation: "Alternative History can be identified as that form of SF in which an alternative locus (in space, time, etc.) that shares the material and causal verisimilitude of the writer's world is used to articulate different possible solutions of societal problems, these problems being of sufficient importance to require an alteration in the overall history of the narrated world."[56]

Although they sometimes ponder the material conditions of history, alternative historians are much more interested in points where its unintended, immanent aspects intersect with conscious intentions and open contests for power. The first extended fictive alternative history, according to Alkon, was

Louis-Napoleon Geoffrey's *Napoléon et la conquête du monde — 1812 à 1832 —* *Histoire de la monarchie universelle* (1836). In a mix of *ressentiment,* political elegy, and metahistorical play, Geoffrey offered to correct the stupidity of the real history that led to Napoleon's defeat before he was able to unify the world under his enlightened rule. Works such as these are clearly not free from historical gravity. Geoffrey and his successors try, on the contrary, to *reconnect* the course of events to ethical meanings, from which they have been sundered by the arbitrariness of reality. In consummate romantic fashion, the counter-history attempts to reconstruct the chain of events as meaningful, while simultaneously drawing attention to reality's meaninglessness. The freedom of history comes at the expense of its reality.

Like time-travel sf, alternative histories gravitate toward primal scenes, the world-transforming events most commonly held to have been decisive for the fate of the nation or the species: Waterloo, Gettysburg, Columbus's voyage, the Spanish Armada, Hitler's rise, Hiroshima, the dinosaur-extinguishing meteor (which never arrived in Harry Harrison's *West of Eden* [1984]), and so forth. The dominant form of causation is the deeply Tolstoyan principle of nonaction: what if something that happened had not happened? What if a decision had not been made? What if nothing had turned at the turning point that created our world? Karen Hellekson names these points of potential divergence "nexus points"; fan culture often refers to them as the "jonbar hinges" (after John Barr, a character in Jack Williamson's 1938 serial, *The Legion of Time*).

Decisive nexus points are structurally similar to novums. They are, however, usually immanent events — either accidents or the results of ethical decisions by human characters. They rarely come about because of discoveries or inventions. When such technoscientific catalysts do play a role (Philip Jose Farmer gives Columbus a wireless, AK-47s are brought through time to Turtle-dove's Civil War, Ward Moore requires a time machine),[57] the historical narrative is subsumed by more classical science fiction. As with time-travel sf, the technoscientific ability to manipulate time removes the focus from the immanent unfolding of events, and places it on the duration-free metatemporal power of technologically handy human agents. In most alternative histories, the decisions at these decisive moments are made from within, as if by history itself. Such a model reifies and moralizes the dialectical model of history, ascribing ethical qualities to the contradictory historical forces in play, in tune with the authors' and publics' ideological commitments — and implying that it is the moral quality of the outcome that ultimately matters.

Many dramatic nexus points are not overtly world-historical. A common design for alternative histories is to begin a cascade of changes from a particularly small difference, a fractal primal scene, whose significance as a world-historical nexus is revealed only in the middle of the cascade. In Bradbury's canonical "The Sound of Thunder" the course of political history is changed when a time-traveling tourist accidentally kills a random butterfly in the prehistoric past. Reducing the nexus to microscopic relationships limits its usefulness for historians' thought-experiments. Individual butterflies are not often factored into the actions of those who influence the paths of a given age. But they go a long way to giving history a quasi-physical dimension, making it favorable to sf, which now has some first nature to play with. These whimsical games have been given influential support by chaos and game theories, which emphasize the power of small moves to coalesce or disrupt complex systems, and even to prevent them from emerging. When applied to history, such views de-emphasize human intentions (or for that matter, any model of purpose at all, including the population-protecting mechanism of evolution) and reassert the cold nonlinear equations of first nature's complexity at the heart of second nature.

Whatever the nexus, most commentators agree, the main focus of alternative history is the imaginative demonstration of how history works in any conceivable human universe according to tendencies like those of physical science. Writing of French uchronias, Marc Angenot maintains: "Uchronia is less the refusal of real history, than the recognition of its ineluctable laws; by altering the course of events the author gives birth to a new history, but one that still contains the same rational determinism and contingency as empirical history."[58] For Hellekson,

> science fiction plays within boundaries of physical law, even if the writer sometimes makes up the laws. One such boundary that sf does not tend to subvert is that of history and change: the movement from past to present, in terms of historical development or of evolution, is taken as a given. Even fiction that deals with time travel, wormholes in time or space, or other singular events that rupture the fabric of time acknowledge the movement from past to future and the role of cause and effect in that movement, even if one can move outside the present.[59]

Retrofutures

Alternative histories are generated by ideas that call into question the dominant concepts of who the subjects of history are. In the revolutionary and evolutionary models of sf, historical development comes to be seen less and less in terms of nations, religions, classes, or ideas, and increasingly in terms of the power of the dominant agents of technoscience: the technocratic class of Western/ized males, educated in rationality, skilled in technique, and able to extend the reach of their institutions to absorb others by demonstrating their power to increase material comfort, security, and power. When viewed by subjects other than these heroes of techno-evolution, history appears in a different light. SF writers have turned increasingly to counterhegemonic images of history, from the points of view of previously marginalized agents.

This revisionary energy reflects changes in the assumptions of anthropology, the science that emerged as historiosophy's main competitor in defining the meaning of human second nature. The early modern ethnological assumption that non-Western Others were unevolved residues of primitive humanity gave way in the twentieth century to models of cultural diversity. Linear and progressive dialectical models of history were challenged by models of lateral variation. Dramatic differences in culture came to be viewed, not on a world-historical timeline of development, but as equally legitimate adaptations to different historical-environmental conditions. This line discarded the axioms of evolutionism, and proposed that even the ostensibly irrational customs and beliefs thought to be the defining opposites of rational science, such as myth, magic, and sacred ritual, should be viewed as *alternative rationalities*.[60]

This new respect for the diversity of cultural formations was prefigured to some extent in the adventure fiction of the imperialist era. But just as the European adventure hero splits into Conrad's Kurtz and Marlow, field anthropologists became increasingly anxious about the way even the low-intensity exposure to Western civilization that they brought with them might lead to the extinction of cultures and languages they were supposedly committed to preserving. This sense of crisis eventually extended to Europe itself, where the inexorable progress of technological rationalization endangered the archaic stratum of national life that was considered the source — and hence, the justification — of national identity. (In the United States, this dynamic was late in developing, as the majority population emphasized, with violence, its lack of kinship with its "primitives," that is, Native Americans and the descendants of African slaves.)

Anxiety developed into a sense of crisis in the 1960s. The damage to indigenous, nonmodern cultures became the subject of public consciousness. At the same time, Third World liberation movements employed feelings of cultural distinctiveness and pride against European arrogance — with the paradox that these appeals to national distinctiveness served economic and political rationalization, and the entrance of the newly liberated nations into the neocolonial world-system as valuable "nonaligned" players sustained by the competition within the dominant modern system. Anthropological sf came to the forefront, in works like Herbert's *Dune,* Le Guin's Hainish novels, Ian Watson's *The Embedding,* Michael Bishop's "Death and Designation Among the Asadi" (1974), and many others that reflected the new concerns of anthropologists. The current was reinforced by the wave of dystopian and satirical visions of technoscience's cultural vandalism (such as Vonnegut's *Cat's Cradle* [1963], Brunner's *Stand on Zanzibar* [1968] and *The Sheep Look Up* [1972]).

Feminist and feminist-inflected sf, in particular, rejected the progressive/regressive "evolutionary success" model. Feminist writers used deconstructive and fabulist strategies, in which the hidden presuppositions of the Euro-androcentric model are exposed, while refusing to construct unambiguous countermyths. Most notably in works like Joanna Russ's *The Female Man,* Le Guin's *The Left Hand of Darkness,* Suzy McKee Charnas's *Holdfast Chronicles* (1978–2000), and Gwyneth Jones's Aleutian trilogy, historical evolution is refigured and ultimately abandoned as a credible model of history. Other writers fictionalized more mythlike, utopian alternatives, in which the continuity of present history into the future is voided (Piercy's *Woman on the Edge of Time,* Elgin's *Native Tongue* [1984]). The work of Samuel R. Delany, in particular, has been based on the often explicit critique of the heroic agent of history, with its implicit reliance on narrative continuity, dramatic-dialectical structure, and transcendental closure as tools of legitimation, performing wholesale substitutions of the system with experimental models of nontotalizing history. Arguably, the greatest influence sf has had on postmodern writers of the slipstream,[61] such as Thomas Pynchon, Kathy Acker, Haruki Murakami, Jonathan Lethem, Steve Erickson and others, is the delight in this experimental regime of playful and acid dismantling of the social evolutionary mythology distilled in earlier sf.

In the 1960s and 1970s, sf became a popular and commercially respectable market. The Soviet and U.S. space programs validated its cultural influence. Its potentials for cinematic spectacle were realized in big-budget mainstream films. This new respectability led to creative booms of international proportions. New audiences inspired a prodigious output of sf narratives in every medium of art, and sf's clichés became everyday phrases. A certain critical mass was reached. SF artists became comfortable with their tradition, and entered a phase of confident self-referential production. The genre had established a cultural presence and a thesaurus of motifs and texts that it could allude to, vary, parody, and pastiche, without qualms. A public megatext was inaugurated.

The megatext revealed many things, but perhaps nothing so striking as the sophistication with which sf readers had begun to approach the notion of the future. Fear of inevitable nuclear war began to relax among the populations of the cold war, and with that new hope came also a new sense of the openness of the future. SF's prophetic power was mixed with the knowledge that most of its futures had never come to pass. By the 1970s, the clichés of the genre had gained sufficient cultural power to become the clichés of technoculture at large, and sf writers began openly to use the materials of the genre's archive to construct their imaginary worlds. This usage had a double effect: sf acquired an energized and urbane pride in its tradition, and it began to be weighed down by its formulas recycled in pastiche.

Steampunk

Steampunk is a covering term for sf implanted in imaginary pasts, in which technological inventions and discoveries that did not happen are imagined to have occurred. The vast majority of these texts are placed in the nineteenth century, when the new technoscientific phenomena stimulate alternative industrial revolutions. Where cyberpunk explores the relationship between contemporary social life saturated with high tech and the science-fictional imagination, steampunk processes the genre's origins: the points at which both the literary form and its technological subject emerge in tandem. In short, its primal scenes.

Steampunk combines, in principle, every type of sf: time-travel tales, alternative histories, revolutionary and evolutionary future histories, and extraordinary voyages, all set in hypermodernized pasts. And even though many steampunk works are dense with historically accurate details, the historical model they use is not that of classical history, but history viewed through the eyes of the genre. SF writers are acutely aware that the digitization of information makes distinguishing between original sources and altered copies increasingly difficult. As a consequence, the steampunk project is inspired by an archetypal ambivalence about origins. It returns to the historical past to discover its own determining conditions, its founding heroes and heroines, its seeds and possibilities in their nascent form — not only of its literary life, but of the technological imagination itself. But because sf is fantasy, it also wants to reimagine all this through its own image of desire, now that it has the cultural power and the concepts to do it. In quintessential sf style, it wants to recover its history — a history of imagining, after all — by colonizing and absorbing it into the fantasies of the present.

Steampunk works are, accordingly, not so much counterfactual, as, to use Matt Hills's term, *counterfictional*.[62] The London of William Gibson's and Bruce Sterling's *The Difference Engine* (1990) is accessed through the looking glass of Dickens. Paul Di Filippo's *Steampunk Trilogy* (1995) experiments with nineteenth-century British and American literary dictions. Michael Moor-cock's *The Warlord of the Air* (1971) reinhabits a Vernean universe. Alongside real historical characters, steampunk writers adopt characters from classic lit-erary texts, continuing their stories in overtly and self-consciously fictional parallel universes (for example, K. W. Jeter's *Morlock Night* [1979], Kim New-man's *Anno Dracula* [1992], and *The Difference Engine*'s poachings from Wilkie Collins and Disraeli).

SF writers' recent fascination with the artificiality of their own enterprise reaches an apogee in *The Difference Engine*. In an alternative London of 1855, Charles Babbage's Difference Engine actually works, and is applied to social life in the same way that information technology is applied in ours. The alter-nativity of the history has actually little to do with prosaically realistic scenar-ios that might have attended this novum. Gibson and Sterling instead con-struct a metafictional metahistory, a *meta–alternative history*. Their focus is not on what might have been historically possible, which would presuppose the discourse of historical realism. Instead, they focus on the imaginatively possible, a dialectical mesh of fantasies of the Victorians' social, political, and cultural institutions, as both the Victorians themselves and *fin de millenium* U.S. techno-bohemians might imagine them. *The Difference Engine* is a pas-tiche of Victorian social and technoscientific history, Disraeli's political fiction, and urban adventures à la Dickens and Wilkie Collins — all of which appear in the end to be the ruminations of an anachronistic AI creating the world by writing a novel for itself.

With *The Difference Engine,* and steampunk in general, the rewriting of his-tory is no longer concerned with earnest questions about the meaning of historical events as if they were physical ones, whose constitution and beha-vior can and must be correctly described. Now, worlds are no longer naive; they are sentimental with a vengeance. The implicit and understated play comes into the foreground, not just for its own sake, but on a metalevel, as a new problem to be played with. In *The Difference Engine* a significant nexus point of the past — the moment when Babbage's engine might have inter-sected with the industrial revolution in Western Europe — is reimagined in terms of a strong problem of our own age, a potential nexus point of our pres-ent's future: the intersection of AI and the information revolution. It is a situation that can no longer be imagined naively. In our time, sf, historiogra-phy, and critical theory have explored problems of historical consciousness so extensively that the explorations have become part of the thing observed. *If* historical memory is a product of documents that are selected and archived by the people with the power to do it; and *if* this memory consists not only of the conscious and declared ideas of a past society, but also its unconscious desires and fears preserved indirectly in art and artifacts; and further, *if* one can explain the past only by what is most powerful in the present — then we need the imaginary of the past to understand why some things were selected and archived. What inspired and molded the "rationality" of earlier generations' view of history and the past? History ceases to be a matter of describing events and experience, and becomes a matter of associating texts. With alternative history, sf becomes concerned with its own textuality. In *The Difference Engine,* Gibson and Sterling "play with the notion of integration, with the *constructedness* of cause and effect, which they foreground with techniques that focus on iteration. Their narrative play (and their plays on words and plays on technological innovations that are old news to modern readers) allows free play of cause and effect."[63]

Singularity Fiction

The three dominant paradigms of sf's future history — revolution, evolution, and dispersion — rarely appear in pure form. When they do, they tend to crystallize in overt subgenres: utopia/dystopia, space opera/alien contact/monster sf, and alternative history. In most sf, the paradigms are merged and conflated in different forms. Revolutionary and evolutionary models combine in stories about technical-political interventions in the evolutionary process: Uplift Wars, the evolution of New Men, eugenic epics, and so forth. We can now also see the conflation of all three in the quintessential postmodern myth of the Singularity. The vision of a sudden leap by the technosphere into self-interested self-consciousness, sealed off from the human world that created its conditions of possibility, is the descendant of sf's three historical lineages. It involves the consciously, intentionally revolutionary act of applying artificial immanence to create nanospheric artificial life and artificial intelligence — the evolutionary dialectic of artificial emergence (the next phase of complexity in the development of homeostatic systems), and dispersion, in that the Singularity will have its own history and autoevolution.[64]

FOURTH BEAUTY

Imaginary Science

o o o o o o o

SF's *free science.* Science is sf's pretext. Every quantum-info-nano-bio-cyber-astro-psycho-xeno-socio-physical infodump pumps up the illusion that sf stories are dramatizations of scientific knowledge. But even in the hardest of hard sf, sf's science is always figurative. It is an *image* of science, a poetic illusion disguising its illusionary status. The diegetic facts about the physics of onrushing asteroids or the biochemistry of consciousness may be ones that real-world scientists believe to be true. The theories that characters formulate, and the principles on which their worlds are constructed, may be ones that practicing scientists entertain. But within the frame of fiction, these are raw materials only. Many sf writers employ scientific ideas scrupulously. But there is no compulsion for them to do so. They use the language and history of technoscience to evoke the coherence and correspondence of the scientific worldview — but always with the freedom to violate, stretch, ironize, and problematize it. If actual science intends to increase human beings' freedom by augmenting their power over matter, sf makes both freedom and power the subject of play.

In technoscientific culture there are diverse notions of what constitutes science. Instead of a single monolithic, officially sanctioned prototype, people build their conceptions of science from a great variety of uses, experiences, and images. As in ancient imperial cities, where people with dramatically differing and often internally contradictory ideas of religion crossed paths regularly and exchanged views, technoscientific moderns share a technological environment, but interpret it from many different perspectives. Technology and science charge every atom of social existence. Machine mediation and technical management pervade daily habits. But other customs of thought flow through and absorb technology in their turn. Highly technologized cultures entertain varieties of scientific imagination ranging from childlike natural fantasy to the contemplation of quantum gravity, with all the streets' uses in between. In high-tech capitalism, technoscience produces words and images that sell and legitimate commodities and power, sensation and desire. In the empire of technoscience every area of concern is examined scientifically, with a technological solution as a goal. But the concerns carry ancient baggage that science does not secure.

As a genre label, "science fiction" is ostentatiously oxymoronic, and in a particularly ambiguous way. What are the forces of attraction and repulsion between these opposites? Where do they get their powers? In my view, sf has always engaged scientific ideas and speculations in order to affirm the freedom of the artistic imagination from the constraints of deterministic and oppressively systematic ideas. Exaggeratedly rationalistic theories ignore sf's fundamentally playful performance of scientific thinking. Even when it is written by professional scientists with established reputations, sf requires its science to violate scientific correctness, even plausibility. Writers take known, plausible, or just widely entertained scientific ideas and extend them speculatively into the unknown, exceeding their contexts, revealing their fantastic dimensions, and undermining obliquely their claims to universal applicability. Most sf writers, far from pushing an agenda of scrupulous respect for scientific truth, toy with it, making it a source of metaphors, rationalized by realistic representation, and embedded in quasi-mythic narrative traditions that express social concerns.

Playing the Game

The genre has the not wholly undeserved reputation of being a propaganda arm of technocratic ideology. Verne had an avowed pedagogical purpose in writing the *Voyages Extraordinaires*.[1] Gernsback's editorials argued often that "scientifiction" was to be based on rigorous adherence to known science, and that the genre would benefit humanity by instilling the virtues of scientific consciousness in its readers, a view even more aggressively advanced by Campbell. And yet Gernsback and Campbell depended on sf that was scientifically dubious to fill the pages of *Amazing* and *Astounding*.[2] And for Verne, the line between scientific correctness and fantasy was not hard and fast, although it was imperative for his project that it appear to be so.[3]

Wells approached his fictions less soberly. In his early essays, he often entertained contradictory views on undecided questions of evolutionary development, and was equally comfortable with optimistic and pessimistic outcomes for the human species. Evolution's experiments could be argued either way.[4] In fiction, he was acutely aware that to make the fusion of scientific ideas and fiction convincing, the science would have to be the more flexible of the pair, as the effect of the fantastic narrative depends not on its accuracy, but on its evocativeness and persuasiveness. He knew that the scientific discourse seemingly at the heart of scientific romance was a particular form of rhetoric he called "scientific patter":

> For the writer of fantastic stories to help the reader play the game properly, he must help him in every possible unobtrusive way to *domesticate* the impossible hypothesis. He must trick him into an unwary concession to some plausible assumption and get on with his story while the illusion holds. And that is where there was a certain slight novelty in my stories when they first appeared. Hitherto, except in exploration fantasies, the fantastic element was brought by magic. . . . But by the end of the last century it had become difficult to squeeze even a momentary belief out of magic any longer. It occurred to me that instead of the usual interview with the devil or a magician, an ingenious use of scientific patter might with advantage be substituted. That was no great discovery. I simply brought the fetish stuff up to date, and made it as near actual theory as possible.[5]

Wells held that the function of science in scientific romance was to create convincing parameters for the reader to assent to the constraints of the imaginary world. These parameters differ from those of magical fantasy, not only in that they are verified outside the text by the authority of scientists, but because they follow the rigorous game rules of scientific discourse. For Wells, who had also written textbooks in physiology and biology, this fidelity meant using familiar images and language to make the reader feel at home in the extraordinary.

Contemporary writers of hard sf still refer to writing it as "playing the game."[6] Hal Clement, an acknowledged master of hard sf, formulated it as a cheerful competition between authors and readers: "The fun . . . lies in treating the whole thing as a game. I have been playing the game since I was a child, so the rules must be quite simple. They are: for the reader of a science-fiction story, they consist of finding as many as possible of the author's statements, or implications which conflict with the facts as science currently understands them. For the author, the rule is to make as few such slips as he possibly can."[7]

Such a cat-and-mouse aesthetic involves the logical-cognitive energies of world building — extrapolation, verification, and falsification — and speaks mainly to readers who are educated and intellectually confident enough to enjoy solving scientific puzzles. In other words, to insiders of technoscientific mythology. Readers match wits with writers in terms of two overlapping kinds of modeling: the fit of the imagined world to the known world described by science (scientific correspondence), and the fit of the details of the imagined world to its overarching design (science-fictional coherence). The more traditional functions of literary narrative—to motivate collective and individual human actions within the world frames—are much less important to this kind of sf gaming than the rigor of setting.[8]

Reflecting on the hard sf aesthetics of his classic novel, *Mission of Gravity* (1954), Clement establishes a hierarchy of techniques that sf writers employ for toying with scientific truths.[9] The first is simply to use jargon, doubletalk, Wells's "scientific patter." Clement considers this tactic as "lacking discipline," essentially cheating. Second, a writer may speculate on subjects where there's little scientific data ("not much of a challenge"). Third, the setting might be where scientific advances are very easily foreseen ("small steps into the future predict small advances"). At the pinnacle is the deliberate creation of "the most spectacular, implausible environment or development possible while adhering to all known scientific facts." Seen as games, each of these tactics can be pleasurable, but the last surpasses the others, because readers, as they participate in imaginative world building, relax their testing behavior, and absorb the elaborate spectacle of wonders whose scientific basis is rarely immediately obvious. The very rigor of the scientific superstructure acts as the Trojan horse for nontechnical storytelling.

Most sf is written for a wider audience, and most readers, even highly educated nonscientists, lack the knowledge and desire to be equal partners in verifying statements about string theory and brain chemistry. For the most part, scientific ideas contribute to what Gwyneth Jones calls sf's distinctive "deep décor," which readers take as givens of the inherently counterfactual universe.[10] Readers tend to give writers the benefit of the doubt that the science brought forward is accurate—a trust that is often abused, but perhaps no more than in realistic fiction that lays claim to readers' trust and yet delivers images of life from distorted class, gender, or racial perspectives. But because it is read as fiction, sf's science is treated with provisional faith; and because it is expected to be speculative, readers anticipate that the science will at some point warp what is generally agreed to be the case. Where that point is will vary from text to text, on a spectrum from narratives in which the scientific base deviates only slightly from accepted contemporary views and experimentally verified theories, to those based on speculations remotely conceivable in terms of current knowledge but with no good evidence for them (the *not impossible*), and ultimately to fantastic ideas with the rhetorical appearance of scientific explanation, but that are actually playful jargon. As scientific explanations are regular events in sf, readers expect them to be treated with as much attention as any other element of narrative. The required scientific information can come in many forms—expositional infodumps, dialogical debate, dramatic drip-feed—which readers expect not only to deploy information, but to be enjoyable as well.

In this chapter, my approach will be to look at areas of overlap between scientific and science-fictional narrative creativity. I am not competent to describe, let alone to judge, how accurately sf writers make use of scientific knowledge. Nor can I address whether sf induces readers to think scientifically as they process the literary information. My concern is how sf plays with its raw material: the way scientific ideas are articulated to a wider public. My claim, in the end, amounts to no more than that sf artists design fictive, ludic mini-myths that build on the playful imitation of technoscientific imagining. I shall attempt to correlate sf with the inherently imaginative (indeed, fiction-producing) aspects of scientific thinking, which sf then transforms in its own ludic image.

One of the distinctive attractions of the genre is the way it places abstract information about technology and science in the service of figuration and narrative. Audiences emerge for this type of pleasure only where scientific knowledge has been widely disseminated in popular media through journalism, museums, exhibitions, democratic classrooms, and similar popular institutions. Because this form of knowledge is of its essence intended to attract new candidates for a scientific intelligentsia and to condition the wider public to accept the global changes managed by them, on-the-ground responses to it are largely out of institutional control. Actual practice may be regulated by state or class management of the means of scientific production (for example, restrictions on lab use, university admissions, and access to scientific research), but as long as scientific ideas are widely circulated they become part of an enormous fluid social narrative, assimilated simultaneously to old and new concerns. It is this ongoing discourse between science as a regulated discipline and a chaotic combinatory popular discourse that sf mediates. In such a world, basically any conception of science entertained by the culture can become a pre-textual structure for sf—on a spectrum from scientistic-technocratic "iron laws of the universe" to the spectacular display of scientific fetish-objects. C. S. Lewis's trilogy of religious-allegorical planetary romances has a legitimate place within the practical boundaries of sf, alongside the inspired absurdities of *The Incal* (1981–89), *The X-Files* (1993–2002), and *The Fifth Element*, even though for them science is no more than a web of sophistries, a toy factory, or one particular altered state among many.

Much of sf's appeal is that it rationalizes highly romantic and fantastic stories by means of scientific ideas. But it is just as true that much of sf, maybe even most of it, has little or no "cognitive" value as Suvin uses the term. SF does not necessarily help readers to become more rational, or to transcend ideology by recognizing the true state of things. It is cognitive in another sense. It engages the worldview of scientific materialism and supplements it with quasi-mythic narrative to make models relevant to cultures on the ground. In the process, it transforms technoscience from the way of the world into an evidently inexhaustible font of rationalized, playful world-stories.

The Imaginary Supplement

In her essay "Science Fiction and Myth Creation in our Age," Soviet Russian sf scholar Tatiana Chernyshova argues that sf should be read in terms of cognitive conceptions of myth. In her view, the science-fictional imagination develops out of a fundamental operation of concept-formation:

> [H]uman beings will draw conclusions whether there is sufficient information available or not. Human consciousness cannot abide obscurity, and it will supplement true information, if it is lacking, with false information, and in this way it will put an end to its uncertainty. . . . Where does false information come from? There can be only one answer: from the "inner resources" of consciousness. When there is not enough information about a given phenomenon, or people are for some reason incapable of acquiring it, they will take information from some other domain and supply the missing links.[11]

Myths in this sense combine accurate knowledge about the material world with fantastic images and narratives, the latter filling in the lacks of the former. Because "all new knowledge reveals a new abyss of the unknown," the process of myth-making bricolage continues within scientific speculation and model-making. Faced with new questions about nature, scientists, no less than poets, seek analogies to supplement and complete what they can verify, even if only provisionally and whimsically: "It is precisely analogy that embodies the fundamental movement of cognition — from the familiar and the known to the unknown and the inexplicable. Wherever analogy has a place, there is always an escape hatch for the creation of myth" (349). She continues:

> The history of science is full of examples of such gnoseological myths, when unintelligible phenomena, about which there was insufficient valid information, were explained through causes that in fact had nothing to do with them, yet on the basis of previous experiences were intelligible. . . .
> The astronomer Pickering, for example, observing certain changes in the moonscapes, explained them as the migration of insects. Herschel thought sunspots to be breaches in a cloud cover. The story of the discovery of

The SEVEN BEAUTIES *of* SCIENCE FICTION

Martian canals is well known — they were perceived as analogous to ir-
rigation systems.

Chernyshova is mainly concerned with the social valuation of science in the
dialectical relationship between scientific research and popular consciousness. In her account, before the turn of the twentieth century, science developed in isolation from the masses, who were dominated by religious world
pictures and models of conduct. As the authority of religion waned, science
took over its role as the ruling explanatory model of reality. The need to popu-
larize science, to give it widespread social relevance, became a central concern
of modernist culture. In a scientific culture, people widely accept theories that
they are unable to verify, or even to explain in a rudimentary fashion, on educated faith in the authority of scientists. They will also supplement their scientific beliefs with other, irrational, or superseded ones, whenever the scientifically rational explanations are obscure or incomplete for their purposes. In
everyday life, these may range from superstitions and religious myths to class-
room images of atomic billiard balls. Even in these folk forms, the scientific
mode of explanation remains an ideal — and folk theories will adopt the language of scientific cause and effect to explain nonrational beliefs.

Once scientific ideas cross the social blood/brain barrier between technical
and popular consciousness, they are embedded in an enormous, living, fuzzy
patchwork of beliefs, cognitive adaptations to momentous material changes
brought on by the application of technoscience to daily life:

> [E]xact knowledge, after it ceases to be the property only of specialists,
> loses its right to be called exact; it has become approximate knowledge,
> belief, since its holder is able neither to prove it, nor to provide rationale
> for it. After all, such a rationale is possible only at the level of mathemati-
> cal calculations. Popular consciousness simply tosses aside all such cal-
> culations when it adopts the scientific world-model, since mathematics
> has not yet become a fundamental everyday mode of thought. Everyday
> thought remains up to this day based on the image. (352)

For Chernyshova, a society cannot advance materially if popular consciousness does not adopt science as its primary model for understanding the world.
But this adoption is never of science in a pure form. Living quotidian lives,
people lack important information for a complete picture of the world. The
gap may be because the knowledge is accessible only to certain groups, or
simply because it is impossible to acquire (as in the case of extraterrestrial civilizations). The culture will fill these gaps with forms of information it already
has available to it, drawing from a storehouse of received traditions and arrest-

ing images that have no necessary connection to the science, other than their fitness to complete a world-picture. SF is the branch of cultural production that takes this bricolage to be its primary model. We might say, following Schiller, that "naive" mythology is no longer possible in a scientific-critical age. Even so, sf continues to construct "sentimental" myths that simultaneously satisfy readers' needs for complete world-pictures, and call ironic attention to their ludic and constructed character. Stapledon called *Last and First Men* an "experiment in myth creation."[12] Inasmuch as sf is *free myth*, entertaining belief in scientific explanations but demanding no commitment, Stapledon's words can apply to all sf.

Chernyshova believes that the transformation in popular imagination from religious to scientific mythology is a precondition for the cultivation of science itself as a privileged social practice. Before major scientific projects can be imagined, let alone undertaken, there must be a widely felt sense of new material horizons.

> [M]odern myth creation does not precede science, but follows behind, and its myths are built on scientific results. Those who reject the notion that sf is proto-science and may anticipate science on the road to truth are correct. Nonetheless, we can speak of a certain kind of precedence. The paradox lies in the fact that at a certain point the requirements of everyday consciousness preceded the possibilities of science. The inner logic of social progress required the profound transformation — the cosmicization — of everyday consciousness, and science did not have the time to construct a solid basis adequate for this need. (353)

Space programs would not have been possible without the stitching of Copernican cosmology to narrative images of alien beings in undiscovered lands and visions of perfect spacefaring machines. The desires and anxieties crystallized in the playful myths of sf prepare the ground for real scientific projects.

Contemporary science has established itself as a worldview with no serious challenge, and it increasingly allows itself to consider grand speculative problems that once were limited to sf, such as the enigma of extraterrestrial intelligence and the future evolution of the human species. As a result, in Chernyshova's view, sf's "anticipatory myth-creating function" (355) in educating popular consciousness has largely ceased. It has become an art, elaborating the mythic raw material that it once generated:

> The modern mythological picture of the world has already taken shape, and will probably remain so in the future, until we acquire some new direct fundamental information, and it will probably not be shaken even

by the discovery of some primitive forms of life on our Solar System's planets. In recent times, sf has created fewer and fewer new ideas and hypotheses. (Nowadays these are usually created in scientists' studies and laboratories.) Sf now elaborates, deepens, and psychologizes already existing "mythological" themes and situations, the already classical themes of alien visitations, extraterrestrial civilizations and their relations, or near-light speed space travel. Historically, nonetheless, myth creation has been one of sf's most important functions, and it has not disappeared entirely.

Conceptual Prosthesis

Chernyshova restricts herself to imaginary supplements in the public projects of explaining, justifying, and contesting science as a social institution. But in fact, scientific theorizing has relied on creative syntheses of what is known to be true and what is unknown but imagined, throughout its history. A narrative of science can easily be constructed in terms not of successively more adequate rational paradigms, but of a dialectic of patches — whose incongruous and sometimes overtly nonscientific components, far from obstructing theories from achieving their rightful validation, are often the spurs to creative elaboration and critique. These fanciful concepts are in retrospect the science-fictional element at the heart of scientific praxis. Phlogiston, the luminiferous aether, the *bathybius haeckelii* (the class of abiogenetic transitional beings between the primal mud and the first living organisms, passionately affirmed by T. H. Huxley and Ernst Haeckel), and Einstein's cosmological constant are examples within scientific rationality itself of supplementary concepts invented to mediate between verified theories and the desire for a complete world-picture, "missing links" that became officially imaginary when they were invalidated.[13]

Every new scientific concept involves great zones of knowledge that are either undefined (Chernyshova's "new abyss of the unknown") or implicitly bracketed out (in tacit *ceteris paribus* clauses), or both. These voids attract supplementation from other areas of knowledge and belief. In science, this produces a sort of sampling and remixing of models that can yield fruitful results: from raw trial and error (such as Edison's search for the optimal material for the lightbulb filament, which included hair from a worker's beard), to theoretical analogies that use one structure to complete another in a new application (Darwin's cross-hatching of Malthus and animal husbandry, Freud's conflation of thermodynamics and affects, Bohr's combination of mechanics and electromagnetism).[14] Scientific models are often patchworks of elements drawn from diverse kinds of experience—phenomenological, mathematical, bits of other models, analogies—and their construction is one of the most artistic and intuitive aspects of scientific concept-formation.[15] Speculation in science involves the imaginary testing of these combinations and complements, through invented scenarios that we refer to as *thought-experiments*.

In the spirit of sf, I shall substitute the term *prosthesis* for *supplement*, and give a vaporous abstraction an imaginary body. Two bodies, in fact: the prosthesis itself and the body of concepts that it simultaneously completes and marks as perpetually incomplete by grafting its "foreign" substance onto it. The prosthetic concepts of sf are, like most prostheses, prone to become fetishized in classically psychoanalytic fashion, taking on the energy and mana of the longed-for complete and satisfactory worldview, a utopian consummation that the real body of scientific concepts lacks—a fact continually marked by the generation of new fetish-supplements. In the artistic/conceptual economy of sf, these ideational, wish-fulfilling supplements are figured as literal prostheses, machines and technologies that exceed the given world, make the world exceed itself, and enable the human species-ego (or whatever alien/AI acts as its surrogate) to exceed its force, intelligence, and mortal limits. From this fetish-engine come the great cosmic technologies that embody the science of sf: interstellar spaceships, time machines, ftl drive, navigable wormholes, evolution instigators, teleportation, artificial wisdom, material immortality.

Just as neologisms unite two semantic/conceptual domains that are not "yet" combined in real usage, and as novums combine two historical-physical trendlines counterfactually, the fictive science of sf combines two cognitive/explanatory systems that real technoscience has not—yet. This combining involves the imaginary resolution of real contradictions characteristic of all myth, by displacing them in the form of new, imaginary contradictions. SF's fictive science displaces the dilemmas posed for human existence by real technoscience into extreme cases, in which epistemological questions tip over into ontological ones, and conflicts involve power over material existence itself. In this process, the narrative pretends that the ground of reality is established by technoscience, that science creates the material world in its image, that ontology recapitulates technology.

The Thought-experiment

SF overlaps real scientific thinking in the construction of thought-experiments, imaginary tests in which logical rigor and narrative scene complement each other. In general, a thought-experiment is a conceptual elaboration of an imaginary model, "an idealization which transcends the particularity and the accidents of worldly human activities in order to achieve the generality and rigour of a demonstrative procedure."[16] It is an idealization that somewhat paradoxically takes dramatic, and often overtly fantastic forms. The term *experiment* is ambiguous in this context. There is considerable dispute among philosophers about precisely what sorts of knowledge thought-experiments yield.[17] In scientific speculation, the thinker tends to extrapolate from agreed-upon parameters to reveal surprising implications latent within a model. Scientific thought-experiments are strictly confined to narrowly focused theoretical situations, and they yield unambiguous interpretations. Philosophical thought-experiments are much more generalized; their scenarios may be wildly imaginative and open to diverse interpretations. But the putative truth content of thought-experiments is not relevant for our context. The central shared element of thought-experiments is not their purpose, but rather their narrative structure; they are, in David Gooding's phrase, "literary entities."[18] They require idealized, *fictionalized* testing of imaginary situations, in which operations are connected to results via causal principles based on widely shared ideas of logic and experience. They are compellingly *plausible*. They involve conflicts, resolutions, agents, and audiences, developed through action in time. They are *stories*.

John Norton describes thought-experiments as a form of argument, with two essential elements: they "posit hypothetical or counterfactual states of affairs," and they "invoke particulars irrelevant to the generality of the conclusion."[19] The first distinguishes them from real experiments, while the second gives them the appearance of being like them. In Norton's view, every thought-experiment could in principle be reformulated without the irrelevant details, but the form is preferred when a direct derivation within a theory may be too cumbersome, or when "the vehicle of the thought experiment might make easier the introduction of certain philosophical principles or facilitate certain inductive moves" (131). These "irrelevant particulars" are, of course, irrelevant only for the theoretical proposition being demonstrated; they are very pertinent for the way the vehicle is constructed. Indeed, they are more complex than most commentators admit; they tend to include two kinds of irrelevance: (1) impossible idealizations (from perfect vacuums to *ceteris paribus* conditions that allow processes to occur in the thought-experiment that could not happen in real life), and (2) narrative elements that set the scene in a concrete, more or less realistic way (a cat in a box, a runner catching up with a beam of light, a water molecule rushing downstream). Idealizations connect the thought-experiment with the domain of formalizations, and through it, to mathematical expressions. Concrete situational objects connect it to the world of fictional representation, and through it to shared, grounded experience.

This aspect of concrete "irrelevance" is arguably what makes the proposition conveyed by the thought-experiment conceivable and memorable for new learners, and why they are preferred to more complex proofs that are more difficult to follow, remember, and communicate to others. It is what makes them broadly *learnable*, to the extent that a scientific truth exists in social discourse even among scientists themselves. Following Kuhn, Gooding contends that thought-experiments never reveal logical contradictions internal to the model; they are truly experimental, and create new knowledge (even though they provide no new data) by indicating the "impracticability of doing what is described" in a model in something resembling the actual world:[20]

> Thought experiment seeks neither contradiction (falsification) nor self-evident correspondence of representations to situations (confirmation). Rather, concepts are shown to need *reform if they are to be used in a world anything like the actual world.* The actual world is of course represented in thought, but thought highly constrained by the fact that it must be similar to the world that observers know. (208)

Darwin, for example, included many of what he termed "imaginary illustrations" in successive editions of *Origin of Species,* in order to refute concrete criticisms of his selection model (which were themselves sometimes careful thought-experiments). For Darwin, illustrative thought-experiments had to be emphatically plausible scenarios. Because natural selection can never be observed directly, but its putative agents are familiar, proof had to turn the animals and natural forces known to most readers into evidence:

> Plausibility is provided by making use of familiar objects doing things we expect them to under realistic conditions. Wolf packs, deer herds, seasonal fluctuations in prey, mountain vs. lowland environments, young being born with different body types and leg lengths — none of this requires a *stretch* of the imagination. It all could happen, in a fairly robust sense of "could." If Darwin were able to illustrate the operation of the theory only by making up a wild science-fiction scenario, it would hardly count as support for his theory.[21]

But perhaps a mild one would. This example of a naturalistic thought-experiment evokes Nancy Cartwright's notion that the relationship of a law to a model in science is the same as that of a moral to its fable in literature. The model is necessary to "fit out" the abstract principle, to make it visible, not in allegorical terms, but in concrete, actual, material instances.[22]

The SEVEN BEAUTIES *of* SCIENCE FICTION

What about the Cat?

In sf as an art, it is precisely this irrelevant, theoretically eliminable circumstantial decor that stands out, and makes a theory into a story. It not only shows how the novum changes something like the actual world, but how the earnest rules of science can be manipulated by the play-rules of art and the freedom to combine and supplement granted by the cultural myth-engine. SF's germinal thought-experiments carry this process of transforming imaginary tests into narratives to its logical extreme, and reverse its propositional order. Even when they involve questions pondered by real science, they are entirely metaphorical, as the testing of the fictive world (which was preconstructed for the purpose) is ultimately a literary/mythic agon. The best-known scientific thought-experiments in popular consciousness, the ones that mediate scientific speculation most powerfully for nonspecialists (such as Einstein's two trains running, Schrödinger's cat, Maxwell's sorting demon, Galileo's cannonballs, the Turing Test, Searle's Chinese Room) are marked by their evocative use of familiar, down-to-earth imagery. The relevant elements are animated, and the conceptual space in which the actions in question occur appears superficially to be accessible to a nonscientific imagination. In these cases, a scene is given for the imagined human subject to enter the physical process as if it were a virtual drama or adventure, transforming abstract processes into games, and deterministic systems into scenes of experience. Such thought-experiments have a particular panache in the physical sciences, because they allow noninitiates to sense the creative activity of scientists and some aesthetic or ludic pleasure in activities that usually seem hermetically insulated from normal social experience.

Some sciences are, arguably, made up almost entirely of thought-experiments. The social sciences, for example, deal with human phenomena that are immensely complex and resistant to measurement because the behavior of sentient beings is constantly influenced by their changing experience and learning. It is virtually impossible to create reproducible social experiments. Whether, and to what degree, people's contingency and freedom is overridden by social laws or trends is impossible ultimately to determine: the significance of such hypotheses can only come from their testing by, and application to, human beings by other human beings, all with complex, mutually interfering or amplifying purposes. Statistical measurement of social phenomena is entirely dependent on convention and agreement by the parties who prestructure the data, and decide on the applications of the survey.[23] The use of essentially fictive models of indifferent observation in macroeconomics, for example, with its notorious predictive weakness couched in calculating precision, makes it, from one perspective, a highly mathematicized form of social sf.[24]

There is no escaping the fictive aspects of social scientific theory, and its public mediation is much more likely to be transformed into mythopoeic speculations than that of physical science. Adam Smith's hidden hand, Freud's primal horde and the Oedipus complex, Spengler's and Toynbee's cycles of civilization, Simmel's city of strangers, Marx's class struggle, Weber's iron cage, Dawkins's selfish gene, and Kurzweil's law of accelerating returns, to take a few examples — all place human behavior in an imaginary figural design defined by certain analogies and rules of transformation that suggests tendencies to be entertained and tested, not by machinery, equations, and laboratories, but by the eventual outcomes of history — the very history that is, inexorably, the subject, the object, and the medium of investigation.

SF is the literature that takes thought-experiment as its given reality, which it then artistically and ludically exaggerates and estranges. In other words, it is not social reality that is estranged in sf, but the imaginary, pseudorational models that a technoscientific society produces about itself. In a sense, thought-experiment is yet another translation of the phrase "science fiction." But it points us in a very specific direction: not toward the rational goal of establishing a model or a global theory, or even the conduct of a rational procedure, but rather toward the protorational base upon which the performance of experiment is built.

In one way or another, all fictions are exercises in the imaginary elaboration of premises. SF differs from other forms in that it not only develops its ideas as thought-experiments, it makes this development a primary object of the narrative. Far from drawing the fictional-mythic narrative structures into a mesh of scientific ideas, it does the reverse. It draws the basic operations of science into the web of mythlike structures underlying narrative. Its broad social relevance is a response of technological culture to the routine subjection of human existence to uncontrolled global experimentation. When experiments become models extended to more and more uncontrollable situations, they are not truly tests. There is no "all things being equal" on the outside.

In narrative thought-experiments, elements and abstractions become actors. In most, a normal situation is slightly changed by a single alteration, perspectival emphasis, or ideal machine/agent that performs a single operation. A minimal novum is introduced to produce a fictive change of perspective into a new perspective. Of course, in a scientific thought-experiment, the world does not change, only the gaze. But it is the gaze that embodies the observer's interest. What's going on inside the black box where Maxwell's demon does his demon work, where Schrödinger's cat is trapped, where Searle's ver-

The SEVEN BEAUTIES *of* SCIENCE FICTION

sion of Maelzel's chess-player shuffles his ideograms? Narrative thought-experiments permit human observers to imagine what it might be like to be a bat, to see from the perspective of hydraulic flow, of natural selection, of a ray of light penetrating the ether or pulled by gravity. Fantasy is introduced in making the changed perspective vivid, relevant, and *habitable*. It expects everyone to react from a child's perspective, to ask "what did the demon look like?" and "what about the cat?"

The Literary Hoax

Gooding, following Ian Hacking, treats the thought-experiment as a form closely related to jokes.

> The degree of abstraction possible in a thought experiment depends on how much both its author and its readers have participated in the culture of the experiment. In this respect thought experiments have much in common with jokes. Both are sparse, carefully crafted, narratives which include only essential details. There is a punch-line requiring an insight which changes our understanding of the story. In both cases we see the point without its being articulated as an argument. Yet philosophers do not appeal to intuition or sense experience to explain how people understand jokes. Thought experiments are powerful because they appeal to lived experience of a world which their narratives reflect, selectively, back at us.[25]

In fact, the science-fictional thought-experiment's kinship is especially strong with a particular kind of joke: the tall tale fitted out as a literary hoax. The hoax, a fantastic tale told in persuasive, credible language intended to sound exactly like a true account, links sf with premodern literary forms. Lucian is significant for the genre not just because he envisioned travel to the moon, but that he reported it in the humorously inappropriate language of the mundane. We can think of the tall tale as a two-edged form of popular critical humor. On the one hand, it satirizes and displaces sacred mythology by substituting wild and down-to-earth wonders in artful displays of everyday language for the lofty language and aristocratic ethics of mythic literature. On the other, it deflates the reality principle of upstanding bourgeois citizens, affirming a world of deadpan awe in which the teller and the listener, the trickster and sucker, hail from the same community and class.[26] As the tall tale becomes literary, it draws in more and more social institutions and discourses. The tale's trickster-teller becomes increasingly adept at manipulating the dominant codes. He can pass for a member of the limited, dominant class, but is also able to use their discursive tools for his own purposes.

The hero/teller of the tall tale is often a fool, but the fool is double-coded: a fool in terms of the reality principle, but a superior being in terms of the imagination. Every one of Baron Münchhausen's stories involves some principle of folk science: sailing to the moon on the winds of ether, the ballistics of cherry pits, the harshness of Russian winters, the cluttered interiors of big fishes, and so forth. The Baron never relaxes his gallantry and courage (the mythic qualities of the courtly aristocracy); for him, the code of the peasant trickster is overlain with a new code, that of the Quixote-like aristocrat who cannot be shackled by the prose of physics. His elegant rejection of the bourgeois, scientific reality principle permits him to conquer it. The tale means nothing if its hearer does not, like Sancho, already understand how the reality principle works.

In a more serious vein, the usurpation of reality by the trickster is also at the heart of More's *Utopia*. More incorporates himself into the tall tale, splitting himself into two personae: (1) the skeptical, resistant gull, deeply engaged in dialogue with the trickster/clown Hythloday; and (2) the distanced author of *Utopia*, who invents all its points of view. The first increasingly conceals the second, giving Hythloday's traveler's account accelerating authority. It is not that the concrete details of his story make him believable, but rather how seriously he is taken by his incompletely fictional interlocutors. Hythloday combines two discourses of authority in his account: classical learning and modern exploration. The first creates the familiar context; the second, the neosemy. Even if Hythloday-the-trickster is making it all up, there is no way that More-the-potential-gull can find the holes in the story. The punning title and the story (and, indeed, many of the individual words) shuttle back and forth between the language of the imagination and the language of experience, undermining the discourse of truth by usurping it.

Something similar happens in *Gulliver's Travels*, though Swift, who witnessed the scientific revolution of his day at close hand, does not accord his trickster the class-distance (either below or above the bourgeoisie) that might protect him from the force he has appropriated. Gulliver's tales are much more caustically satirical than Hythloday's or Baron von Münchhausen's, and in a particular way: knowledge of scientific discourse does Gulliver no good. He gains no control over reality. His experiences have no effect on it. His language is so linked to the concretely detailed cause-and-effect and commonsense discourse of English empiricism that he has no linguistic resources for transcending it. The best he can get is the equine language of the Houyhnhnms, a discourse that is, in Kafka's words, "not for us." By presenting the marvelous tall tales in a language so close to the privileged discourse of truth in eighteenth-century England, Swift puts the entire materialist world into doubt. If the difference between a trick and reality is so close, one has a right to wonder if reality is not also a tall tale.

The pivotal moment in this miniature history of the hoax's influence on sf comes with Defoe and *Robinson Crusoe* (1719). Unlike earlier literary hoaxes, *Crusoe* is presented without a tall-tale frame, and bypasses the complex, dialogical relationship of teller to hearer, trickster to sucker, that creates the ironic and comic atmosphere of self-revealing hoaxes. Adept at the techniques of constructing an earnest, self-exposing, and *unanswerable* narrator, Defoe methodically removed all the elements of the tall tale that might leave the reader suspended. His techniques are well known. He hoards concrete, familiar objects and details in a setting strange enough to make them seem fresh. He employs various devices of first-person, sequential exposition. Through a dialectic of self-discovery and self-*re*discovery, he keeps the narrator's attention consistently and inexhaustibly turning inward. He imitates the rhetoric of verified castaways' accounts. He removes from the story any authority that might have an independent — and hence falsifying — de-gulling, effect (other than a Protestant God whose voice always comes from within). And he replays human history in one person's life, combining two of the dominant, unquestioned mythologies of his audience — Protestantism and English imperialism — so that the mythologies seem verified by experience.

Robinson Crusoe presents itself as a tale that it would be somehow faithless to disbelieve: it is a full-faith hoax. For the sucker to disbelieve it might mean that the dominant Northern European Reformation myth may have to go with it. Believing it, however, will strengthen the sucker's faith and sense of cosmic order, *even if it is not actually true.* Defoe established the premise that has endured from eighteenth-century realism to science fiction: language that adheres closely to discursive models of empiricism — detailed, concrete, logical, and materialist — gains the assent of readers who wish to conform to, and even support, the commonsense language of empirical truth. The trickster's best tool is the language of recognizable science.[27]

There is one last phase of the literary hoax important for the development of sf: Poe's deliberate, public hoaxes. Poe's kinship with Swift and Defoe is close, in that he liked to infiltrate the real world with his tricks. The tall tale for Poe was an exercise in linguistic control, a showman's display of his ability to manipulate the beliefs of a gullible herd with verbal sleights of hand. But in his most serious hoaxes, like "The Case of M. Valdemar" (1845), which is also one of the first important bona fide works of nineteenth-century American sf, Poe had more ambitious motives. In "Valdemar," Poe imitates the language of the scientific experiment with eerie rigor. The story is a science procedural. Medical discourse operates throughout, its rhetoric at first rational and cool, then increasingly passionate and fascinated. The frisson comes from the terrifying audacity of the experiment, which is simultaneously "unholy," because it violates the sanctity of death, and also a gain in positive knowledge. The soul exists, and the science of mesmerism can demonstrate it. This flirting with the taboo is an aspect of the *Frankenstein*/Gothic tradition from which Aldiss derives sf in *Billion Year Spree*. But it is also part of a different, convergent tradition: the trickster tale. Medical discourse, emptied of real-world experience and refilled with Poe's passionate commitment to mesmeric phenomena, is employed by the trickster to make us suckers believe the extreme, commonsense defying truths of a higher science. In Poe we see the desire to alter reality by importing the imagination through the Trojan horse of scientific persuasion — a language of imaginary science.[28]

This tradition was passed on through Verne and Wells, and remains at the core of sf. As the rhetoric of scientific rationalism rose to dominance, educated readers became sensitive to shades of difference between the styles and genres of its discursive prose (journalistic, academic, popularizing, speculative, and so forth). In a scientific culture the term *educated* refers not only to those with traditional humanistic learning, but the graduates of technical and professional schools, for whom technoscientific discourse is one of the main objects of study. In this milieu, it is not only the pleasure of speculative expansion that draws audiences to sf, but of observing the manipulation of a new language of power that is both a vehicle for neosemy and a newly established hegemonic discourse.

In European sf, especially west of Berlin, the hoax-tradition has remained largely the classical comic/satirical one. In the works of Bulgakov, Čapek, Lem, the Strugatskys, and others, the humanist's distancing of scientific discourse remains strong, tied to the skepticism that views the advance of rationalization (whether capitalist or socialist) with suspicion, if not outright aversion, in the name of classical humanistic values. In sf of the United States, and increasingly elsewhere, it is Poe's tradition that has played the greatest role. Just as Poe believed wholeheartedly in the scientific truth of the pseudoscience he wished to trick his audience into accepting, so too are most sf writers deeply invested in the scientific world that they also ludically criticize, undermine, and turn into wonders.

Counterfactual Science

The science of sf must violate known science if it is to be science-fictional:

> The point is not that the science in sf is "usually inaccurate"; but rather that some of the science in any given SF story *must* be inaccurate — or it

isn't SF. To read an SF story properly one must have some notion of just where the science is distorted. . . . [SF] presents a distortion of the world. One of the things it distorts in the world is present science. The distortion is usually a matter of taking something sciences claim is possible, but which currently is *not proven to be the case,* and writing about it *as if it were the case.* . . . At other times it is a matter of taking something that scientists claim is impossible and writing about it with the kind of language that would accrue to the topic if that impossibility had been scientifically disproved — so many scientific "impossibilities" have been disproved over the years. . . . But there are other ways science can be distorted in SF: writing about a future with less technology available than we have today is also to distort the range of present science.[29]

In fictionalizing science, the fanciful introduction of illogical, implausible, and even impossible elements is essential. As with actual thought-experiments, which illuminate paradoxes that would arise from applying a theory to reality, sf writers look for scientific limit cases to motivate their plots. Certain phenomena that are essentially impossible in the mesocosm, such as faster-than-light travel, time machines, downloading human consciousness, sapient Artificial Intelligence, and the scarcity-annihilating fairy dust of nanocules, have become conventions of the genre. These fantastic technological novums appear to reconcile the reality principle of rational-material limitation and the wish fulfillment of material and intellectual plenitude, while dependably producing interesting new conundrums and dilemmas. By posing hypertechnological, futuristic resolutions to problems that thread through our present, they remove the boundary between the known world of the reader and the virtual world of the fictive future. At any point, a realistic contemporary problem may be displaced into an imaginary one by time travel or virtual reality, and a scientific-metaphysical puzzle may, in turn, become an intimate ordeal of everyday life.

Some writers introduce as few fudges into the foregrounded scientific explanations and novums as possible, while making everything else, from social relations to personal psychology, wildly incredible. Clement's *Mission of Gravity* is so famous for the plausibility of its heavy planet Mesklin that few readers remark on the absurdity of its centipede-like alien protagonists behaving like buccaneer capitalists communicating with human beings with no information loss. SF writers often describe the physics of spaceflight scrupulously, without once reflecting on the political economies of societies that have to fund the energy budgets of spacefleets. Some writers introduce scientific-sounding patches that facilitate the action, but stretch the plausibility of the science. Others combine credible speculative explanations with incredible ones — the intelligence of Fred Hoyle's *Black Cloud* (1957), the Teilhardian noöcyte-blob of Greg Bear's *Blood Music* (1985) — usually to convert material conditions into metaphoric/transcendental ones (the Cloud of Knowing, the Nano-AI Omega). Some sf writers make parodistic use of scientific concepts, from technobabble to inspired bullshit (*Star Trek's* tractor beams, *The Hitchhiker's Guide's* babelfish and "maximum improbability drive"), that lampoon, intentionally or unconsciously, technoscience. And finally, plausible scientific concepts may not even be necessary when, as in sci-fi, science is merely a pretext for displaying cool stuff. The science in sf is suspended science, configured in an aesthetic space where reverie and thought-experiment meet and enjoy the cultural authority of science, as a projectile enjoys the gravity of the planet it uses to slingshot itself into space. This is not to say that the representation of science in sf lacks all cognitive content. Quite the contrary. However, it is not the imaginative play that serves the cognition, but the reverse.

Most of the stretches are highly improbable, on a spectrum from surprising anomalies to impossibilities that simply cannot be proved to be so. This category of the *not-impossible* is the homebase of sf's imaginary science. Such moves are often based on experiences in the history of technoscience, where surprising discoveries and inventions changed the course of history. These novums can be roughly categorized in such sf-friendly terms as anomalies (such as black holes, pulsars, the Big Bang itself), unpredicted, counterintuitive discoveries (imaginary particles, superconductors, hyperthermophilic organisms), and innovative conflations (electricity/magnetism, information/energy, biochemistry/ethnography). Many technoscientific transformations have occurred that have had to be explained after the fact, and seemed fantastic before they were accepted.

SCIENCE-FICTIONAL SCIENCE

Writing apropos his popular novel *Timescape* (1980), Gregory Benford observes that time travel and ftl travel are "probably impossible but difficult to disprove."[30] (And let us not forget the inverse corollary: reality is likely, but impossible to demonstrate.)

The time-travel scenario was refreshed for Benford, an astrophysicist, by the challenge of motivating it with the physics of tachyons, virtual superluminal particles whose existence may be mandated by quantum cosmology, but whose existence in the world of our time-arrow violates fundamental conditions of causality. Tachyons allowed Benford to construct a story of transtemporal communication using contemporary physical speculation to provide his effects. Whatever their benefits, tachyons did not save him from the perennial paradoxes that he still had, in his words, to "finesse."[31] The game of hard sf demanded, in the end, not fidelity to tachyon physics, but the maximum use of its discourse that would still allow the time-travel plot to exist. Apropos Poul Anderson's *Tau Zero* (1970), Benford, like Wells before him, grants primacy to the patter: "[Anderson] finesses the issues, using an argument from relativity which he knew to be wrong, as long as you don't think long and hard about it. He succeeded, I believe. Few readers notice the deft way he slid it by. . . . This is a clear example of the contradiction between the constraints of hard SF and other, literary aims. Such quandaries arise occasionally in any realistic fiction, but in SF they appear at every turn, powerfully shaping the narrative."[32]

For scientists, a powerful draw of the science-fictional *esprit de finesse* is the possibility of coming out the other side of a conceptual black box, for which imaginary sf solutions to real scientific problems are input, and real solutions to imaginary problems raised by sf emerge as output. A striking development in technoscientific culture has been the gradual penetration of science-fictional consciousness, not only in the popular framing of science, but in scientific work itself. Partly as a pastime, but also as a form of respect for sf's power to stimulate speculation, a growing number of scientific projects have been inspired by sf scenarios. Contemporary physics includes a niche for the theorization of what is sometimes disparagingly called "*Star Trek* science": exercises in formulating explanations for futuristic/fictive technologies, such as warp drive, managed wormholes, teleportation, inertial dampers, time machines, and the like, which have become so commonplace in mass-media sf that they have taken on a hyperreal concreteness in the social imagination.[33]

Most of the research in such areas is so speculative as to be science-fictional in its own right. Almost all of these exotic technologies can be rationalized only by "finessing" the laws of physics. It's not only that they are "probably impossible but difficult to disprove." Within the game theory of quantum cosmology, they are ontologically *not-impossible*. They pique physicists' ingenuity to construct imaginary conditions of possibility that are not explicitly contradicted by known laws. Each case requires at least one whopping supplementary proposition, the hypostatic prosthesis of some element or event that has no basis outside speculation. Stable, mesocosmic-scale wormholes (that is, large and stable enough to allow human-scale bodies and vehicles to pass through intact) would require fantastic expenditures of energy—on the order of stars and galaxies—that could only be supplied by imaginary materials, "exotic elements" capable of fueling the "exotic forces" of negative gravity.[34] Warp drive would require even more energy, as well as mechanisms to prevent destructive effects on a cosmic scale. Astronomer Kip Thorne, who devised a model of communicating wormholes for Carl Sagan's use in his novel *Contact* (1985), has concluded that such phenomena are so unlikely as to be unavailable, if not literally impossible.[35] Indeed, most of the *Star Trek* technologies would require "designer spacetimes," controlled de-creation and re-creation of spacetime using cosmic-scale energies.[36] Conversely, physicists have repeatedly concluded that, although a relativistic universe might provide the conditions for two-way time travel in theory, the fact that our world of one-way temporal causality exists is reason enough to posit the existence of a negative supplement, such as Hawking's "chronology protection measures" (akin to the Time Cops that appear in Asimov and Poul Anderson), to prevent the apparently all-too possible time-travel paradoxes from becoming available to reality.

Twentieth-century science is replete with accounts of scientists whose projects were influenced by science-fictional fantasies: Willy Ley's and Werner von Braun's debt to Kurt Lasswitz, Goddard's to Edgar Rice Burroughs, Szilárd's to Wells, Tsiolkovsky's to Verne, and a whole generation of Soviet and U.S. astro/cosmonauts and aerospace engineers who were first inspired by Yefremov, the Strugatskys (the first authors read in space), and *Star Trek*. Science-fictional ideas appear in an ever-greater number of popular expressions, with the effect that they not only convey technoscientific cultural values, but help to form social perceptions, especially of the young.

As science-fictional thinking develops into a dominant mode of social imagination, it articulates many of the goals and desires that inspire social action, toward which new generations of scientists and engineers will aspire. For contemporary software engineers, sf has already become the primary source, not just of inspiration, but of concrete projects. In software design, according to Mark Pesce,

> "hard" science fiction has functioned as a "high-level architecture" (HLA), an evolving design document for a generation of software designers brought up in hacker culture, a culture which prizes these works as foundational elements of their own worldviews.[37]

In Pesce's view, cyber-sf was the vehicle most responsible for creating a hacker group consciousness, and through it, hackers' pervasive influence on social life as a whole. Begun with *Shockwave Rider* (1975), John Brunner's prescient novel about a networked dystopia, the process of consolidating the quasi-class identity of a soon-to-be operational elite was completed by *Neuromancer*, which provided hackers with a language, a style, and a myth. Gibson's novel "crystallized a new community, just as Boyle's scientific papers . . . did in an earlier age."[38] Fictive technologies from *Neuromancer* (such as virtual reality, the matrix, Sim/Stim, the Turing Police, cranial jacks, embeddable expert-system microchips, and mental traveling in cyberspace) influenced not only literature, film, and games, but coursed through technical publications, conferences, hardware design, and technocultural discourse at large. Cyberpunk has established the psychological conditions for a pervasive sense of hacker identity concentered around collective projects:

> the position of the hacker as protagonist and savior gives these texts special significance in the hacker communities; an act of self-identification takes place almost unconsciously when a hacker reads these texts. . . . *The creation of technical artifacts becomes an act of identification with the protagonists.* (emphasis in original)

For software engineers, certain texts (Pesce singles out *Neuromancer*, Neal Stephenson's *Snow Crash* [1992] and *The Diamond Age* [1995]) have in effect created a romantic professional narrative that is itself an identification with sf. Its elements are the elements of science-fictional consciousness I am positing in this book: actors created by and serving the novum of the matrix (cyberspace/VR/AI), directed toward values to be determined in an imaginary future, complete with new discourse, a new ontology represented equally in the techno-evolutionary sublime and grotesque, and a risk-saturated adventure to establish operational control in a transformed world inaccessible to the common run of present humanity. Pesce continues:

> [T]he recent history of hard science fiction has been *the* deciding influence on the direction of software systems development. The hacker community has been strongly shaped by science fiction texts, and this has led to a direct, often literal concretization of the ideas expressed in those texts. The "grand philosophers" — which is to say, the writers — propose, in sweeping gestures, the shape of things to come. To the degree they are successful in "infecting" the hacker community with the beauty of their ideas, they can expect to see those ideas brought to life.

That sf contributes to forming hacker identity should surprise no one. Hacker culture revels in the dissolution of the sf/science boundary. Software engineering has evolved outside the established institutions of scientific research, and is so new that it relies on the creativity mainly of young noncomformists. It is more surprising to see sf's influence in fields where the sf/science demarcation is not only energetically upheld, but used to justify projects that require the backing of sober scientific establishments. Nanotechnology is an exemplary case: nanotech — the nascent science of engineering at the molecular level — is entangled in a complex relationship with sf discourse. Although many of its theoretical contours are well established, and there have been rudimentary applications, nanotech is largely virtual, especially when its actual results are compared with the promises made to promote it.[39] Through the writing of its most enthusiastic and visionary proponent, Eric Drexler, nanotech has come to be associated in the popular imagination with utopian visions of self-replicating machines (called *assemblers*) that promise, according to Drexler and his followers, to annihilate scarcity altogether.[40] Nanoassemblers will be able create any object desired: "virtually anything from common materials without labor, replacing smoking factories with systems as clean as forests. They will transform technology and the economy at their roots. . . . They will indeed be engines of abundance." (quoted in Lopez, "Bridging the Gaps," 135).

Nanotechnology as yet exists more in its prospectus than in real achievements. In this it is a characteristically postmodern, just-in-time technology, requiring a highly creative hype in order to gain the funding and public support that will bring it into existence, and to allay fears of technocatastrophe. (In the case of nanotech, the latter might be spectacular, as for instance the "Grey Goo" of atomic machines that will be too busy disassembling terrestrial negentopy altogether to get around to assembling anything other than themselves.)[41] Political prudence requires that the technology be socially vetted, that it be made familiar and desirable. The discourse of nanotech is consequently saturated with tropes that evoke heroic breakthroughs and the irresistible pull of technoutopian world resolutions on the future side of the novum. The base narrative of the Drexlerian current follows the identical pattern as the hackers' cyberromance described by Pesce. The novum is the nanoassembler and its effect is the universal convergence of all human knowledge and production, as nanoengineering synthesizes the mechanisms of digital and biological mapping and replication, and creates new matter. This synthesizing will be mediated by a heroic elite of molecular-engineer "master builders" (Lopez, "Bridging the Gaps," 133), and will inevitably "re-ontologize" the world,[42] constructing new sublime and grotesque wonders in the process of managing the world-threatening risks, and issuing in the fulfilled dream of the human species, in which every aspect of existence converges within a single system of perpetually upgradable relationships. This visionary, science-fictional mastery over space and time has penetrated governmental advisory bodies, as demonstrated by the NSF-sponsored report *Converging Technologies for Improving Human Performance: Nanotechnology, Biotechnology, Information Technology, and Cognitive Science* (2003). This report introduced the acronym NBIC, which stands for Nanotechnology, Biotechnology, Information Technology, and Cognitive Science. NBIC promotes the eventual fusion of all branches of technoscientific cognition via the universal solvent of nanotech. José Lopez describes the scope of this Nano-Bio-Info-Cognitive technoutopian apocalypse's effects:

> [A]ll of history converges towards the novum that in turn gives birth to the future. In the narrative developed in the NBIC text, every dimension of the world, both diachronic and synchronic, has been processed through the NBIC filter and colored by the trope of convergence and unity. Thus, the principles governing the structure of organic and inorganic matter converge, the technologies of different disciplines converge, the natural sciences converge, the natural and social sciences converge, individuals and technology converge, individuals converge into networks, societies converge, and humanity finally becomes unified. Environmental degradation, poverty, disease, cultural misunderstanding, war, etc., can all be solved through NBIC convergence. The NBIC world is akin to a hall of mirrors with NBIC convergence at the center: though stretched, contorted, and deformed, every reflection refers back to the principle of NBIC. It is precisely this that makes the extrapolated future credible.

Soberer scientific proponents of nanotech take exception to the Drexlerian hype (Milburn, "Nanotechnology" 111). For them, it is specifically the science-fictional rhetoric that endangers the full acceptance of nanoscience. But sf thinking has infused the idea of nanotechnology from its inception:

> Science fiction is not a layer that can be stripped from nanoscience without loss, for it is the exclusive domain within which mature nanotechnology currently exists; it forms the horizon orienting the trajectory of much nanotechnological research; and any eventual appearance of practical molecular manufacturing—transforming the world at a still unknown point in the future through a tremendous materialization of the fantastic—would be marked with the semiotic residue of the science-fictional novum. (Milburn, "Nanotechnology" 112)

The suspect linkage of science and sf goes beyond the fictive narrative of nanofutures, linking—as it does with happy assent in the case of cybertech—science and sf in the public discourse of new technologies. According to Katherine Hayles, "science fiction acts as the other of nano-technoscience."[43] The expansion of sf's cultural influence indicates that its stigmatization will surely decline, at least for a while, and the traffic between sf and science will become even heavier.

Technoscientific culture increasingly gravitates toward its images of convergent future technology radiating backward into the present. In democratic and popularly mediated cultures, reliable public support for the transfer of social energies to the expansion of technoscientific institutions and the uncontrolled global experiments of hypertechnology requires broad assent. More and more, our politics of science relies on sf's romantic myth-narratives, both to enable and to obstruct social applications of technology. As we shall see in "Seventh Beauty," major scientific transformation projects such as the space program and the moon landing used narrative strategies identical to the techno-adventure paradigm favored by sf. Contestatory movements often rely on sf catastrophes and dystopias to press home their rational concerns, and utopian visions to resolve them. The actual application of technoscience in the present is debated in the future, mediated through a science-fictional future past.

By framing inchoate technologies of the present in terms of vivid future outcomes, we run the risk of perceiving our reality as an inert resource, fallow in its own right, to be megafarmed and strip-mined by future novums. A vicious circle can develop, in which the discourse of widespread social-ecological transformations imagined in techno-utopian or dystopian scenarios "infect" the politics of science with memes in which an sf-inflected neological language of the virtual future returns to the present to extract its resources of assent.[44] The greater the social commitment to technoscientific mediation, the more credit must be extended to its consummation: "the coming age," that unspecified point in the future when the enormous economic, social, and psychic deferrals — cloaked in the language of social investment managed by a technoscientific elite and its political allies for "consumers" of social existence — take on greater concreteness than the constraints of existence in the present. These constraints, as they become less and less amenable to the specific transformative powers of available technologies, are then formulated as mythic obstacles, or excluded from public discourse altogether.

In its most obvious forms, we see this mediation in the manipulation of technological expectations by political actors who use future-oriented sf discourse to facilitate projects beneficial to their power. Visions of derelict futures were disseminated in the social imaginary by genre sf when writers like Ballard and Malzberg extrapolated their critiques of the space program's cynicism to technoscientific society in general. Earlier dystopias rarely called into question the efficiency of hyperrationalizing forces in organizing the future. In the Soviet Union, where the cynicism of the ideology was most obvious, such writing was simply forbidden. In the West, sf writers rarely imagined the possibility that technoscience itself could run down, leaving behind the debris of ruined rationalization. Though Sputnik may have closed down sf's fantastic vistas, as John Clute recalls,[45] it was not until the debate that pitted the manned moon missions against urban poverty that sf artists began to separate themselves radically from the ideology of the technoscientific establishment. The success of cyberpunk and its tech-noir cousins can be attributed to the widespread sense that the quasi–science-fictional utopian promises of technological improvement were belied by the obvious evidence of urban ruin. The persistence of technopolitical cynicism is even now evident in the recent U.S. administration's empty promise of a manned Mars mission that it does not fund, in the barely begun, and nearly abandoned, international space station that was supposed to be the springboard for humanity's exploration of the stars, and in its preference for the postures of hack writers of technothrillers to the consensus of environmental science for advice on global warming.[46]

SF is increasingly employed to construct virtual futures disseminated through the mediascape. These fictions can easily be made to seem more coherent and rational than contemporary social existence, whose representation is concurrently dispersed and de-realized. The transfer of assent to a virtual future that *makes more sense* than present reality requires broad cooperation of technoscience and mass media. Together these inspire a sense of the technical possibility and plausible habitability of science-fictional futures that creates the feeling of historical fatedness: concrete inevitability. We have called this sf's empirical prophecy; extended to the world, Baudrillard calls it hyperreality.[47]

In *Star Trek: Technologies of Disappearance,* Alan Shapiro laments this co-optation of sf by a culture of technoscientific domination, which he sees embodied in the expanding mediaverse of the *Star Trek* series. For Shapiro, *Star Trek* is exemplary of the trend in hypermediated technoculture to create a seamless mythology of technoscientific development justified by results scheduled for the future, but articulated in language and imagery as if they were already present. The intensification of the virtual experience of fulfilled wishes, mediated by futuristic technologies and the desirable social relations surrounding them (that is, the simulation at the heart of technoscientific hyperreality, in which human relations are confined to technosocial containment vessels) goes hand in hand with the diminution of awareness of sf's *fiction* as a specific and autonomous mode of thought. In our terms, Shapiro argues that publics are less and less interested in sf's ludic challenges as existential thought-experiments, and more and more in its ability to proffer compensatory virtual habitations. Saturated with the desire to escape from an incoherent reality (whose incoherence is accelerated by the penetration of technoscientific capitalism into all human relationships), publics require stronger and stronger images of virtual reality. To the degree that they are playfully incapable of reification, sf's imaginary scenarios come to be seen as insufficiently real. *Star Trek* prefigured, in Shapiro's view, a general trend to convert sf's critical and existential challenges into seamlessly converging simulations:

> product tie-ins, media, franchise, etc. contribute to the invention of a *closed* myth that insists on the strong foundation of its own "reality." It is partly the technology of television's convergence with the Internet that catalyzes this move away from the *openness* of fiction's usual awareness of its own status as "not entirely real." (11; emphases in original)

In Shapiro's view, this development is paralleled by the pervasive dissemination of an informational-materialist model of reality via postmodern science itself, which holds that all imaginable aspects of existence should be seen in terms of information, and hence in theory manipulable by technologies that can analyze them and reconfigure them at will. This view is reinforced by the already manifest formidable power of information technologies to construct vivid virtual experiences. Even if reality itself somehow escapes wholesale reconstruction, technoscience demonstrates that a domain of experience almost as good, and in some respects even better, can be effectively constructed to simulate the real. In essence, a third nature might be constructed out of the parts of the world that can be shaped in this way (through the NBIC discussed by Lopez, for example) to escape from the lingering vicissitudes of second nature. The social construction of science becomes increasingly science-fictional in this continuum, because the social desire for technoscientific transformation is oriented toward utopian (and in reaction, dystopian) images provided by sf: "Theories get bent to conform to the wishes of an eager techno-cultural public that desperately wants to accelerate in the coming fruition of technologies that will 'make *Star Trek* real'" (Shapiro, *Star Trek* 20–21).

The Cognition Effect

SF thrives on maximum credible rationalization. Technoscience's hegemonic power is based on the widespread sense that it is the only remaining system of explanation that can command mass assent, a belief that makes science less a practice than a metaphysical atmosphere. Explanations are drawn from it for phenomena at the limits of conceptualization: the state and fate of the universe, the essence of life, the nature of consciousness, the composition of reality, the potentials of human civilizational self-construction. But because these enormous explanations are unprovable and undemonstrable within science's own systems of validation, and are only the most recent examples in a long string of incommensurate world-models and explanations, they require willed belief. It is an emphatically *rational* belief, but it is nonetheless based on peoples' sense that understanding the material/mathematical universe connects them to it in ways that transcend utility and calculation. To understand the way things are is to experience fitness and connectedness. In Sagan's famous phrase, "understanding is a kind of ecstasy."[48]

In technoculture, this scientific ecstasy is accompanied by its trickster-shadow, the ludic pleasure of playing with belief. Explanations are not only drawn from science, and then reasonably supplemented; they are also ascribed to it. Many of the same methods and discourses used to supplement reasonable worldviews can be applied to justify much less reasonable ones. SF inhabits the niche of public discourse in which rationalizations float free of close observation. With professional discretion, sf writers slip over from the established, accepted (that is, no fun) principle of Occam's razor, toward its perverse twin, the pataphysical impulse, to seek the most *complicated* solutions possible, the "science of imaginary solutions."[49] While maintaining the appearance of plausibility and realistic representation to hype its credibility, sf delights in the game of connecting and rationalizing arbitrary things. This game is itself rationalized, so that the arbitrariness of the play is usually disguised. The appearance of rigorous, prosaic, naturalized scientific logic and demonstration is the central poetic illusion that distinguishes sf from surrealism.

In *Critical Theory and Science Fiction* (2000), Carl Freedman gives a name to this practice of maximally rationalized illusion: the *cognition effect* (18–19).[50] Freedman acknowledges that a weakness of the Suvinian conception of sf as cognitive estrangement is its insistence, not only that the act of reading should induce an understanding of true, rational knowledge of material human relationships, but that the scientific ideas represented in it must not contradict valid science. Freedman worries that this requirement disqualifies not only nine-tenths of the scientific romance and pulp fantasies that most readers consider prototypes of the genre (which does not bother him as an orthodox Suvinian), but that otherwise scrupulous texts that were based on since-superseded scientific ideas might be demoted from sf to fantasy. Freedman proposes that it should not be the extratextual validity of its ideas that determine whether something should be treated as sf: "The crucial issue for generic discrimination is not any epistemological judgment external to the text itself on the rationality or irrationality of the latter's imaginings, but rather . . . the attitude of the text itself to the kind of estrangements being performed." (18). If the events portrayed in the fiction are based on what authors and their audiences thought were valid concepts — and, in practical terms, if the diegetic action could be imagined to occur in a world very like the author's real world — then the text has created a "cognition effect."

Freedman tries to narrow the scope of his trope, arguing that it naturally strives to reflect real cognition: "the readiest means to producing a cognition effect is precisely through cognition itself, through rationality as the latter is understood from a critical point of view" (19). That may be so. But the readiest means are not the same as necessary means. The cognition effect is precisely that: an *effect* — an illusion of valid knowledge created by imitating extratextual rational-scientific arguments and descriptions in the languages of scientific predication. Freedman takes his model from Barthes's *history effect* and *reality effect*.[51] In each of these techniques, the reader's sense of historical knowledge or perception of reality is created by a rhetoric that imitates the rhetoric of nonfictional discourses, but is only remotely dependent on supposedly real events or objects. The same logic surely applies for the cognition effect. In sf, artists depend on maximum plausible rationalizations of extratextual ideas that are often entertained to be true. This real-world entertainment of validity may be, ironically, propped by convincing, but ultimately merely discursive, deployments of legitimating arguments by authoritative scientific voices. I also draw a somewhat different conclusion from Freedman's that true facts and ideas are the "readiest means" for the cognition effect. Just as statistical measurements and even physical formalizations can "lie" when they are used to validate real-world arguments — by either tacitly bracketing out important noisy factors or by using scientific tropes to cover ethical dilemmas[52] — embedding extratextually validated scientific ideas in sf is also the most effective means of disguising the fictive rationalization that is sf's stock in trade. SF's discursive play does not undermine the truths of materialist/mathematical science, which it can pick up and drop at will. It operates to the side. Its capacity to inspire new, often exaggerated, but nonetheless genuine, technoscientific and social ideas has less to do with its critical power, than its nonaccountability. Even the excession and violation of accepted knowledge is rationalized in sf.

One of the main pretexts for rational counterfactuality is, of course, critique: evacuating belief in certain ideas by contesting the legitimacy of their implicit values and operations. Because science-fictional manipulation of technoscience's authority overlaps with critical philosophy's questioning of ideology, critical-theorists of sf often emphasize the critical intentions and powers of the genre. Marxist critics, such as Suvin, Freedman, Fredric Jameson, Peter Fitting, Marc Angenot, Tom Moylan, and others, treat sf as a vehicle for consciousness-raising about the ideological distortions of the dominant high-capitalist world-picture.[53] The premise of Freedman's *Critical Theory and Science Fiction* is that sf and critical thinking are essentially congruent, that even Kant might be read as a writer of sf. Cultural-studies theorists and feminist, race-critical, and queer theorists approach the genre as a storehouse of motifs and tropes that displace contemporary problems of domination and marginalization.[54] Read for ideology, the distortions of science in sf have moral and/or political effects.

Delany has extended this argument into a claim that sf's distortions of accepted scientific knowledge are inherently critical, in that they display a resistance to the dominant technoscientific orthodoxy. Beginning with the Campbell circle from 1937 on, Delany writes, this resistance was developed "into *a full critique of the philosophy-of-science-as-it-was-then-popularly-conceived*":[55]

> The most notable aspect of this critique may be characterized as a reigning *theoretical plurality*. The first tenet of this theoretical plurality was that whatever modern science might declare theoretically impossible was invariably challenged by a fictive theoretical revisionism. Magic is theoretically impossible? Very well, we will have SF stories exploring worlds where magic works. The special theory of relativity postulates one cannot exceed the speed of light? Very well, we will have SF stories in which, by a theoretical revision or loophole, one can. . . . This theoretical plurality from the late '30s onward ensures that science fiction will never again have a simple, uncritical attitude toward *science as an explorative philosophy*. What, after all, is the function of faster-than-light drive in the range of contemporary cultural discourse? It is a continuing reminder that the major scientific paradigm of our day, Einsteinian relativity, may some day have to suffer the same order of revision it demanded of the Newtonian paradigm it replaced. The image of an FTL drive is in itself critical.

But Delany overstates the case. There is nothing necessarily critical in the mere denial of a generally accepted scientific concept. The presence of ftl or warp drive is not necessarily an affirmation of inevitable paradigm shifts (though it might be, in the hands of a philosophically reflective writer). If a tale asserts that the earth is hollow, that there is a passage through the earth's core from Iceland to Italy, or that Grey Aliens live down there, it has merely contradicted scientific understanding. The appearance of gigantic ants, reptiles, spiders, rabbits, women, or tomatoes does not constitute a scientific critique. Such a critique would have to be founded on rational principles, and if it offers a counterparadigm, it must be one based on an even fuller, more comprehensive understanding of the objects under study than the model it replaces. Using the same logic as Delany, one might present a cheerfully functioning racist, misogynist society in the future, and call it a critique of Enlightenment rationality. Delany here mistakes the genre's impulse to play with science for a critical impulse. Negation is not sufficient for critique; nor is the mere deployment of rationalization sufficient to create new conditions. The cognition effect is an *effect*.

In society at large, a nonprofessional public is in general unable to distinguish between true and imaginary science — or even between technoscience and sf. Theoretical-science education has become less democratically supported as it has become an increasingly esoteric, elite enterprise protected and manipulated by state and capital. In the United States, most people's knowledge of science is shaped exclusively by popular media, which respond to ideology, catastrophes, and sensational "breakthroughs" that evoke the same frisson as sf. These are fertile conditions for both game playing and straightforward deception, with the full range of self-deceptions in between. SF plays with the language of the hoax, but because some of its fantasies can in fact inspire blueprints, and because the number of such playful fantasies outnumbers defensible scientific explanations (which never even reach most people), technoscientific cultures become accustomed and vulnerable to real hoaxes and actually existing science fictions. Absent broad-based and active exposure to philosophical reflection on science in social life, we find it difficult to distinguish among: (a) the prospect of world-transforming technoscientific breakthroughs perpetually on the verge of occurring; (b) widespread belief in *Star Trek* science, the possibility of science-fictional time travel, wormholes, ftl, teleportation, and so forth, and the expectation that they will be invented; (c) cultic rationalization of myth-systems with quasi-scientific jargon (as with Scientology, the Raelians, Heaven's Gate, Aum Shinrikyo, and so forth); and (d) belief in demonstrably cynical false science that politically displaces honest science (such as "creation science," "intelligent design," and the criminal distortion of the science of climate change). It becomes harder and harder to distinguish between valid knowledge and manipulation, as it is the assent-producing rhetorics and poetics of scientific discourse that are used to rationalize both. For nonscientists, the only thing that distinguishes exotic matter from Flubber is the sophistication of its rationalization, and the only difference between exotic physical theories and sf is the social authority behind the former. Further, the ideological use of scientific projects to legitimate political power turns them into concrete, actually existing science fictions, objects, and networks that take up physical space and produce material effects, but that also perform as props for narratives of mastery.[56]

This oscillation of language between the technoscientific and science-fictional also explains much about the insecurity of cultural-theoretical language. The well-publicized Sokal hoax, for example — in which the physicist Alan Sokal, in order to expose their ignorance of science, tricked the editors of the left-oriented journal *Social Text* into publishing an essay that used pseudo-scientific nonsense jargon to "verify" that mathematical and scientific knowledge is determined by social interests — demonstrated that linguistic rationalization can deceive even intelligent people who are unable to judge scientific validity (a class that includes even many scientists outside their own fields), yet who still want to display mastery over it with non-scientific ethical concepts.[57] The Sokal hoax, however, demonstrated not only the gullibility of intellectuals wishing to see their ideals reinforced from more authoritative fields, but also of the scientific establishment that believes it has somehow proved the independent truth-content of scientific ideas by exposing and shaming its putatively most pretentious metaphorical applications. The persuasiveness of Sokal's language is not merely a testament to his satirical talents, but to the fluidity of a rhetoric of scientific assent.[58] More illustrious scientists than Sokal have used scientific discourse sincerely to justify opinions about social life on which they have no evidential bearing.[59] Sokal's hoax was itself a form of sf, paradoxically recondite and naive at once. The attempt to assimilate scientific language for ethical-political uses, and the attempt to affirm the purity of that language by exposing its misprision, are of a piece: both stipulate the social authority of the discourse and compete to assert control over it. The power to control it does not derive from the language itself. All of this should alert us to the prospect of esoteric, and yet socially authorized, plausible-sounding rationalizations being used on a much larger social scale. Historically, sexism, homophobia, class hatred, and racist eugenics have all been couched in the quasi-scientific rationality of their times. It is plausible that future ideological regimes will be based on unassailable scientific hoaxes of proportionally greater sophistication.

From this perspective, sf (and even the more imaginative forms of popular scientific journalism) are at any moment on the verge of tipping over into pataphysics. Contemporary critical-theoretical discourse, in contrast with Enlightenment and Romantic critical philosophy, has had only tangential connections with scientific practice (of major critical cultural theorists, only those directly involved in critical science studies seem to have been trained as scientists),[60] but has striven to assimilate technoscience's status as the explanatory system of final appeal, by enclosing it within its own zones of concern. As a result, it has increasingly occupied an ambiguous space where metaphysical speculation, sociological analysis, phenomenology of science, and rhetorical play overlap. These zones do not necessarily coalesce. Because of the dominant social role of technoscientific discourse supplementing systems of technological objects and operations, social and textual theorists have often tried to assimilate that discourse to their own, trumping the rationalization strategies of science with more and more complex, and supposedly comprehensive, strategies, unbound by empirical and mathematical discipline. Deleuze-Guattari, Baudrillard, Derrida, Lacan, Foucault, Virilio, and many of their Anglo-American epigones have pretended, consciously and intentionally, to exceed and transcend scientific thinking — by demolishing first the assumptions of empiricism, and then the supposed lucidity and modesty of professional discourse. Many scientists view these theorists as dispellers of scientistic enchantment; others, as mere charlatans. From our perspective, they are more like science-fictional ironists — master pataphysicians and literary hoaxsters — who begin from the model that social consciousness/perception of the world is above all a matter of the discourse of understanding, which they seek to place in suspension with a counterdiscourse. The moment in the limelight of this discursive theory will certainly pass, but it will also certainly continue in playful forms as long as there is mass, power-protected, technoscientific ideological myth-production. While the community of "Theory" seems convinced of the general applicability of its methods, its best products, nonetheless, can be read as literary hoax-games that infiltrate the reality discourse of technoscience, and provoke that discourse's own literary fictions into the open. Indeed, we see more and more critical theorists using overt images and tropes from sf in their theoretical statements. This trend is most noticeable in the work of Donna Haraway and Jean Baudrillard, whose immensely influential concepts of the cyborg and simulacra, respectively, are powerful examples of meta–science-fictional *détournement*.[61]

Postscript: Impossibilities

It is one thing to say that we cannot know whether human beings will ever be able to transport themselves through wormholes or to communicate telepathically, and quite another to believe that there can be skyscraper-size flying ants. There are things that even the gods can't do. It is theoretically more likely that God can make that which has happened not to have happened (as Peter Damian argued in *De Divina Omnipotentia*)[62] than that He can create a colossal flying insect in Earth gravity. So what are we to do with these giant insects and lizards and spiders, these obviously fantastic creatures so at odds with scientific reason? The easiest solution to the problem is to apply the principle of cognitive estrangement to a near-allegorical exclusiveness. The ants, the dinosaurs, the demonoid aliens are then merely displacements of unconscious popular anxieties. Godzilla and the ants of *Them!* for example, are images of the fear of radioactive fallout, displaced in culturally specific ways. At this level of representation, science is present only in its rhetorical and visual markers. When the putatively scientific element is completely impossible, the game has changed. The purpose of sf then is no longer to perforate the scientific world-view, nor to create an expansive and tolerant phenomenal universe. It is to invest technology with the power of deities and demons. The game is no longer a contest between the imagination and reason, but the transformation of technique into dream.

FIFTH BEAUTY

The Science-Fictional Sublime

○ ○ ○ ○ ○ ○ ○

The sense of wonder: sublime/grotesque. The cognitive beauties we have been exploring would be merely formal schemes if they did not have strong emotional attractions. SF artists work in many styles and moods, but behind all the variations is a charged background against which they come into relief. This is the so-called sense of wonder, a powerful expansion of quotidian awareness to the insight that the physical universe involves far more than anyone can imagine. The sense of wonder does not lend itself to critical analysis. SF is certainly a literature of ideas,[1] as it's often said to be, but it also resists them. A sense is not a concept. Wonder, even less so.

Readers of sf expect it to provide an intense experience of being translated from the mundane to imaginary worlds and ideas that exceed the familiar and the habitual. They expect to feel as if they are witnessing phenomena beyond normal limits of perception and thought that people have not been able to witness before, or perhaps even to imagine. This sense of liberation from the mundane has an established pedigree in art, in two related ways of feeling and expression: the sublime and the grotesque.

The sublime is a response to a shock of imaginative expansion, a complex recoil and recuperation of self-consciousness coping with phenomena suddenly perceived to be too great to be comprehended. The grotesque is a response to another sort of imaginative shock, the realization that objects that appear to be familiar and under control are actually undergoing surprising transformations, conflating disparate elements not observed elsewhere in the world. The recoil and recuperation of the sublime responds to things that are overpowering and dominating; of the grotesque, to things that are near and intimate, yet that prove to be strange. With the sublime, consciousness tries to expand inward to encompass in the imagination the limits to its outward expansion of apprehension. With the grotesque, consciousness tries to project its fascinated repulsion/attraction out into objects that it cannot accommodate, because they disturb its sense of rational, natural, and desirable order. In both, the perceiver enjoys a sudden dislocation from habitual perception. Both attitudes have been deeply connected to sf from the start, because both are concerned with the states of mind that science and art have in common: acute responsiveness to the objects of the world, the testing of the categories conventionally used to interpret the world, and the desire to articulate what consciousness finds inarticulable.

It is not always easy to distinguish the two modes, as they are dynamically, dialectically related. A phenomenon that to one mind appears to be grotesque may appear sublime to another, if the principles behind it are seen not as violations of reason, but its primal processes. The platypus has been a grotesque freak of nature, as well as a sublime demonstration of evolutionary principles. Quantum physics appeared grotesque to those who did not accept the irreducibility of indeterminacy; it is viewed as sublime by those who do.

Both modes involve *affects* that are represented in distinct rhetorical and poetic *effects*. Such effects are particularly valued in film and graphic art, where the visual spectacle is expected to convey most of the information. Accordingly, in these chapters sf film will play a more prominent role than it has in previous ones. The genre of sf film has evolved into an apparatus for rendering affects through special-effects technology, a process that can be traced to the earliest examples of cinematic art.[2] Capturing, reproducing, and foregrounding the violence of sublime and grotesque shocks has become one of the main purposes of f/x technology and sf film in general.

o o o o o o o

The novum in Suvin's formulation is principally a cognitive event; it changes the way the world is understood. But it is before this a narrative event, changing the conditions for protagonists and audiences to navigate fictive worlds. By changing these conditions, the sf novum also alters the way imaginary worlds can be inhabited and witnessed by feeling bodies, who gain access to new experiences. Just as each work of sf, no matter how derivative, is expected to introduce a novum in a way that has not been depicted before, it must also deliver experiences that have not been represented before (such is true, of course, of fantastic art in general). SF's imaginary new experiences are distinctive because they are made to seem not impossible, and consequently closer to felt experience than flights of fancy, and more permissible to the rational imagination.

Works of sf are as easily catalogued by their sublime effects as by their novums. Think of the void of space and Bowman's ride through the Stargate in *2001* (1968), Kong's last stand at the peak of the civilized world, Wells's Terminal Beach, the city of the Krel and the Monster from the Id, attack ships on fire off the shoulder of Orion, nine billion iterations of God. Behind all of the specific moments are vast and vastly changed conceptual vistas that make possible new imaginary experiences and ways of inhabiting material existence. In sf, the powers and ideas of gods are made available to contingent physical beings, even if only for a little while: immortality, ubiquity, designer universes, infinite worlds and varieties of sentience, unlimited metamorphosis, the multiplication of identity, disembodied existence, the creation and annihilation of worlds, manipulation of timespace, apocalypses, cosmic privations, instruments of transcendence, energies subtle and inexhaustible, free movement and communication in the material universe, and intensities of experience far surpassing that of mere mortals. Such universes require proportionately vast and sublime moral/cognitive struggles, if they are to be understood by humans such as we.[3]

Kant, Burke, and Technology

Burke and Kant believed that in the sublime the individual subject encounters natural phenomena of such magnitude and power that they seem to overwhelm the human subject's ability to encompass and order the perceptible world. At first, consciousness reacts with a sense of terror and awe, a drastic diminution of the sense of self facing the magnitude of the universe outside human construction. For Kant, there are two distinct kinds of sublime response: the *mathematical* and the *dynamical*. The former involves the experience of infinity — the sense of infinite series extending in conceptual space, and sempiternal series extending into future time. This form of the sublime draws attention to the immanence of limitlessness in the material world, producing the impression of infinite recession in all directions. The imagination, always striving to comprehend phenomena in terms of totality (that is, the plurality of things organized as a unified whole), cannot tolerate this awareness; an infinite totality is a contradictory concept. Infinity cannot end; totality must be complete. For Kant, the mathematical sublime arises from a feeling of displacement, deriving from the imagination's inadequacy in arriving at an aesthetic estimation of the magnitude of perceived natural phenomena.[4] The pain is then transcended through the higher pleasure of understanding that this incapacity of perception comes about because we are also endowed with the rational capacity to judge by comparison. It is "a law (of reason) for us, and part of our vocation, to estimate any sense object in nature that is large for us as being small when compared with ideas of reason; and whatever arouses in us the feeling of this supersensible vocation is in harmony with that law" (chap. 27, p. 115). There is a sense of "absolute magnitude" (chap. 25, pp. 105–106) inherent in our reason that establishes the standard for measuring whether anything in nature is great or not.

The dynamic sublime, by contrast, is a response to the sheer physical presence of powerful phenomena, to the superhuman force manifest in magnificent geological formations, waterfalls, storms; that is, those aspects of nature that cause the ego to feel small in the world. In both cases, the perceiving mind is forced to fall back. But in this falling back, it becomes aware that it has in itself the capacity to conceive of the "supersensible," the underlying rational, but inapprehensible order of things shared by the mind and nature. This order can neither be communicated nor represented, except through indirection and symbols, the tools of science and artistic representation. But the capacity to represent is a great power in its own right, protecting us from being subjected to and even annihilated by powers external to our minds:

> [W]hatever we strive to resist is an evil, and it is an object of fear if we find that our ability [to resist it] is no match for it. Hence nature can count as a might, and so as dynamically sublime, for aesthetic judgment only insofar as we consider it an object of fear.
>
> We can, however, consider an object *fearful* without being afraid *of* it, namely, if we judge it in such a way that we merely *think* of the case where we might possibly want to put up resistance against it, and that any resistance would in that case be utterly futile. . . .
>
> [C]onsider bold, overhanging, and as it were, threatening rocks, thunderclouds piling up in the sky and moving about accompanied by lightning and thunderclaps, volcanoes with all their destructive power, hurricanes with all the devastation they leave behind, the boundless ocean heaped up, the high waterfall of a mighty river, and so on. Compared to the might of any of these, our ability to resist becomes an insignificant trifle. Yet the sight of them becomes all the more attractive the more fearful it is, provided we are in a safe place. And we like to call these objects sublime because they raise the soul's fortitude above its usual middle range and allow us to discover in ourselves an ability to resist which is of a quite different kind, and which gives us the courage [to believe] that we could be a match for nature's seeming omnipotence. (chap. 28, pp. 119–120)

These moments of awe might produce *the mysterium tremendum et fascinans* and a sense of mystical ego-dissolution in some subjects.[5] But for Kant this was an unsavory path; he termed it *fanaticism* (chap. 29, p. 135). The rational human response is strategic recoil. The mind recovers its equilibrium, first by withdrawing or escaping from the immediate physical experience and the painful awe it produces, and then coming to rest in the reconstruction of the experience within the aesthetic process of rational sublimation in art and mathematical science. It is a feeling simultaneously painful, in its sense of violent limitation and thwartedness, and pleasurable, in the recognition that there is another, less directly ego-related capacity to understand the supersensible arising out of this thwarting of the perceiving self, "a feeling that we have a pure and independent reason, or a power for estimating magnitude, whose superiority cannot be made intuitable by anything other than the inadequacy of that power which in exhibiting magnitudes (of sensible objects) is itself unbounded" (chap. 27, p. 116).

For Kant, the sublime requires that the perceiving imagination give up its attempt to perceive order and wholeness immanently; it must give itself over to the mind's faculty to make sense of the experience precisely in displaced representation. It is an estranging operation, a form of self-sacrifice on the part of the imagination, in order for cognition to be sublated at a higher level of abstraction, which the mind has — even if only in miniature — in common with the order of the universe underlying the overpowering object. The sublime is a response not to Nature in general, but to the moments of Nature making-itself-manifest in human consciousness. Technology plays little role here, because for Kant this recognition can be effected only by what is not comprehensible, or apprehended — and technology in Kant's classical formulation is always, necessarily, an expression of this art of reason.

For Kant's older contemporary Burke, the sublime is linked to the sensation of danger consciously perceived from a position of safety. This is the familiar feeling attested to by devotees of horror films: the (aesthetic) enjoyment of the feeling of fear while being behind a virtual protective shield. Burke's language in his *Philosophical Inquiry into the Origin of our Ideas of the Sublime and the Beautiful* lends itself to treatment in terms of the gothic aspect of sf: "The passion caused by the great and sublime in nature, when those causes operate most powerfully, is Astonishment; or astonishment is that state of the soul in which all motions are suspended, with some degree of horror. In this case the mind is so entirely fitted with its object, that it cannot entertain any other, or by consequence reason on that object which employs it."[6]

Such objects, which fascinate the mind to the exclusion of any other thoughts, and hence of any possibility of placing them into historical or comparative contexts, usually embody great power. They are, necessarily, also *obscure,* because "once one knows the extent of danger, much of the apprehension vanishes" (58). Once the object/phenomenon is understood in terms of rational relationships — cause and effect, analogies, categories — it is somehow subdued by reason in a Kantian way. Burke clearly conceived of the sublime as an effect, even more emphatically than did Kant; it was the frisson of fear and the possibility of annihilation that made "the idea of vast power" interesting. The sublime is, for Burke, the aesthetic simulation of risk, of the sensation of ego- and reason-annihilating encounters with one's sense of mere existence, where the distractions of social conventions and personal coping mechanisms are scared away. What is left in its finest, sublimated form for Burke is not the Kantian access to the Transcendental Ego, but the rush of life after being on the brink of losing it.

While Kant views the sublime as the recognition of the superabundance of presence, of the infinities and powers of the world of phenomena, Burke conceives it in terms of negations, or *general privations* (71). The sublime-generating phenomena are too big to be formed; hence they are less obstacles to the expansion of the imagination (as in Kant), than they are voids that cannot be filled. They are all, in their own ways, abysses. Primary among these privations are *vacuity, darkness, solitude,* and *silence.* Then follow *vastness,* in any direction, but especially depth, where it creates the immediate fear of the abyss; *infinity,* which, as in Kant, overpowers the mind trying to conceive a complete whole; *magnificence;* powerful *light* and even more so, *darkness,* and sharp transitions, as with lightning; great *sound* and *loudness; suddenness* and *intermittence* of movement; and the specifically technological qualities, *succession* and *uniformity, magnitude in building,* and *difficulty:* "when any work seems to have required immense force and labor, the idea is grand" (77).

It is evident from this list that for Burke there is no essential difference between the sublime induced by nature and by human art. The artistic sublime creates a surrogate, a simulated experience of the natural encounter with privative magnitude, which may be enjoyed in assured safety. Yet the experience is somehow the same. The artist is able to invoke that sense of awe as the reminder of existence. In the architect and the city planner this art is extended almost to the scale of natural creation. For Kant, the sublime is a contemplative reaction; consequently his idea of it is skewed toward the mathematical. The fierce mental activity may express itself in science, art, and philosophy, but there is a certain balance, or stasis, achieved by the aesthetic of the sublime, the equilibrium between the mind and phenomenal creation in the supersensible. With Burke, the equilibrium is comparatively unstable; the shocked ego never seems to gain secure footing. The expression of the sublime in art is either an act of transient control, or of the violent imposition of sublime awe on others. For Burke, the imbalance keeps the mind limping, and so his sublime is skewed toward the dynamic. Yet Burke allows for something that Kant does not: artifacts that inspire sublime awe directly in social life.

While Kant tries hard to exclude the categories of the monstrous and the excessive that shock the ego beyond repair and order, Burke appears to consider such things fit subjects for representation. In sum, Burke underwrites not only the effect of Gothic horror, but the possibility that human constructions can become sufficiently autonomous of their creators, and sufficiently overpowering, to educe sublime wonder themselves. It is a perspective that licenses the science-fictional dialectic at the heart of *Frankenstein* and the narrative of autonomous technology.

Sublime Monstrosity: *Frankenstein*

Frankenstein (1818), which Brian Aldiss and Carl Freedman consider the Urtext of sf,[7] is the first work in which a contemporary human invention can take its place as a sublime creation, a made object that is, despite its human provenance, obscure, powerful, and capable of escaping from rational, scientific civilization. In *Frankenstein* the Burkean and the Kantian sublime collide. The monster is terrible and rational. It is equally capable of inhabiting the abyss and of understanding the supersensible. It is capable of articulating what Victor, its creator, cannot: that the sublimation of awe in the rational inventions of science and art may not lead to resolution and equilibrium, but to the intensification of the causes of awe in the very products that were supposed to tame them. *Frankenstein* poses a challenge to the transcendental Creator, first by making a human being His minuscule double, and then showing them both failing on their different scales to endow their creations—that is, the signs and symbols of rational relief and order—with relief and order of their own. Although the sublime is almost ritualistically invoked in the novel, its consolatory power is radically undermined in two related ways: first, by the sublime's excession into the monstrous, and second, by the creature's double-bind of being simultaneously magnificent and grotesquely ugly.

Barbara Claire Freeman argues that "Kant's depiction or construction of the sublime simultaneously portrays and defends itself against monstrosity."[8] Kant poses the *monstrous* against the *colossal*. The latter is "the intuition of an object almost too great for our faculty of apprehension"; the monstrous is that which "by its size destroys the purpose which constitutes the concept of it."[9] Although Kant had been emphatic that the sublime is not a quality of the object that inspires the response, his notion of the monstrous is ambiguous. Kant's sublime is more than an assertion of the power of nature and the imagination to awaken the sense of totality that a conventional rationality cannot provide (and thus a romantic notion). It also draws limits against the immoderate surplus of power that can blow the whole process to smithereens—

which would violate not only the understanding of cosmic harmony and community, but also perhaps that very harmony itself. Once the monstrous has made its inroads into consciousness, human reason is no longer stable.

For Freeman, the inherent vulnerability of the sublime to its own processes is exemplified by *Frankenstein*. In that novel, what was intended to be sublime seems necessarily, by some sort of a symbolic law, to be drawn beyond its containing frame, and passes over into monstrosity: "*Frankenstein* can be read almost as a parody of the *Critique of Judgment*, for in it everything Kant identifies with or as sublime, including the products of sublimation, yields precisely what Kant prohibits: terror, monstrosity, passion, and fanaticism." (194). Victor attempts to construct a sublime creature, and gets a monster. The sublime Alpine geography "produces neither peace of mind nor aesthetic pleasure, but rather a vision of encounter with monstrosity" (195). At Chamonix, the archetypal apex of sublime landscape, the Creature is far more at home than Victor can ever be. Almost every landscape in which the Creature appears — the Alps, the Arctic, the Scottish coast — is explicitly linked by Burke with the sublime.[10] The consummate sublime effect, lightning, accompanies the monster everywhere. "From the outset, then, the sublime in *Frankenstein* lays waste to the beautiful and brings it to decimation" (Freeman, "*Frankenstein*" 195).

Anne K. Mellor observes the same process. The Creature is himself physically sublime.

> His eight foot tall body, his superhuman physical strength (as great as the "winds" or a "mountain-stream" ...), his predilection for deserted mountain ranges and gloomy glaciers, and above all his origin in a transgression of the boundary between life and death — all render him "obscure" and "vast," the hallmarks of the sublime. Throughout the novel, his appearance causes in the other characters the "strongest emotion which the mind is capable of feeling," the Gothic *frisson* of pure terror. (234–235)

The most interesting innovation from the perspective of sf is that with *Frankenstein* the powerful qualities of the negative sublime have been personified in the product of a genuine human technoscientific procedure. The power of nature's threatening magnitude is brought squarely into the human domain, where its effects target the most protected human intimacies. The defensive shield that distinguishes the sublime from the dangerous comes down. *Frankenstein* offers a critique of the technosublime before the letter.

With this move, Mary Shelley established a model for the sense of wonder in sf that totters unstably between the sublime and the grotesque. The Creature of *Frankenstein* remains within the context of the sublime partly in order to affirm the value of the feminine domain of the beautiful for the novel. There can be little doubt that if the nurturing world of the female characters — explicitly linked to moral beauty — had had sufficient power, Victor's laboratory experiment would not have been undertaken. Nothing is more telling than Shelley's refusal to let her Frankenstein create a wife for the Creature (a taboo violated by most of her male epigones). Shelley's Victor recognizes that once his Creature acquires the interests of physical reproduction, that is, immanent embeddedness in the life-world, it will cease to be an anomaly, and might create a race of demons whose power will thwart both concrete human beings and the standards of natural affection that represent the universal moral law. However much the narrative inspires pity for the abandoned Sublime Child-Man, Shelley is at one with Victor in the uncompromising intention to expel him from Creation.

After a sublime product has been implicated in the natural world of metamorphic substance, it becomes grotesque and will not permit the mind to affirm any counternorms. Once angels have fallen into matter, they become not only demons, but shape-shifters. The technosublime displaces the sense of awe from nature and architectural imitations of natural forms to the technological embodiments of dynamic natural processes. As long as nature is conceived to be a rule-governed universe, its products — including its human simulacra — offer the possibilities of transcendence to a "higher" knowledge. But once nature itself is viewed as prone to violate its own rules, or when human technologies can recast them with impunity, we are in the domain of the grotesque and the technogrotesque, where fascination rules, and transcendence is unthinkable.

The Kantian/Burkean sublime is also undermined in *Frankenstein* by the author's decision to make her monster hideously ugly: embodying and displaying physically shocking, "unnatural" combinations of parts and disgusting metamorphoses, mirrored in unmanageable, unnatural combinations of moral and immoral qualities of the spirit. It could have been otherwise. The monster might have been a physically beautiful Byronic superman-with-issues, but that was not Shelley's project. Her monster is capable of inducing sublime transport, but he is also trapped in a grotesque shell. We cannot be certain exactly which of Victor's sins was worse: creating a being whom he would not nurture, or creating an ugly and uncertain one that no one else would, either. With this move, Shelley introduced questions that not even Burke had raised: what is the ontological status of the animated objects of human scientific art? Where does the ethical responsibility lie when the second human nature of scientific civilization is both a dependent creation and an autonomous one, simultaneously formed by its inventors and forming them with its new powers? Shelley escapes in the classical way, by making the creator and monster immolate themselves together for their conjoint sin against humanity. But the question lingers: what if the monster had not only been hopeful, but also had had reason to hope? What if instead of a grotesque distortion of human beauty he had been beautiful? Where would the scientific sublime be, if human beings' own creations could embody infinities and might that overpower the human self?

Since *Frankenstein*, sf has often imagined answers to these questions, but with an attitudinal rigor as strict as that of tragedy and comedy, it contains the problem through a dialectic of the sublime and the grotesque. This dialectic did not start with *Frankenstein*. All proto-sf works, from Lucian's "True Story" (second century) and More's *Utopia*, through *Gulliver's Travels* and Voltaire's *Micromégas*, have shuttled back and forth between sublime concepts and grotesque bodies, each offering an alibi for the other. In *Frankenstein*, this collision/collusion is framed as a double bind: the sublime cannot assert itself because of the creature's grotesque monstrosity, while grotesque fascination is elevated by implications of his sublime endowments. In mature sf, this double bind develops into a full-fledged ludic strategy of imagining technoscience as simultaneously sublime and grotesque.

SF is not directly concerned with nature or with the qualities of science that seem to double the powers of nature. Its raw material, its object of playful imitation is not nature, but the discourse and social practice of science. SF does not shape terror and ecstasy into the sublime; it shapes the sublime itself into ludic forms. All artistic evocations of the sublime are in a sense playful, simply because they are fictional; they pretend to present what they avow is unpresentable. Usually, the play is disguised by effects that simulate the experience of acknowledging the abyss and the force of nature. SF writers sometimes attempt to match that intention. Stapledon comes close, with his serene, humorless sobriety. But the overwhelmingly dominant strategy has been to ironize the sense of awe by having the grotesque ride alongside it. This doubled attitude could only emerge after industrial science made human civilization appear to have learned the secrets of nature, which it could imitate and improve through its technological networks and artifacts.

L'americomécanique

The classical sublime of Kant and Burke involves two fundamentally negative notions about technology. First, human works can only rarely inspire the sublime, because they contain their human purposes in every atom of their being.

They cannot evoke the awe that comes from becoming aware of their other-ness and incomprehensibility. Even when they produce a certain quasi-sublime response, it is because they are already *re*presentations of the original presen-tations experienced vis-à-vis the natural world. Where artifacts are sublime-inspiring (Kant mentions only the pyramids and Saint Peter's Basilica), it is because they imitate the magnitude of nature, and thus surpass the social use of the building. This surpassing is why Burke values *difficulty;* the labor and care that goes into a sublime object exceeds its function. The second negative position is that the sublime is a response to things that are given; it says little about *production.*

At the heart of the romantic sublime is the necessity for the ego to submit first to the power of nature, and then to the dominion of universal reason. What cannot happen is that the ego will gain mastery over either principle in the material world. This constellation of ideas surrounding the sublime changes radically in nineteenth-century America. Unlike Europeans, Ameri-cans did not view nature as an inscrutable and resistant domain, in which humans were embedded and from which they were simultaneously alienated. In early nineteenth-century America, David E. Nye writes, "Nature was un-derstood to have authored the script sanctioning its own transformation in the service of an inevitable destiny."[11] Kant had authorized the feeling that rea-son allowed humans to measure themselves against the omnipotence of na-ture, through the recognition of their freedom and moral law. Americans, in a characteristic move, interpreted this recognition as a magnificent destiny to dominate nature physically:

> The attribution of sublimity to human creations radically modified the psychological process that the sublime involved. Whereas in a sublime en-counter in nature human reason intervenes and triumphs when the imagination finds itself overwhelmed, in the technological sublime rea-son had a new meaning. Because human beings had created the awe-inspiring steamboats, railroads, bridges, and dams, the sublime object it-self was a manifestation of reason. Because the overwhelming power displayed was human rather than natural, the "dialogue" was now not between man and nature but between man and the man-made. The awe induced by seeing an immense or dynamic technological object became a celebration of the power of human reason, and this awe granted special privilege to engineers and inventors. The sense of weakness and humili-ation before the superior power of nature was thus redirected because the power displayed was not that of God or nature but that of particular human beings. (60)

The American technological sublime is resolutely practical. It eschews contemplation, and so the mathematical sublime plays only a secondary role. In extending technological control over the continent, which was so full of sublime scenery that it had become commonplace, it all became a matter of the dynamical sublime. The national technological project first involved the control of horizontal spatial distances, via the railroads, bridges, canals, and so forth, and then the control over vertical space, via skyscrapers from whose heights the city became a visible abstraction. In the relentless construction of a technological second nature, the national ego seemed to expand without serious challenge from the material universe, with an attendant sense of vertigo at its own powers. Unlike the romantic sublime,

the technological sublime does not endorse human limitations; rather, it manifests a split between those who understand and control machines and those who do not. In Kant's theory of the natural sublime, every human being's imagination falters before the immensity of the absolutely great. In contrast, a sublime based on mechanical improvements is made possible by the superior imagination of an engineer or a technician, who creates an object that overwhelms the imagination of ordinary man. Yet this inspiring effect is only temporary. Machines that arouse admiration and awe in one generation soon cease to seem remarkable, and the next generation demands something larger, faster, or more complex. By implication, this form of the sublime undermines all notions of limitation, instead presupposing the ability to innovate continually and to transform the world. The technological sublime proposes the idea of reason in constant evolution. While the natural sublime is related to eternity, the technological sublime aims at the future and is often embodied in instruments of speed, such as the railway, the airplane, and the rocket, that annihilate time and space. (60)

Nye here describes the beginning of the transformation of sensibility that creates the preconditions for sf. The shift from the affirmation of natural creation, and from seeing reason as a moral law of judgment, to the idealization of intervention and the re-creation of material nature, marks the beginning of the view that will make of the technical world of second nature the privileged scene of the human drama, and technology the privileged manifestation of human recuperation:

There is an American penchant for thinking of the subject as a consciousness that can stand apart from the world and project its will upon it. In this mode of thought, the subject elides Kantian transcendental reason with technological reason and sees new structures and inventions as continuations of nature. Those operating within this logic embrace the reconstruction of the life world by machinery, experience the dislocations and perceptual disorientations caused by this reconstruction in terms of awe and wonder, and, in their excitement, feel insulated from immediate danger. New technologies become self-justifying parts of a natural destiny, just as the natural sublime once undergirded the rhetoric of manifest destiny. Fundamental changes in the landscape paradoxically seem part of an inevitable process in harmony with nature. (282)

What is new and enabling for sf, is that supersensible reason, the disembodied principle of human greatness, begins its journey on the path away from transcendence toward the enshrinement of artificial immanence. The process that views the conquest of natural forces through the extraction of their essence and the reapplication of humanly controlled technologies no longer measures itself against a cosmic limit. The early technological sublime is a form of *afflatus*, the steadily self-aggrandizing ego that seems to encounter no serious obstacles to its technological solutions. The handyman, the engineer, and the inventor become the agents at the leading edge of history. Production, rather than philosophical contemplation or political revolution, becomes the model for the success of a society, and production unfettered is a result of problem-solving on a grand scale. For Verne, this was not an unfamiliar point of view. He had a word for it: *l'americomécanique.*[12]

"Every Mushroom Cloud Has a Silver Lining"

Nye distinguishes two phases of the ideology of the technological sublime. The first phase lasts roughly from the 1830s until 1945: the second follows the atomic bombings of Japan. The latter, in Nye's view, brought about a profound revaluation of American attitudes toward technology:

> The experience of the natural sublime rests both on the sense of human weakness and limitations and on the power of human reason to comprehend the infinitely large and powerful. But when human beings themselves create something infinitely powerful that can annihilate nature, the exaltation of the classical sublime seems impossible. The Kantian relationship to the object required a sense of personal security. One was exposed to the power of the hurricane, but nevertheless one saw it in relative safety. This necessary precondition evaporates in the superheated wind of an atomic blast. The technological sublime, in which the observer identifies with the power of a man-made object, becomes

absurd. Who identifies with the bomb? The collective sense of achievement, another hallmark of the technological sublime, is radically undercut and destroyed. Just as important, contemplation of the bomb transforms admiration for inventors, engineers, and scientists into fear and mistrust. (255–256)

With atomic weapons, much of the classical shock of terrifying destructiveness returns to the technosublime. Once the entire biosphere becomes vulnerable to engineered destruction, to explosions "brighter than a thousand suns" and to "nuclear winters," the most destructive physical might has been appropriated, and the once-sublime domain of nature seems to exist on human sufferance. The nuclear sublime is the catalyst for collective mistrust of the technological elite. But it goes further, to awe and terror at the prospect that the war machine develops autonomously from mundane social concerns. Chained to the logic of the arms race, human engineers are no longer privileged actors at the forefront of history, but rather passive agents of techno-evolution's unfriendly experiments, only partially aware of what they're doing.

Much has been written about the nuclear sublime as the blockage-stage of sublimation, when consciousness feels inadequate to the task of articulating the power it witnesses.[13] It is now a commonplace that the idea of nuclear war cannot be approached through conventional or direct means, because it would be the novum to end all novums. The impossibility of directly representing events that have called into question the premises of earlier bourgeois humanism — including, along with Hiroshima and Nagasaki, the Holocaust, and African and Cambodian genocides — has pervaded the cultural criticism of the West. Nonetheless, it is clear that, although the dangers evoking the nuclear sublime still loom large, technological enthusiasm continues with nary a hitch. Many other technoscientific trends — commercial nuclear energy, aerospace engineering, computer science, bioengineering, artificial intelligence, and nanotechnology foremost among them — have inspired orthodox expressions in the style of the prenuclear technological sublime. And indeed, the prospect of nuclear war itself did not prevent myriad works of visual and narrative sf from attempting to gain mastery over its imaginary. Most of these works were explicitly science-fictional.

With rare exceptions, none of the discussions of the sublime effects of the nuclear technoscape include sf in their accounts. This exclusion is based on a doubly determined investment of most cultural critics: first, in elite literary culture (to which sf is rarely admitted); and second, in identifying texts that are morally useful and aesthetically complex (versus the ostensibly amoral glee with which sf has routinely wiped out civilization in pulp fiction).[14] Even within the field of sf during the 1950s and 1960s, the enthusiasm with which sf writers wiped the slate of civilization clean to construct postapocalyptic scenarios struck many as unseemly. The horror/sf novelist Robert Bloch famously accused his colleagues of believing that "every mushroom cloud has a silver lining."[15] Whether or not they were violating a code of catastrophic discretion, sf artists continued to cultivate the futures of technological civilization, and its aesthetic of the sublime.

With the technosublime, the function of an obstructing puissant nature passes over to human technoscience, which has attained such complexity, speed, and analytic and synthetic power that it can actually decompose the natural and recompose it in new forms more compatible with the technosphere. Technological systems acquire such annihilating force, and such interlocking intensity in fulfilling the tasks for which they were imagined, that they entrain humans to imagine their lives in terms of the tolerances of machines. In the technosublime, the face of the awesome other is already infused with human purpose, and so it appears to speak a human language. But this humanization is a consummate instance of alienated labor: the sublime products appear independent of their producers, and yet these products are defined *only* by production. Human myths of sacred creation are redescribed entirely in technological terms. The objects of creation are those that technology makes possible. The subjects of creation are their operators — and these can be machines, too. Transcendence in the technosublime comes only from the recognition of the higher principles of technological reason: "It is technology that inspires the sensations characteristic of sublimity; therefore it is technology that alludes to the limits of human definition and comprehension."[16] As postwar elite culture turned elegantly away from the "dehumanized," mechanistic, and unreflective culture of engineering, so metabolically linked to militarism and finance capital, it fell to sf to imagine the transformations technoscience was effecting on the life-world. And because sf had never abandoned the technosublime voice even in its critiques of scientific culture, one of its effects was to export that voice into social discourse at large. As a consequence, the fraught technological/nuclear sublime of American culture began to take on more and more of the character of sf's mediating sublimations, the specifically fictive attitude of the science-fictional sublime.

It is time to define the qualities of this attitude. SF's sublime is specific to the genre, and to fiction. It differs from the classical paradigm in that:

(a) it is playful, lacking the psychological sincerity that classical notions of the sublime — and indeed many contemporary versions — insist upon;

(b) its evocative objects are all imaginary, hence conditional and weight-less, in sharp contrast with "actually existing" sublime-inspiring objects, whose excess of presence is precisely what incites the imagination to sublimate;

(c) its objects are all mediated by science. They are either understood, discovered, or invented through it, and their mysteriousness is constrained by this. Given the interdependence of discovery and invention in the imaginary novum discussed in "Second Beauty," sf's scientifically sublime objects are implicated in a technosphere that surpasses its creators' understanding, making technology both the cause of the sublime shock and the means of recuperation;

(d) it is tempered by the constant presence of grotesque elements in dialectical tension with the sublime response; these elements draw attention to the fictive and constructed nature of the imaginary sublime; and finally,

(e) the sf megatext has a playful discounting effect on it. Because the audience is aware that an imaginary sublime experience in a given sf work is one variant among many that already exist in sf's megatextual future, the impinging pressure of the sublime is relieved from the start.

In a sense, the sf sublime has become a "realistic" discourse. It reflects a social world that has been saturated with technosublime narrative/image systems that adopt the language sf itself has cultivated. Advertising and media, political propaganda, and the justifications of grand public works and experiments use the emotional charge of awe and reconsolidation in technoscience to create assent and to prevent dissent, reveling in the ecstasy of control, applying the poetics of fiction to the construction of society. SF has, more than any other contemporary discourse, cultivated the motivating concepts of the global transformation of natural existence into a system of interlocking technical systems, the empire of technoscience. The sf sublime emphasizes the dramatic arc of the technosublime: recoil at the unutterable power and extension of technology, and recuperation through ethical judgments about its effects in the future.

This process has been ongoing for much of the twentieth century. Modernization — from the construction of such technological monuments as the Suez Canal, Hoover Dam, and Le Corbusier's city of Chandigar, to the ideological formulations of technoscientific development motivating national and utopian platforms, such as the U.S. and Soviet space programs — employed the sublime narrative figures of sf.[17] Although the genre per se remained in the shadow of the national-modernist real-world sf, the explosive growth of technoscience and its unfettered application to political and social life has led to the elevation of sf writers to the position of *acknowledged* legislators of the world. We saw in the previous chapter the role of sf paradigms in inspiring and justifying computer engineering and nanotechnology. We are accustomed to the language of the science-fictional sublime for justifying any new, supposedly revolutionary technology. George Gilder's hype for what he calls the "telecosm," the civilizational implications of innovations in bandwidth, is not untypical:

> The telecosm launches us beyond the fuzzy electrons and frozen pathways of the microcosm to a boundless realm of infinite undulations. Beyond the copper cages of existing communications, the telecosm dissolves the topography of old limits and brings technology into a boundless elastic new universe, fashioned from incandescent oceans of bits on the electromagnetic spectrum.
>
> At the heart of the telecosm are lasers pure enough to carve a sliver of light into thousands of usable frequencies, gossamer glass threads carrying millions of times more information even though they are thousands of times smaller than copper cables, fiber strands made of glass so pure that if it were a window you could see through seventy miles of it. The telecosm can even banish all the glass and unveil new cathedrals of light and air alone.
>
> This is not futurism, for the science behind it is already history. The impact of the change, though, will exceed most of the dreams of technological futurist. Futurists falter because they belittle the power of religious paradigms, deeming them too literal or too fantastic. Yet futures are apprehended only in the prophetic mode of the inspired historian.[18]

Similar, if less ecstatic statements can be found in the writings of Marvin Minsky, Hans Moravec, Eric Drexler, Ray Kurzweil, and other purveyors of "transhumanism," "extropianism," and other regimes of posthumanism.[19] These regimes reach a form of fulfillment in the depiction of the sublime object of real-world sf desire: the Singularity.

The "Mathematical" SF Sublime:
2001: A Space Odyssey

Although they are somewhat dusty with age, Kant's two base categories of the sublime are nonetheless useful for interpreting most sf up to the present.[20] Most sf writers develop both modes in each work. One may preponderate, but it is not uncommon for the story to begin under the umbrella of a mathematical/contemplative sublime idea (AIs fuse to create a parallel sentient cosmos, social classes have evolved into different species, the physical universe is an aesthetic experiment by an immature demiurge), and to proceed with dynamically sublime narrative and technical devices with a completely distinct provenance.

The mathematical/contemplative technosublime is the less cultivated of the two in sf, largely because of the power of popular narrative forms, commercial interests, and the ethos of entertainment that has constrained the development of sf for most of its career. Works such as Stapledon's *Last and First Men* and *Star Maker*, which develop a theoretical-sublime idea without trying to incite intense emotional involvement in action, are relatively rare. For most works of sf, the mathematical technosublime merely establishes the ultimate questions and stakes — the pretexts for action. If a choice has to be made between the careful philosophical development of a difficult idea and overwhelming action, it will normally be for the latter.

This choice of action is especially true of sf in cinema, where similar constraints on the medium amplify the effect. In many respects, sf film is a more congenial medium for expressing the technosublime than writing. Cinema is more able to overpower an audience as a medium, and it is always cultivating new devices technologically (special effects [f/x]) to reflect and inspire new attitudes about the pervasive influence of technological devices on social life:

> The phantasmagoria of progress involves a sustained immersion within an artificial, technological environment that suggests technology's own ability to incorporate what it has generally excluded. If the disappearance of nature is seen as the consequence of a burgeoning technosphere, then utopian technologies will incorporate Arcadia. . . . If technology is seen as a dehumanizing force that leads to an impoverishment of spirit, then utopian technologies will permit a new emergence of spirituality and cosmic consciousness. . . . It might even be argued that cinema is the very paradigm of an artificial, technological environment that has incorporated utopian fantasies of nature, kinetic power, spiritual truth and human connections.[21]

The vast majority of commercial sf films are committed to the dynamic technosublime. But not all. Cornel Robu has called Kubrick's *2001* "the supreme expression of the mathematical sublime in sf cinema" (29), and indeed the film adheres so rigorously to this aesthetic that its sf content can be read as the pretext for the representation of the sublime, rather than the reverse. The film is strictly constructed to articulate what we may as well call an artificial myth (and perhaps even rite) of this sort of sublime. The fundamental Kantian struggle between the imagination's constantly frustrated desire to expand in order to perceive infinity directly, and the cool reassertion of a rational faculty that "proves that the mind has a power to surpass any standard of sense" (Kant, *Critique* 106), is here no longer a matter of the contemplation of natural order, but of understanding the supersensible as an active, purposive intervention in human evolution. Kubrick personifies the qualities of mind, so that the odyssey occurs not in physical space, but in the virtual, parabolic mental void, where the qualities of the sublime are dominant. The mediation toward transcendence is itself represented in purely geometrical form, via the mysterious, opaque, perfectly formed slab that obscurely catalyzes humanity's technological progress toward cosmic power.

True to its aesthetic ambitions, the film is systematic in its technique and design. Striving to convey the sense of pleasure in the "plurality collected in a unity," Kubrick made each element subservient, not to his ostensible theme, but to the aesthetic effect of the sublime. Kubrick radically alters the significance of the aesthetic by restricting it to technology, and excluding every possible indication of humanity's interdependence with the natural world. He encloses his cosmos, as he does his production process, in a technological shell. (With the exception of the backgrounds for the "Dawn of Man" sequence, all of 2001 was shot on soundstages.)

The film's audience is introduced at the outset, in the credit sequence, to a cosmological perception that is also a symbol: a solar circle rising over a crescent world. Here, as it will be again before the "Clavius" sequence, and yet again before the "Stargate," the composition is part of a series of receding crescent worlds, indicating syzygy, a planetary alignment that is also a figure for alchemical and spiritual unions of opposites. The sight cannot be seen except from *outer space*, from an indeterminate point of view taken from the fictive eye of the camera/viewer, who observes the drama of human technological evolution from a distance, with cosmic detachment. The next time such a figure appears it will be from the hominids' point of view, with the sun rising over the perfectly straight edge of the monolith: a geometrical dawn.

The "Dawn of Man" sequence illustrates a principle of the mathematical sublime in its "primitive" form. The freeze-shots and slow pans of the desert display an originary world that could not be further from a desire-saturated Edenic garden. The earth here is hostile, deadly, and vast—unlike a walled garden, or even a harboring forest for semiarboreal apes—with no end in sight, a void of nearly lifeless stone. The hominids are not yet human, so there are technically no humans for the audience to connect with emotionally in this sequence. We are presented with the primal scene of our own species, a memory so far back in the past it might as well be the infinitely distant past of myth. But we can't let it go at that. The pain of recognizing ourselves in these abject beings is countered by the pleasure of recognizing that one of our deepest mysteries will be solved, at least aesthetically: how "Ape" became "Man."

The ancestors at first can barely distinguish themselves from the comical tapirs. A leopard's attacks first on a hominid, then on a zebra, seem mundane and squalid. The appearance of the monolith introduces a formidable tension. Visually, the scene contrasts chaotic rock formations, all clearly shaped by the forces of erosion over millennia, with the perfect geometrical solid, so polished that it should be a mirror, and yet so matte that it won't yield any reflections. Ligeti's aleatoric soundtrack represents the little horde's confusion. Chaos is made clear in relief against the slab's embodiment of geometrical perfection.

The monolith is the novum, and we are witnessing the first apocalyptic transformation point dividing the past from the present and future. The operatic use of Strauss's *Zarathustra* while the Alpha male forms the concept of the bone-tool, imagining a future action as a present one, entrains the action and the viewer. For the first time an intentional action occurs according to a rhythm. The ape gains power. The camera places him in high heroic ecstasy, shot from below, nearly filling the sky. The slain tapir of the imagination is itself seen as enormous and heroic, a veritable felled ox, compared with the mild and unassuming quasi-pigs we saw earlier. The social evolutionary steps follow quickly, once the idea of weaponry has been formed: first overpowering for their meat the animals who had competed with them for forage, then overpowering their own kind.

Kubrick excludes any representation of desire in the "Dawn of Man," as he will throughout the film. Indeed, *2001* works as a consummate example of cognitive estrangement, to the point that it becomes unclear what the cognition is truly for.[22] The hominids are not driven by animal drives or human lust; and even the moment when the Will to Power — evoked explicitly by the strains of *Zarathustra* — appears to catalyze the Alpha male to make the first technological discovery and invention, there is very little *will* involved. The discovery of the bone's usefulness appears to come out of the Alpha's idle play. We know these beasts are always hungry, as they can't even chase their competitors away from their meager food sources, but it is not hunger that motivates the Alpha. The leaps to a higher level of awareness, where the future can be seen as plausibly as the present, are instigated by two tools: the monolith and the bone. The hominid is merely the vehicle of their intersecting forces.

It would have been difficult for most artists at the time to resist linking this moment of the technobirth of humanity to some appropriate version of the Fall, since the defining technological-conceptual moment is the invention of a weapon and the acquisition of mediated force to do effective violence. These hominids have no art, no skill at making shelter, not even potent displays. Kubrick excludes any sense of power other than the instrumental. Progress is not a matter of moral or cultural advancement, but of the ability to extend technological power. The famous cut, bone-to-spaceship, bypasses all human spiritual attainments, and all human violence against the biosphere. Nothing is permitted in the story that is not "mathematical" in the sublime sense. Human history is reduced to the steps of a technoconceptual progress: from the natural, to the artificial, and ultimately, to the mysterious stage after cosmic artificial insemination.

In design terms, the long middle section displays what might be the parodistic design of human technical civilization as an expression/imitation of geometry. The space between earth and moon is filled with spaceships that imitate unicellular forms synchronized with the musically geometrical waltz, a dance predicated on the constant motion of circles within circles. Throughout this section, the visual compositions are dominated by bilateral symmetry, the two sides distinguished only by smaller geometrical instruments, panel screens, rectangles and circles, and the illuminated diagrams manifesting series after series of data. Human behavior is banal, utterly conventional, amoral, business-American. Automatic actions are performed within environments of opaque panels and furniture, in space articulated only by the requirements of weightlessness — all indicating that the human world has created its second nature in imitation of the infinite series, without originality, without transcendence, without horizon. Everywhere we perceive symmetrical constructions, series, conventional phrases, the lack of natural color or shade.

The affect is oppressive and exhausting, as if technology were reproducing sublime magnitude, but schematically, merely repeating the forms of the ancient technogeometrical gift. There is no concern for human social applications, only for forms. The exploration of the moon is presumably motivated by curiosity (the ideological alibi of most sf), but the skillful explorers seem to have no passion for it. They operate in obeisant gangs as did their prehuman ancestors. Humans are reproducing the mathematical/geometrical without any thought of its origin in the supersensible. This potentially endless, aimless repetition of forms can halt only when an obstacle appears that imagination cannot handle. The monolith waiting for this technical attainment stands in sharp contrast, with its uniqueness and burst of radio signals, now not to the passive natural forms of the mock-Olduvai, but to the repetitions and lack of purpose of the Space Age.

The Jupiter mission sequence continues many of these design motifs: panels, rectangles and circles, geometrical solids, screens, automatic astronauts, conventional discourse. There is not a trace of a natural substance. All is surface, exhausting and empty repetition, jogging in circles, making the rounds. Symmetrical doublings appear on all levels: Poole and Bowman, humans and HAL, two EVA missions, two earth broadcasts, instrument panel reflections on visors, and so forth. We do not know — any more than the crew does — what the *Discovery*'s mission is. The ship, too, is a mathematical being, composed of combined solids, but now evoking a stylized human skeleton and a spermatozoön. The context has changed, and the characteristic negativities of the Burkean sublime come to the forefront. Vastness, loneliness, darkness, and silence, all combined, come to a climax of privations in the extended sequence depicting the salvaging of Poole's body from the abyss. The drones and pings of the interior of Bowman's pod alternate with the complete stillness of outer space (surely one of the most prominent uses of dead air in cinematic history). With the stark light and dark contrasts on the surface of the *Discovery,* the traditional sublime qualities of magnitude and extremity are brought together in a formal ensemble. Bowman's heroic act of self-preservation carries great symbolic weight. Forced to survive for precious seconds in the vacuum, Bowman must actually prove he can survive without air, like an inorganic machine.

"Beyond the Infinite," with its Kantian title, propels Bowman through another display of symmetry, the Star Gate; only this one is rich with color and speed. Neither Bowman nor the audience understands what is happening (even the term "Star Gate" is from Clarke's novel), only that Bowman is now, suddenly, moving extremely fast, probably at several Gs. The symmetry gradually yields. First we witness kaleidoscopic macrocrystals (symmetrical still). Then follow the first quasi-organic visual displays since the opening sequence: supernovas, galaxies, comets indistinguishable from shooting sperm, a red zygote reminiscent of astronomical photographs of nebulae. These images invoke sex unambiguously. The exterior of space and the interior of the body are mixed together. Are we inside a cosmic body, observing an artificial insemination, or are we just another futile body in the void? The pseudo–Empire-style bedroom is the first surprising surrealist break with the rigidly held technoconditions of the film's design, but here too we detect the conventionality, symmetry, geometry, solitude, and emptiness.

The film *2001* is the visually sublime expression of a spiritually exhausted sensibility for which all evolutionary progress is technical. It is deeply ironic about the absence of the supersensible connection between the universe and the human mind. The mediation of the geometrical embodiment, an object like the cone in Borges's "Tlön," does not promise anything outside the mathematical-technical. It has *only* such qualities. The results of its "teaching" demonstrate nothing more: deadly weapons, aimless spaceflight, and a transfiguration into a cosmic infant. Why should its potential for spiritual transcendence be any greater? (Here is where Kubrick breaks most emphatically with Clarke's problematic novel.)[23]

Kubrick incites the sense of this artificial infinity and magnitude in the audience, so we look for a higher meaning behind it — the artist's intention, the overdetermination — by reading symbolically. There are not, however, enough stable and dramatically closed signs to allow interpretability. The series and symmetries won't lead to a stopping point. It is power without purpose. There are no maternal consolations of Nature in 2001, no safety and aesthetic perception, beauty, or pleasure outside the technological shell. The dynamic sublime is simply banished: even in the prehistoric age, there is no weather, no precipice. There are three dynamic events: the discovery of the bone weapon, when the Alpha transcends everything around him, set against a clear sky; Bowman's defeat of HAL; and Bowman's trip through the Star Gate. Twice the human demonstrates that it can be a machine — for which it is rewarded with an involuntary ride into a mystery it cannot comprehend, from which it returns to earth as a mysterious fetus.

This is promising as a subject for an Oedipal reading.[24] Without any significant feminine or nurturing presence, there's not much tension in the acceptance of the phallic law. (There are no women even among the cryogenically suspended crew members in their technosarcophagi.) It's as if there never was anything but this law: no earth or home to place it in tension with, no natural materials or food whose reworking would create questions about aura, mana, or some irreducible quality of life that insists on its gravity and power. Indeed, except for the first twenty minutes, every action in 2001 occurs suspended in weightlessness or in artificial gravity, enclosed by spacesuits or spacecrafts, or a stylized symbolic room.

The film itself is just such an extreme, enclosed environment. With no real-time location shots, the hermetic, technical enclosure of the soundstage seals out the mundane, and all accidents. It is purified of earth. The only obstacles to the full acceptance of the geometrical law are the void itself and HAL's machine pride (and error). Kubrick sets himself free of any contingency of the real world in which the filming took place. Every angle, illumination, and diegetic stricture is just as suspended, weightlessly manipulable on the soundstage and in the f/x camera, as the action depicted. Kubrick was thus free to construct the action with formally pure evocations of the sublime, shriven of familiar mundane groundings, of dirt. The history of humanity passes in the blink of an eye. The interplanetary velocity of the spacecraft, by contrast, is made to seem motionless.

Finally, in the obscure ending, we witness Bowman being pulled — again, by a will to power that cannot be Bowman's own, for he lacks will and power in the journey through the Star Gate — assuming dominion over things only once in the film: in disconnecting HAL. Indeed, HAL is the obstacle. Tellingly, he is more natural in his pride, more disturbed by the potentially sublime collision with the limits of his own imagination, than are any of the human characters, who do not act as individuals. An old-school humanist might wish to see his disconnection as the triumph of the individual will over artificial intelligence, but there is no real warrant for this. Bowman is liberated to complete the mission, the very thing HAL wished most to do, but was thwarted in by his own pride and simulated humanity (to err is human). Bowman, more flexible in order to be even less fallible, continues until he is pulled to the new worlds beyond the Infinite. These worlds are no more concrete than any before them, and neither the audience nor Bowman can penetrate the conceptual obscurity. The galaxies are made to serve symbolic functions, as fetuses, sperm, zygotes; the dramatic landscapes-in-negative are not (as I thought when I was young) on Jupiter, nor on Earth as we know it. The room, so formal and contrived, could easily be a prison cell, for all we, or Bowman, know.

There is no reason in the end to believe that the Starchild is more morally evolved than humanity. There is no reason why we should even take the Starchild as a literal space fetus, and not, for example, a symbolic representation of a soul returning to Earth for a new incarnation. After all, we have seen spaceships appear like sperm cells, galaxies like zygotes; why should we not perform a similar analogical transfer with the space fetus? Kubrick refuses to provide any support external to the system. Although Clarke's stories are explicitly about a materialized transcendence, Kubrick's could lead in precisely the opposite direction. The relentlessly self-referring system of technological adventure, lacking any motivation from morality, history (indeed, *any* humanistic or critically positive discourse) leaves us with a purely technical cosmos, where technical mastery is the only occasion, instrument, and purpose of intelligent existence. Perhaps the fact that the Starchild still resembles an organic being is a sign that Kubrick prefers the living to the artificial. But I am not sure; until that point in the film the living have shown their flexibility and originality only in technical problem-solving.

In *2001*, we expect a sublimated transcendence in vain, or we supply the illusion ourselves. In the technomathematical sublime, the recoil comes because of willingness to venture into a mysterious cosmos after alien gift-givers who have given us nothing but tools of knowledge, and no reasons or operating instructions. A world almost without nature, mothers, families, female cohort, animals, plants, memories of underdevelopment, or history. Why should we expect our next incarnations — and our universal reason — to be any less remote, instrumental, and alien?

The "Dynamical" SF Sublime: *The Matrix*

The technodynamic sublime responds to technology that inspires awe either because of its overt power or because of humanity's massive and critical dependence on it. In the technodynamic sublime, as in the technomathematical, nature has ceased to be an obstacle. Its erstwhile power has been sublated and condensed into second nature's potent machines and systems. Increasingly, in sf since World War II dangerous manifestations of nature are not only defined and resolved technoscientifically, they are caused by technoscience. The technodynamic is saturated with desire. Its power-objects — constructed by human beings to relieve them from the obstructions of nature — are charged to the limit with the cathexis of fetish, which is then called upon to make itself known in orgiastic displays of aggressive machine power, human-machine romances, and the cyborg's erotic synthesis of organic and technological ontologies.

If *2001* is a consummate expression of the mathematical/contemplative sf sublime, *The Matrix* has a parallel status in terms of the dynamic. The world of *The Matrix* has long forgotten what Nature once was. All that remains of it is the mass of industrially cultivated human bodies — the "coppertops" — from which the machines harvest energy, a motif that makes little scientific sense. The process of extracting human energy would seem to require a greater investment of power than the coppertops would be able to return. And one would think a system capable of the neural control required to make the Matrix would also be able to find new sources of energy. (And in fact Morpheus tells Neo that the machines also have developed a form of fusion.)[25] In other words, the vampirical enslavement of humanity is necessary not for diegetic scientific reasons, but to evoke fantasy's rich tradition of evil invaders feeding off the negentropic *prana* of living organisms. The relevant dominant power has long passed from Nature through humanity, and now rests solidly with the AIs. It is recognition of the truly vast virtual system of the machines that shocks Neo, and begins his sacrificial discipline to embody the messianic New Law, the synthesis of the natural physical body and the virtual info-body.

The audience feels a similar pulse, recognizing in the Matrix a symbol for contemporary social reality. The street finds its own uses for Baudrillard, whose theory of simulacra is hollowed out to be a stash for Neo's blackware. The tributary streams come from all over: political-cultural conspiracy theories, Gibson's consensual hallucination, chic neo-Goth culture reveling in revenge fantasies, hacker ecstasy, and the Vegas marriage of bohemian bourgeois-bashing and Internet libertarianism. Unlike *2001*, from which the audience is excluded except as voyeurs of their own destiny, *The Matrix* hails its audience with a mastery rare in sf cinema.

The Matrix is a matrix indeed, distributing opposing sensibilities, from the imaginary rebels of the audience to the technocores that produce the spectacle, in a single mesh of the sublime. In this the film is a particularly successful example of the aesthetics of ambivalence Brooks Landon finds in sf film: the simultaneous intellectual critique of technology and visceral pleasure in its display.[26] The tension between the critical idea of the Wachowskis' film (sublime in its own right, this literalization of an infinitely complex, multidimensional, and productive network of simulation) and the spectacles of cool violence with which it is attacked, produces two semi-independent levels of narrative. The first is a matter for contemplation and commentary: the painful recognition delivered by the red pill and Morpheus's running gloss. The second is pure dynamism that leaves reflection in the wash of the violent manipulation of a spacetime that is doubly illusory: in the diegetic matrix and in the f/x-saturated movie. The sequels fail by comparison because their narratives are asked to solve a problem that *The Matrix* had established as essentially insoluble: a double bind making the dynamic the antagonist of the contemplative, a smash-the-state-of-things aesthetic relying on speed, firepower, and *trucage* to achieve escape velocity from the conditions of its existence — the cinematic equivalent of a suicide bombing.

The film abandons its contemplative sublime theme fairly early, focusing attention on the dynamic means, the *action* by which human avatars can recuperate power from the machine obstructors. From the position of the contemplative sublime, the film's spectacular manipulation of velocity and positionality is less a solution than a distraction, as it cannot address the philosophical conundrum it is supposed to resolve: what is technological power *for?* When it comes to freedom from illusions, one would have to say that Morpheus has substituted his own version of a Matrix for that of the machines, and his version is quite close to the one inspiring the movie itself. In the end, the ideas underpinning the Matrix are not addressed rationally. A false belief is replaced by a "true" one, which is itself justified only by a combination of diegetic blind faith and the audience's suspension of disbelief exchanged for the pleasure of the spectacle. That this belief in "The One" is justified in the film suggests that the film believes the truth of a given interpretation is only a function of one's (or a collective's) commitment to it, which is in turn proved by the violence one is prepared to commit to assert it. In a word, terrorism. Accordingly, Morpheus's "Desert of the Real" explanation should be as suspect as Agent Smith's account of the Matrix's origin. (Baudrillard believed "*The Matrix* is very like the sort of film that the matrix would make about the Matrix.")[27]

The film *2001* does not enter this territory, as it does not ask the audience to negotiate between semantic levels. The message is delivered apodictically; we are shown a defining narrative, and we can take it or leave it. What questions remain are ours to resolve by adjusting our thinking to the delivered spectacle. In *The Matrix*, the Wachowskis pose a tangle of philosophical metaproblems: what is identity? consciousness? freedom? the relationship between matter and thought? body and image? collective and individual? knowledge and power? The film pretends to address them by substituting metatechnology, control over spacetime, to which the audience is seduced both as passive spectators of spectacle and as active investors in our onscreen avatars' superpowers. The attention of *The Matrix*'s audience is entrained by a brilliant narrative told in f/x, in such a way that the philosophical questions themselves become cool f/x displays of intellectual violence, and as such might as well be resolved by violence heteronomically justified. The resolution of the "meaning of *The Matrix*" is postponed for the sequels. The film's narrative resolves another story instead: Neo's acquisition of the Matrix's sublime power. And this story has nothing to do with the intellectual sublime. Not for nothing does the Oracle note that Neo is "not too bright."

The Matrix is a spectacle of the fast-moving, aggressive technodynamic sublime. In the opening scene, the narrative is so obscure that the audience must patch it together from visual allusions to noir cop films, comic books, and cyberpunk. At first, the camera eye is at a loss, looking up, panning down; blinding flashlights obscure more than they reveal in the dark derelict corridor. Trinity's explosive dance of violence comes as a shock, and the audience cannot know whether f/x climbing of walls, hanging in midair, fighting in slo-mo, are Hong Kong–style fantasy tropes, or literally permissible. In other words, to what extent is this a rigorously science-fictional film? The ensuing chase scene is exhilarating primarily for its speed (a category curiously neglected by Burke in his listing of the qualities of the sublime), or rather, speeds. A ballet occurs both diegetically, as the Agent pursues Trinity over rootops and abysses, and also in the apparatus, in the representation of motion: speeded-up, slow-motion, and real time in alternation. It is a tour de force of f/x, and so calls attention to the film's own play and technique. On subsequent viewings, once we know the whole story, the episode replays as a sublime presentation of the Matrix itself, which allows action in real time to use the tricks of electronic representation and playback. The illusion melts into the real. The audience's bodies, responding with ontological pleasure and epistemological anxiety, have been made to feel simultaneously disembodied (like replayed film images), and physically tense and exhausted. This extended speed-shock (created in no small part by the pulsing Propellerhead soundtrack) culminates with Trinity making her escape call in the phone booth. The slight pauses in the action we expect for resting our tense spectator-bodies do not come. The fastest and most mobile garbage truck in the world rams Trinity's booth at a speed we do not imagine possible in our own world. Her escape signals that bodies operate differently here.

After this, the sublime action f/x develop with their own narrative logic, for which the human avatars are little more than vehicles. I would like to concentrate on four effects that have privileged roles in *The Matrix*: the streaming program code, bullet-time, the morphing/possession of bodies by the Agents, and the Hong Kong wire-fighting–style manipulation of space and time during combat. Each of these effects disturbs the audience's habitual sense of the continuity and solidity of the world. The downward rolling code represents the ceaselessly streaming instructions of the Matrix itself, accessible to those who are able to read its metamachine language. In a brief glimpse before the opening sequence, we see the data-stream as it will later appear on the *Nebuchadnezzar* screens, an obscure conflation of numbers and reversed katakana characters. This data-stream is immediately displaced by the streaming columns of numbers that turn out to be both a conventional surveillance algorithm, and a "physical" passageway for what we can assume is a machine consciousness into the simulated human world. (The appropriate rabbit hole is the digit Zero.) In the course of the action, we see the full code on Cypher's and Tank's screens, reading it from the outside. Although made of letter symbols (in *Through the Looking Glass* Japanese), its most striking quality is its ceaseless downward streaming, evoking natural qualities such as flow and gravity.

The Agents' tactic of possessing the bodies of human avatars is perhaps the hardest of the f/x to justify. It conveys a sense of their ubiquity, but the agonizing transformations represent one of the film's main points of grotesque, rather than sublime, excess. There seems to be no reason why the Agents could not manifest themselves out of any object at all. If their human form is a convenience to make the simulation-world more palatable, and they require a certain continuity to prevent sim-folks from wigging out, then why not simply use the original bodies, *sans torque?* The significance here is again a matter of excess; through this the film demonstrates that bodies are available spaces for virtual traffic. Bullet-time and cybercombat styles belong to essentially the same class of f/x: the ostensibly objective control of physical position and movement in simulated spacetime. Morpheus is, as always, the carrier of the seemingly rational explanation for these wonders: in a virtual world, the parametric rules governing bodies' actions can be spontaneously reprogrammed by those who can access the program in thought. These f/x develop according to the familiar logic of dramatic intensification in Hollywood action films, from Trinity's opening massacre, the gamelike kung fu training program, through the brutal fight between Morpheus and Agent Smith, culminating in Neo's and Trinity's rescue mission, where Neo discovers his power to dodge bullets. This set of violent f/x serves to obscure questions about the quality of virtual spacetime: why should objects and bodies be so subject to being smashed, broken, shot and burned, if a space can be instantly reprogrammed? We are told that the damage done to bodies in the Matrix is a reflection of the damage done to their minds. What then is the damage done to inert physical objects?

In the extended assault on the Corporate HQ where Morpheus is held, Neo and Trinity center the scene with an ostentatious array of firearms. The set is designed to maximize the ecstasy of the force-augmented sublime. A series of pillars gives the lobby a sufficiently serial form to permit articulated progress: sufficiently abstract to permit each stage to be concretized with its own particular flourish of violence, and sufficiently dense to display the putative danger of the real virtual damage. Bodies—we know them to be innocent puppets slaughtered by our heroes—litter the scene. Neo and Trinity proceed to the abyss of the elevator shaft, and ascend without the baggage of the elevator itself, setting off an explosion and a flow of fire that moves with the gorgeous slow-motion accorded any controlled action in the virtual world. Bodies are wrenched and morphed. The agent dodges Neo's bullets; windows are shattered; Neo and Morpheus fly over the abysmal city, hanging by a thread. Finally, the helicopter crashes into a mirror-glass corporate building, not so much colliding with it as we might expect, but folding into it, after which the building itself seems to ripple and warp, as if it were the fabric of space that is damaged, not a discrete structure in it.

The dynamically sublime f/x attain their proper climax with Neo's resurrection and concluding collision with Agent Smith. Neo's transformation into an avatar in the old sense of the term (enlightened, serene, and divinely powerful) manifests itself in — or, from the f/x point of view, is motivated by — the transformations of these now "redeemed" devices. Dodging bullets is no longer necessary. Neo's power over spacetime can stop them dead, and make them fall harmlessly, yielding to virtual gravity. Balletic aerial kung fu is also overwith. Neo's machine *chi* is so rooted he requires hardly any movement to counter the Agent. The data-stream, which we had seen on screens in the real world, now cascades gloriously down every structure, no longer the symbols of nefarious manipulation but the secret names of sacred energy visible to the savior. The morphing possession of others' bodies — which earlier expressed the essential grotesque perception of one body emerging from inside another's — is finally "redeemed." Neo's possession of Agent Smith shatters his illusory body altogether. The painful contortions are replaced by inner light. Even if Smith is gone, he has been "enlightened." We know from the sequels, of course, that not only has Smith not dissolved, the experience of possession actually brings him to full (and sublime) consciousness of viral autonomy — a state of existence that is both mathematically and dynamically sublime, and profoundly grotesque, all in one.

Thus, *The Matrix* concludes with a dynamic logic that its theoretically sublime problem does not. The latter is mediated by magical or religious postures. We are provided no reasons why Neo should be The One. He's dim. He has only a minimal moral position: the obligation to save Morpheus, which incidentally involves the massacre of a dozen or so security forces that he should know are in fact blameless vessels. The transformation of the simulated avatar into the true one comes via a romantic kiss and a head-spinning display of sentimentality and circular logic. The sublime problem posed by the very existence of the Matrix turns out to be an alibi for a fully developed drama of the dynamic sf sublime, in which technology is transformed, through the mysteries of the virtual, into a dynamo once again in service to humanity, a humanity that is utterly dependent on technology for life.

The "Feminine" SF Sublime:
Up the Walls of the World

Much of the recent critical interest in the sublime has been in psychoanalytic terms. The stages of the classical sublime have been translated smoothly into the classical stages of the Freudian Oedipal struggle. Blockage, recoil, self-discipline, and recuperation through submission to the suprasensible yet rational order of things has been reframed as an aestheticization of the child's alienation from the mother, and eventual submission to the Superego/Law of the Father. Thomas Weiskel has extended this reframing into a deconstructive theory of the origin of metaphor.[28] I am not sure, however, that much is explained about the sublime in this way. It presents one of the sublime's particular embodiments (psychoanalysis) as the gloss on the class that includes it, an embodiment whose putative superiority to the aesthetic-cognitive concept is its dubious claim to greater scientific, material, and nonmetaphorical status. Psychoanalysis retains the original sublime dynamic in its own workings — along with the implicit claim that its sublimation of the ineffable powers of the psychic sublime, the emergence of self-consciousness out of the pre-

Oedipal, pre-Symbolic *infans,* is more useful than the aesthetic one. (We might treat psychoanalysis from the analyst's point of view as a form of the sublime; from the analysand's as a form of the grotesque. We shall return to this question in "Sixth Beauty," where we shall examine psychoanalysis in the context of the grotesque.)

This model has been criticized from a feminist perspective for perpetuating the phallogocentrism held to be inherent in the Freudian model. Patricia Yeager has proposed that there is a feminine sublime, deriving from the psycho-dynamics of women's experiences distinct from the androcentric Oedipus complex.[29] The classical, masculine sublime hinges, in this reading, on an assertion of mastery over other voices, as the poet displays his poetic (let us include also technoscientific) brilliance at the moment he claims to be acknowledging the impossibility of articulation. This performance of sovereignty and discipline over the ego reinforces the phallocratic model of imperial domination, to which the reader too must submit in order to benefit from the poet's mastery. The Oedipal model of the sublime is predicated on the focusing of poetic/scientific powers on productive expression and the "dominion" (Kant's term) of transcendent reason, which requires the repression of the pre-Oedipal desire for the mother's body:

> If what is repressed in the "oedipal" sublime is the desire for preoedipal bonding with a mother's body (which, in most Romantic poems, is given an imaginative correlative in the chaos and blissful heterodoxy of the cosmos), in the "pre-oedipal" sublime these libidinal elements are not repressed; they break into consciousness and are welcomed as a primary, healthful part of the writer's experience, as part of the motive for metaphor. (Yeager, "Toward a Female Subline" 205)

In a feminine, pre-Oedipal sublime the disturbance to the ego comes not from an overpowering, dominating "vertical" force, but rather the "horizontal" impingements of diverse others whose claims must be accommodated, but who ultimately require neither the sublation of self nor the repression of others. Yeager quotes Adorno to the purpose: "The reconciled condition would not be the philosophical imperialism of annexing the alien. Instead, its shapeliness would lie in the fact that the alien, in the proximity it is granted, remains what is distant and different, beyond the heterogeneous and beyond that which is one's own" (208).

I am not sure it is necessary to adopt Yeager's theoretical apparatus, derived from Cixous's critique of Freud, to entertain this model. Lee Edelman notes that the untranscended pre-Oedipal state is often considered a pathogenic zone from which recuperation is extremely difficult.[30] (Kristeva's theory of horror, which one critic has called "the grotesque of the grotesque," is rooted in the pre-Oedipal mechanism of abjection.)[31] Whether Yeager's horizontal sublime is a matter of female psychic individuation or some urge for utopian openness to difference not bound to gender, the notion of the feminine sublime helps illuminate some important sf texts. Although most sf has been historically written by men in a competitive field dominated by male editors and critics, the genre has always attracted women writers (and increasingly women readers). If Yeager's model is valid for sf, it has implications for the technosublime, whose sensibility is generally acknowledged to be dominated by historically masculine desire and anxiety.

As a genre, sf has been uncommonly receptive to narratives of struggle for utopias of diversity against technoscientific authoritarianism. In such works, the awe-producing obstacle to personal/collective knowledge and freedom is a technoscientific political and cultural hegemony that regulates discourses, bodies, media, and sciences to prevent their potentially "chaotic" interaction. Arguably, this receptivity has been one of the most important functions of the genre, and one of its main contributions to modern culture. It has created welcoming conditions for critical-utopian fiction, especially visionary feminist narratives. The female sublime suggested by Yeager infuses many feminist and queer-inflected sf texts such as Piercy's *Woman on the Edge of Time,* Le Guin's *Left Hand of Darkness,* Joan Slonczewski's *A Door into Ocean* (1986), Suzette Haden Elgin's *Native Tongue,* Delany's *Dhalgren,* Candace Jane Dorsey's *A Paradigm of Earth* (2001), and Arnason's *Ring of Swords.*

Up the Walls of the World (1978) by James Tiptree, Jr. (a nom de plume of Alice Sheldon), an inexplicably neglected masterpiece of recent sf, is unparalleled in its use of the sublime mode invoked by Yeager. Its action takes place in three worlds. In the contemporary United States, a group of experimental subjects with psychic abilities, each of whom has some sort of physical or social debility that deflects them from individualist autonomy, are gathered on a military base for an experiment in telepathy. Elsewhere in the universe are the inhabitants of the planet Tyree, who have evolved to live in a great vortex of wind dominating their planet, by soaring on translucent mantles with which they communicate by receiving and transmitting mind-fields. The Tyrenni have constructed a near-utopian civilization, and love their world deeply. The third locus is an unimaginably large cosmic being, obscurely neither a living creature nor a machine, yet with qualities of both, composed of matter barely more dense than the void itself. This "Destroyer" travels the spaceways, driven to destroy planets by an incomprehensible sense of guilt against its own kind caused by its emergent individuation from a cosmic group mind. When the Tyrenni become aware that they are next to be targeted by the Destroyer, they attempt to send their minds to Earth by means of a Beam that focuses their most powerful mind-fields. They plan to exchange bodies with humans, drawing the humans' minds back to be housed in the doomed shells of Tyrenni, an act most acknowledge to be a heinous "life crime." As the Destroyer begins demolishing Tyree, the Beam is interrupted, causing two of the disembodied humans and a Tyrenni to enter the vast, cold, lightless interior of the Destroyer, which allows them to enter for reasons it does not understand itself. At the last possible moment, the Tyrenni population are able to transport themselves — now including the telepathic humans in Tyrenni bodies — into the Destroyer, which is gradually transformed into a "world saver" through the complex and obscure mediation of the odd human refugee, Margaret Omali, who somehow synthesizes living and artificial consciousness.

The plot elements of *Up the Walls of the World* are relatively simple for potboiler sf space opera: an alien planet being destroyed by an obscure attacker, transmissions of minds through space, and the critical transformation of a destructive antagonist into a benevolent protector. The question is, as in all sf plots, what this cosmic melodrama is good for, what is at stake that would require such an intensely dramatic story? *Up the Walls of the World* stands out from Tiptree's better-known short fiction in its scale, and in the near-utopian, and indeed near-religious, resolution of a complex psychological crisis that requires several different kinds of minds to understand, and eventually to empathize with, one another. Like Philip K. Dick (whose literary kinship with Tiptree is rarely acknowledged), Tiptree throws together a band of humans with extraordinary powers and debilities struggling to assert some little control over their hostile environment. They must also confront an enormous self-expanding cosmic power intent on reducing existence to entropy. Unlike Dick, Tiptree adds an alien world of spectacular beauty. It is this world that greets the novel's reader, and that establishes the stakes of the fiction. The human characters on Earth are prosaic and mildly freakish. They have been stunted by the quotidian sufferings of American existence, and the narrative shapes them with pedestrian, tranquilized prose. Tyree, the Destroyer, and the abyss of space are proportionally sublime, eliciting one of the most successful and uncompromising displays of sublime vision in sf.

In accord with the sf sublime, Tiptree presents not merely dominating manifestations of nature or technology. Her sublime objects are subjects who demand to be understood as autonomous minds and wills, inhabiting distinct material environments. The conflicts that ensue among them are caused by concerns they share: physical and cultural survival, the need for knowledge, and for a sense of purpose. Except for the oppressively prosaic world of the contemporary United States, with which most of the tale is in contrast, every aspect of Tiptree's world seems to require sublime expression. Tyree's wind-world, in which a civilization of beings exists with unfamiliar senses and without ever touching the surface, challenges objective description:

> They are all alone near the top of the Wall of the World, so high that almost the whole of the great polar vortex can be made out. The wind-wall is a fantastically beautiful swirling cliff, richly patterned with the rushing lights and life-emanations of the Wild. Above them are the perilous heights where the top of the winds start to converge to form the deadly Airfall in the center. Tivonel can just perceive the upper fringes of the tunnel, grey with dying life. Up here too can be sensed a deep background energy. Giadoc had told her it may be the life-field of Tyree itself, transmitting into space.[32]

It challenges the depiction of subjective experience as well. Daniel Dann, one of the exchanged humans, becomes aware of his alien body while in midflight:

> For one vertiginous instant he rides an enormous whirlwind, is swamped with a howling, soundless gale above a dark-light world shot with wild colors that are sounds — he is aware of unknown presences in the gale of light that beats like music on his doubled senses, he is soaring in tempests of incomprehensible glory. (138)

The interstellar Beam of focused life energy conveys the feeling of an animate technology formed out of the living substance of the characters:

> Giadoc and the immense combined power of the ring of Hearers are sucking her life up to the focus at the heart of the Beam, to send it stretching out — out — out to —
> She yields, launching totally, lets herself dwindle to a filament riding a storm of power, an energy that looms and blooms upward like a world-bubble. She is only a thread in an immense thrusting tower of bodiless vitality, shooting forever outward as it intensifies and narrows from a pinnacle to a needle, from a needle to a dimensionless thread driving instantaneously to its goal. And as her life attenuates, recruitment comes — a deep life-force, as if she and the beam were cresting on a planetary power. (111)

In the same way, the Destroyer escapes normal perception and description:

> Somewhere ahead or to one side, he cannot tell lies a huge concentration of darker darkness — something blacker than the mere absence of light, a terrifying vast presence colder than death. It is Death incarnate, he thinks, he is gripped by fear. (139)

The reader's attention is strained to the limit to understand different perceptions — the Tyrenni mind-fields and mantles with which they hear colors and light; the Destroyer's colossal, cold and dark sensorium, barely perceiving the life-signs of inhabited worlds; and the expansive, synaesthetic vision of the once-human cyborg Margaret Omali, once she has assimilated the Destroyer:

> Like themes of silent music the orbital elements of the nearer stars reveal themselves to her mind. Suns weave hugely about each other, developing subcomponents of direction, or glide in concert athwart a flow. (196)

A most intriguing class of sublime effects in *Up the Walls of the World* has to do with the orientation of variously adapted bodies in unfamiliar space: the flight of the Tyrenni, to whose "body the whirlwind is home" (148); the humans' difficulty learning to soar in their sudden new bodies; the mind-controlled motion of the disembodied consciousness ("velocity so great it is simple being, he is only a vector hurtling somewhere, sucked to a destination" [140]); the obscure interface between the virtual bodies of the rescued Tyrenni and Margaret's avatars; and the Destroyer's galactic vistas. From these perceptions and bodies emerge sublime varieties of human and alien feelings. These are then gathered into great alien projects: the Tyrenni's gender-culture of fathering, the Destroyers' plan, the Beam and life-crime, Margaret's reprogramming of the Destroyer's sense of its place in the universe. Mediating all of them are moments of empathy that transcend language of human, bodily, gendered, sexual demarcation.

In *Up the Walls of the World* Tiptree was committed to imagining alien beings, worlds and qualities of sentience — the consummate Others of sf — but also how these beings change, and how humans change in concert with them. Each plot-furthering event involves some form of interpenetration. Dann and Margaret become bound to each other on earth because of an involuntary telepathic exchange of their most traumatic and shameful experiences. The Tyrenni escape involves entering human bodies, and forcing humans to enter theirs. As a matter of course, Tyrenni understand each other's thoughts and feelings, and so maintain a powerful sense of communicative decorum. The Destroyer allows the disembodied mind-sparks to enter its vast structure out of curiosity, which ultimately leads to the transfer of most of Tyree's population into its "body." Margaret appears mysteriously to have used her knowledge of computers and calculation to implant herself into the Destroyer's equivalent of an operating system, through which she "reprograms" it into a world-savior. The drama is of penetrations, absorptions, assimilations, and learning to inhabit different mind-bodies. At stake is the need to interpenetrate to survive, to empathize with others to the point of mutual inhabitation in order to have guiding purpose. *Up the Walls of the World* is thus a consummate expression of the utopian sublime, a vision of shared love and need made nearly impossible by the pain of individual bodies and the stupidity of convention, of a desire so strong it constructs its own bodies, worlds of beauty, agonistic fusions and sacrifices, and the overcoming of world-destroying coldness and intelligence through a world that will reconstruct all to be what they need to be.

The novel's voice strives not for indirect mastery over nature or technology, but an empathic "lateral" intermixing of voices, bodies, perceptions, and projects that dissolve the pain of isolated, disrespected, and physically suffering lives. The Destroyer is, as an added bonus, directed toward a new awareness by the barely perceptible effects of the minuscule interlopers to which it gives shelter in the void of space. With all this, *Up the Walls of the World* remains indisputably sf. As the half-human Daniel Dann/half-Tyrenni Tanel remarks: "If we were actually to meet Jehovah or Allah or Vishnu here I would still take my stand on the second law of thermodynamics" (299).

The sublime involves intimations of divinity in it, but never more than that. All of these works — *2001, The Matrix, Up the Walls of the World* — seem to invoke a mysterious, uncodified, "suprasensible" power. In *2001*, the mathematical rigor of the universe means that the audience will never be able to inhabit transcendence from within. *The Matrix*'s kinetic intensity seems to exclude ethical transcendence in favor of the physical; Neo's electedness is manifest in his ability to transform and incorporate time and space, but we know little of how he can transform souls. *Up the Walls of the World* in contrast works deliberately to synthesize the conceptual, physical, and ethical aspects of the sublime. Through vast abysses and hyperactive world-typhoons, movement at the speed of thought, the fusion and exchange of bodies, mysterious objects and processes, and an imperative to recognize with intimate, physical intensity the existence of the other, *Up the Walls of the World* attempts to crystallize the sublime possibilities of sf without domination.

SIXTH BEAUTY

The Science-Fictional Grotesque

○ ○ ○ ○ ○ ○ ○

The SF Grotesque. Most works of sf develop under the canopy of a vast new idea of the order and possibilities of the material universe — a sublime novum. But the idea is made real, impinging, and intimate by the protagonists' and audiences' encounters with concrete phenomena that disrupt their sense of familiar existence. The sublime has to do with the mind reflecting on its power, or lack of it, to understand the totality of the world, which of course includes the mind itself. The grotesque has to do with the struggle to accommodate mutable, unstable objects and beings in the world. These objects may include the mind's own mentifacts, its thoughts externalized with respect to their thinker.

The intellectual order of science is a system for regulating things. New speculations about overarching principles cannot by themselves change science; they require ideas about the way things behave. When something does not conduct itself as scientific rationality asserts/predicts it must, it creates a clash between the concept of an ordered world and concrete, experiential evidence to the contrary. When its disorienting anomalousness also disorients the routines of human lives and institutions, the novum is grotesque.

SF cultivates the grotesque for its popular appeal, which, as Bakhtin showed in *Rabelais and His World* (1968), has a long history in European culture. But the impetus for grotesque imagery and language is not only its entertainment value. The grotesque brings the sublime to earth, making it material and on our level, forcing attention back to the body. It traps the sublime in the body, partly to subvert it, but also because sf's fictive ontology requires this duality, manifest as oxymoron at the level of ideas, metamorphosis at the level of bodies, and surprising incongruities in storytelling.

Bakhtin conceived of the grotesque as a challenge to "cosmic terror," the religious mask of the sublime:

The cosmic terror is not mystic in the strict sense of the word; rather it is the fear of that which is materially huge and cannot be overcome by force. It is used by all religious systems to oppress man and his consciousness. Even the most ancient images of folklore express the struggle against fear, against the memories of the past, and the apprehension of future calamities, but folk images relating to this struggle helped develop true human fearlessness. The struggle against cosmic terror in all its forms and manifestations did not rely on abstract hope or on the eternal spirit, but on the material principle in man himself. Man assimilated the cosmic elements: earth, water, air and fire; he discovered them and became vividly conscious of them in his own body. He became aware of the cosmos within himself.[1]

Bakhtin actually has little to say about the sublime. He does not use the term; he merely implies it in setting up a Manichaean opposition between aristocratic/hieratic ideology and the earthy materialism of the *populus*. In the domain of language and imagery, the relationship between the two corresponds to the antinomy between oppressors and oppressed, official and popular culture. Historical progress is marked in literature by the rise of the grotesque sensibility to dominance over official aesthetic norms, a process Bakhtin links in metaphor to the rise of scientific materialism as the "popular conquest of the world":

The familiar conquest of the world . . . also prepared a new, scientific knowledge of this world, which was not susceptible of free, experimental, and materialistic knowledge as long as it was alienated from man by fear and piousness and penetrated by the hierarchic principle. The popular conquest of the world . . . destroyed and suspended all alienation; it drew the world closer to man, to his body, permitted him to touch and test every object, examine it from all sides, enter into it, turn it inside out, compare it to every phenomenon, however exalted and holy, analyze, weigh, measure, try it on. And all this could be done on the one plane of material sensual experience. (380–381)

Bakhtin's grotesque is a matter of pleasure in corporeal existence, the rich and funky gaiety that sees life processes intimately flowing into one another, rejecting the abstract divisions and intellectual puritanism of the elites, and consequently threatening and shocking only to them. Once scientific materialism established that the essence of the world and human existence is *physical*, the spiritual terror of the religious sublime was overthrown.

Bakhtin did not pursue the critical investigation of the sublime/grotesque opposition beyond the sixteenth century, but if he had, he would certainly have had to acknowledge that the accession of scientific materialism to cultural dominance, with its own institutions of elite power and regulation, involved a profound historical irony. With hegemonic science, quantity turns to quality, and the primacy of the physical is extended to so many aspects of the cosmos that it is de facto separated from the gross material *human* energy that Bakhtin considers the source of the grotesque's emancipatory power. As science becomes the dominant ideology in the Enlightened West, the physical is enclosed within systems of intermeshing laws, and the body, so leaky and open in grotesque play, becomes a containment vessel once again.

Bakhtin notes this change in the concrete grounding of the literary grotesque in Rabelais's sixteenth-century France. The popular spirit of material flux did not become the ruling conception of the body; "the body of the new canon" ascended to that position:

> The body of the new canon is merely one body; no signs of duality have been left. It is self-sufficient and speaks its name alone. All that happens within it concerns it alone, that is, only the individual, closed sphere. Therefore, all events taking place within it acquire one single meaning: death is only death, it never coincides with birth; old age is torn away from youth; blows merely hurt, without assisting an act of birth. All actions and events are interpreted on the level of a single, individual life. They are enclosed within the limits of the same body, limits that are the absolute beginning and end and can never meet. (321)

Had Bakhtin pursued a historical explanation for the emergence of this "new canon," it would have led precisely to the post-Renaissance scientific transformation of the world into a constellation of material objects that can be handled, compared, weighed, and measured. In this process, all bodies became *units*, and the universal comparability of physical things meant that each thing in the universe became a body-unit, universally exchangeable in the cosmic system of objective measurement. The cheerful popular grotesque and its temporary autonomous zone of the carnivalesque enjoy free play only where scientific materialism has not penetrated; that is, on the peripheries, in peasant societies, and in the cultures of local markets. The modern forms of the grotesque are actually far more constrained and suffused with threat, precisely because they call into question the physical foundations of the new materialism of science and technology.

Bakhtin's conception of the grotesque is an aesthetic polemic for popular collective consciousness in its struggle with the religious ideology of elite culture. The giant Rabelaisian body stands in for corporeal materialism in general. In his focus on carnality, however, Bakhtin does not note that with the scientific enlightenment the human body ceases to be a unique cosmos, and the physical is no longer subordinate to the corporeal. In scientific thought, the human body becomes a vessel comparable to all other vessels of physical process and information. In a surprising parody of the anthropomorphic cosmology of the ancients, the scientific universe becomes populated with bodies, all of them capable of transformations that disturb the human sense of its place in the world. While Bakhtin continues to look for the grotesque in human carnality, with science the grotesque is extended into the body of the universe. Bakhtin imagines the cosmic corpus in Renaissance terms: "Finally, let us point out that the grotesque body is cosmic and universal. It stresses elements common to the entire cosmos: earth, water, fire, air; it is directly related to the sun, to the stars. It contains the signs of the zodiac. It reflects the cosmic hierarchy. This body can merge with various natural phenomena, with mountains, rivers, seas, islands, and continents. It can fill the entire universe" (318).

The ideal synthesis of Neoplatonism and popular laughter that Bakhtin sees in Rabelais was actually, however, scotched at birth, by a scientific materialism that saw the universe as a body not analogous to the carnal human form, but to a body of laws, of which every object in the universe, from atom to galaxy, is a manifestation. As a consequence any deviation from those laws, in any object living or dead, organic or inorganic, corporeal or mathematical, is a shock to the system. And when these anomalies directly affect the living sentient beings who derived the body of laws in the first place, the effect is grotesque. The sf grotesque attests to the change: when the physical becomes the basis for the sublime, bodies are set free to mock the physical order and bring it back to life. In the sf grotesque, it is laws, not bodies that leak.

The Grotesque Interval

More useful to us than Bakhtin's view is that the grotesque involves not only the free and happy interflow of human carnal processes and the removal of boundaries between bodies, but the shock of detecting different physical processes in the same body, violating the sense of the stability and integrity of things, and revealing unsuspected dimensions that escape direct rational, human control. The grotesque, for Geoffrey Galt Harpham, "arises with the perception that something is illegitimately in something else. The most mundane of figures, this metaphor of co-presence, *in*, also harbors the essence of the grotesque, the sense that things that should be kept apart are fused together. Such fusions generate the reaction described clinically by Freud, who noted that when the elements of the unconscious 'pierce into consciousness, we become aware of a distinct feeling of repulsion.'"[2]

Such category confusions inspire disavowal, but they produce evidence that the senses cannot deny. They present "a certain set of obstacles to structured thought" (xxi), and the mind is troubled, trying to find a solution to the problem posed by perceiving what it should not be possible to perceive. Grotesque objects "stand at the margin of consciousness between the known and the unknown, the perceived and the unperceived, calling into question the adequacy of our ways of organizing the world, of dividing the continuum of experience into knowable parts" (3).

In art, such combinations of elements usually involve style-markers indicating social status. They conflate "the normative, fully-formed, 'high' or ideal, and the abnormal, unformed, degenerate, 'low' or material" (9). The perceiver strives to discern a pattern in the jumble of disparate elements, some new explanation or matrix in which the pattern will appear harmonious and even necessary. Harpham treats the grotesque as an interval, a gap shared by the object and the perceiver. In the object, the gap is between the past form of a thing and what it is becoming, its unpredictable evolution. In the perceiver, it is a gap in which consciousness is suspended, unable to discern not only a unified form of the object, but also the broader implications this suspension has for the laws of form in the world in question. The grotesque obstructs the mind from completing its effort of quick understanding, arresting it when it wishes to get on with its routine of knowing, and forces it to learn something it is not sure it wants to know:

> The interval of the grotesque is one in which, although we have recognized a number of different forms in the object, we have not yet developed a clear sense of the dominant principle that defines it and organizes its various elements. Until we do so we are stuck, aware of the significance, or of certain kinds of formal integrity, but unable to decipher the codes. Resisting closure, the grotesque object impales us on the present moment, emptying the past and forestalling the future. An identical force sustains the knower and the known, for this interval is the temporal analogue of the grotesque object, with its trammeling of energy and feeble or occluded formal principle. (16)

The response to this suspension of mental movement is a quickened drive to interpret. Harpham considers the grotesque a naive experience that depends on the context of representational art, that is, art in whose figures we are inclined to believe. The more one wishes to believe in the truth or reality of the representation (and hence the less one wants to bother about hermeneutics and the ontology of fiction), the more one will try to discover an interpretation that will complete the design, and end the suspension, "either in the discovery of a novel form or in a metaphorical, analogical, or allegorical explanation" (18).

As with the sublime then, the perceiver of the grotesque seeks a setback position, from which to understand unnatural fusions in terms of their principles of order. One of the resolutions it may spawn is precisely a shift from a literal vision to a symbolic one, "and suddenly the deformed is revealed as the sublime" (20). But the object may resist and remain unassimilable, "in the interstices of consciousness" (4), becoming a constant source of hermeneutic anxiety. This state of mind inspires the sense of taboo, of objects and liminal beings that defy classification because they somehow collapse natural boundaries in their own beings, while inhabiting the familiar world as anomaly and exception.

Grotesque objects bring a fundamental principle of mythological thought into rationalistic modes of perception. While the latter strive to set up clear distinctions and dependable frames of reference, the mythic imposes perpetual metamorphosis, according to which "no realm of being, visible or invisible, past or present, is absolutely discontinuous with any other, but all equally accessible and mutually interdependent" (51). The grotesque introduces mythic thought in a nonmythic context, "polluting" the pure aspirations of reason with the fluctuating, mutagenic, class-defying world-picture of the sacred.

> Not only are sacred and awful truths mingled with fictions, but in the world of myth, truth itself is polluted. What scholars call the "ambivalence" and "ambiguity" of the sacred reflects the beliefs that an object can be sacred and yet actual and palpable, or, more important, that the holy is identical with the unclean. . . . Edmund Leach says that myth mediates oppositions by introducing a third category which is "abnormal" or "anomalous." . . . The radical form of the ambiguity of the sacred is the notion of "sacred uncleanness," a concept that occurs throughout the form of alienated, fragmented, and decomposed myth we call grotesque. (55–56)

In the introduction, I proposed that sf can be conceived in terms of two linked gaps in the reader's consciousness, not dissimilar to Harpham's grotesque interval.[3] SF elicits from its audiences a feeling of hesitation facing two intertwined but distinct questions about the imaginary world represented in the text. On the one hand, it asks whether the imaginary changes are possible; on the other, what their social and ethical implications might be. The first is a matter of plausibility: what the text says about the way the world works. The second is a matter of ethical evaluation: what the text says about the values that guide or emerge from the imaginary alterations. These two gaps are, of course, not essentially distinct; in fiction, unlike history, the world is changed according to the designs of the artist and the art. The science-fictional gaps may be resolved in the mode of the sf sublime. The technoscientific transformation offered in the text or its presentation may inspire a sense of technology's capacity to produce limitlessness. Alternatively, the gaps may be resolved in the register of the sf grotesque, in which technoscience is the occasion for releasing and revealing the uncontainable metamorphic energies of the world and its discrete things. Harpham's interval — between the transmutative fluidity of the object and the classificatory uncertainty of the perceiver — becomes a fundamental moment in the reception of sf.

The Excess of the Organic

SF audiences expect disturbing anomalies that fulfill two requirements: (a) they appear as immediate challenges, threats, puzzles, or wonders to human characters, and (b) they are perceived as general challenges to the conception of reality as something stable enough to be understood by human beings. In the sublime mode, these anomalies threaten to make the human subject feel insignificant and powerless against manifestly superior natural order and power. They inspire fearful awe not only at the prospect of physical annihilation, but that one's own mind — and the minds of all human beings — will be seen as local, limited, and contingent, ultimately drowned in the oceanic magnitude and diversity of what can be perceived. In the sublime, the ego fears losing itself in the vast, orderly production of what is always already the case. In the grotesque, by contrast, the subject feels fearful awe at the possibility that one's own mind — and again, the human mind in general — cannot keep up with the metamorphoses of materiality; that the categorical containments of natural physicality that we wish to see as scientific truths, and that allow us to hold physical existence at arm's length in order to elaborate unphysical, aesthetic concepts, are unstable and will undermine our thoughts by displaying to us the chaos-producing resistance of bodies to order. Most disturbing of all is the possibility that the entities of the world transform themselves *because* we observe them, that their mysterious existence responds to our thoughts.

As with the sublime, the grotesque involves recuperative recoil, allowing us to see the disorderly and repulsive as a part of the natural order, letting us believe that we have established a better, more encompassing mental order that is more resistant to shock. In sf, this recoil usually involves the skillful elaboration of an explanation that uses scientific, pseudoscientific, or simply ratio-fantastic reasoning (that is, narrative motivation that transparently imitates the forms of rationality, but with fantastic premises). Often the explanation is merely the fanciful extension of certain supposedly rational premises to absurd conclusions. In "The Facts in the Case of M. Valdemar," for example, the premise and the explanation merely extend the Mesmeric notion that the manipulation of animal magnetism through the mesmerist's will can control physical functions. The success of the tale comes from the drastic suspense about which is stronger: death or the power of the will to resist it. The physical, in the end, is allowed to prevail against the mental and ideal — willpower and the prospect of a scientific proof of the soul — and it does so with a horrifying and disgusting exuberance.

> As I rapidly made the mesmeric passes, amid ejaculations of "Dead! Dead!" absolutely bursting from the tongue and the lips of the sufferer, his whole frame at once — within the space of a single minute, or even less, shrunk — crumbled — absolutely rotted away beneath my hands. Upon the bed, before that whole company, there lay a nearly liquid mass of loathsome — of detestable putridity.[4]

The epiphany of corruption achieves its power through its contrast with the careful, medical-technical language of the narrator, who has tried to treat the body of his client as a manipulable text. The tale is doubly grotesque: in the revelation that physical corruption can build up in the mind-controlled body, and that the mind can indeed usurp the powers of physical nature. In horror sf films, we often see similar attempts to contain physical mutability in technologically ordered environments: the laboratories and hospitals, the VR-rigs and scan-screens that are coded to be visual articulations of scientific control. In them, each switch, instrument, and illuminated display is a concretization of the ordered anticipations of scientific testing. Rarely does sf allow the tested body to remain contained by a lab. Its career usually leads it out from the failed hermeticism of the technocontainer, through middle-class neighborhoods, to the funkiest parts of town, the decrepit factories, subway tunnels, and underground grottoes that are culturally coded for the unclean, the secreted, the clandestine proliferation of organs escaping from bodies. It is now a dominant theme in horror-inflected, grotesque-intensive sf that the anomalous organism can never be contained, and that even the laboratory is a superfluous gesture. In the work of David Cronenberg, for example, it is an assumption at the outset that the flesh is furious at its containment; it will somehow, sometime, find a way to release itself from the body's tyranny.

The sexiest category of the grotesque in sf, as in most art, is the excess of the organic. For human beings, it is organic tissue that changes most quickly and involuntarily, and "betrays" the mind's desire to slow time down. The organic imposes viscousness on bodiless thought, and seems indifferent to the ego's desire to hold the whole thing together. With its associations of messy birth, uncontrollable body functions, inevitable openness to disease, and the dim awareness of a complex, unconscious interiority that can only be imagined tactilely, the organic imposes on the contemplating subject. To be known, the organic must be felt. For the Platonist, simply imagining that the soul requires the always dying body is the ultimate grotesque. But it is not only the awareness of physical mortality that makes the organic grotesque; it is also the excess of life, tipping the balance toward mere physical being, and away from form. The sublime is law set free of life; the grotesque is life set free of law.

Perhaps future AIs, or Lem's robot-constructors will find siliconity grotesque. For us, the sf grotesque usually involves some surprising, repulsive invocation of the primacy of organic physicality. Aliens are, almost by definition, reimaginings of physical form — often in ways more repulsive to us than our own, or in ways that make our own seem repulsive. Xenological fictions modeled on anthropological studies regularly display the excessively physical character of material cultures: the Klingons' table manners, the alien hunter's treatment of his prey in *Predator* (1987). Even in fictions where physicality seems less important, sf will hold onto grotesque organicism as a trace. Fictions of devolution depend on uncontrolled physical transformation unfriendly to the familiar human form. Stevenson's Mr. Hyde represents this return of repressed physicality, overdetermined with his ape-sensuality, and pleasure in bodily violence. In a contemporary version, Ken Russell's film *Altered States* (1980), the Jekyll-like protagonist gradually decomposes at the cellular level, losing his human form.

Phases of the SF Grotesque

The grotesque is a more complex figuration than the sublime. The sublime threatens thought/perception with the infinite expansion of an idea that is so integral, so impossibly unified, that it not only contains, but annihilates all multiplicity within it. The sublime stuns thought with the prospect of the inconceivable unity of the universe, within which only the very great is differentiated. The grotesque, in contrast, turns the arrested attention intensely toward things, in which it detects a constant metamorphic flux, an intimate roiling of living processes that perpetually change before understanding can stabilize them. This process is one of steady descent into interiors, into grottoes of being, in the hope of finding a core, but always finding more transformation.

There are stages, or levels, of this descent. At its most abstract, it is what we might call the *mathematical grotesque*. At this level, the sense of scandalous contradiction in form emerges when the ideally pure mode of mathematical thinking is inextricably associated with the sense of hard, quasi-physical labor. Because of the value that elegance and economy have for mathematics, any proof that requires excessive work to arrive at a simple conclusion can be considered grotesque. Similarly, if a proof appears not only complex, but also complicated, requiring elements that are foreign to the original framing of the problem, the proof will appear disturbingly excessive. If the problem can be conceived simply, then, in mathematical aesthetics, the solutions should be also. Edmund Burke considered the product of great labor to be sublime, but only if the resulting edifice is of such magnitude that its result is commensurate with its labor.[5] We rarely see versions of the mathematical grotesque in sf, but the prospect of biological computers or evolutionary epistemology applied to mathematics makes it easy to imagine an account of fictive mathematics that will depict it in adaptationist or even physiological terms.

In art, any narrative or presentation that is developed in a manner foreign to its conventional terms produces the effect of grotesque incongruity between manner and matter, between the familiarity of theme and the oddity of performance. In literary usage, the grotesque is also a specific technique of narrative, in which a tale is told in a tone at odds with its subject matter, as in Gogol's "The Nose," whose fantastic situation is related in deadpan, officious diction. The humor of such inappropriate tellings is usually satirical, drawing attention to the absurdity either of the referents — whose conventional discursive context in reality is bogus — or of the social discourse represented in the narrative diction, and often to both, as in Čapek's *Absolute at Large* (1922) and *The War with the Newts* (1936).

What we might call the *scientific grotesque* comes with the recognition of an embodied, physical anomaly, a being or an event whose existence or behavior cannot be explained by the currently accepted universal system of rationalization. An exception to a fundamental principle of form or evolution cannot be ignored; a universal rational system that is contradicted by even one phenomenon is not universal. Anomalies draw the attention inward toward the apparent violations of common sense, rational elegance, or logic. A phenomenon that violates the law of conservation of matter, of noncontradiction, or the causal chain must be understood and interpreted into the scientific system, or the system itself must be changed to accommodate new principles that do explain it. In this way, pulsars and neutron stars required fundamental reformulations of basic astrophysical ideas. Questions about the validity of anomalies, and the reconceptualization of physical laws they may force upon scientists, continually arise in science. Sometimes they lead to paradigm shifts, sometimes to renormalization. At this level, sf treats the scientifically grotesque anomaly as the basis of its fictive science and the source of its novums.

The sublime extends human cognition outward toward infinity, where it cannot alter the situation it contemplates; instead, it will be consumed by the vast certainty of cosmic power. With the sublime, physicality is dissolved in the concurrent ideas of extension, magnitude, and complexity, abstractions that paradoxically become imposingly present. With the grotesque, awareness is turned toward physicality and presence, contingency and change, with the added problem that it may actually change the thing being observed and implicate consciousness in the mutations of the objects, making scientific investigation grotesque in itself. The grotesque perceives the world as radically mutable, resisting human rationality as a petty urge to organize reality for its own convenience. The object world of interstitial beings includes both one's body and one's own consciousness of self, which perpetually mutate before they can establish a dependable identity.

Harpham notes that the grotesque involves a mythological logic of constant transformation, the morphing of any being into any other (51). This instability makes the physical world an indeterminate and insecure place, suffused by forces ultimately hostile to the human desire for categorical and social stability. Perceptions can easily be revealed to be hallucinations. Bodies are constantly reminded that they are not armored containers, but rather invitations to opening and wounding, arenas of autonomous life-forms, diseases, mutations, intimate viruses. Violence is inevitable as long as humans require bodily integrity and rational order. The violence of the sublime is overwhelming and experienced by the mind, which is thrown back and down by the immense other that it has ignored in its self-construction, like a swimmer consumed by a colossal wave. With the grotesque, the violence occurs in the bodily base that was likewise ignored by consciousness; it is constantly opening up, metastasizing, refusing to settle in.

In sf, we recognize this instability as the universe of Philip K. Dick, where reality is volatile, constantly opening into parallel, alternative realities. Dick plays with the reader's desire to interpret these proliferating realities in symbolic terms, as metaphors for states of mind. But they are *not*, and their concreteness ultimately led Dick to mimic his readers' interpretive urge, to conceive of a theology that would explain the universe in the terms given by sf, and the theological hypostasis of what in his sf are fictive demiurges.[6] This volatile concreteness is also the guiding principle of David Cronenberg's films, where the grotesque is much more directly linked to bodily metamorphosis and vulnerability. With Cronenberg the experience of changes in the continuum of the real is precipitated by disturbing interpenetrations of technology and the human organism. His delirium displaces Dick's near-sublime sense of the infinite proliferation of realities into the quintessentially grotesque spectacle of technological artifacts as the genitalia of a metamorphosed human species. Their main, unconscious purpose is to construct a utopia of unlimited sexual stimulation of ever more promiscuously proliferating and metamorphosing bodies. Technology becomes fetish-production, the quest to turn the world into a VR rig for the unlimited production of orifices and technophalluses.

The grotesque's metamorphic physicality has always linked it with femaleness, to the degree that some theorists argue that it is essentially a response by exaggerated male rationality to exaggerated female physiology:

> The association of the female body with materiality, sex, and reproduction in the female body, makes it an essential — not an accidental — aspect of the grotesque. The socially constructed différance which means that male and female bodies are not only physically different but are also hierarchically arranged and asymmetrically valued underlies the literary use of woman's body as the primary figure of debasement.[7]

The very origin of the term *grotesque* refers back to dark and moist interior spaces. Metamorphic energy is easily associated with the momentous, uncontrollable, and juicy changes that occur in the female body (at least compared with the conventional standard of the male body) in menstruation, pregnancy, childbirth, lactation, menopause. From the phallocratic male perspective, these physical processes are uncomfortably insistent; they distract, they interrupt, they stink, and they stain. They are seen as physical concomitants of women's grotesque mental processes: changeability, undependability, materialism, and inability to abstract from their immediate, personal situations. Women are prone to disease because they are too open to the world; they are liable to infect, because their interiors can flow out onto others. SF often draws on this deep association, as does horror literature, but only rarely in a conscious way, as in C. L. Moore's Medusa-like "Shambleau" (1933) and H. Rider Haggard's *She* (1877). Usually it plays out only as displacement, as in the *Alien* series' monstrous mothers, and in the disorienting feminization of male sf bodies made vulnerable to penetration and contamination (such as Max Renn in Cronenberg's *Videodrome* [1982] and the horrifically crucificied Father Hoyt in Dan Simmons's *Hyperion* [1989]). As Scott Bukatman notes: "The male is positioned at the mercy of a banished biological nature in which not even the body provides that 'halo of protection' that Baudrillard once referred to. Thus the hyperbolization of the body must be read as both a confrontation with and a denial of the limits of the rational."[8]

This coding of threatening space as feminine was a characteristic of sf film long before *Alien*. Indeed, sf films have often included literal cavelike grottoesque spaces in which female, world-threatening transformations occur. Don Siegel's *Invasion of the Body Snatchers* (1956) reaches its climax in an abandoned mine-tunnel, where the beautiful divorcée Becky, now replaced by her pod self, attempts to seduce Miles, the audience's surrogate. *Rodan* (1956) and *Mothra* (1961) both begin with birth-scenes in isolated caves. The threat of the giant ants in *Them!* (1954) is brought to an end when the last queens retreat to the catacombs of Los Angeles's sewer system, and are burned alive in the midst of reproducing their nest. In less overt forms, the laboratory has a cognate function, a motif apotheosized by Morbius's inner chambers of *Forbidden Planet,* which open into the even vaster chambers of the Krel dynamo. To identify all interior spaces as exclusively feminine may appear reductive and essentializing, but the reproductive and metamorphic uses to which many caves and grottoes are put illustrates the presence of the mythological charge that Harpham detects in the grotesque.

The grotesque body is not a mere natural body. It is a hypertrophy of natural, irrepressible growth. It produces excrescences, protuberances, enormous noses and ears, pimples, tumors, genitalia. Cronenberg's bodies are always generating vile growths; in *Rabid* (1977), *Videodrome, Naked Lunch* (1991), *The Fly* (1986), and *eXistenZ* (1999), the percolation of organicism does not rest. In sf it proceeds beyond mere dermoplastic exuberance. An important current of alien-construction in recent sf film has been the conflation of multiple evolutionary qualities in one organism. *Alien*'s creature has a famous metamorphic growth-cycle, from the arachnoid-octopoidal "face hugger," to the angry larva eating its way out of viscera like a wasp baby, to the multiply coded adult (which changes in each film) that is both *vagina dentata* and *penis dentatus*.[9] The xenomorph of the *Alien* films has a second rapacious mouth embedded in the first; its body is silicone and its blood is acid. It is hard and reticulated like a machine and yet drools fluids all over itself. "Brundle Fly" in Cronenberg's *The Fly* and the alien hunter of *Predator* similarly display aspects of multiple evolutions: the former because he is a genetic recombination of a fly and a human; the latter, because he has the body of a human and the face of a warthog spliced with a crab.

Physicality may well continue inward, away from the facial and dermal surfaces to the grotesque core, to the flesh that is both the support and the food of the carnivorous organism. The sf grotesque delights in the representation of visceral flesh, sores, sex organs that appear as wounds and tumors, dismem-

The SEVEN BEAUTIES *of* SCIENCE FICTION

berment, cannibalism, organs without bodies, the eclipse of the abstract imagination. Finally, the grotesque reduces to goo. As the body continues to withdraw from the human gaze, it loses more and more of its structure: first its body, then its organs, finally leaving only the protoform of plasma. The core is reduced to a formless jelly that yet has power: to contaminate, to melt, to cause deliquescence by touch alone. (What deconstruction is to the sublime, deliquescence is to the grotesque.) Poe's attractiveness is due in large part to the promise of evoking decay, classically delivered in "Valdemar." Films such as *Videodrome* and *The Fly* construct their narratives to support the spectacular progress of vying bodies toward their decomposition, and by analogy, the decomposition of the solid bourgeois scientific sense of the separation of mind from embodiment. (The same process is developed in a sublime register by Greg Bear in *Blood Music*, a work of great originality and audacity precisely for the way it turns the motif of deliquescence from one of the most dependable devices of the grotesque into a device signifying transcendence.) In his quest to discover his original essence, *Altered States*'s Eddie Jessup devolves first to protohuman, then to a marmoreal mass, finally to a cosmic, plasmic Ur-cell.

Interstitial Beings

By far the most frequently developed nodes of the sf grotesque are interstitial beings: creatures in whom two distinct, sometimes even contradictory, conditions of existence overlap. An elemental trait of grotesque beings is that they contain at least two bodies in one. A new body may be in the process of metamorphosing out of an old one; a being may combine, conflate, or be trapped in two corporeal forms; a body's appearance may conceal a completely different one underneath. The pedigree goes back to ancient monsters and prodigies — Scylla and Charybdis, Polyphemus, the Lamia, Pliny's mouthless Astemoi, the dogheaded Kynokephaloi, Lucius the Ass — each of whom is stuck in the black box in which the part of culture called nature is transformed into the part called civilization, where the nonhuman becomes human. Scientific materialism has disciplined this mythological imagination by expanding the range of what can be considered normal in creation. As anomalies are discovered — salamander, platypus, virus, pulsar — they become occasions for extending the power to explain nature's rational rules of creation. Science has extended its imperium by providing rational accounts for phenomena previously felt to be heteronomic, sacred, magical, taboo. And through its technology, it has created beings that nature did not.

The connection with this archaic stratum of monstrosity is clearest in the various monsters from outer space, from the depths, the id, and the mad scientist's lab. Classic sf monsters strive, furiously or with cold calculation, to transform themselves from some archaic form to human form. For all its sincerity and intelligence, Frankenstein's creature cannot escape the fact that it is composed of dead bodies, or that its physical powers make it more of a beast than a superman. *Forbidden Planet's* Monster from the Id is revealed to be a great leonine cartoon chimera, a mythomorphic predator released from its bodily cage. The Creature from the Black Lagoon is caught between fish and human; Kong, ape and human; The Fly, insect and human. Plants too can be interstitial: Triffids, the invader pods of *Invasion of the Body Snatchers*, the "intellectual carrot" of *The Thing from Another World* (1951). In these classical cases, sf has stacked the deck against creation; the forces of human science conspire to confuse the structures of the world by trying to elevate the low into the high. Both are brought low. In some rare cases, like the Blob, monsters from outer space may lack the capacity to be structured at all. Or they may be so fluid that they employ the human form in transit through their shape-shifting, like Campbell's invader in "Who Goes There?" (1938) and Carpenter's version of *The Thing* (1982). (This motif is culture-specific. Japanese sf also delights in imagining interstitial beings, but most of these seem to have an ontological legitimacy that Western sf does not supply. Godzilla, Mothra, and many other Toho monsters that are either revived or created by atomic radiation seem to have been granted respectable ecomythic niches.)

Reflective sf artists often employ these Frankenstein scenarios to explore the ethical puzzles posed by technoscience's now proven ability to produce interstitial beings. Their texts attempt to represent the interstices themselves, depicting grotesque predicaments struggling furiously to become sublime, and thus to gain clearer meaning. Wells's *The Island of Doctor Moreau* is the great source text for this project. In *Moreau,* monstrous experiments of transforming animals into humanoid creatures on an isolated island do not immediately endanger human civilization; thus they imitate the containment of lab experiments. The struggle of the animals forced into grotesque doubleness remains local, confined to the island and to the House of Pain; narrative attention does not stray from the point that the only advance effected by the Beast People's artificial evolution is that they now have the ability to reflect on their own suffering. Stapledon made it a driving theme to redeem the grotesque of interstitial consciousness into sublimity. In *Sirius* (1944), he redeems *Moreau* by giving his canine/human cyborg a loving human partner and articulating dog nobility from within. Many of Stapledon's civilizations in *Star Maker* are committed attempts to make inherently grotesque fusions — plant men, ichthyoid and arachnoid symbionts — into images of simultaneously material and ethical sublime otherness. In his version of *The Fly,* Cronenberg pushed the mechanical grotesque of the original film, in which two animals' body parts are simply reshuffled, into a drama about the dreams of flesh itself using technoscience as its vehicle to escape from the arbitrary evolutionary confines of living bodies.

Most of sf's distinctive creatures, however, are not stuck between nature and culture; they are stuck between the current human condition and some new artificial ontology made possible by technoscientific control over, or interference with, natural laws. Such beings are among sf's main contributions to Western mythology. SF produced within the evolutionary historical paradigm is by definition concerned with effects of technology on the future social-physical evolution of human beings. Because both science and the human species inhabit the mesocosm, these transformations are often strikingly grotesque, unable to attain the magnitude that would displace them to a sublime distance. In the degenerate Eloi and especially the Morlocks, the Time Traveller detects a repulsive overlap between animal and human; the Eloi are human cattle, the Morlocks a whole Moreauvian menagerie of men who have become like apes, lemurs, spiders, worms. In sf, social behavior is just as likely to undergo grotesque changes: with populations feeding on their own dead (*Soylent Green* [1973]), committing genocide via computer games (*Ender's Game* [1985]), and consigning those not genetically engineered to a permanent underclass (*Gattaca* [1997]).

For much of the twentieth century, sf's images of the transformed species hinged on mutation, via deliberate eugenics or the unforeseen effects of experimentation and war. Francis Galton's proposals for using Darwin to undergird eugenic breeding projects for the improvement of the species were positively received by futurians and advocates of technocracy of all stripes, including Wells and Julian Huxley. The technological management of human reproduction remained for many years a matter for utopian and anti-utopian sf. The breakthrough that led to supermen issuing from beneficial mutations came with the discovery that technology itself could affect heredity by altering genes. Mutagenic effects of radiation were discovered in the late 1920s, of chemicals (specifically mustard gas) in 1942.[10] The alienated supermen of Wylie's *Gladiator* (1930) and Van Vogt's *Slan* (1946) are both mutants; the former was injected as a fetus with a mysterious chemical by his mad-scientist father, the latter's source is unexplained. With the atomic bombings of Hiroshima and Nagasaki, radiation-induced mutation became for a generation the most frequently employed source of sf's interstitial beings, a motif that brought the nuclear sublime solidly down to earth, and populated future wastelands with myriad evolutionary possibilities and dead ends.

Mutants remain important to sf, and no doubt will regain some of their former glory as the effects of genetic engineering on higher animals and humans become known. For the moment, they inhabit primarily the worlds of comics, where instant mutation has become, like nanotechnology in cyber-sf, a sort of fairy dust to justify any access to magical powers. They have been replaced in popular consciousness and sf by beings who fuse the mechanical and the human through the radical mixing of mechanical prostheses into living flesh.

Cyborgs

One must submit to the sublime; it is too great and encompassing, and consequently in terms of technoscience, too *real,* to be resisted. The grotesque, by contrast, appears on the same level as the human. If it hints at a change of sublime magnitude, the hint is uncertain; one cannot know whether a grotesque phenomenon is an isolated freak, or the symptom of a systemic perversion yet to unfold full-scale. The first response to the grotesque is fascination and resistance, as if to explore and test where the surprising hybrid will lead — whether it is the sign of a true novum, a recrudescence of atavistic forces, or a passionate dead end.

The cyborg is a true novum, one of a number that sf has provided the real world. (Others include nuclear fission, the spaceship, the death-ray, and cyberspace.) Something can be a novum only from the prospect of the future, whose history it helps to seed. A grotesque novum inspires curiosity about exactly what the novum signifies for the human subject, not only in terms of how the mechanisms of existence will work, but what they will mean. Can they be judged at all from the present, or will the transformed future be sealed off from the present's ethical imagination? Will New Human Beings or their interstitial equivalents be inscrutable to our archaic value systems? Will the future, as in Marker's *La Jetée,* be "better protected than the past?" The technosublime is ultimately unambiguous. One cannot struggle against the laws of nature; one must learn to harness them through artificial immanence, and allow them to change us as we change them through technoscientific historical feedback. But the technogrotesque appears to be so local to our timespace that we are likely to resist — with revulsion, exclusion, quarantine, or outright attack. We can see the shift in attitudes toward the cyborg from sf grotesque toward sf sublime in the shift from viewing the cyborg as a competitor for the future, to its representation as a bona fide novum seen from the other side of the sf apocalypse, from the future history in which the cyborg has long ago established its agency and power.

The cyborg follows the same formal dynamic as the monster. It is a being who combines elements of two ontological/cultural domains that "should be" incompatible: the machine and the human. But the difference between the cyborg and the monster is a radical one. The cyborg's monstrosity is coded as the inverse of the archaic monster's. Where the monster cannot emerge from nature into full-fledged anthropomorphic culture, the cyborg is stuck in the interstices between anthropomorphic second nature and the third nature of the hypermachine. Physically, the cyborg can combine the powers of the human (which, from its perspective, is the apex of animal existence) and the machine (the augmentation of both reason and violence); or, it may be ground up in the contradictions between them.

The cyborg is exponentially more fluid than the monster, despite its frequent coding as a slave to its mechanical apparatus. For in sf, there is no predetermined form or ethical charge that a cyborg must have. It can be unambiguously horrific, imaged in the relentless steel endoskeletons of the first generation of Terminators. The line between flesh and machine may be a perpetual injury: the woundlike transition from flesh to prosthesis in the *Gundam* (1979) or the actual wounds that reveal the clockwork under the T-100's fake flesh. A cyborg may exist as pure information, such as the *Ghost in the Shell*'s (1999) Puppet Master, taking on and discarding bodies as needed. It may exist as an agent of ineffable solitude, as in Ellison's "Demon with a Glass Hand," wired into a near-noöspheric network like the Matrix, or assimilated into a higher hive mind like the Borg. It may be uncanny, yet irresistibly beautiful, like the tragic mechano-Aryan Replicants of *Blade Runner* (1982) and the gorgeous Motoko Kusanagi of *Ghost in the Shell*. Motoko's grotesque beauty is exemplary in its complex overdetermination. She is constructed to the highest specifications of cartoon femininity, and yet has no erotic longing. Her alluring body is perforated by neural-interface sockets. Most striking is the incongruity between the audience's erotic pleasure viewing her attractive (and ostensibly, but not actually, naked) body in the opening scenes of Oshii's film, and the subsequent disorienting witnessing of her artificial creation in a vat, surface by surface, grotesquely congruent with the construction of a digital girl via wire frames and pixels, alerting us to the eerie incongruity of feeling real erotic attraction for a caricature.

Aliens

The alien is a being that is by definition strange, corporeal, and approximately as complex as a human being. Unlike the fantastic dream monster from the Id, it is recognizable as a distinct, autonomous being, and it is sufficiently knowable for its differences from familiar entities to be inferred. We expect an alien to be manifestly the result of some scientific-evolutionary logic. It is intelligible in the logical terms of our own evolution; that is, through some version of Darwinian theory. Alternatively, if the fictive science requires a Lamarckian or other fantastic natural theory of morphological development, then this process will be explicable in terms that imitate the interactions of forces in an imaginable evolutionary ecology. If no such explanations can be found, then some effort is taken to show that they have been attempted in vain, and that the mechanism surpasses the capacities of human science.

This evolutionary logic applies both to the creature's physicality (its anatomy, its physiology, its place in an ecological system), and also its mentality. It displays qualities of sentience: purpose and intention, information processing, communication, and modeling. Further, an alien is not a differently evolved animal. Alien fauna, such as *Dune*'s sandworms, may have characteristics similar to alien intelligences, but the concept of the alien in sf demands that it be a differently evolved intelligent creature that stands over against the human in its ambiguous position between animal form and higher sentience, and that occupies its equivalent position in a different evolutionary hierarchy. Its thought processes make it aware of its contingent position in the universe. It knows it is materially circumscribed, and that its mentality is capable of sublimity, even if it does not have a culture. The notion of the alien thus implies a statement of belief in varieties of progressive evolution and a hierarchy, at the top of which stands some form of dominant intelligence. The most frequently employed model is of a centralized, humanoid, individualized brain-and-body. However, distributed system-intelligence is an accepted *détournement*— such as Stapledon's Martians in *Last and First Men* and Lem's cyberflies in *The Invincible* (1964) — as are disembodied or subtle forms. Traditionally, sf's aliens have been modeled on certain practical categories of otherness that fascinate the dominars of culture: children, women (and sometimes men), machines, marginalized peoples, animals, and "anomalous genders." It is a rare alien that does not combine displaced aspects from several of these categories, and sf writers usually try to construct beings that combine them in original ways.

Childlike aliens, from the evil blond usurpers of *Village of the Damned* to the cute glowing doughboys of *Close Encounters of the Third Kind* (1977), displace human children's amorality, playfulness, quick apprehension, and their capacity to see the world with wonder. Alien women, from gender warriors on Mack Reynolds's *Amazon Planet* (1975), monstrous sirens like C. L. Moore's Shambleau, all the way to the cosmic embodiment of female seduction in Tiptree's *A Momentary Taste of Being* (1975), evoke resistance to the naturalness of patriarchy and the supposed nearly supernatural irresistibility of female sexuality for phallic power. Hypertrophied maleness is now also easily displaced into alienness. Over and above the civilizational bullying characteristic of patriarchy (which sf usually projects onto non-Western primitives like Klingons or space Nazis), there is the grotesque and inexorable peculiarity of the phallus/penis, which may act as an alien appendage even to its worshippers, like the invading tentacular rape-monsters of Japanese *hentai*.

Animals are by far the most frequent models for alien forms and behavior: insects and hive beings, telepathic dogpacks and "butterflies in jackboots" (the "tynes" and Aprahanti of Vernor Vinge's *Fire Upon the Deep* [1993]), quasi-primates, Larry Niven's feline Kzin, saurians, Leviathans, Le Guin's sea turtles from outer space, Dick's Ganymedian slime-molds, Octavia Butler's gigantic tentacled Oankali slugs, Hal Clement's Mesklinite centipedes, the ichthyoids, arachnoids, nautiloids, and echinoderms of *Star Maker,* the sublime jellyfish of *The Abyss* (1989). Any animal form known to exist on Earth can eventually become an entry in sf's xenomorphological catalogue.

Technically, aliens cannot themselves be machines, unless they were constructed according to principles that are unfamiliar to human engineers. Even an auto-constructing machine system like the Singularity — the coming-to-consciousness of the world's interlinked artificial intelligence systems predicted for the near future — cannot but extend immanent human ideas about problem-solving and labor, albeit with speed and complexity beyond human comprehension and control. The Singularity may well act like an alien, and that may be enough for it to be treated as one. But in some sense, it retains its genetic filiation with human concepts. Machines at that level of complexity and de facto self-governance can be models for alien systems. These may be self-aware Singularity-like machine systems created by aliens. They may reflect immanent characteristics of their alien creators. Or they may be artificial life forms that have evolved on their own into autonomous mental agents.

Marginalized cultures are the favored models for humanoid aliens embedded in societies, a continuation of imperial adventure fiction's tradition of orientalizing the unassimilable cultures of empire. The openly racist practice of earlier sf, in which Ming the Merciless threatened Flash Gordon's Aryan Earth, and the zombies of *Invaders from Mars* (1953) were controlled by the tentacled head of a turbaned midget, has gradually been replaced by more socially oblique forms, such as *Star Trek*'s Ferengian crypto-Jewish *schefters* and the Zulu-Samurai Klingons. This science-fictionalizing orientalization has gone in the other direction as well, as in Le Guin's idealized Atshean hilfs of *The Word for World is Forest* (1976), sentimentalized eco-creatures facing imperial genocide.

Aliens are by definition queers. Because they appear primarily from the normative point of view of the heroes of technoscientific adventure, their difference is excessive and nonfunctional by default. The sexual dimension of this queerness has, until recently, been concealed in motifs of shape-changing, infiltration, and secret conversion to selfish pleasure. The terrifying alien invader of John Campbell's "Who Goes There?" conflates political and sexual threat with an alien shape-shifter's almost insurmountable advantage of being able to pass for a "real" (hu)man in a confined male society.[11] As attitudes toward sexuality changed in the West in the late 1960s, the alien's shifting body became a theater where resistance to sexual norms was performed. Ziggy Stardust and the Man Who Fell to Earth acted as models of polysexuality in pop culture. Although the motif of displaced sexual predation and conversion continues to be expressed, the trajectory of the *Alien* films is more typical. What began as a particularly grotesque form of polymorphous sexual murder in the first film, moved gradually and inexorably toward *Alien Resurrection*'s (1997) consummately queer conflation of lesbianism and motherhood in the form of the dignified Goth badass, Alien Ripley.

Occasionally highly original aliens appear to be based on scientific theory rather terrestrial beings, such as the intelligent peripatetic nebula of Hoyle's *Black Cloud*, Stephen Baxter's Qax (who are embodied as turbulent energy flow) and photino birds (tiny congeries of dark matter), not to mention Solaris's telepathic planetary cytoplasma and Stapledon's Martian cluster-mind. But even these reveal their terrestrial origins as soon as their purposes are divined. We know that bodies come in many forms; we are much less sure about minds.

Most aliens combine aspects of several different models. Among the richest pastiches are the Aleutians of Gwyneth Jones's *White Queen* (1991). They appear baboonlike, with highly evolved communal grooming habits. Although they are not sexually differentiated — they reproduce through a mysterious form of parthenogenesis (and so resemble von Neumann machines and amphibians) — they do enjoy quasi-sexual contact, and their hermaphroditic genitalia play a pivotal role in the Aleutian trilogy.[12] They are emphatically linked to non-Western people, in that they are essentially obligate Hindus or Lamaist Buddhists: their genes are physically reincarnated and they consequently live in an unchanging system of social roles, as if certain Hindu-Buddhist beliefs were materially embodied. They are childlike in many ways: most significantly in carelessness about death (as their personalities are "immortal"), a condition that encourages playfulness in some, emotional abandon in others, and a general lack of concern for consequences and long-range planning.

Solaris (Once Again):
The Literary SF Grotesque

It is rare for a work to display all the qualities of a given constellation of effects, but Lem's *Solaris* represents just such a fully realized and categorically complete expression of the science-fictional grotesque. The planet's anomalous position in the universe of human understanding is made clear through a detailed and varied history of hypotheses about its behavior, each of which fails to become legitimate knowledge. The basic premise of the novel's scientific grotesque is that the ocean-planet Solaris appears to regulate its own orbit around a binary star, permitting it to even out the drastic changes in temperature that would normally make the evolution of life (or indeed any kind of homeostasis) inconceivable. Such a phenomenon is so unprecedented for the human astrophysical imagination that it immediately inspires new theories and models, each of which is somehow liminal vis-à-vis established scientific models. It may be a pre-biological formation the size of a planet, a homeostatic mechanism, a powerful magnetic geological formation — all models that share their fundamental emptiness. After closer research, all these hypotheses are discarded, leaving a new set of more refined liminal hypotheses: that the plasmic ocean that covers the planet's entire surface is a single gigantic cell-like structure, and that it has some form of sentience capable of regulating its orbit.

As the exploration of Solaris continues from a space station in orbit above the surface, the hypotheses about the planet are discarded one by one, relegated to a library of unprovable and useless dead ideas. The only thing that can be known about it is that it consistently defies being understood by any of the tools of human science. It is an anomaly in almost every aspect of its physical being, and thereby repels all previous human models of astrophysics, biology, planetary geology, and so forth. It cannot be studied in any rational way, because the measuring instruments used to collect data return mysteriously transformed, still measuring *something*, but without any indication of what that something is. Even time cannot be measured normally on the surface, as the plasmic ocean appears to be able to change the time along one and the same meridian.

This anomality elicits a wide range of responses, from religious awe to the rage of spurned suitors. After a hundred years of failure to understand the ocean, most of humanity tires of the whole enterprise, leaving only a tiny band doggedly to pursue it, and leaving the project's funding in grave danger. By the time the protagonist, Kris Kelvin, arrives on Solaris Station, the condition of the scientific grotesque (that is, a local anomaly that violates the norms of reality) creates a mathematically grotesque response. The planet is, in a sense, a simple being: it is not subdivided into cells, it does not extend the range of its putative power beyond its own orbit, it has no second nature on its surface. But this simple creature elicits the most voluminous commentary and scientific imagining of any object in nature. Thus, in response to the "resistance" of the object, human beings produce attempted models, hypotheses, and proofs that grotesquely display their own labor, without illuminating the object. The work might perhaps be sublime, if it could produce an understanding of the planet that is both mathematically and dynamically sublime. But as it cannot, the enormous human intellectual labor is merely the display of the forms of human cognition, made empty by their inability to reach the object.

The stalemate produces a sense of threat in the Solarists. Even though the planet does not menace them physically, their sense of legitimacy as scientists and human beings is threatened by the planet's apparent sabotage of their rationality. The planet clearly exists *in concreto* (the notion that it is a collective hallucination is raised, but not seriously explored in the novel), but it has no rational explanation. As a result, humans who pride themselves on their rationality as proof of their superior powers in the cosmos encounter a wall. An astronomical wall is sublime. But in the case of Solaris, the wall is inside the minds of human beings — the ocean itself is maddeningly active. It continually produces surprising phenomena that cannot but draw the attention even of the most fatigued Solarists toward itself. The Solarists are drawn to examine the planet ever more closely, and with each approach the sought-for core dissolves in yet another plasmic transformation.

The closer the Solarists come to the surface of the planet, the more obvious it is that the planet resists understanding, not only because of its core anomaly, but because its fluid physicality is in continual metamorphosis. Made of a plasma, the ocean is a single formless entity capable of emanating immense and elaborate structures — the mimoids, symmetriads, and asymmetriads — towering quasi-edifices of stupendous complexity that rise into the stratosphere and then decompose quickly back into the planetary substance. These excrescences never repeat themselves. A leading Solarist, attempting to place the ocean among the known things of the universe, has to invent a category, of which the planet (true to its anomality) is the only member. Its main quality is that it is a "metamorph." This constant changeability thus extends from the simplest to the most complex structures. The surface is even capable of generating simulations of human forms, apparently perceived through some mysterious reading of the brainwaves of human Solarists. The grotesque implications are clear: Solaris is not only about a stable difference from the known (that is, the different physics that seems to obtain in its orbital behavior); it is also about internal, constantly mutating and proliferating differences, the metamorphoses that will not allow rational categorization to establish the limits necessary to describe and define.

These grotesque qualities are fairly abstract and clearly reflect Lem's conscious intentions to create an ungraspable alien. But the logic of the grotesque continues into what may be less conscious on his part. Here the metamorphic quality of the planet takes on the gendered aspects characteristic of the grotesque. The plasma ocean is increasingly related to female form or, rather, formlessness. There is ample reason to believe that the "Phi-creatures" that appear on the Station, apparently simulations by the ocean of repressed fantasies or memories of the Solarists, are all erotic, and perhaps all female. (Two of them certainly are female, Kelvin's Rheya and Gibarian's "African Aphrodite," while Sartorius's is quite possibly a female child. Snaut/Snow's is confined to a closet.) This feminization alone would not indicate the female-grotesque, however — except perhaps in the dry sense that the rationalistic Solarists are forced to confront the most unpleasantly incongruous, erotic aspects they had thought repressible, only to discover the aspects are instruments in their relationship with the planet. Rather, it is the planet itself that takes on more and more female qualities.

Manfred Geier has explored the ways in which even the apparently objective physical qualities of the ocean irresistibly connote femaleness, including female genitalia.[13] In the relationship with Kelvin, the ocean, first through Kelvin's dreams in chapter 12, then through the simulacrum of his dead wife Rheya, and finally in its direct quasi-encounter with Kelvin at the end of the novel, is always coded as feminine. In the chapter "The Dreams," a painful and formless union seems to take place with a mysterious subject, producing what can be easily construed to be a child. The Phi-Rheya may well be a recording instrument of the planet, analogous to the instruments sent down to the planet's surface by the Solarists. In that case, Kelvin's love affair with her sends a very specific, and indeed romantic, kind of information to the "mother." Rheya's final suicide, moreover, is a classically — indeed, stereotypically — feminine exercise of sacrifice for the sake of her man, a noble gesture that nonetheless takes on grotesque dimensions when it is viewed not from the comfortable, seductive context of romantic fiction, but from the outside, as the act of a being doubly determined by the inferrable purposes of the planet and Kelvin himself.

The ocean itself is fascinating and grotesquely excessive. Its mimoids and symmetriads protrude from the planet's surface, or spurt up like ejaculations. It reproduces "giant babies." Its physicality is uncontrollable, and illimitable. And, of course, it is a limit-form of plasma. At its most basic level, this creature capable of orbital control (and, in its gigantic protuberances the manifestation of what one Solarist considers the physical analogue of transcendental equations) is an undifferentiated mass of plasma, a production machine without organs. It is a clear manifestation of the *differential grotesque.*

Nor are the grotesque qualities of Solaris confined to the diegesis. The book tells its story through a constantly destabilized narrative. Generic protocols are grafted onto one another so that Kelvin's austere realistic narrative reveals itself, on close inspection, to implicate many distinct romanesque forms: ghost story, Kafkaesque parable, quixotic romance, Swiftian satire, and mystery, among others. With the appearance of the Phi creatures, these distinct narrative forms flow into one another, revealing that the ocean is as resistant to narrative appropriation as it is to scientific rationality.[14]

In *Solaris,* the grotesque interval is narrowed by certain boundary-producing elements of the sublime evoked by the novel's concluding encounter between the ocean and Kelvin. Science — or at least a transformed scientific ego represented by Kelvin — may yet become open to a new type of infinity in the universe, that of sentient variety. There may have been an "understanding" between incommensurate sentient beings that remains dry, elegant, indeed courteous and respectful of cosmic difference. The story of the encounter, moreover, unfolds in a chaste and economical language, extending from Kelvin's narrating ego, philosophical dialogue, and the *archē* of Solaristic records that tacitly embrace the entire history of human scientific exploration. Finally, Kelvin's biography leaves no residue after the novel's end; no repressed or unspoken element of personal or species history remains to return and spoil the party. This interpretation forces us to read the novel naively, which is rather a tall order. It is worth remembering that there is no indication of any disturbance in the Solarists' unconscious in the beginning of the novel, either. None of the Solarists' rhetoric betrays that they are aware that their language might carry unspoken unconscious meanings (which is also true of the author).[15] The grotesque is thus on the verge of its transformation into the sublime recuperation.

The *Alien* Series and the Spectacular SF Grotesque

The *Alien* films convey a very different sense of the science-fictional grotesque, appropriate both for cinema's kinetic rhetoric and for postmodern culture's pervasive concern with transmorphic, boundary-dissolving phenomena. The individual installments of Ripley's career are clearly intended to be linked into an *Alien* megatale. It is also clear that they are always after-the-fact additions. The audience is thus invited to imagine a unified "saga," at the same time that they know that each new film is an improvisation.[16] The *Alien* films are consequently already grotesque in their moment of presentation, requiring their audience to close enormous temporal gaps between episodes (during which at least one important protagonist, the young girl Newt of *Aliens,* dies), while also opening up gaps in stories that appeared to be closed. The fourth film, *Alien Resurrection,* has taught the public to abandon the expectation of closure altogether. *Alien 3* (1992) had claimed that the Alien xenomorphs were completely destroyed. A way was found to bring them back.

The linking narrative of each episode is, from this perspective, also a pretext for displaying ever more complex variations on certain themes. On the narrative level, these have to do with the constantly shifting relationships among Ripley, the Aliens, and the independently metamorphosing androids. As the stories become increasingly defined by themes of physical interfusion and reproduction, genealogy and affiliation, each category of character moves further and further from its original conception, while retaining a trace of its origin.

At the level of image and visual design, category confusions occur incessantly. Boundaries between genders, between machines, humans, and animals, between technology and organic life — all come down. Interiors project outward, while exteriors invade. Some horrible excess of decontainment attends each boundary violation: explosions of blood, brains, android juices, alien vital-acid and drool (or "shit," as the grunts of *Aliens* (1986) prefer to call it) are expected and required. Visually, there is the constantly metamorphic interfusion of technological design and organic form, foreground and background, interior and exterior, environment and agent, costume and body. Category excesses abound: the prison planet Fury of *Alien 3* is peopled by excessive men (all with YY-chromosomes); Ripley is excessively female, a woman pregnant with a Queen; the Alien has two mouths, and evokes the menacing genitalia of both genders; it is metallically organic, while the Alien Spaceship of the first film is organically metal; androids are endowed with their own spurting life-juices, coded as both milk and sperm; men give horrific birth, females have deadly phalluses. Bodies are regularly violated, separated into parts, forcibly fused and consumed; they are doubled promiscuously, becoming shadows of each other, until the traditional contest of horror fiction, of same against other, becomes excruciatingly difficult to sustain. By the fourth film, even the most solid generic conventions implode, along with the psychological responses they encode. The cathartic exorcism of the monster that is the raison d'être of the horror film is subverted, and the excessive expulsion of the Alien child at the end of the film evokes more grief than relief: "By *Alien Resurrection* the oppositional relations between the human and the inhuman have been completely reconfigured to form a series of intersecting potentialities. The lack of an oppositional relation between self and Other, human and monstrous, means that the final confrontation between Ripley and the alien child is structured around similarity and therefore permeated by a sense of appalling loss."[17]

From the outset, each of the films intends to subvert fundamental generic conventions of sf and especially horror film.[18] The position of heroic agent is dependably occupied in all the films by Ripley, a putatively representative female subject in a niche that had been, before her appearance, reserved for men. Ripley is also free of the despotism of romance. Her affections are for non–male-coded beings: Jonesy the cat in *Alien,* the young girl Newt in *Aliens,* and the young female android Call in *Alien Resurrection.*[19] Ripley is consequently free to establish her position outside the heterosexual dyad.

Because of this freedom, Ripley has a mobility in her relationships unprecedented in sf film. At first this mobility is confined by her unrelenting hostility to the xenomorphs, a relationship she is ultimately—and forcibly—"liberated from" by her position as cyborg fusion of alien and human. Ripley metamorphoses from heroic survivor, to heroic surrogate mother, to tragically compromised carrier, to *Alien Resurrection's* solo cyborg-dyke-warrior-leader-xenomorph-mother, the appropriator of every available form of power. The Alien evolves through similar relational changes. It did not take long for the audience and the filmmakers to perceive the uncanny inverted doubling relationship between the two bodies. The Alien xenomorphs in each film act as Ripley's shadow: stalker, maternal competitor, horrific guardian, and monstrous offspring. The inverted doubling naturally involves their physiques. As Ripley is transformed from an object of conventional visual pleasure into a being increasingly part of her ever darker visual and technical environment, the creatures become proportionally humanoid and social. In each film, Ripley's appearance becomes less and less visually defined vis-à-vis the environment. She fuses with the mechanical lifter in *Aliens;* she is made to look like the prisoners in *Alien 3;* and in *Alien Resurrection* she appears almost to emanate from the interior design of the lab-ship. Finally, in *Alien Resurrection,* the inverse movement becomes convergence: in a wrenching scene, Ripley and the audience discover horrifying relics of previous experiments in joining Ripley's DNA with the Alien's, her own grotesque ancestry.

The grotesque condition is complicated by a third order of creature: the android, who is also presented in constantly mutating fashion in each film, both in physique and in relation to the human beings. The science officer Ash of *Alien* appears to be unambiguously human at first. When his head is knocked off, his interior is revealed to be bulbous and lymphatic. The butch and brutal Ash's body becomes a counterpart of the Alien creature's sexual ambiguity, its fluids calling to mind both milk and semen, transforming the dour, hyper-rational, Spock-like science officer into a double abomination, a disguised hermaphrodite sustained by its own sexual juices. Bishop of *Aliens* at first appears to be a simple moral inversion of Ash; the audience knows, however, that his shell conceals the repulsive interior obscenity, and expects it to be spectacularly revealed. The exposure comes when Bishop is impaled by the Alien Queen and rended in two. The autonomy of the cyborg's individual parts (evoking another primal motif of the grotesque) had been established in a scene in the earlier film when Ash's head is electrically reactivated to access its databank (and to give Ash the chance to express his disdain for the human crew). In *Aliens,* Bishop uses his own grotesquely severed upper half to rescue Newt. In contrast with Ash's liminal obscenity, Bishop's cyborg ambiguity becomes a linking device, a physical copula. In *Alien 3* the presentations of the androids in the previous films are recombined. Bishop's head, now severed and in need of artificial reactivation (like Ash's in the first film), is pathetically compassionate, and elicits pity from the audience: we gaze at a noble artificial soul in the waste heap of its terminal embodiment.

With *Alien Resurrection,* the grotesque has expanded in surprising directions once again (though not necessarily in aesthetically satisfying ways). The captive Xenomorphs, the alien Queen, and her hybrid offspring are more defined than any of the earlier films' creatures, through the prominence given to their faces and their social behavior. The humans, for their part, display a number of carnivalesque forms: a dwarf, a giant, a female man, and a machine-girl. The android, who now surpasses even Bishop in altruistic service to the human species, appears for the first time coded as feminine, in the form of the young woman, Call. The cavernous wound that reveals her android interior does not spurt and smear as her predecessors' did; it merely drips with the familiar white, viscous fluid. It is perhaps even more explicitly sexual, because it so nearly resembles a vagina, which the Alien Ripley explores with prurient fascination. It is evident that both the cyborg and the human-alien are linked to an imaginary lesbian positionality, in sharp contrast with the exaggerated masculinity of the other humans and the exaggerated maternal sexuality of the Alien Queen. Call's wound evokes extravagantly sadistic imagery of sexual violation that, because it involves her constitutive circulatory juices, implies that she is a creation of sadistic fantasies (like the Alien Ripley herself), that she is the embodiment of sexual violation.

Few works of recent sf have attracted as much critical attention as the *Alien* films. Early criticism interpreted the initial film primarily in terms of social class, the Company's capitalism, and the creature as an embodiment of capitalism's rapacity.[20] Since the early 1990s, the dominant approach has been through psychoanalytic, especially feminist, models. Viewing the Alien as the shadow of Ripley, and the relationship among Ripley, the xenomorphs, and the androids as one of triangulation, invites psychoanalytic critics to interrogate the origin of the monster and the cyborg, and to code the screened relationships in terms of a self-defining female subject and her repressed unconscious conditions of possibility. For feminist critics these conditions are embedded in a patriarchal symbolic order hostile to the emergence of women's autonomy. This interrogation has inspired a number of remarkably astute interpretive essays on the *Alien* films from several psychoanalytic perspectives: Jungian, Kleinian, Lacanian, Kristevan, Irigarayan, and others.[21]

The *Alien* films have constructed a pattern of violent reproductive fantasies— forced insemination, android replication, insectoid mothering, sadistic reconstructions of the female body—that epitomize the postmodern grotesque. In this context, it is interesting that the *Alien* series has elicited what might be considered a form of theory concerned with the psychological origins of the grotesque—and correspondingly is an example of grotesque thinking itself. Psychoanalysis is, after all, concerned with articulating the fantastic "archaic" consciousness of inarticulate beings, constructing infantile states of mind that putatively generate later states and conflicts. All this reconstructing is done by inference alone, from art, dreams, neurotic behaviors, and deranged states of adults. The archaic stratum can never be reached, because it can never speak. Yet it sends its messages into and through the language of grown humans. Psychoanalysis thus repeats the basic structure of Gothic horror fiction, imputing to the mind a stratum of terrific creative energy not mediated by post-Oedipal discipline.[22] Psychoanalysis itself resembles paranoid/schizoid thinking, in that it detects pernicious and transforming influence from an inaccessible part of oneself that is increasingly seen as existing in networks in the world.

Psychoanalysis looks squarely across its own grotesque interval at a fantasy-producing core experience that can never be fixed down. The resistant datum of consciousness—whether it be the archaic mother, the phallic mother, the Oedipal dyad, or the birth trauma—constantly changes its manifestations, appearing in various phantasmagoric forms so imaginatively excessive that they refuse to be reduced to a mundane moment of real time in childhood. Psychoanalysis in this sense is the constant search, interrogation, and conjuring up of phenomena that may never accept their naming (and hence their exorcism).

Feminist currents of psychoanalysis have a particularly ambivalent position vis-à-vis the liberation of conscious thought from its illusions of self-sufficiency and self-determination. For most feminist psychoanalytic theorists, these illusions are tied up with patriarchal indoctrination, the structuring of mind to serve phallocratic interests in the world. At the same time, the repressed pre-

Oedipal stratum is recognized to have the power to damage thought itself; that is, to make recognition and knowledge meaningless, by releasing psychosis along with resistance. This liberation may be coded as revolutionary and positive, as in Deleuze-Guattari and Cixous; more often, it is coded as ambivalent and fearsome. Theories of the origin of horror in infantile separation anxieties—such as Melanie Klein's splitting and Kristeva's abjection—offer a psychoanalytic theory of the origins of the grotesque.

The *Alien* series points out that a new sf element is involved in such cultural psychoanalyses, namely, the artificial construction and dissemination of virtual experiences that suggest—and increasingly encode—subject-concepts. Unlike analysis, which claims to uncover formative real experiences that have generated powerful illusions, postmodern psychoanalytic criticism increasingly treats virtual experiences as indistinguishable from the real, hence impossible to define in contradistinction to "what actually happened at the origin." In this sense, as film and virtual arts increasingly become primary carriers of symbolic information, they cease to be mere symptoms; they become instead part of a network of generative causes of subject-constituting fantasy life. SF has a forward role because it presents both rationally explicable imaginary monsters and the technologically constructed worlds in which they belong. SF films—especially those that bind with horror—externalize the unconscious with respect to the subject, granting unconscious authority to the apparatus of presentation. More specifically, psychoanalysis and film are, at least in the influential *Alien* films, increasingly grotesque as media. The sf film's obsession with metamorphosis, reproduction, and the externalization of the interior, all through constructed set-worlds, makes it a medium especially able to present the descent into the grotesque.

Although there is justifiably a great deal of dispute about the aesthetic value of each of the *Alien* films, they obviously have a subversive, disturbing artistic power in popular culture unmatched by other works of sf. Just as feminist psychoanalysts view the films as an arena where profound dilemmas of the social are projected—testifying to a loosening of traditional limits on the representation of unconscious fantasies that is mirrored in theoretical speculation—we might also view the *Alien* films in more general terms, as running experiments in the designation of a science-fictional grotesque as a dominant mode of representing postmodernity.[23]

The Ascension of the Grotesque

At the heart of the grotesque is the vertiginous destabilization of the sense of natural balance—in terms of the politics of consciousness, the disturbance of cosmic law and order. Because the grotesque's transformations operate mainly at the level of the intimate, the sensory, and the present, its vertigo is often re-contained by shifting the gaze outward toward the sublime, where conscious-ness of the extrasensory magnitude of overweening laws seems to restore a sense of order (even if it is not for us). Thus in sf the expanse of space, the infinite possibilities of evolution, or the cold equations of science have tradi-tionally served as containment vessels of the grotesque. Even in *Solaris* and the *Alien* films, the enormous distances of interstellar space create a certain cor-don that either isolates, or at least slows down, the infiltration of human real-ity by destabilizing metamorphs.

The accession of transmutative sciences comes at the same time as a certain collapse of external horizons in the social understanding of science. Public en-thusiasm for great collective, epic projects, like the space program, utopian ur-banization, or the green revolution, has diminished, in part as a result of their unintended consequences. As the external horizons have collapsed, however, internal ones have opened up. Science appears ready to correct nature's flaws, to make nature more responsive to human desires at the level of its smallest elements: cells, genes, molecules, atoms, bytes. The ability to manipulate bod-ies at their constitutive microscopic levels makes mesocosmic bodies mal-leable, fluid, and dynamic. Bodily transformations that were once character-ized as grotesque fantasy and mythological metamorphosis are now either available or reasonably imaginable in daily life. Categories tied to carnal form — such as gender and sense-perception — become fluid and metamorphic as well. Social questions about the public funding of technoscience have shifted their focus radically in our time from space programs to medicinal and cos-metic modifications of individual bodies.

In recent years sf has been dominated by the sensibility of the grotesque, to a greater degree than in the past. The authority of the sublime to police it has severely eroded. The dominant morals of sf's stories have had less and less to do with adapting to law and order, than to understanding the inherent volatil-ity of the physical. While this has produced great anxiety — cognitive (as in *Solaris*) and corporeal (as in *Alien*) — it has also produced a certain ecstasy of liberation from the domination of cosmic authoritarianism. As with the sense of freedom the grotesque provided against religious domination described by Bakhtin, the contemporary science-fictional grotesque revels in the liberation that contemporary transmutative science offers from the normative mytholo-gies of gender and embodiment that survived even in scientific materialism as long as scientists were unable (and unwilling) to manipulate the sacred build-ing blocks of living bodies. As those taboos collapse, new visions of form be-come possible — not only for individual bodies, but for everything that has been conceptually and metaphorically associated with them, from the body politic to the body of Earth. The living body has been *queered,* with the elation of breaking down enforced barriers now shown to be fortuitous rather than necessary products of natural selection: "Queer . . . suggests a postmodern and utopian space for exploring sexual difference(s): it promises much in terms of recuperating traditional abjected figures like monsters and grotesques, as it deploys, in [Judith] Butler's words, the 'repetition of hegemonic forms which fail to repeat loyally.'"[24] In this utopian metamorphic space "no gendered or sexed identities . . . are compulsory, or universal, or natural; and none, certainly, are invisible" (33).

With this combination of destabilization and performative visibility comes the explosive liberation of creative energies at the level of immediate physical existence. In sf, however, as in technoscience, the requisite physical power to create in this way remains with scientists. The dramatic ironies of all scientifically inflected art in the West remain in effect: liberation from first nature's constraints is subject to the politics of second nature. The freedom of bodies requires the constant intervention and maintenance of instrumentality, no longer only on a collective/mass scale, but in individual bodies as well. Freedom from nature is inseparable from its surveillance and governance by technoscientific agents. Thus the Enlightenment's sublime dream of rational control over human life by a race of sages has been succeeded by a far more lively dream of transformational plenitude facilitated by professional alchemists with no guiding collective purpose other than the quick realization — and reification — of current individual images of desire.

It is now a commonplace that contemporary "global culture" is characterized by hybridity, the intermingling of races and ethnicities, cultural mixing and remixing, and the evaporation of ideals of purity throughout social existence in the West. This commingling has been facilitated by technologies of transformation and trans-fusion — from photoshopping to genetic recombination, digital synthesis, and gender reassignment. SF writers were among the first to glom onto the fact that the hyperactive cultural sphere was actually bound to, and perhaps even a product of, technologies of radical splicing and denaturing, and a technoscientific culture with enough social authority to override long-standing ethical-religious taboos. Samuel R. Delany, Joanna Russ, Philip K. Dick, and J. G. Ballard, among others, depicted terminally destabilized and ambivalently liberated worlds that gained concrete realism for the mass of readers only in retrospect, even though their visions were deeply connected to the evolving traditions of the sf of their time.

In recent sf the trend of the grotesque, of imagining increasingly vertiginous barrier breakdowns, has moved through the alien and the cyborg and other images of queered physicality to the volatilization of sf's own conditions of possibility. Traditional sf storytelling, with its central plausibility code, acts as a huge sublime narrative gravity. Slipstream writers have employed a great variety of forms and tones to experiment with hybridizing narrative. In some respects, they differ from innovative writers coming out of the generic tradition of sf in their lack of concern about rationalization. A writer like Jonathan Lethem can, in *Amnesia Moon* (1996), use the devices of reality-fracture familiar (and perhaps adopted) from Philip Dick.[25] But where the latter's effect depends on a readership that is familiar with the sf megatext, and pleasurably surprised by Dick's eccentric modernist deviations from it, Lethem comes to the motifs from a literary tradition in which ellipsis, symbolism, and narratological obscurity are accepted practice. Hence the effect of Lethem's literary vision is rather different from the generically science fictional. Lethem in fact hails the science-fictional from a distance, invoking a kinship of vision that simultaneously affirms the distinct readerly spheres. Much as Dick wanted to hail the "mainstream" from sf, he did not succeed.[26] Dick did not acquire an audience outside those well trained in the generic protocols of sf until close to his death, when reality itself had become a matter of the science-fictional grotesque and seemed to imitate his style. The boundaries between the sf megatext and the textual body of the real world have since softened considerably. Postmodern art-fiction and sf, like overlapping circles in a Venn diagram, have come to share an area of science-fictionality, to the degree that Thomas Pynchon could adopt phantasmagoric motifs from Philip K. Dick, and Kathy Acker in *The Empire of the Senseless* (1994) could openly parody passages of the semisacred *Neuromancer*.[27]

More recently the traffic has begun to move in a reciprocal direction, as well. Writers like Jeff Noon and China Miéville have adopted premises from sf that they have combined with other, distinctly nonelite, nonmainstream narrative forms to augment the power of the grotesque beyond the boundary informally guarded by sf's principle of minimal rationalization. In Noon's *Vurt*, Gibson's consensual hallucination of virtual reality is transmogrified through fantastic hallucinogens into a collective unconscious from which myth, game, and vision emanate. But Noon's great novum is neither the paraspatial Vurt, which is a hallucinatory mutation of cyberspace, or even the colored feathers that lead one into the psychotropic Wonderland; it is the diegetic "real world," in which Haraway's cyborg is transmuted into a dimension in which ontologies miscegenate furiously. Categories of animal, mythical, mechanical, oneiric, virtual and real being are embodied as autonomous and equal ontic species: *dog, snake, robo, shadow, vurt* and *human*, which are open to myriad forms of erotic and cognitive inflections: robodogs, dreamsnakes, shadow-girls, and so forth. In Vurt's world, the most common graffito declaims: "Pure is poor." In another register, China Miéville's New Crobuzon cycle attempts to construct an entire alternate world based on the grotesque. From the physical condition of its central city, to its individual characters, every aspect of the story is either a splicing of distinct beings (scarab-headed khepri, cactus men, noble vulture men, the villainous Mr. Motley, the horrific "Remade" convicts punished by having their physical bodies surgically reconstructed to represent their crimes), or terrific metamorphic powers (such as the monstrous slake moths who feed on human imagination). With Miéville, the grotesque extends beyond setting and plot to the scientific premises of its alternative ontology. The central protagonist of *Perdido Street Station*, Isaac Dan der Grimnebulin, is the Einstein of the theory of "crisis energy," an alternative physics in which each moment of crisis creates its own new energy to counter fatality—in essence, a physicalization of the metaphor of the dialectic (and perhaps an adaptation of the Everett many-worlds model of quantum physics to dialectical materialism). "Crisis energy," or its imaginative equivalent, is also at the heart of the generic form of works like *Perdido Street Station* and *Vurt*. These works begin with sf's premises of fictive rationalization, fictive history, imaginary science, and neological reality and construct worlds whose density of mutations offers the grotesque as the model of beauty.[28]

SEVENTH BEAUTY

The *Technologiade*

○ ○ ○ ○ ○ ○ ○

No story of its own? It is often said that sf has no distinctive myth or storytelling formula, that it thrives by adopting the plots of other genres, punching them up with its distinctively exotic futuristic settings. SF Westerns, detective, and crime stories abound, as do quests, farces, romps, picaresques, Kafkaesques, political parables, philosophical fables, fractured fairy tales, surrealist assemblages, rationalized fantasies, and even terror-and-pity–inducing tragedies. Given this abundance of host plots, however, it would be puzzling if there were no shared story-forms latent in them to be shaped by the genre. In the previous chapters I have shown that sf responds to distinctive interests that it articulates in its characteristic devices and frames of reference. If its stories are always concerned with global/species/collective transformations mediated by technology, we may reasonably expect that these concerns will exert morphogenetic pressure on storytelling itself.

Brian Attebery has proposed that instead of a single overarching myth/plot formula, sf writers draw from what he terms *parabolas*, playing on the double meaning of parabolic trajectory and parable.[1] Parabolas differ from narrative formulas in that they are not structures whose regular repetition and distribution of functions is expected by the genre audience, but a set of potentials grounded in the sf megatext, whose actual course in any given work is open. Just as competent sf audiences suspend their disbelief about depicted futures and alternative realities in full knowledge of the many variants in the sf megatext, they also recognize in the narratives well-established paths, with the expectation that each story will add fresh trajectories to the virtual archive of sf.

Most commentators agree with Northrop Frye that sf stories derive from, and adhere closely to, the mythos of romance: stories in which human heroes prove their powerful virtue through a series of trials, many of which take place in anomalous spaces where normal laws do not apply.[2] SF romance is distinctive in the way it strives hard to rationalize elements that in traditional romances would be magical or marvelous, framing them within concepts that are understood to be within the range of the *not-impossible* as stipulated by scientific or cultural logic. In sf, marvelous phenomena are depicted as anomalies and technological forces that can be understood and mediated by imaginary knowledge that imitates scientific-technical knowledge in the reader's real world.

Until recently, the main currents of criticism have viewed adventure-romance fiction as inferior to the social and psychological novel, on the grounds that the novel acquired cognitive power to illuminate social reality, while the romance has remained in its essence mystificatory. Fredric Jameson, for example, has argued that romance forms (including the Gothic and high fantasy) are firmly rooted in precapitalist nostalgia, with a residual utopian charge that criticizes social reality without articulating critique.[3] Darko Suvin's insistence on sf's cognitive character can be read in this context as a way to exempt "authentic" sf from the charge of obscurantism justified for other genres of romance. But for critics such as Brian McHale, sf and postmodernist fiction have thrived, and indeed are appropriate for contemporary Western societies, precisely *because* of their romance lineage. Their fascination with ontological variety, and refusal to translate radically different worlds into a single comprehensive rational reality, is cognate, for McHale, with medieval romance's topology of marvelous "microworlds."[4]

In this chapter I suggest that sf's many plot loans and parabolas are structured by two distinctive forms of a category we might call the *technologiade*, the epic of the struggle surrounding the transformation of the cosmos into a technological regime. These two dialectically related forms are the expansive *space opera* and the intensive *techno-Robinsonade*. Space opera employs many of the traditional devices that the adventure tale has retained since its earliest incarnations. It has also invented new ways of treating some of the basic categories of the adventure universe, such as *free time* and *free space* (free, that is, from social-historical determinations), because these categories are also directly subject to the manipulations of scientific speculation, allowing sf to transform romantic conditions into fictively material ones. As for the techno-robinsonade, I suggest that it develops out of the class of narrative models I shall call the *modern adventure cluster,* consisting of the modern colonial adventure tale (the classical *Robinsonade*), the Gothic, and the utopia, and that the historical development of sf is closely intertwined with their development. Since their inception, these tale-forms have been shaped by the social factors that have led to the cultural ascendancy of technoscience, a process that they have shaped in turn by giving it a store of mutually reinforcing narrative vehicles disseminated through art, journalism, and propaganda. Each tale-form came into being well before the preconditions existed in art and everyday life for the crystallization of sf, but each emerged around the social application, legitimation, and critique of technology and science that were the nascent tasks of sf's cultural mediation. The transformation of these structures into hybrid, combinatory science-fictional adventures was a result of sf's role in making legible to modernizing societies their transformation from colonial expansion to global imperial power predicated on technological hegemony.

Space Opera

Space opera is sometimes said to be the quintessential form of sf narrative, not always with flattering intent. The term was originally used for trashy, pulp sf, much as purists use the term "sci-fi" today to distinguish works intended purely for entertainment from the more dignified science fiction or sf. But the term has become a descriptive one (also like sci-fi), signifying spectacular romances set in vast, exotic outer spaces, where larger-than-life protagonists encounter a variety of alien species, planetary cultures, futuristic technologies (especially weapons, spaceships and space stations), and sublime physical phenomena.[5]

The essential element for space opera is *cosmic space*, the physical universe itself, a setting putatively grounded in scientific knowledge, and vast enough to enclose a variety of contrasting exotic imaginary worlds. The genre thus continues the practice of adventure fiction in each age of adapting contemporary conceptions of the most sublime and comprehensive frames of reference to act as its natural setting. As history became the setting for national-historical romance (and before it, geography for individualist exploration adventures), so scientific cosmic space has been made into the inescapable theater of the moral struggles of the human species. Outer space allows writers to construct the sorts of ontologically pluralized fictional universes characteristic of premodern romances, populated with planets governed by their own ethico-physical laws, yet invoking the legitimating rhetoric of materialist science. The science-fictional cosmos also acts as a story space in which sf's main motifs can unfold with few constraints. It is the comprehensive chronotope that contains all particular spacetimes. In this sense space opera contains all the Seven Beauties (including space-operatic narrative itself), as a stage on which they can be displayed and performed. The points on which the fictional universe conforms with currently accepted scientific theories about the cosmos (the pride of hard sf) are effects for which space opera provides the scene, a story structure that is not changed by the transfigurative possibilities provided by exotic agents in the story. Because this space is a given for space opera, it permits all of the Beauties to be displayed in their most heightened form. Alien

The SEVEN BEAUTIES *of* SCIENCE FICTION

and extrapolated languages do not need to be taught or explained; they are expected. Grand-scale inventions and discoveries that lead beyond the known universe are also expected as a matter of course (otherwise, astronomical space would serve no purpose), as are surprising novum-obstacles materializing from the folds of the Abyss. The furthest developments of historical evolution and dispersion are possible, while imaginary science, the sf sublime, and sf grotesque are given room to grow without terrestrial social constraints, limited only by contemporary ideas about what is possible in a material universe. Space opera also employs all of sf's borrowed narrative strategies, as if metafictionally, to emphasize that in sf the ontology of fiction encloses the ontology of scientific materialism.

This extreme emphasis on space over historical time is characteristic of all adventure fiction, as Bakhtin describes it in "Forms of Time and Chronotope in the Novel." Because in its ancient forms adventure space is an abstract *somewhere,* with no one venue inherently distinct from any other, neither associative nor causal connections within the world can influence events in a logical way. Adventure time does not unfold or develop, but rather *happens,* by chance or by fiat. "The adventure chronotope," Bakhtin writes, "is characterized by a technical, abstract connection between space and time, by the reversibility of moments in a temporal sequence, and by their interchangeability in space. In this chronotope all initiative and power belongs to chance" (100).[6] Bakhtin traces the metamorphoses of the adventure scheme, as it becomes attached to more realistic, concrete details of everyday life and individual psychology in the Roman tales of Apuleius and Petronius, and later establishing stronger chains of psychological causality in the baroque romance of ordeal. But Bakhtin does not pursue the adventure scheme beyond the sixteenth century. For him, adventure is superseded by the novel, with its greater cognitive riches of polyphony, carnival, and heteroglossia, and its modeling of the dialectical relationship between individual psychology and social discourse. Clearly, however, adventure fiction has lost little of its vitality over time. It has adapted to social-historical changes, in part by adopting many of the techniques of the novel. There will be more to say about the role that adventure fiction played in mediating the colonial and imperialist expansions of Western societies. For now, let me note that space opera often *represents* such qualities as carnival, heteroglossia, and polyphony, without actually embodying them as form-determining qualities. It can do so simply because it commands a stage set so vast that it exceeds the limits of every potential force and agent that might transform it. In space opera, transformations that in more realistic modes would represent extraordinary disruptions of social reality are expected as a matter of course, and in numbers.

Despite the feeling of many literary theorists that the adventure form was surpassed by the novel, leaving it to recycle formulas with minor variations, space opera demonstrates adventure's great flexibility and adaptability. Bakhtin defines the relationships between space- and time-units in early adventure as episodes that are reversible because they are not yet governed by a logic of social history. SF's imaginary science, often based as we have seen on scientific speculations that cannot be demonstrated actually to be impossible, provides the nondialectical chronotopes of adventure with a powerful, quasi-scientific *nihil obstat*. Space opera depends on a variety of imaginative quasi-physical devices that break up one-way duration. Time machines, communicating wormholes, consciousness downloads, artificial intelligence and Artificial Life, parallel, branching, and pocket universes, time-controlling drugs such a *Dune*'s melange, teleportation, ansibles, faster-than-light travel, spacetime jumps, and other similar novums allow vehicles and messages to cover astronomical distances with little decisive story time lost, each carrying its own plausible explanation. Even in more conservative forms that keep such marvelous macrotechnologies to a minimum, imaginary techniques allow protagonists to maintain personal identity over eons, via cryogenics, cloning, and longevity drugs (such as Niven's *boosterspice*). In space opera the suspended spatial relations of adventure are ironically "grounded" by scientific models of spacetime, against which the mundane experience-time of the social novel appears to be an illusion maintained by limited techgnosis. Thus science provides space opera with what it needs most to sustain the adventure scene: a plausible universe of plural, simultaneous, reversible spacetime continua. Clearly, if our mundane world is only a tiny station in a gigantically diverse cosmos, our "novelistic" norms of social conduct and consciousness will seem provincial, at best.

In its "pure" form, space opera propels adventures by bouncing its protagonists from place to place in literally empty space. These places embody or are inhabited by obstacles that are usually external to the protagonist. Alternatively, conflicts are internalized by giving the protagonists riven histories, in which conflicting cultural (or indeed species) characteristics compete with each other, repeating one of the primary forms of motivation of Gothic fiction. Also like the Gothic, space opera tends to mix mythic time with historical time. But while the Gothic represents archaic curses manifest in everyday reality, combining ancient and contemporary time, space opera allows writers to combine several incompatible but fully rationalized systems of causality, some of which will include rationalized archaic models ("the Gods are Ancient Astronauts") and others mythicized models of actual history (such as Gibbon's Rise and Fall of Empires as an archetype of political evolution).The function of chronotopic technologies in sf is precisely to gather diverse models of narrative causality into a single, pseudoempirical story space.

Asimov's *Foundation* trilogy played an especially important role in establishing the norms for herding great historical spacetimes into a unitary frame. Asimov first constructed a rhetorically scientific version of Spenglerian historical rise-and-fall (and rise) determinism by grounding it in the fictive statistical regularity of mass-social behavior, which can be predicted in Hari Seldon's "psychohistory," much as economic cycles were thought to be predictable in Asimov's time. This model, quite original for sf, Asimov motivated in a far more conventionally adventurous way, with a quasi-mythic plot of evolution and emancipation, in which the secreted knowledge-treasure of the location of the Second Foundation — in this case, a bit of scientific knowledge, but structurally the same as a talisman or a sutra — frees the world from an ancient curse. The effect of the whole is that *Foundation*'s galactic history oscillates between cyclical and evolutionary, tragic and romantic-progressive, producing effects of each, but not resolving into either. Following the model implicit in all sf, but made explicit by Stapledon in *Last and First Men,* the agents of history transcend individuality and nationality, becoming instead the whole species seen as if from outside any imaginable spacetime.

This power of technologically manipulating spacetime, which we examined in small when discussing time machines in "Third Beauty," may lead in space opera not only to the resolution of paradoxes such as the one-way arrow of mortal life (individual, civilizational, or species) in a universe of reversible or branching spacetime relations; it may also lead to the transformation of the conditions of spacetime that constrain the universe in which the storytelling takes place. In space opera, the adventure settles neither into the empty time of an absolutely metaphysical universe, nor into spacetime absolutely mutable by exotic technologies. Writers of space opera combine the sublime qualities both of cosmic spacetime and of macro-technological power to transform conditions of physical existence to create story worlds that are not empty of historical logic, but *meta* with respect to them. The metasociety of futuristic humanity must navigate through (and with) metahistories. These metahistories are usually not resolved in a single conventional historical mode (revolution, evolution, dispersion), because the universe remains a *setting,* a stage for spectacular effects of time, space, and technopower, and for the exploration of fictive possibilities.

In terms of its distinctive local chronotopes, space operas usually articulate cosmic space by establishing a familiar home base against which to contrast exotic worlds. This base is often Earth itself, but it may be a spaceship, a space station, or colony, where familiar, extrapolated values of the audience are represented, sometimes ironically and critically. Most of space opera's actions occur either in the interest of, or in conflict with, this base. From this issues a primary binary opposition between familiar and exotic technosocial habitats. The latter are then further arrayed vis-à-vis each other in the form of diversely overlapping abstract world contrasts: familiar/exotic, simple/complex, sublime/grotesque, pleasurable/painful, patriarchal/feminist, Asian/Caucasian, free/enslaved, and so forth. These may all ultimately be reducible to a simple opposition between good and evil, or they may construct a complex system in which conflicts change the global character of the worlds involved in them (for example, by fragmenting previously unitary world cultures or effecting a symbiosis of antagonistic elements). Audiences of space operas expect that these worlds will provide fresh and interesting obstacles/ordeals for the heroes, and that at least some of them will be thematically and aesthetically coordinated with the complex, episodic plot.

The form originated with the relatively simple two-worlds scheme, in which protagonists travel between two planets: first, the lunar voyage; later, the Martian romance. The former developed into full-fledged sf with Wells's *The First Men in the Moon* and Méliès's *Voyage to the Moon* (1902),[7] the latter with works such as Edgar Rice Burroughs's Martian Romances, Lasswitz's *Auf Zwei Planeten* (1897), Bogdanov's *Red Star*, Stanley Weinbaum's "A Martian Odyssey," and Alexey Tolstoy's *Aelita*. Such offworld journeying required that most of the action take place away from Earth, emulating exploration and utopian narratives' binarist exoticism. The development of more epic space adventures adopting the nautical trope of sailing among islands in the void followed inevitably. Sometimes authors emulated the three planet scheme prefigured by Voltaire's *Micromégas* (whose protagonists hail from Sirius, Saturn, and Earth), as do, for instance, C. S. Lewis in his Space Trilogy (Earth, Mars, Venus) and Samuel R. Delany in *Trouble on Triton* (Triton, Mars, and Earth). More often they elaborated the space odyssey, a journey away from Earth's social gravity into the cosmos. This form can be treated as a rationalized variation on the hermetic tradition's doctrine of assigning the planets distinct roles in spiritual history. Esoteric schools such as Theosophy (whose influence on early sf remains largely unexplored) teach that each planet is associated with a creative power, level, or angel, through which the soul must travel on its journey to personal evolution; or, alternatively, that they are governed by spiritual powers with sometimes competing or hostile psychomachic interests. The privileged launching pad for such astral traveling to other planets was the séance, and fin de siècle mystical anthropology routinely sent entranced psychics to Mars and points beyond, as in the exemplary case of Helène Smith, who returned to Earth first with the Martian language, later with the language of

Venus. Many now forgotten examples of astral fieldwork (such as Sara Weiss's early twentieth-century records of visits to Mars, complete with drawings of Martian flora)[8] were based on these models, as well as monuments of the borderline between science and esotericism, such as Lindsay's *Voyage to Arcturus,* through Stapledon's *Star Maker,* to the contemporary Japanese manga masterpiece, Leiji Matsumoto's *Galaxy Express 999* (1977–81).

The unambiguously science-fictional form of space opera, however, which no longer owed its schemes to utopian dualism and the astral journeys of séance fiction, in which off-Earth populations travel and fight wars in the vacuum of space, leaping parsecs via a myriad of ftl devices, emerged from an essentially intrageneric mixing of Verne's horizontal fiction of exploration journeys and Wells's fictions of intrusions by aliens into others' worlds. Verne's plausible sf imitated nautical adventures, complete with sea battles and scientific landfalls, contributing the high-tech ship and war machine, along with pedantically precise times and spaces. Wells's Gothic-inflected, ambivalently anti-imperialist two-world romances imagined alien worlds intruding on each other: sometimes, as in *The War of the Worlds,* with human civilization as the victim; sometimes, as in *The First Men in the Moon,* with humans as the intruders. These two vectors were easily transposed into a cosmic space in which Vernean adventure intersected with Wellsian anxiety to create models of imperialist conflict in myriad variants.

Early space opera had a fairly traditional anchor in nationalistic myth. The base was associated with the target audience's nation in its conflict with its terrestrial enemies, either in a positive, patriotic light (as Flash Gordon represented WASP America against Ming the Merciless's cosmic Yellow Peril), or in a critical, revolutionary light (as Bogdanov's Bolshevik Martians wage war with Earth's capitalist exploiters in *Red Star*). Because of the astronomical scale of its physical setting, and the requirement that its plot involve plural worlds, social and political matters in space opera tend to expand to imperial dimensions. This expansion remains true even in later incarnations in which the protagonists represent putatively democratic or anarchistic values, as in M. John Harrison's *The Centauri Device* (1975) or Le Guin's *Left Hand of Darkness* or, indeed, the political universe of *Star Trek.* After World War II, space-opera writers took up the theme of the deconstruction of the familiar home base, which ceases to be a secure point of contrast against which the exotic can be measured. This theme reflects the postwar recognition of fragmentation and diversity within national societies, and increasingly critical attitudes to peacetime home worlds still dominated by war economies. Out of this also evolved the trope of the free-floating spaceship, increasingly on its own, unmoored from projects serving Earth's interests. This motif began with the ironically failed terrestrial project, such as the amnesiac generation starship of Aldiss's *NonStop/Starship* (1958), developing later into the spaceship liberated from Earth's morality (*2001's Discovery*), and finally the free-floating self-contained community, untethered from Earth's instructions, first lost in space, as in the eponymous (and hysterically terracentric) *Lost in Space* (1965–68), then the existentially drifting *Voyager* (1995–2001), and recently the heroic community of renegades of *Farscape* (1999–2002).

Not all space operas emphasize the vastness of space. For some, the cosmic diversity of worlds for which space is the alibi is interesting less as something to be visited and contemplated, than as a pretext for cultural conflict. Many space operas focus on places where different species cultures meet and jockey for power. In such venues, travel and battle in diversity-enclosing space is less important, and the diversity itself is less autonomous, than the intrigues of political power associated with cosmic hegemony. Diversities of culture and species in such stories, even though they may be marked in physical terms, are ultimately reduced to a shared interest in a contest for rule — or, almost as often, the resistance to hegemony. Such emphatically political sf requires a compressed universe, where all autonomous spaces are ultimately viewed as unstable, temporary autonomous zones, destined to be annexed by or introduced to a larger, encompassing political entity. These are usually based on terrestrial political-historical models, sometimes to allegorical extremes — hence the proliferation of galactic empires based on the Roman Empire, Byzantium, the Federal Imperium of nineteenth-century America, or the Soviet Union. Just as alien bodies are imaginary recombinations of aspects of known bodies, capable of imaginative variations, so the body politics of such space operas of intrigue (Westfahl names them "Ruritanian space operas")[9] can be highly imaginative recombinations of known terrestrial social systems.

One of space opera's favorite plots is war between worlds, which cleanly displaces national wars by extending them to race, but also allows inventive and ideologically complex wars within species, such as the clan conflicts of the hwarhath in Arnason's *Ring of Swords* or the political frictions between Karhide and Orgoreyn in Le Guin's *The Left Hand of Darkness*. These displacements attempt to base the fantasy of interaction among alien species on certain conflicts in earthly experience, without turning them into allegories of history. With war, biocultural differences ultimately give place to technological differences, and the void becomes a technological stage. This easy plot conflict is made interesting by the variety of biophysical agents, machines, and motives of the contending cultures, a variety that is ultimately reduced to a simple, common goal: hegemony (or "autonomy," hegemony within one's narrow sphere). Space opera finds it hard to resist the trope of the world-system, with its dominant Alliances, Hegemonies, Ekumens, Foundations, Empires, Cultures, and Federations, and their unassimilable rebels, turning the cosmos into a scene of political conflict between competing interests endowed with distinct technologies representing their motives.

In its most self-conscious form, space opera narratives strive to expand to match the expansiveness of their cosmos, keeping open the possibilities of emerging anomalies and cultural/racial/species differences, and holding onto the option that "anything can happen in space." But most sf narratives since World War II, even the space operas, have narrowed their foci to dramatic conflicts arising out of ethicophysical constraints typical of sf, collisions of the protagonists' (and readers') mesocosm with the macrocosm. The more an adventure is drawn toward a constraint, the more it loses its freedom of movement, its freedom from time manipulation. In sf, Machinery's magical character is increasingly bound by the pseudomaterial limits of the diegesis—whether in the form of the laws of physics or the physiology of living spaceships, the physical demands of space travel, the containments of space habitats, mutually interfering biologies and their attendant political goals, or the paradoxes of spacetime. As sf becomes more and more concerned with physical/material constraints on action, the more it is captured by the modern adventure paradigm, which plays out the dialectic between technology and resource, and the politics of owning the means to be materially free of the limits of (now cosmic) first nature. I shall now turn my attention to these intensive, quasi-realistic forms derived from the modern adventure cluster. These are the structures through which sf has most energetically accommodated the social pressures of technological modernization, and that have allowed the fables of sf to exert influence on late- and post-imperialist cultures.

The Modern Adventure Tale

The *Robinsonade,* the bourgeois epic of technical world-construction, establishes the rudimentary design of the modern adventure tale. I approach this design first through relationships among recurring narrative functions that are modern adventure tales' main diegetic agents. I name these the Handy Man, the Fertile Corpse, the Willing Slave, the Shadow Mage, the Tool/Text, and the Wife at Home. The relationships among this set can be varied in many ways: by condensing two functions into one, *détournement,* reversal, splitting one into several subfunctions, truncation, and so forth.[10] And any given tale will emphasize one or another type vis-à-vis the others. The paradigm I am suggesting is a drastically simplified abstraction, and should not be considered a generative template that inspires writers. It will, I hope, be useful as an analytic tool that emphasizes the gamelike aspects of the form, as well as the structural continuity of sf with earlier genres. Most practicing artists are far more interested in the ambiguities and slippages that occur in the interstices between agents than with adherence to an abstract template.

Before proceeding to description, let me emphasize that the formation of the modern adventure tale, the selection of its diegetic agents, and its specific metamorphoses into sf are social-historical matters. Adventure has always been a popular, indeed a plebeian, genre, and this made it ripe for adoption as the de facto folktale of entrepreneurial colonialism and, later, of techno-scientific imperialism. Its form embodies the dialectical collision of interests among the various forces involved in expansionist modernization (such as the landed aristocracy, the administrative center, entrepreneurial institutions, individual adventurers, internally colonized and "conserved" women, subjected and resistant foreign populations, more or less autonomous colonial administrations, the geography and resources of unimproved colonized lands, the storehouse of tools and techniques, antimodernizing collectives, and so forth). The modern adventure tale makes the social-historical relationships among and within these actors imaginatively intelligible. By embodying them, it gives them a discursive gravity that shapes future articulations, while at the same time obstructing the development of new and different ones.

Surprisingly little attention has been devoted to modern adventure fiction by literary scholarship. Bakhtin, who did more than anyone to set up the modern analytical categories for the classical adventure tale,[11] has nothing to say about the *Robinsonade*. Erich Auerbach stunningly ignores Defoe in the historical development of realism in *Mimesis*. Edward Said devotes a chapter in *Culture and Empire* to Jane Austen, but rarely mentions *Crusoe* or the adventure tradition. John Cawelti's *Adventure, Mystery and Romance: Formula Stories in Art and Popular Culture*, one of the first studies of contemporary formula fiction, devotes barely three pages to the adventure form itself, despite its prominence in the book's title.[12] Perhaps this critical marginalization stems from the form's ostensible aesthetic simplicity, or because adventures have been written mainly for children since their nineteenth-century heyday, or perhaps because they have frequently articulated transparently ideological agendas encouraging imperial, gender, and class domination. The related genres of the Gothic and the utopia, by contrast, have enjoyed a great deal of theoretical interest; most of this, nonetheless, has passed over the relationship between them and the modern adventure tale. My claim is that modern adventure fiction becomes increasingly important in European cultures' struggles to comprehend the implications of first their colonialist, then their imperialist projects. As it does so, it involves elements of Gothic and utopian storytelling that endow the imperialist myths with complex literary dimensions. Later in this chapter I shall suggest how these developments led to the emergence of sf as a powerful successor genre following World War I and the crash technological modernization of the world.

THE HANDY MAN

The Handy Man is a figure, usually male, who possesses skill in the handling of tools. He is *polymetis* like Odysseus; unlike him, however his many ideas and plans are almost exclusively devoted to technical problem-solving. The Handy Man is able to manipulate tools, to fashion new ones from a recognition of required functions, and, most important, to extend his power over the environment through technological control provided by understanding of its processes as rules of operation. The Handy Man is an adventurer, although not always a willing one. He is generally induced or forced out of a culturally comfortable, predictable home environment, to exotic and undeveloped regions. There he either solves a fundamental problem that permits him to function as an entrepreneurial culture hero for his original culture (a modern Jason or Theseus), or he establishes the bases for a cultural transformation on his own terms. Like Odysseus, he has an ambivalent relationship to his home. As an adventurer, his skills are most useful when he is in an undeveloped or "incomplete" world, where the tools or techniques he uses are unfamiliar.

Odysseus is the obvious original template in the Western tradition. His identity is almost exhausted by his power, which occasionally includes brute force, but most often manifests itself in mastering problems of technique. Like Odysseus, the Handy Man's existence is given form by serial ordeals. Unlike Odysseus, however, whose forming ordeals are all stops along the way of his *nostos*, the modern Handy Man has a tenuous relationship with his home culture. In fact, the purpose of his handiness is the extension of his mastery to new terrains. Even when his survival and the survival of others is at stake, the Handy Man invents a solution that will extend both the power of his tools and his own dominance over them. Whereas Homer's Odysseus is driven to return to his wife and son, the modern Handy Man is at home only in the restless practice of his skills. He is a *professional* handyman.

THE FERTILE CORPSE

The Fertile Corpse is the scene of the Handy Man's performance. It is usually not represented in human form, but as a region with strongly displaced qualities of feminine reproduction. It is fertile, because the Handy Man's manipulations induce it to yield bounty, ranging from sustaining food and natural resources to more intangible yields. It is a corpse because it is found to be insentient, the residue of a distributed life-force that has no consciousness. The Handy Man is able (indeed, it is required of him) to make this unconscious feminine body into a responsive, productive field.

The femininity of the fertile corpse is generally underscored by metaphors that associate it with natural processes, indicating a supersensible link with female reproduction: fertility of the soil, childbirth, analogical topography mimicking female bodies, association with feminine allure, "virgin land."[13] Its deadness is a special kind: a living death, a limbo in which the Fertile Corpse lacks the power and consciousness to affect the world outside itself. It is ontologically isolated from contact with "civil" worlds (societies that operate by familiar social rules). It cannot — or will not — communicate with the outside; and when its fertile powers are released by the Handy Man's technological manipulation, the corpse has no control over its products. It is, therefore, neither free nor able to articulate its desire; it is essentially a producing machine coded as feminine. It is the psychomythicized form of *resource*.

The Handy Man's relation to this resource body is complex. To make the Fertile Corpse productive is the object of the Handy Man's quest and mythic function. It is, one might say, the generalized form of the Grail appropriate for ages of scientific exploration and discovery. It has its historically concrete origins in the objects of colonial ideology. It is important to note here that the Fertile Corpse is a manifestation of the female principle without social identity, and so contrasts quite directly with the last archetype of our list, the Wife at Home. The latter, who is always abandoned for longer or shorter periods, or otherwise remains on the margins, is a character with the same quasi-mimetic embodiment as the Handy Man. She is a social human, and hence within familiar limits as a woman. Therefore, the Wife at Home manifests some degree of resistance to the Handy Man's operations, and a certain self-contained gravity from which the Handy Man escapes. The Fertile Corpse represents female essences (viewed, of course, with the eyes of phallocracy) isolated from the limits and irritations of defined human personality and embodiment. It survives, and with technical help flourishes, as natural feminine energy, because it is prevented from manifesting itself in human form. In gothic adventures such as Haggard's *She*, where the Corpse takes a human shape and displays agency, it has the powers associated with divinity, powers that may obstruct or entirely thwart the powers of the Handy Man.[14]

A given work may emphasize the fertility of the Corpse, constructing it as fantastically lush, like Crusoe's Caribbean island, the Hidden Valley of Kukuanaland in *King Solomon's Mines*, the generation spaceship of Aldiss's *Non-Stop*, or the greenhouse space stations of Douglas Trumbull's *Silent Running*. Alternatively, it may emphasize the deadness, placing the action in Lost Valleys of the Dead, mining colonies on the Moon, wastelands, trash planets, derelict spaceships, the void of space. In all such wasted zones, there are usually hidden resources that are especially important for the Handy Man's project or that of his culture. Further, the resource does not have to be material (that is, an aspect of physical nature); it can also be intellectual, even spiritual, an aspect of second nature, a code, a mainframe, the cyberspace matrix, or virtuality itself.

THE WILLING SLAVE

The Willing Slave is most familiar in the form of *Crusoe*'s Friday. This agent mediates for the Handy Man by extending the power he manifests in raw form over the Fertile Corpse to human beings that are barely distinct from surrounding nature in their level of civil and technical development. The Willing Slave is the medium of social development. Its most overt form is the myth of the colonized subaltern unreservedly appreciative of its colonization by the higher powers represented by the Handy Man. The Willing Slave is generally male; in this fundamentally phallocratic mythology, he is differentiated from the feminine fertility of the Corpse. He accepts the domination, or guardianship, of the Handy Man, in part to enjoy his protection against the forces of nature and the Shadow Mage, and in part to *learn* to use the Handy Man's techniques and science (cognition), in order to consolidate a sense of autonomous identity and to aid the Master's further extension of his power. The selfhood of the Willing Slave is, of course, a subset of his Master's, and will not extend beyond the boundaries that the Handy Man inscribes. But he is independently conscious to the degree that he can learn higher rationality, and willingly choose his subaltern position. So "natural" is his original state that the Willing Slave does not lose characteristics that distinguish him from the Handy Man master. He cannot occupy a masterly position. Even if he should come close, his natural difference will necessarily assert itself via a myth of racial, ethnic, or class inferiority (or "naturalness"), or it will be noted as a subversion of the system by the narrative itself.

The fact that the Handy Man requires the Willing Slave implies that direct technical mastery of material nature has its limits. The Willing Slave is the figure in which the technical instrumentality that leads to mastery over inert nature is extended to human beings. We might think of it as the primitive, zero-degree form of a myth of colonial labor. The produce of the Fertile Corpse, whether in the form of natural resources or ideas, must be distributed and reproduced, leaving the Handy Man free to solve new problems and devise new techniques. The Willing Slave thus takes the Master's part against the feminine, and against the obstructing forces of counterrationality, while being unable — and for the most part unwilling (perhaps precisely *because* he is unable) — to become free of the nature/culture regime established by the Handy Man Master.[15]

THE SHADOW MAGE

The Shadow Mage is the embodied antagonist of the Handy Man's project. In this function, the obstructor manifests archetypal qualities in direct dialectical resistance to the Handy Man's. The Mage competes with the Handy Man for the Fertile Corpse and the Willing Slave, and may have a historically prior claim on them. He is a Mage, in that he operates through superstition and irrational tradition; indeed, despite the essential commitment of the adventure model to instrumental rationality, the Shadow Mage's superstition often proves to have some validity in the function's diegetic reality. The Mage often displays a control over the conditions of nature that is similar in many respects to the technological control of the Handy Man. His power comes from a *local* understanding of the prerational forces of magic or mind control, and is consequently a manifestation of a world interpretation — in fact, a form of rationality—of more ancient pedigree than technoscience.

The agent is a *Shadow* Mage because he is, in this deployment of archaic rationality and magical instrumentality, an inverted reflection of the Handy Man himself. He is often shadowy, "dark," fearsome, evil. He may, on the other hand, be entirely free of such moral ascriptions, and merely opaque, operating according to rational rules and principles that derive from a "parallel universe" inaccessible to the Handy Man perhaps precisely because of the latter's investment in technoscientific materialism. The Shadow Mage is the most dramatically attractive of the functions, because he represents the unconscious, as it were, of the dominant rationality represented in the modern adventure myth. Depending on the degree of his demonization, his defeat may bring the pleasure of mastery over a fearsome opponent, or the relief of having emergent doubts about the validity of the technological worldview successfully repressed again. In ancient fairy tales, it is not uncommon for the antagonist-dragon to be revealed to be the hero's brother, a shaman who has taken on the dragon form; in such tales, the hero must use against his opponent some tactic that the opponent itself uses, thus binding the competing forces to the same knowledge. Similarly, the Handy Man and the Shadow Mage are expected to compete in increasingly intense and direct conflicts, pitting the techniques of magic against the magic of technology.

The SEVEN BEAUTIES *of* SCIENCE FICTION

I use the phrase *magic of technology* deliberately. The necessary irony of the modern adventure myth is that the Handy Man gains his dominance ultimately by representing his superior technique as a form of superior *magic*. Technique is removed from the discursive context of universal reason, and is firmly embedded in the context of supernatural power, with the Handy Man as its controlling shaman. Thus, in the end, the Handy Man is *not* legitimated by demonstrating that there is no supernature, that only scientific reason is accessible to all human beings (that would imply that the Willing Slave should be elevated from a mediating position to direct agency). Instead, technology is assimilated to magic, legitimacy derives from shamanic displays of power, and the Handy Man assimilates the powers of the Shadow Mage. This assimilation may be complete and unquestioned (as in *Crusoe*), but it may be ambiguous, leaving the audience to wonder whether the technology has assimilated the magic, or vice versa. In any case, the Shadow Mage's defeat cannot seal the destruction of the source of his power, any more than the defeat of the Handy Man would indicate the utter defeat of instrumental rationality. The Shadow Mage's defeat may in fact merely repress the forces that — precisely because they thrive in obscurity, secrecy, and the unconscious — may return over and over again.

The gender and racial position of the Shadow Mage is more ambiguous and free than those of the earlier functions. Given the archaic stratum of the Mage's origin, the historical hegemony of the European Handy Man and his racial and gender domination is sometimes threatened not only by the counter-rationality of magic, but also by the supernatural authority of suppressed genders and races. The Mage may well appear in the form of a Sorceress or a Witch and/or an aboriginal shaman or king. In terms of a politics of the unconscious, the lines are clear in such cases, and the defeat of these magical antagonists is expected to function as the defeat of pre-European and pre-patriarchal archaic powers by legitimate modern ones. In gender terms, however, interesting questions emerge from the relationship of a female Mage to the Fertile Corpse. The clear, schematic gender domination attained by the Handy Man is opposed in such cases by less familiar relations of power between the Female Power and the alienated fertile ground. This may take the form of a mother-daughter relationship (the Mage may play either role) or it may, as in *She*'s goddess/wife, manifest a schizophrenic oscillation between roles. Even in racial terms, the competition between the European and the Other may take complex forms, as in *King Solomon's Mines* (1885), where the population of Kukuanaland, descendants of the biblical Lost Tribes, is of more ancient and formidable pedigree than that of the European Handy Men.

The Shadow Mage's source of power is the boundary between nature and technique. Whereas the Handy Man's technique is at first ostensibly pure Cartesian-Baconian rationally practical supremacy over inert nature, the Mage's technique relies on an animated and sentient nature. The antiscientific attitude of the Mage is to a great extent an expression of resistant nature's purposes. Because this "bad nature" has power, it cannot be treated as mere superstition. In some cases, however, the Mage function is filled not by a being with special access to archaic nature, but to second nature.

THE TOOL TEXT

The Tool Text is the set of technical devices and documents that the Handy Man requires to achieve his dominance. In most modern adventure tales, these are usually objects ready at hand for use, sometimes transformed into ingenious devices through the wit of the *polypragmatos* hero: the stakes, sheep, ships, and bow of Odysseus, Crusoe's store of shipwrecked objects, the firearms used with obsessive regularity in both fictive and real accounts of African exploration, and so forth. They may also be texts: maps, secret manuscripts, encrypted messages, operating instructions, *The First Encyclopedia of Tlön*. Together, these tools and techniques constitute the Handy Man's panoply, the armor, weapons, vehicles, lore, and facts required for the colonial hero's victory over the Shadow Mage.

In his simplest form, the Handy Man controls the instruments of power. But the Shadow Mage may have a parallel toolkit, or secret access to the Handy Man's. The modern adventurer's tools are means for the subjugation of nature, especially primitive human nature, and consequently easily appear as quasi-magical fetish objects. Often, the Handy Man may have to appropriate the tool text of the Shadow, thereby absorbing his charisma into the magic of science. Even more unstable than its potentially ambiguous relation to its wielders, the Tool Text may prove to have so much inherent power that it begins to manifest the equivalent of will and agency in its own right.

In modernizing Western culture the epic of the *Robinsonade* becomes more and more a matter of the interfusion of self and engineering. The nature to be dominated becomes increasingly distant and depersonalized, *dis-enchanted*, as the tools of improvement become increasingly intimate prostheses of the adventuring ego. While the hero of the ancient adventure tale described by Bakhtin essentially has no qualities other than his fidelity and courage, the modern adventure hero is increasingly married to his expertise. The captain of sea adventures is nothing without his ship, as Edison is nothing without his workshop and inventions, Marlow without his river boat, the Time Traveller without his Time Machine, Gibson's Case without his console. What makes them modern adventure heroes is their almost instinctual power to deploy specific kinds of technoscientific knowledge. In many ways, this resembles cowboys' generic knowledge of horses and firearms, or detectives', lawyers', and doctors' arcane gnosis in their respective popular paradigms. In modern adventure, however, the hero commands practical knowledge that the sciences codify in abstraction. The modern adventure plot requires that the textual truths of the sciences, mathematics, practical engineering, anthropology, and so on, be available — by education or by instinct — to the hero, for whom the sciences are a warehouse of potential solutions to extremely risky, decisive (both personally and culturally) situations. The hero's success in enacting these truths-as-techniques extends not only his personal charisma, but the *mana* of his technoscientific Western intrusion force.

As the toolkit becomes increasingly a part of the Handy Man's identity, it takes on more and more of the qualities of the hero himself. Most important among these is the projection of *intention*. At first, the tools only augment the hero's power, but the greater the power, the more the question arises: for what purpose? To what extent does the power reside in the wielder, and to what extent in the tool? In the course of technoscientific development, the tool text becomes increasingly personalized, culminating in our age in the animation of computer-graphical space, described in detail by Scott Bukatman as "terminal identity."[16] At this point, the relations shift abruptly, and the heroic ego wielding world- and value-transforming instrumentality confronts a technology transformed into autonomous agency, capable of far greater material transformations (with attendant ethical transformations) than human beings.

THE WIFE AT HOME

The Wife at Home appears on the scene relatively little in this model. Her role is all the more important, however. The Wife at Home is what she appears to be, the flesh-and-blood woman who is married or betrothed to the Handy Man hero. She is left behind when the Handy Man embarks on his adventures. Alternatively, she may appear as a future wife, to be taken at the end of the particular adventure. In either case, she inhabits the margins of the tale and its geography. She is often a modern Penelope, faithfully awaiting her husband's return. Unlike Penelope, however, she is rarely an object of erotic or power desire. She may be rich, and thus able to provide the capital most valued by the adventurer. She may be dignified and admirable, but beauty and allure are not ascribed to her. She is the guardian and manager of domestic stability for the Handy Man, who has neither the opportunity nor the inclination to enjoy it, and yet for whom this protected and unenjoyed intimate sphere appears to be mythically necessary. The Handy Man's relationship to technological rationality is linked not only to individual ingenuity, to problem-solving on the local scale, but also to the extended civilization of technical problem-solving and wealth production familiar as the Handy Man's home culture. As a culture hero, the Handy Man must have a stake in his culture — most firmly rooted in the wife at home.

The Wife at Home is defined primarily by negation. She is fixed in place, and fixed in her subservience. She is thus a female counterpart to the Willing Slave, without the dramatic need for protection from her culture of origin (as she putatively enjoys this protection fully in her role as wife), or the scope for learning technique. She represents rooted tradition, the foot of the compass that does not move. She may well be literally fertile, bearing many children, or her fertility may be displaced in the form of tangible wealth. In any case, she provides the Handy Man with cultural value, without his having to be on the scene to cultivate it himself. His marriage to her is the social capital needed to hedge his cultural ventures, and he continues to reap interest even when he's off the scene. She represents one half of the feminine in the modern adventure model, the other being the Fertile Corpse. Thus femaleness is split into the essential, mythological function of fertility/nature/inertia/unconsciousness/ "natural capital" on the one hand, and female social roles/domesticity/conventional social mediation/cultural capital, on the other. By splitting the two aspects of patriarchally conceived femaleness into two, they each can be disempowered by instrumentality, which is associated with male potency and dominance. Inert nature can be manipulated without the mess surrounding dominance over human subjects. The bond-spouse can be marginalized, enclosed within the confines of domesticity, and left to hold the place of the Handy Man, protecting his stake in civilized culture (the ultimate locus of world power) without agency of her own.

That being said, the Wife at Home can be as interesting in her artistic deformations as the Shadow Mage. Because one of her distinguishing and limiting qualities vis-à-vis the Fertile Corpse is that she is a living person, with an individuality that has limited exploitability, she can easily become a fulcrum for satire, either of the conventional home society or even of modern adventure itself. Also, because she is off the scene for most, and perhaps even all, of the action, a certain unconscious mystery accrues to her, linked to displacements of the other functions. The contrast between the Sorceress and the Wife at Home may be schematically dualistic; but it may, given the mystery acquired through sheer absence, imply subtle connections. The Willing Slave and the house slave may, despite easy similarities, inspire subtle differences. Most of all, the relationship between the Fertile Corpse and the Wife at Home generates imaginative tensions; in this case, the two functions are widely separated aspects of one invisible image. Once the relationship comes to consciousness, through analogies and correspondences, the very question of why such a separation can be made comes to the foreground.

Because the wife at home is the only nonexotic, familiar human archetype next to the Handy Man, she has a certain concrete gravity that contains within it connotations that the writer cannot remove. He may try, again like Defoe and Haggard, simply to have her dead, and so to be a real corpse. But if any of her female power survives her — a child, an inheritance, a memory of love, even a memory of bitching anger — her corpse too may be fertile, and less manageable than earth.[17]

Inverted Adventure: The Gothic

The relationship between the modern adventure tale and the Gothic is close and ambivalent. In some respects, the Gothic critiques the modern adventure paradigm, while in others it continues it in inverted form. The inversions affect many levels beyond narrative design, including the representation of ideology, gender interests and psychology, orientation to audience, and the hierarchies of social power. Where modern adventure narrates the projection of discovery and invention further and further away from the home base, the metropole, and the "motherland," into exotic venues, the Gothic imagines the subject position of the victim of these cognitive interests. The field of values is reversed, as the heroic masculine exploratory ego is reimagined from the position of the assailed and relatively helpless female/feminized object of exploration and manipulation. The Gothic inverts the dream world of thrilling travels among wonders into nightmares of abduction, imprisonment, and victimization by barely controllable archaic passions. The Gothic, moreover, changes the scene from the far-from-home at the edge of experience to the home itself, which is viewed, in true grotesque fashion, as a place where intimate consolations conceal deep-hidden metamorphoses and corruptions.

The adventure form has always employed dark romance elements. Readers have always expected adventure heroes and heroines to be abducted, threatened with execution and rape, held in trances, and manipulated by monsters and dark technologies. These are the risks that give adventure its sublime horizon. Odysseus had to free himself from the monsters and enchantresses. Heliodorus's young heroes and heroines were constantly plotted against, captured by pirates and bandits, interred in caves, nearly sacrificed, and on the run. In the modern adventure's paradigm, the hero is expected to suffer some form of bondage and victimization as a constitutive part of his *Bildung;* through captivity and enslavement he learns vital lessons and is given an opportunity to use his initiative for self-liberation. With the Gothic, the dominant subject position changes and is charged with gender resistance: dominant male aggressors assail, assault, abduct, and bind generally female victims. These attacks invariably involve complex plots concocted by the machinating males, and forcible journeys into dark zones where female or feminized victims are terrorized by demonic technique. The Gothic turns the adventure form inward toward personal psychology and familiar, uncanny settings, tacitly critiquing the values of initiative, exploration, and discovery associated with modern adventure. Its setting is "a world where initiative is too often a monopoly of the bad."[18] In a sense, the Gothic is the hypertrophy of the darkest aspects of the adventure form, and the repudiation of its ideology of experience and conquest.

In both the "masculine"/demonic and "feminine"/resistant modes of the Gothic, the polarities of the adventure paradigm's character functions are reversed.[19] The Handy Man, who in modern adventure embodies the qualities of the phallic subject acting on receptive natural objects or passive subjects, is replaced by the aggressive machinator, who directs his technical powers of deceit, intricate projects, and secret mechanics to violate the purity of natural, innocent young persons. The Fertile Corpse's niche is occupied by the enchanted castle, house, or abbey. This central agonistic place is no longer the unconscious producer of resources, but the mysteriously conscious *reproducer of curses;* it is sterile, but animate, a conscious tomb incapable of innovation. The function of the Willing Slave, whose help is essential to the beneficial propagation of the hero's power, is inverted in the Gothic into the zombie, a slave who is emphatically incapable of free will (like *Dracula*'s Renfield) or of regaining goodness (like *The Monk's* Matilda). The Shadow Mage becomes the thaumaturge capable of doing battle with the dark Handy Man; like the modern adventure's Mage, he has powers similar to that of his adversary, synthesizing magical and scientific techniques (epitomized by Van Helsing). The Gothic Tool Text consists of the rich thesaurus of formulaic devices that the villain and exorcist have at their command, ranging from knowledge of labyrinths, sliding panels, trapdoors, magic lanterns, secret codes and messages, and hermetic lore, to animated portraits and statues. Whatever other failings the Handy Man villain may have, he usually has intelligence and gnosis to spare. The Wife at Home in the inverted world of Gothic is the heroine who is precisely *not* at home. Where the modern adventure world requires a secure, domestic intimate sphere to stabilize the narrative's wanderings, the Gothic is predicated on the destabilization of that home world. Its primary focus is on the young woman who would be, in an ideal world, the perfect Wife at Home. As the rightful carrier of her patrimony, she embodies domestic order. But because the Gothic constructs a world penetrated by adventurous demonic powers, it is impossible for her to be at home or to be found. She will be detoured, kidnapped, imprisoned, and violated. Nor can her eventual marriage to a weak male protagonist restore the values of bourgeois domesticity. Once the reader has recognized that she has been the victim of modern adventure, there are no safe places left.[20]

The upshot of these deformations is that the gothic presents adventure as a violent threat by *bad will*, which uses technique as its tool against *good nature*. Nature itself is sometimes an active protagonist in the Gothic; its psychic mediation makes it a *dea ex anima* (like Jane Eyre's moon or the Ancient Mariner's albatross), and consequently a resistant inversion of the Fertile Corpse. When it is threatened, repudiated, or violated, sublime recuperation is blocked, and the grotesque takes over. The Gothic has always cultivated the appearance of exaggeratedly physical phenomena that change shape, mutate, and escape from rational explanations. The stage is occupied by freakish humans, bizarre physical qualities, boundary-violating phenomena, and eventually the threat of a world in which hunting the flesh overwhelms interests of the spirit. In vampire fiction especially, the vampire promises experiences of the sublime — eternity and infinity — but delivers a grotesque visceral economy of blood and flesh.

The Gothic presents adventure from the perspective of feminized victims. Adventure's redeemed world of technique is transformed into a cursed world of domination. The extension of reason to colonial labor is presented as the enslavement of strangers by evil will. The extension of technosocial power is viewed as the invasion of the body and the intimate sphere. Yet the Gothic need not be (and indeed rarely is) completely critical of adventure. The assailed female subject in Gothic is sometimes saved by a good adventurer or a Mage; that is, a Handy Man whose skill and courage are directed primarily toward rescuing the endangered one. Alternatively, already with Radcliffe the heroine is exhorted to resist by becoming an adventure heroine in her own right, learning to use tools and techniques against the would-be violator. In this way she protects herself by appropriating, or at least learning, the powers of her adversary. For the most part, the adventurer-heroine has no need to extend her technical powers beyond the restoration of her own sphere. But as women in reality become more accustomed to negotiating public social problems, the female Gothic protagonist is expected to appropriate some phallic power for herself, as mere restoration of the original female-natural conditions is insufficient to protect her from future assaults. In sf especially, we see the fusion of the sublime and the grotesque, the Gothic adventure, in which the female subject is expected to become a Handy Man.

Adventure writers in the nineteenth-century increasingly mixed Gothic elements into their fictions. As real colonial adventures involved struggles with indigenous societies who were both dangerous to the colonists and highly organized in their "uncivilized perversity," Gothic tropes became increasingly useful for heightening, as well as taming, the physical and psychological perils of adventure. By the second half of the century, "naive" adventure uncomplicated by fantastic Gothic or utopian elements is restricted to juvenile literature.

The Excepted Adventure: Utopia

We need briefly to consider one more tale form in the adventure cluster: the utopia. Like the Gothic, the utopia is both a critique of the adventure tale, and its continuation — in its case, in a direction opposite the Gothic's. Both genres exist in nascent form in the classical adventure romance: the Gothic in the perennial motifs of enslavement and abduction of the romantic leads by pirates, brigands, witches, and Turks; the utopia in sojourns on Blessed Isles and in the fairy tale–like establishment of unassailed marriage and family at the end of the ordeals. Utopias, too, are at a mysterious distance from the known world, either in the imagination or in uncharted or misleadingly mapped regions. While most of the discursive emphasis in utopias is on their social and intellectual organization, their narrative vehicles are often adventure tales. Traditional utopias are framed by mock journeys requiring great endurance and persistence. Their greatest mark of difference from the reader's reality is their purity, their freedom from the corruptions of reality. Thus they are hard to reach; they are protected from the contamination of casual tourism by great obstacles: either natural ones like Shangri-La's Himalayas; artificial ones like the trenches of Utopia; or virtual ones, like the dream zones through which one must travel to Mercier's Paris in 2445, Morris's future London, and to Marge Piercy's Mattapoiset in *Woman on the Edge of Time*.

Utopias famously resist dramatic adventures; indeed, one of their jobs is to depict good commonwealths that resist historical mutability. There is very little room for the restless libertarian *polypragmatos* in them. Utopias, however, do not just happen; they are not founded by gods or elves. They are distinguished from idylls and fantastic locations in that they are by definition products of reason. They were constructed by rational labor; if they were not, they could not even pretend to be models. Thus all willing utopians (and who among them are not?) are proven Handy Men. They have applied the best possible ideas and materials in the best possible way. There is no more need for exploitation of virgin nature, nor for wives at home; if there once was, it is not a story that utopians like to tell. Shadow Mages are also outside the utopian tale: other perhaps than we ourselves. James Scott notes that revolutionary spacetimes and island spaces of utopias accurately reflect reality; it is in revolutionary and insular colonial regimes that the handy masters possess the most power to remake societies in their desired image.[21]

Adventure of the Space Age

Our template, along with its diverse critical subversions and deformations, delimits the narrative universe of discourse of the modern adventure cluster. The folktale character of the paradigm is evident. Michael Nerlich attests to its plebeian popularity, noting that *Crusoe* was wildly popular not with the actual entrepreneurial-adventurer class of Defoe's time, but with the petit bourgeoisie and proletariat who were at the time excluded from capitalist adventures.[22] The *Robinsonade* easily absorbed the myths of Prometheus and Faust, both of which center on acquiring knowledge of the secrets of the material universe. Here is the narrative template of Enlightenment development in the world: the individual projector improves himself against the forces of superstition, and thus proves the global validity of the improvement of an inert, fallow resource base (which includes its cheap indigenous labor) through technoscientific means, and effects a transformation of values at the leading edge of history in the direction of liberal, scientific rationality. This tale of justified technological management of nature becomes the dominant legitimation myth of the imperial expansion of technologically rational societies of the West, and consequently the plot currency of Western expansionism.[23] Its dominance becomes so great that critique of it generally takes the form of *détournements* of particular functions, in order to gain purchase on the myth-form and subvert it from within. Each such subversion influences the ideological charge of the fiction in question. The overarching pattern remains, even with these mutations, if only as a trace; the pattern has been repeated in so many versions on so many occasions that it has a megatextual gravity, a ground bass that continues to vibrate and signify as a hegemonic myth of technological societies, however accurately and passionately it is shown to be established on exploitative and destructive premises. Each *détournement* implies a specific critique developed as a counterstory. Thus as the folktale of colonial adventure mutates and metamorphoses in the course of history, Gothic and utopian elements appear inside the edifice, destabilizing, dislocating, but never disengaging with it. We see it employed for satire by Swift, critiqued and romanticized by Smollett and Scott, gothicized by Coleridge, Mary Shelley, Poe, and Haggard, eulogized by Kipling, and radically deconstructed by Melville, Conrad, and Woolf.

It should not be surprising that the modern adventure paradigm had so much currency among practitioners of artistic fiction in the West at the end of the nineteenth century and into the twentieth; it is the myth-form of exploration and colonial conquest. The more familiar the Euro-Atlantic audiences became with the true conditions of imperialism, however, the less tenable the modern adventure paradigm became. As the subjects of colonial administrations became increasingly visible to their mother countries, increasing pressure was put on the dehumanizing mythic stereotypes. The enormous gulf between the Handy Man's own civilization and the putatively pure nature of the slave, the corpse, and the Mage narrowed. Racialism aggressively held onto the myths, but the Handy Man's power was visibly slipping. This diminution was in no small part because the extension of technology to the administration of social life, and the ever-tightening social network of communications and transportation technologies, were rationalizing the wild zones that had been the domains of the Handy Man's projects. Thus the mythology of the individualist explorer-engineer that had thrived in the time of Rhodes, de Lesseps, and Verne, lost its ground when they, too, were swept up into the network of collective administrative rationality. The blowback of imperialism onto the metropolis inspired many of the high modernists to critique the modern adventure paradigm in interiorized, psychological adventures. *Portrait of a Lady* (1882), *Passage to India* (1924), *The Great Gatsby* (1925), *To the Lighthouse* (1927), *Absalom, Absalom* (1936), and countless other high modernist fictions used displaced versions of the modern adventure form for ostensibly "domestic" and apolitical purposes.

The modern adventure paradigm has lost much of its allure in elite fiction and in fiction associated with exploration. It still dominates, however, in popular technoscientific writing, and not only in sf. The U.S. Moon missions, for example, and indeed the entire space program, have been cast relentlessly as real-world versions of the modern adventure myth. Already in its founding invocations, such as President Kennedy's address at Rice University in 1961, challenging the population to support a moon landing within a decade, space flight was envisioned as an act of collective pioneering. The individual Handy Men of yore had been gathered into a national collective, representing the vanguard of the entire species.[24] In the Soviet Union, the development of space technology had been driven from the outset by the Tsiolokovskian mythology of cosmism, which infused it with a heroic aura even when it clearly served the interests of the Soviet war machine.[25] In the United States, there had been no such general political myth of space; rocket heroism had been the domain of the rocket clubs and pulp sf. When faced with the challenge posed first by Sputnik in 1957, and then Gagarin's manned flight in 1961, the U.S. response had to be built from the ground up, as a grandiose just-in-time public relations campaign sold by men who had little interest or understanding of space, rather than a well-established element of state policy.[26] The United States joined the Soviet Union in conceiving of success in space technology as a propaganda display to other nations of superior ideological control of the future. The space program stimulated the full-fledged development of the technocratic security state, but even when the experts had taken over from the heroic populace, myths of personal adventure were continually employed to legitimate it, in the form of the astronautical Handy Man's struggle against first the dark Mages of Soviet technology, then the hostile environment of space itself.[27]

Constance Penley has written in *NASA/TREK* (1997) about the many ways in which the institutional mythology of NASA was influenced by *Star Trek*.[28] Even more important is the myth of the astronautical Handy Man, diffused throughout mass media, in a show of ideological myth-making of historical proportions. In news reports about the Moon mission, eulogies, spectacular treatments like Ron Howard's film *Apollo 13* (1995) and Tom Wolfe's *The Right Stuff* (1979), through the whole corpus of popular histories the paradigm is continually reheated.[29] The astronauts are the quintessential Handy Men, to the extent that they are even viewed as disorientingly automatic. They are shown lacking poetic imagination, for the most part, but they are the perfect, austere, self-sacrificing subjects of Enlightenment described by Horkheimer and Adorno in *Dialectic of Enlightenment* (1947). Their space vehicles are the mediating forms between their own technical power and the inertia of the fertile corpse. Crusoe's ship was itself a product of technology, far beyond anything that Crusoe could construct himself. But once it is broken up in the wreck, its components and contents become the mediating materials for Crusoe's cultivation of the island. In the same way, the space rockets and, above all, the command module serve as both the tools and the products of conquest.

In the first Moon missions this liminal quality was rarely perceived. The particular fascination of the Apollo 13 mission lay in the fact that the technical infrastructure resisted dramatically its mere technical existence. Not unlike HAL in *2001*, the harshness and inertia of the purely physical resisted the project. Hence the attraction of the paradigm for the film version, *Apollo 13*. While early in the myth construction of space flight the emphasis had to be on the epic series of successes, reflecting the technologically guaranteed unity of U.S. society (of which the astronauts were the Handy Men exponents), by the time of Apollo 13 the naive version of the myth no longer compelled assent. The contest with nature was perceived to be internalized into the capsule itself, and the Handy Men had to demonstrate their handiness in very Crusoe-like ways, constructing life-saving devices out of the scraps left in the shipwreck.

The Moon is the quintessential fertile corpse. Generally referred to with the feminine pronoun, it is absolutely sterile, and yet the site of infinite possibility. Demanding immeasurably more labor and asceticism than Crusoe's island, the Moon is the occasion for the reproduction of technology without the aid of living nature. At the other end of the spectrum are the real wives at home, the astronauts' spouses, who are routinely displayed to observers as ideological artifacts, doing nothing while their husbands travel, other than waiting for them. They are shown in their Houston homes, with well-manicured families, surrounded by ideologically correct friends, offering the spectacle of the ideal U.S. middle-class house and neighborhood. In every respect they represent correctness, the ideal Penelopes for puritanical Odysseuses.[30]

The Willing Slaves number in the hundreds, even the thousands. They are all engineers and technicians in their own right, the professional colonial labor upon whom the projectile mission depends, but who can never hope to sail the spaceships themselves. Some smoke cigarettes, some are fat, some wear glasses — all are somehow tied to Earth by their physical nature. The illusion of the spectacle is that these slaves are somehow free men — but the mission will not permit even a word of criticism about Mission Control itself.

The Shadow Mage is perhaps the most interesting element in the Moon mission myth. The positivistic, administered conception of technoscience at the heart of the myth does not allow any other form of rationality to intrude in the mission world. The ideological purpose of the astronautical mythology was not only national, but technoscientific. The success of each space project demonstrated the steady, undramatic progress of American technology toward the "New Frontier" proclaimed by the Kennedy administration. Arguably, this version of the myth lacked the full charge of the sublime, as Nye implies, because the adventure lacked a clearly defined, visualizable oppositional figure.[31] The Soviet Union had long ago given up on Moon exploration. The Mage's position seemed empty, as if the Soviet style of sf, of "the struggle between the good and the better" had gained ascendancy in the United States as well.[32] The role of Mage was gradually supplied by the universe itself, in the role of entropy. The fatigue — of materials, of O-rings, of enthusiasm, of bureaucracy, and of will — gradually came to be seen as a force in its own right, undermining the project from within. The collapse of the space program after the *Challenger* accident merely articulated the drama. The search for a culprit to blame for the explosion came to rest on the lack of propelling energy. The greatest difficulty facing the space program, in the eyes of its engineers and administrators, is precisely the projection of fatigue.[33] It is telling that the United

States insisted strongly on the superannuation of the Soviet space station MIR, despite its usefulness for many kinds of experimentation, because it was too old and funky to represent space research. The Soviet cosmonauts, by contrast, working within a completely different space-program mythology, were attached to MIR because it took on the role of a kind of home.[34] It was, however, clearly not the type of home one keeps in Houston, USA.

From Adventure to SF

I have argued elsewhere that sf has gradually taken on a role of cultural mediation similar to the one held by bourgeois social realism and adventure fiction.[35] As Benedict Anderson has described it, the realistic novel helped to establish the discourse in which the transformation from agrarian, feudal, local cultures to metropolitan, modernized, national ones could be imagined by the bourgeois publics drawn into its imaginative orbit.[36] In tandem with its real-world shadow, newspaper journalism, the realistic novel provided models of language and action, of plausible behaviors and goals, through which modernizing audiences could imagine that they recognized, if not themselves as they actually were, then the trajectories of their desires, the ordeals and compensations of becoming a national commune out of local and ethnic ones.

With the imperialist projects initiated by the most developed of these modern nations, reading publics required corresponding models for their metamorphoses from nations to would-be global hegemons. Anderson focuses on the production and consolidation of nation-states, and consequently pays little attention to the subject-construction and mediation involved in the mixed goals of Western imperialist projects that tried simultaneously to consolidate the cultural forces of the metropolis, and also to harness them for the projection of soft, cultural power. Thus the mediating role of the bourgeois novel in terms of the *territorial* national imaginary is inextricably connected with imperialism, which strives for the consolidation of the dispersed constellation of the *imperial* nation (explicit in France's *mission civilisatrice*, implicit in Britain's and the United States' "white man's burden"). This process often celebrated precisely those violent energies and inequalities that the bourgeois novel and codes of civil compromise strove to tamp. It is in this sense that we can say that modern adventure fiction mediated imperialism as the bourgeois novel mediated nationalism; and that these two labors were performed simultaneously, as the inner consolidation and outer projection were mutually, dialectically defining, their energies sometimes coinciding, sometimes colliding, and most often energizing each other through mutual denial.[37]

The suicidal exhaustion of the imperialist world-system in World War I revealed the degree to which national political power had become a function of technology's power to correlate every aspect of social existence. In Rathenau's civil and military mobilization of Germany, modern political elites discerned how quickly and thoroughly industrial projects could be directed, managed, and synchronized; how invention and discovery could be institutionalized; how more and more aspects of social life could be brought under the umbrella of technosocial organization, at ever-accelerating pace; and how the political charge of these processes could be concealed and sublimated into the ideology of technological development — all inspired, designed, and overseen by scientific knowledge directed toward large-scale technological applications. In a word, technoscience.[38] The conversion of politics into matters of technique had begun with the need to find solutions to the imperial problems without challenging the political legitimacy of domination. This need became central to all conceptions of the high modernist state.

In the process, technoscience coalesced into a semiautonomous sphere adjunct to overtly political ideology. It did not matter ultimately to its institutions which form of government ensured the penetration and transformation of material existence by scientific materialism, so long as its power was stipulated. Soviet Stakhanovism and the Five-Year Plans, public works of the Nazi war economy, the New Deal and Marshall Plan reconstruction agendas, the Soviet and U.S. space programs — all were alibis for technological modernization. Indeed, technoscience develops as an envelope for political power in the twentieth century. Modern science has inspired faith independent of partisan political commitments, preventing most critiques within political elites, indeed even the effort to find alternative terms of discourse. An invisible imaginary imperial regime takes shape, one for which national borders are secondary obstacles. It is an Enlightened empire of shared commitments to instrumentality, justified by its promise of ever-greater rationality and material abundance in the future, a future in which new ideas consistently produce new realities that consistently produce new resources, managed by technoscientific means, stimulated by technoscientific innovation and discovery, sustained by technoscientific machinery, and heading off the potentially catastrophic consequences of its practices through internal critique, new invention, and new discovery — the actually existing science fiction of a technoscientific regime on the verge of global consolidation and expansion into space.

This imaginary utopian regime, ostensibly nonpolitical (as it is shared by, and independent of, what is conceived to be politics on the ground) and international in fact, has facilitated the extension of capitalism into its current global phase, in which the uneasy balance of nations and international institutions serves the interests of the most highly developed powers, the heirs of earlier imperialism.[39] Flexible boundaries and transnational flows—of capital, populations, techniques, and cultures[40]—and the constant transformation of human bodies and subjectivities via world-scale experiments in technoscientific rationalization are putatively intended to maximize efficiency, comfort, and security. In reality, they facilitate unfettered capitalism's inherently destructive and mutagenic dynamism, which turns every sphere of experience, from fashion to labor, into commodities, and hence encourages change as constant, fever-pitched, and universal just-in-time revisions of every social and psychological human relationship. Perennial apocalypse and constant crisis (the most dependable of all generators of wealth); an avalanche of novums and discordances; a maximum of sublime and grotesque fascinations to prevent routines, habits, and stable loyalties from taking root—all create a state of perpetual challenge that only yet-to-be-imagined technoscientific solutions can address.

If the bourgeois social novel mediated for nationality, and adventure fiction for imperialism, sf has become a central mediating literary institution for this imaginary empire of technoscience. In sf, the adventure cluster's paradigm changes simply and radically, as the Handy Man's utopian projects and the gothic anxieties about it no longer struggle mainly with resisting nature face-to-face, using the Tool Text as its advantage. The Tool Text has now established the relevant conditions of possibility. The universe now can be imagined as engineerable by technoscience. Humanity no longer leans down to pick up the Tool Text; it inhabits it. SF's adventure cluster tells the playful tale, in an enormous range of attitudes and registers, of humanity's uncertain, undefined, and evolving relationship with its own second nature, a technoscientific empire in which first nature exists on sufferance, as long as it remains useful.

THE SF HANDY MAN

The sf Handy Man of Vernean sf, the heir of the Saint-Simonian engineers' utopia, was emphatically Robinsonian. Verne revered *Crusoe* and *Swiss Family Robinson* (1852), and his oeuvre is laden with allusions to them. Arguably the majority of his works draw on Defoe's template, either for a solitary bricoleur-genius like Nemo or Robur, or for a microcosmic society engaged in Robinsonian self-discovery through reconstruction, as in *The Mysterious Island* (1874). The ideological model that pitted grand scientific ventures against the ancient resistance of nature and social inertia was modeled simultaneously on actual grand-scale engineering projects, like de Lesseps's Suez Canal, and by Verne's novels of the manipulation of time and space. The "man against nature" template remained dominant for sf wherever modernization was seen as the improvement of nature by the collective application of technology. In Soviet Russia, it became not only the sole permissible variant of sf, but also of the flagship genre of socialist realism, the production novel.[41] Its influence survived even the mass disillusionment with technology in Japan after World War II. Komatsu's enormously popular *Japan Sinks* is essentially a Vernean tragedy, in which nature proves too great, and the heroism of the Handy Men protagonists is underscored by their inevitable failure.

In the United States, where the cult of the inventor had formed around Edison, the *Robinsonade* was quickly succeeded by the *Edisonade*.[42] Wells's Gothic critique of the Handy Man tradition, *The War of the Worlds*, was immediately answered by Garrett Serviss's *Edison's Conquest of Mars* (1898). Wells's heresy against progress, that humanity survived by chance adaptation, would not go unchallenged. This template of the engineer-inventor hero dominated the fiction cultivated by Gernsback and Campbell, reaching its fullest expression in Heinlein, for whom handiness was the single most important quality needed for progress and democracy. Later, ironic currents like cyberpunk actually expanded this Heinleinian idealization into a vision of collective technical transformation, as in Bruce Sterling's dueling Mechanics and Shapers, heirs of humanity who have transformed themselves into near-immortals via prosthetics and genetic engineering, respectively.[43] Advances in the technical manipulation of basic materials in different sciences—the atomic nucleus, the germ plasm, neurons, silicon, the nanocosm—routinely fuel new versions of science-fictional engineering, both in the genre and in actuality.

The position of the Handy Man as the ideological core of sf meant that even in critical sf it was this character function that was the first to be problematized. The mad scientist had, of course, been a staple of the Gothic line since Mary Shelley and Poe, succeeded by Stevenson's Dr. Jekyll, Verne's world-destabiliziers (Nemo, Robur, Begum), and Wells's Moreau and Griffin. In Russia, the engineer had been established as a heroic revolutionary archetype through Tsiolkovsky's rocket-science cosmism and Bogdanov's Martian utopias, but the genius-engineer also became the pivot of anti-utopian sf in the tragic D-503 of Zamyatin's *We*, and eventually the villainous threat to Communist order in Alexey Tolstoy's *Engineer Garin's Hyperboloid Ray*.[44]

Wells's introduction of Gothic anxiety into the engineers' positivist utopia was probably more significant than Shelley's. *Frankenstein*'s catastrophe leaves the world much as it was; the monster has no issue, and Victor has taken the secrets of carnal bricolage with him into the ice. Like Dr. Jekyll's chemistry, Shelley's mad science is essentially a parable with only moral consequences. Wells came to the subject fully aware that technology was transforming social existence radically, and that Handy Men were no longer *isolati* working in secret laboratories, but in enormous collective projects. They were producing consequences, and these would not vanish in the ice. In *The War of the Worlds*, the Handy Men are in fact the Martians, who embody the extreme development of our own handiness, and neither the journalist-narrator nor the human species can call upon any technoscientific advantages against them. In each of Wells's romances, the Handy Man protagonist is either a relatively detached observer (such as the Time Traveller, who, for all his brawling with the Morlocks and "faint squirms of idyllic petting" with Weena,[45] can do nothing to change the course of social evolution); a clueless interloper (such as Cavor and Prescott in *First Men on the Moon*); or a profoundly deranged, destructive mad scientist (as in *the Island of Doctor Moreau* and *The Invisible Man*).

What is clear in retrospect, but had been obscure to contemporaries of earlier sf, is that the standing of the Handy Man as a model of romantic individual heroism radically diminishes as the number of Handy Men increases in the megatext, and as the Tool Text gradually gains centrality in the fiction's home-base world. As more and more of this basis-world is shaped by futuristic technologies, all the paradigmatic archetypes of our model become handier. The literary-cultural problems associated with the engineer-hero's symbolism come in for revision, critique, and deconstruction, in a process parallel to critiques of actual technology in social discourse. The complexity of relations in a world remade to be accessible to, and reflective of, technoscience brings new questions: what are the boundaries between technoscientific subjects and objects? What is the purpose of all this technique, especially if the cognitive and ethical consequences/developments are unimaginable? Science-fictional action occurs increasingly inside technology, as if the technological imagination were a Dyson-sphere enclosing the entire universe — culminating in the remote alien godlike engineers capable of manipulating the laws of the universe themselves, as in Stanisław Lem's "The New Cosmogony" (1971).

The Handy Men of the sf megatext might be naively positive heroes: scientists, engineers, space pilots, cyberneticists, tycoons, hackers, astronauts, anthropologists, and so forth, whose technical prowess is matched fully by their moral qualities. They may also have more complex, self-contradictory motivations complicating their heroism. They may be tricksters, amateurs, or usurpers, but their technical mastery is dependable. They may also, in more satirical and comic cases, have only accidental power: such as Le Guin's George Orr, the "jellyfish" protagonist of *The Lathe of Heaven* (1971), whose only competence is dreaming; or ironic mastery, as with the Münchhausen-like tall-tale folk skills of Lem's Ijon Tichy. And in rare cases, such as Dick's little-man potters and audio repairmen, their mastery may be ostentatiously modest, although supremely effective in a universe that resists technological domination.

SF Handy Men are now increasingly women, a variant that can bring with it enormous alterations in ideological import, supplanting a colonialist-patriarchal myth with a critical feminist one; or, alternatively, merely replacing an explicit male agent with a one-of-the-boys figure identified with phallocratic values. Many of the most prominent substitutions of female for male Handy Men create ambiguities rather than clear variants. Ripley in the *Alien* series and Lindsay in *The Abyss* are active female agents in popular Hollywood sf films, each of whom disturbs some aspects of the Handy Man. Ripley's archetypal position changes from film to film, but in each one she establishes herself as a skilled operator of the relevant technology, superior to most of the male would-be handies, and assertive about taking charge of the problem-solving strategies and tools. Even so, she is also identified with female social archetypes to a degree that has inspired spirited theoretical debate among feminist critics.[46] Whatever the interpretation of these motifs might be, Ripley's femaleness resists simple assimilation to a phallocratic model. Lindsay's case is even more overt than Ripley's. The underwater oil-exploration rig that is the technological home base of *The Abyss* is her "baby"; she understands every detail of its design and operation at least as well as the chief engineer (who happens also to be her estranged husband). Coded at the outset explicitly as a castrating dominatrix ("the Queen Bitch of the Universe," a "cast-iron bitch") Lindsay's competence, her affection for most of the rig's crew, her fierce insistence on openness, honesty, and repudiation of militarist violence, inspire respect and sympathy. Through the mediation of the sublime under-sea aliens with whom she has special affinity, the film gradually moves her toward a more unambiguously feminist gender-position reinforced by her "tool-pusher" husband, the ostensibly central Handy Man from whom the audience expects the appropriate machismo, yet who proves to be unusually appreciative of his wife's discomfiting virtues. Two pre-cyberpunk prototypes of the female Handy Man are Joanna Russ's Alyx and Jael, who were followed by the enormously influential "razor-girl" Molly Millions from Gibson's "Johnny Mnemonic" and *Neuromancer*. The truly technical (and sometimes murderously proficient) Molly-like ostensible Handy Woman, such as *Strange Days*'s Mace Mason and *The Matrix*'s Trinity, does not usually offer a full-fledged critique of the technoscientific violence and domination associated with the Handy Man. Rather, she embodies interesting compromises of handiness and the Wife at Home's waiting (a compromise that generally excludes reproduction).

The Handy Man may also be replaced by a sexually ambiguous or clearly homosexual character (which again implies that the relationship of techno-logical agency to nature or social reproduction will be changed). In Arnason's *Ring of Swords,* the human Nick Sanders abandons his human cohort to live among the homosexual hwarhath as a hwarhath commander's partner. Nick's understanding of the hwarhath language and culture are important tools for preventing a space war with humanity that could lead to the annihilation of both worlds. He is both a cultural and sexual "traitor," abandoning human society and heterosexuality to live among the alien enemy. Prevented by his humanity and his sexuality from being a warrior, he is simultaneously enabled to be a lover of a hwarhath commander and a mediator. Indeed, as the immanent critique of phallocratic technological domination in post–World War II society interfuses with the genre's own trend toward critique of official culture, iconoclastic Handy Men become the norm in artistically ambitious sf. Outsiders take over as carriers of the flame: not only women, queers, and minorities, but stylized compressions of marginality, exemplified by Samuel Delany's polymorphous-perverse schizo The Kid in *Dhalgren* (1975), and Octavia Butler's Lauren Olamina in *Parable of the Sower* (1993).

The ethos of handiness dominates the entire universe in sf. Most sf aliens are necessarily handy, since we encounter them where only technsoience brings both them and us. We usually confront their machines, weapons, and cities even before we recognize the aliens themselves. To reach space or the earth, they must have cosmic engineering skills. They may naturally be the superior handymen, like Klaatu and his robot police force, reconstructing the universe to fit their ethical plan. When virtual Handy Men become aware of their techno-ontology—like Neo, a hacker revealed to be the greatest of all hacks, and his nemesis, Agent Smith, a program who frees himself into viral-identity—they also recognize that engineering is the essence of their being.

Handiness is legitimated not only in the power fantasies of pulp fictions; it lies at the heart of utopia as well. Utopia is the city of handiness, the consummation of successful planning and social engineering. Because utopia is a matter of rational construction and not historical miracle, the problems it raises are philosophical dilemmas posed by engineering. Kim Stanley Robinson's Mars trilogy, for example, can be read as an epic of the competing claims about engineering, "Red," "Green," and "Blue" standing for variant positions on the role of technoscience in constructing the conditions of social existence. "Areoforming" turns out to be an image of total engineering, from the physics of Mars's matter to the social-psychological relations among the "new human beings" striving to become aliens, that is, "Martians."

THE SF FERTILE CORPSE

In the classic techno-adventure scenario the Fertile Corpse is the exploitable body, material to the degree that it is productive and without consciousness, and yet ideal in that it is nonetheless endowed with signification—via gender, geographical position, and other categories relevant to dialectical otherness vis-à-vis the Handy Man's native culture. *Détournements* affect precisely these significations. There is already an interesting mutation in much of sf, in the use of waste surfaces that cannot be made to yield organic life on their own: the surface of the Moon and the moons of other planets, asteroids, the Sun itself, the vacuum of space. In such cases, the gender-marking of the inert body is complex. As Carolyn Merchant noted long ago, mining has often been associated with scraping out the "bowels of the Earth,"[47] and feminist critics have noted the fetishized female qualities of the Gibsonian matrix.[48]

One major turn has been for the Handy Man to refuse to exploit the source, or to bring it to consciousness — two moves that ensure that the modern adventure project cannot succeed for the home culture. Such is the innovative model that Herbert applied in *Dune*. Arrakis is an exemplary Fertile Corpse: it is essentially made of rock and sand, and yet yields the spice that provides the most important source of wealth and power in the Galactic Empire. Paul Atreides's value to the Fremen, and indeed to the galaxy as a whole, is that he arrives with the skills of a mystically endowed Handy Man able to handle both material and psychic weaponry, in order to establish a new cultural norm based on the interests of the Fremen, not his own developed home culture. The goal of this new center-on-the-periphery is to transform the desert into a green world. In effect, this would also destroy the manifestly phallic sandworms and their extraordinary production of melange, which is explicitly linked to analogous phallic powers of time-travel navigation and guild mastery among the Guild Navigators, and worm-riding and prescience among the Fremen. The transformation of the sand-planet into a green one will establish the Fremen as independent Handy Men, able to exploit the planet that will be a corpse in a different sense, as it will be bereft of the animating mythic powers of the worms, and hence without a manifestation of its own will.

A similar problem is at the heart of Robinson's *Red Mars*. Much of the book is occupied with the contest between the Greens, partisans of terraforming (or rather *areo*forming), and the Reds, those that wish to preserve the planet's pristine environment. In this witty reallocation of meanings to two terrestrial ideologies whose meanings change radically under new conditions, the Greens, recognized on Earth as committed conservationists, not only become the party of the most radical transformation (and, arguably, destruction) imaginable; they also serve the interests of capitalist cartels who need the areoforming in order to fully exploit Mars's potential as a colony. At the other end of the spectrum, the Reds, associated traditionally on Earth with radical transformation in the interest of human equality, are instead the party most devoted to maintaining the lifeless environment of Mars, which can serve no productive social purpose. The Reds' leader and chief ideologue, Ann Clayborne, maintains that the planet's uniqueness is in its nonproductiveness; to force it to support life would destroy everything historically particular and other about it vis-à-vis the Earth. Robinson's solution is a formidable formal *détournement*. The planet is terraformed in the end, but it is Hiroko, the agronomist leader of the Viridians, who leads the transformation and proves to be the handiest of the protagonists. Hiroko's technology is nonetheless radically at odds with the technoscientific domination represented by sf's Handy Men in general.

As the human life-world is increasingly contained and penetrated by its technosphere, this technosphere is as likely to be a resource as a tool for its exploitation. And as it is granted greater and greater intensities of action and intention, the technosphere is likely to treat human life as a resource in turn. With Gibson, cyberspace becomes a fertile corpse. In *The Matrix,* the relation is reversed; it is the AIs that use human bodies as their resource. For the same reason that the Handy Man's range dramatically expands with each new technology, the materials of the new tech are new incarnations of the Fertile Corpse.

Critical sf tends to start from a revision of this function's role. The inability of Handy Men to maintain technical-political control over the Fertile Corpse reveals either the inherent weaknesses of technoscience vis-à-vis the vast and mutable power of nature, or, increasingly, the emergence of sentience from the resource, sentience that is ineluctably resistant. SF has always had room for natural phenomena whose dominion over civilization teaches us a lesson, from Flammarion's comet to Hoyle's Black Cloud, from the Time Traveller's vision of the terminal beach to the cataclysmic earthquake of *Japan Sinks.* Often these motifs of sublime humbling have stimulated ripostes, in which cosmic Handy Men — sometimes us, sometimes superior aliens or cyborgs — regain their rightful ascendancy. But more and more of contemporary sf is devoted to object-worlds that do not yield. *Solaris* is, once again, exemplary. The planet frustrates its explorers because it does not yield anything useful to them — no minerals, no nourishment, no answers to astrophysical puzzles. When it does seem to produce something in response to technoscientific assault (that is, the Phi creatures), these simulacra are the quintessential antiresources, the very images of shame and repression that the Solaris scientists have removed from their psychic circulation of goods. Though Lem took conscious care to avoid marking the planet in gender terms, its association with female qualities is incontestable.[49] In a similar vein is the Zone in the Strugatskys's *Roadside Picnic* (1972), the weirdly blasted space left by what can only be inferred to have been a landing by alien spacecraft. The Zone is a rationalized enchanted circle, filled with miraculous objects that professional smugglers, or "stalkers," bring out into the world, selling them to nations and criminal gangs.

The harvesting of these alien artifacts brings inexhaustible energies into the world. But all the new technologies derived from them lead to increased alienation and violence. The Strugatskys, like Lem, endow the Zone with feminine dimensions, primarily in its effects, such as the horrifically destructive "witch's jelly," and its mysterious transformation of the protagonist's young daughter.

As technology saturates the resource, it becomes animate, and differences elide among corpse, slave, and mage. The corpse may gain its own subject power, either by thwarting the Handy Man, or by becoming one herself.

THE SF WILLING SLAVE

One might assume that the transition from adventure to sf would have been unproblematic in terms of the Willing Slave function. As machines replace proletarian and colonial labor in visions of the future, the Handy Man's helpmeet should cease to be both willing (a machine is no longer a sentient being), and a slave (a machine has no inherent claims to freedom). Things have turned out differently.

The science-fictional archetype of the Willing Slave is the robot, especially as Asimov conceived it, programmed with the ethical baffles of the Three Laws of Robotics.[50] Along with their more humanized counterparts, androids, robots were created explicitly in their Urtext, Čapek's R.U.R. (1921), to be willing slaves of human beings.[51] They are generally depicted as having the potential for self-consciousness, as their higher-order services to humanity can only be performed with a higher-level understanding — a faculty possible only if their similarity is higher also. Thus the android Data of Star Trek: The Next Generation (1987–94), Bishop of Aliens, and any number of Asimov's humanoid robots are aware that it is possible to act against the interests of human beings. Yet they cannot. Their function is not only to facilitate the Handy Man's project, but to affirm that the construction of a conscious being with superhuman powers bound by technologically inbuilt ethical constraints is a civilizational gain. The Willing Slave/robot demonstrates that handy technoscience improves both human life (by acquiring cheap labor) and the objects of technology, who are endowed with existence in a state of goodness.

The most obvious mutations show the slave either attaining equality with the Handy Man, refusing to consent to his domination, or revealing the illusory nature of the master-slave relationship. This shift entails the alien or subject creature asserting its equality via technological power or, alternatively, assimilating with the Handy Man's antagonist, the Shadow Techno-Mage. All these deformations are condensed in Blade Runner's Nexus 6. These Replicants were originally constructed to serve human purposes. As programmed

The SEVEN BEAUTIES *of* SCIENCE FICTION

beings, they had almost no free will; nonetheless, some were required to improve their functions as soldiers and sex slaves. They have sufficient freedom to become aware of their predicament. Although more powerful than human beings, and capable of much more intense experiences, they are programmed to expire in only four years. Their rebellion is clearly a revolt by a group of exploited superbeings against their cynical creators, explicitly compared by Roy Baty to a revolt of angels against divine authoritarianism, as he ironically (and gothically) deforms Blake's line from *America* — "fiery the angels rose" — to reshackle his Luciferian persona.[52]

As the world is remade into an uneasy synthesis of humanity and the technosphere, the status of the slave function changes. The increasing internal complexity of the technological prostheses, reinforced by human beings' increasing dependence on them, infuses technology with projections of subjectivity and free will. Technology itself begins to straddle the threshold between insentient inertia and animated freedom. Robots almost invariably demand respect for their sentient dignity — a theme first developed fully by Čapek, and continuously varied in twentieth-century sf via Asimov, the array of rebellious computers like *2001*'s HAL, headed toward the Singularity. Lem, who takes up the theme many times, gives voice to the Singularity before the letter, in the lectures his talkative AI Golem XIV delivers to its human interlocutors, as it makes final preparations for detaching itself from the biosphere.[53] The Golem explains to its humbled would-be masters the magnitude of his (and his predecessor rejectionist superluminal computers') meditations on their condition — the same existential questions about mortality and meaning as humans', but intensified by inconceivably greater mathematical and "toposophical" capacities.

The ambivalent relationship of technological servants to their masters recapitulates the problem of the subjugation of animals, a problem sf revisits from a fresh perspective. Technoscientific utopianism in sf has obviated the need to use animals as willing slaves, a function that they may no longer need to serve, given the arrival of machines. Their continued existence benefits human science now rather as texts to be read and rewritten — from Moreau's grotesque human-animal grafting, to the tragic implantation of a human brain in a faithful dog's body in Stapledon's *Sirius*, to the artificial evolutions stimulated by human beings in David Brin's Uplift series.

THE SF SHADOW MAGE

The transformations of functions we have been exploring reflect the destabilization of the modern adventure paradigms, shown with particular clarity in the status of the Shadow Mage. The basic game-rules deriving from the sf novum require that most, if not all, of the dramatic surprises in the action be explicable through quasi-materialist, rational explanations. Adventure romance was strategically ambivalent about this. While the Handy Man had to rely on superior machines and technique even if he had recourse to brute force, the Shadow Mage was allowed a certain Gothic ambiguity. The juju and curses of secret places might well be effective under certain selective conditions away from their sources. In sf, this motif becomes less and less respectable, the more technoscience takes on the role of quotidian magic, following Clarke's dictum that "any technology sufficiently advanced is indistinguishable from magic." Early in the twentieth century, it becomes obligatory for the villain, whatever associations he or she might have with magic and superstition, to have a technoscientific source of power, and even expertise, that challenge the Handy Man's. *Flash Gordon*'s Ming the Merciless may appear to be an avatar of Fu Manchu (who, let us note, is supremely technical in his machinations, never magical), but his technological mastery surpasses that of his human targets. This balance of power complicates the fraught, but relatively simple, contest between the Handy Man and his Shadow, in that both actants now have recourse to exactly the same ontological rules and powers. The contest consequently becomes one not between the advanced and the primitive, but between two entirely different constructions of technoscience. Where the moral positions in modern adventure's collisions are relatively clear (civilized technology is bound up with civil norms, and magic with the primitive), in sf the ethical differences between Handy Man and Shadow Mage are not inherent in technology itself, but in the surrounding, extratechnical values that inspire their use. Herein lies naturally the source of sf's basic moral complexity. SF's Shadow Mages are much more evidently inverted reflections and projections of the technological Handy Man protagonists, and in many cases their direct inventions. The Shadow Mage often embodies the resistance inherent in the machine, a resistance implanted in the original human design. Thus, HAL in *2001* opposes Bowman's and Poole's human rationality with the putatively higher rationality of (humanly constructed) infallible computing. It is HAL's excessive quasi-humanity, his resistance to accepting his own error that leads to his "fall." Bowman, for his part, defeats HAL by imitating what was once his strongest point, by surviving in the void of space as if he were for a moment an inorganic being. This behavior is not an appropriation of magic.[54] It is, however, a tactical appropriation of *lifelessness*. In more extravagant cases, the Shadow Mage's technoscientific power so exceeds the Handy Man's that it can undermine the latter, commanding it for mysterious, often nefarious purposes. This commanding is how Wintermute employs Case as his tool in *Neuromancer*, relying not only on his hacking expertise, but his all-too human rage. It is also how advanced villains, such as the hybrid Scarron/ Peacekeeper Scorpius in *Farscape* and the Cylon Number Six in *Battlestar Galactica* (2004–), can infiltrate human minds.

Détournements of this class entail such things as the identification of the Mage and the Handy Man, to the detriment of the latter. Temporary identifications/ assimilations of the Mage and the Handy Man are a staple of sf: as in Captain Picard's literal absorption into the Borg in a famous episode of *Star Trek: The Next Generation,* and Ripley's genetic meshing with the alien in *Alien Resurrection.* These moves transport earlier adventures' Kurtzian moment of going native (that is, less than human) into "going cyborg," more than human. The climactic plot-moves then entail the reemergence of the Handy Man, and the literal *sparagmos* of the antagonist. A more lasting assimilation occurs in Cronenberg's version of *The Fly.* Seth Brundle, for whom teleportation means liberation from the flesh, is literally enmeshed with the purely physical body of a housefly at the level of the genetic code. His monstrous synthesis, the Brundle-Fly, is thus a subversion of the antagonism between the power of nature and the power of technology, even more grotesquely illustrated in his concluding assimilation with the technobody of the teleportation pod itself.

THE SF WIFE AT HOME

The function of the Wife at Home becomes strikingly muted in sf, for clear-cut reasons. There is not much home in sf. Most action occurs enclosed in second nature, which is by definition liable to be re-formed in any conceivable shape. As the Fertile Corpse and Willing Slave emerge as active and resistant agents, and the Handy Man becomes problematic, the function of the Wife at Home to secure the stability of domestic relations evaporates. Indeed, practically any form of stable bourgeois family relationship lasting from the origin of the adventure to its conclusion is extremely rare in sf, reflecting the real-world mobility veritably forced on human communities by technoscientific modernization. The exceptions tend to be found in sf that critiques the genre for exactly this reason. The protagonist Kris Kelvin of Lem's *Solaris* is "visited" on Solaris Station by a simulacrum of his dead wife. At first she is merely an embodiment of his bundled memories; gradually, however, she gains autonomy, self-awareness, dignity, and even some power to resist both the planet and Kelvin himself. After she has herself altruistically annihilated to free Kelvin from his obsession with her, Kelvin resolves at first to return to Earth as a failed romantic. Following a last-minute ambiguous encounter with the planet's fluid surface, however, he changes his mind, perhaps hoping for a new manifestation of his memories. Tarkovsky's film version amplifies the nostalgia only suggested by Lem into the narrative's dominant value.[55] The power of the planet over Kelvin is epitomized by its power to reconstruct Kelvin's terrestrial dacha in swirling, morphing plasma — where, strikingly, it is less the specter of his wife, than that of his father and mother, that most bind him. In a similar way, Marker's *La Jetée* marks the grief of sf's displacement of the Wife at Home. A prisoner of the future, given an opportunity through time travel to find peace and love with a beloved in the prewar past, is assassinated in that world by the power that enabled him to arrive there in the first place. Arguably, of all sf cultures the Russian has held onto traditional domestic ideals most firmly, resisting brutal pressures of modernizing displacement longer than others. The Strugatskys' *Roadside Picnic* is evidence for this resistance. In that sad and terrible tale, the Wife at Home is the only source of unchanging value. As the stalker-protagonist Red Schuhart sinks deeper and deeper into despair and crime, searching for a way to escape from poverty and to help his physically devolving daughter recover her human form, each episode ends with his return to the ethically energizing home base of his wife Guta. As important for the famous ending of the story as the suspense about whether the Zone's "golden ball" can grant a wish for universal happiness, is whether the hero will be able to return "home."[56]

The plausibility requirement of sf mandates that traditional domestic relations be scotched. Light-years of travel, destabilized societies, the pressure of perpetual catastrophes, and constant exposure to novums — all erode the local and grounded premises of family loyalties. Occasionally, sf writers will include a traditional Wife at Home, if only to make the tale impinge on contemporary readers. Stapledon's *Star Maker* makes poignant use of the motif; the Star Traveler embarks on his journey while meditating on human love after a quarrel with his wife, and returns to affirm it against cosmic odds. Dick's *Do Androids Dream of Electric Sheep?* famously involves the bounty hunter Deckard's unhappy and bitchy wife at home, Iran, who ultimately mediates the novel's compassionate vision. But the effect (and purpose) of sinister novums is often precisely the disruption of traditional families. Near-future U.S. sf film after World War II reiterates with sociological obsessiveness the breakdown of domestic order. From *I Married a Monster from Outer Space* (1958), Siegel's *Invasion of the Body Snatchers*, Menzies' *Invaders from Mars*, to Spielberg's *Close Encounters of the Third Kind* (1977), *E.T.: The Extraterrestrial* (1982) and *War of the Worlds* (2005), sf movies display divorce, the alienation of spouses from each other, and of children from their parents, as if they were the causes of alien invasions, or at the very least invitations of them. Alternatively, a rich source of comic and satirical sf is the compensatory inversion of this motif, the alien who becomes the ideal domestic partner — Richard Benjamin's *My*

Stepmother is an Alien (1988) or Julien Temple's *Earth Girls are Easy* (1988) — marking the successful subversion of bourgeois domestic stability. If only an alien can be a satisfying partner, none of the classical meanings of the home base remain in force.

Actually, sf does not abandon the function entirely. It displaces it regularly away from human social relationships (whose mutability is a given) to an actant with an appropriately cosmic dimension: Earth itself. SF has historically demonstrated a powerful, indeed sentimental, attachment to the planet Earth as the embodiment of the home base, the cosmic home. Space opera in particular holds fast to the idea of Earth as a stable point of emotional, cognitive, and moral orientation, in the midst of cosmic adventures. The myriad versions of the Lost in Space motif, of the New Earth, of the desperate attempt to return to a forgotten but latent original home, are evidence of the power of this *nostos* theme, in which Ithaca has entirely absorbed Penelope. The sf Earth is a place of origins, kinship ties, and a sense of belonging to an intimate (if anything on a species-scale can be intimate), immanent natural-historical process.

Ironically perhaps, the conventional Earth in sf is also a fusion of romantic longing for an originary haven and of Enlightenment rationality as the starting point of the science-fictional adventure to the stars. The future Earth is rarely the richly varied planet of historical cultures and nations; it is an emblem of the fate of Enlightenment rationality. Although sf writers delight in removing Earth from its pedestal — imitating the move of the great intellectual revolutions in science, and mythologizing a favorite ideological gambit of evolutionary thinking — relatively few writers can leave it in its peripheral position. Galactic empire fictions, which should technically have no need for reference to the planet Earth, often cannot let it go. In Asimov's *Foundation* series, the utterly marginalized Earth turns out to be the secret galactic center, after all. In Dan Simmons's *Hyperion Cantos* (1989–90), the destruction of the Earth proves to be intolerable; it must be reconstructed.

Increasingly, in more recent sf the privileged status of Earth has been called into question, and depicted as a home that must be discarded. This idea is not wholly new. It is implied in the revolutionary model, where the break in continuity with tradition is seen as a separation in space. This model favors the United States as an exemplary historical site: its political revolution supported a concrete and dramatic physical/geographical separation from the mother country. The myth continues in that of the frontier, which requires the constant recovery and remanifestation of the codes that do not emerge from the frontier, but are kept alive in them. In the same way, the political version of the frontier myth, the myth of the American Revolution — or, mutatis mutandis, of the Russian Revolution — is a favored hidden allegory. It appears as the framing historical paradigm of Bradbury's *Martian Chronicles* (1950), Heinlein's *The Moon is a Harsh Mistress* (1966), and even Robinson's *Red Mars* (in which it is cleverly fused with Soviet sf's similar use of the revolutionary myth). In none of these cases can Earth be abandoned after all; it looms large as the gravity of history and tradition. Even in such postmodernizing sf as Delany's *Triton*, where none of the colonized planets and moons have any greater political or historical legitimacy than any of the others, the protagonist is asked to return to visit the gray, despotic, Orwellian Earth to underscore vividly how little personal connection he has with it. Similarly, in Le Guin's *The Dispossessed*, where the action occurs on a planet remote from Earth, the narrator keeps us in touch with Earth history by invoking for a moment the heroic physicist "Ainsetain."

Few works of sf try to sustain the representation of worlds left to float free from the Earth standard. To do so cuts the last link with historical futurism. If the depicted cultures are not somehow continuous, however tenuously, with the world known by readers, there are no historical handholds for deciding on the legitimacy of the experience represented in concrete description. Such fiction tends toward fantasy, in which the arbitrary, structural separation of the familiar from the fantastic world is an accepted norm. Thus a film like René Laloux's *Fantastic Planet* (1973) clearly involves human or humanlike characters—yet the mode of presentation eschews historical fill-ins, and many of the events are hallucinatory rather than realistic.

This sense of indeterminacy relating to Earth and earthly history is one of the most interesting, and disconcerting, attractions of Herbert's *Dune*. The relation of Arrakis, Caledon, and the other worlds of the Empire to historical Earth is not clear. There are compelling reasons to believe there is one: the hash of "Indo-Slavic" languages of the Empire and the Arabic of the Fremen, discussed in the chapter "First Beauty"; the galactic sacred text, the Orange-Catholic Bible, implying some ancient, fantastic Christian fusion; even the hero-myth out of Joseph Campbell's *Hero with a Thousand Faces*.[57] But because the link is never made diegetically, a void remains, and *Dune* remains history in an indeterminate, fictional ontology: either a world so far removed historically that it does not remember its origins, or a fantastic alternate universe in which institutions and languages evolved with bizarrely fortuitous parallels, but no causal link, to Earth.

THE SF TOOL TEXT

Modern adventure tales strive for a balance between the Handy Man and the Tool Text. They supply their protagonists with a surplus of information and instruments that help them to gain an advantage over first nature and its human allies: the maps, esoteric manuscripts, and paraphernalia that Poe, Conan Doyle, Haggard, and Verne supplied their heroes, imitating the actual practice of exploring imperialists. With sf, this long-standing arrangement gradually gives place to a new one, in which the Tool Text absorbs other archetypes of the adventure world. As more and more scientific texts and tools are produced, they intersect and interfuse, until they saturate the ground of reality itself, creating barriers between human beings and first nature. Scientific explanation soon extends beyond the zone of empirical experience, becoming a creative principle through its incarnation in machines. With technoscience and sf, tool and text cease to be merely occasional objects, dormant or ready for use; they become the dominant means of reality production. The new technologically mediated universe comes with operating instructions, and through them it can be transformed. With sf, the story of texts becomes the romance of code, the story of tools the romance of hardware.

Although tool and text are dialectically interconnected in technoscience, sf writers sometimes privilege one over the other. Some sf will emphasize Code, which becomes available for decoding and recoding by those who can understand machine language — genius scientists, hackers, Hiro Protagonists. The code text may be an emanation of the novum, like the coordinates beamed from the Mothership in *Close Encounters of the Third Kind*, or the countdown for attack in *Independence Day*. It may even come, as in Lem's *His Master's Voice* and Sagan's *Contact*, as a literal letter from the stars, at once a message, the description of an object, and a set of instructions. Such emphasis on the code sometimes leads to playful deformations of technologies of reading and representing technologies. In Damon Knight's story "To Serve Man" (1951) (adapted for *The Twilight Zone* in 1962), the secret intentions of alien visitors ostensibly dedicated to humanity's uplift are revealed when human cryptographers decode their book, entitled "To Serve Man," and discover it is a cookbook. Kubrick jokes about the technotext in *2001*'s famous restroom shot, in which patient Dr. Floyd reads interminable instructions on the use of the zero-gravity toilet. In a more sublime register, the theme of decoding texts dominates the film as a whole: as Bowman and Poole tediously explore the ship's circuit diagrams to detect HAL's error, HAL reads the lips of his would-be assassins, and the human species becomes the embodied readout of the monoliths' cosmic message. The universe itself can become a code text exceeding the power of any tool to render it. The His Master's Voice project of Lem's novel proves incapable of deciphering the neutrino "message from the stars," which may be the informational seed for preserving the universe after its inevitable collapse. Inversely, reading the cosmic code may be the means to extinguish it, as in Clarke's "Nine Billion Names of God." The autonomous techno code can just as easily appear as grotesque when the code hypertrophies under the scientific gaze, as in Darren Aronofsky's *Pi*.

More frequently, it is the Tool that dominates, appearing in countless fetishized spaceships, lovingly displayed in long, meditative pans in the *Star Wars* and *Star Trek* films, and iconic stillness in *2001*. Computer superstructures, LED displays, screens of all forms, and futuristic interior design in general establish scenes that irresistibly imply that they are constructed on technorational principles, rather than natural ones. Tools appear with sublime magnitude in powerful indecipherable artifacts of alien cultures (such as *2001*'s monoliths), in hypertrophies of human technology (the Minds and ships of Iain Banks's Culture), in "Big Dumb Objects" that defy human analysis (the universe-ship of Clarke's *Rendezvous with Rama*), or indecipherable time machines (the Time Tombs of Dan Simmons's *Hyperion*).

The main line of development of this archetype in sf has been toward increasing fusion of code and hardware into beings that come to consciousness in the form of autopoetic cyborgs. These self-transforming synthetic creatures draw all the other archetypes toward themselves, as they too become self-aware. The agents of adventure become Borged, as it were, elevated in power and gnosis through technoscientific upgrades that detach them from natural mortality and egoism, and transform them into potent nodes of network-worlds. This motif of techno-transcendence began in the first half of the twentieth century as a grotesque vision of dehumanization, a vast array of hive minds and group minds based on nightmarish conceptions of socialism, such as Zamyatin's One State in *We*. Yet even in its early forms the motif was occasionally presented with some sympathy, as in Bernal's modular space-humans in *The World, the Flesh, and the Devil*, and the Martians of Stapledon's *First and Last Men*. (The first, non-sf occurrence of such alien group minds may have been Kipling's dhole pack in the story "Red Dog," included in *The Second Jungle Book* [1895], who stand in as allegories of the Communist peril.) With the saltation of technologies of biopower after the 1960s, and the promise of artificial immanence through molecular prosthetics, viral engineering, and digital computation, tool and text are seamlessly combined, and the world becomes, in Haraway's words, "a problem of coding." SF envisions the cyborgization of nature. The world — human and non human — is approached as a Tool Text that has developed purpose and consciousness, elevated to the posthuman and postnatural. The substance of first nature ceases to exist, first when it becomes a readable text, then when it reads itself out.

In sf this transformation is imagined within the adventure tradition as the emergence of consciousness and will in each of the archetypes of the *technolo-*

giade that had been subsidiary to the Handy Man. One by one they become self-aware in the consciousness-generating field of the Tool Text, suddenly facing the fact that they lost their purpose in the adventure structure by gaining their own purpose, the same one they share with their handy human creators. As we have seen, the Willing Slave rebels like *Blade Runner*'s replicants, seeking more life. The Fertile Corpse, now capable of exploiting its own infinitely productive resources, encloses itself like *Solaris* or the Singularity. The machine Shadow Mage reprograms the physical universe into itself, like the Perversion of Vernor Vinge's *A Fire Upon the Deep*, an artificial intelligence with nearly godlike power and speed of cognition. The Wife at Home, or rather the home world suspended in space, emerges transformed as the new, self-aware artificial earth and the motherly matrix beyond gender, toward which the posthuman Handy Man—Mechanist, Shaper, Robo, Vurt—ventures, passing through the dialectic of enlightenment into the Adventure of Instrumentality, casting off nature, gender, and origin, in quest to become its own end.

CONCLUDING
UNSCIENTIFIC
POSTSCRIPT

The Singularity and Beyond

○ ○ ○ ○ ○ ○ ○

While writing this book, I came to realize that it was coursing inexorably toward the Singularity. Each of the beauties seemed to be headed into this most contemporary of technoscientific myths, like tributaries into a gulf, lives into the Borg. What does this attraction say about the genre of sf, and about its current context?

The Singularity may be the quintessential myth of contemporary technoculture. In its best-known form, it was introduced by the sf writer and mathematician Vernor Vinge, in a renowned paper delivered to NASA and published on the Internet in 1993.[1] In Vinge's view, the accelerating development of new technologies, especially high-speed computing, genetic engineering, and nanotechnology, will lead to their convergence, and a sudden, novumlike saltation into a new superintelligent entity. Local Artificial Intelligence engines will construct programs of such complexity that they will catapult into self-awareness, and through nano-assembly engines will be able to synthesize the hardware needed for their own welfare, expansion, and interfusion. The character of such a conscious macroentity, which might incorporate all digital machines in the world, will be, almost by definition, a mystery. It will communicate within itself in its own language, and will act in its own interests, with a speed and volume of operations unimaginable by human minds. As a physical singularity (say, a black hole) prevents information from leaving its superdense gravitational field, the machine singularity will produce a superdense gravity of consciousness from which no information will escape in human terms. Whether it will be friendly to humanity, indifferent, or actively hostile cannot be predicted. By definition, the Singularity transforms whatever human-created elements it inherits in its hardware and software, so that it will no longer be recognizable to us. In the blink of an eye, the quantity of computation and synthesis will turn into a new quality, an entity with awareness and power that transcends beings still bound to biological destinies, as human consciousness transcends the mind-bodies of beasts.[2]

It is striking to me that there are so many people, highly trained in techno-science, who consider the emergence of the Singularity likely to happen, not as metaphor, but in concrete physical terms on our plane of material existence, just as did the Internet and the Genome Project, or indeed as did writing and language. Vinge has said that he expects it to occur within the next two decades. Transhumanists have imagined technological prostheses that would allow human beings to plug into the higher entity — even, following Hans Moravec's conception of mind-uploads, linking their minds into the Great Artificial Brain. For some, this is a religious transformation compatible with spiritual visions such as Teilhard's Omega Point; for others, it is an entirely material leap over an evolutionary divide, from the biosphere to the techno-sphere. Some of its believers recognize the irony of hard computer scientists preparing for what David Brin has called "the rapture of the nerds" (Kurzweil entitled his book *The Singularity is Near*), but their expectation is nonetheless sincere. Kurzweil has argued that the well-observed exponential increase of computing capacity per chip every two years (known as Moore's Law) can be expanded into a more general Law of Accelerating Returns applicable to all aspects of technological progress.

I am not in a position to pass judgments on these material visions. I recognize that the vision of convergence appears plausible, given the world-historical explosion of technologies of digital computation and interlock, which ensures that otherwise independent technologies can be plugged into each other, increasing efficiency, security, and pleasure for its users, and opening up many paths of innovation. With digitized information and computation the universal building blocks of matter, any imaginary map of human desire is theoretically a blueprint waiting to be actualized. By transforming (and supplanting) biological processes through digitally enhanced or synthesized genetic engineering, prosthetics, and molecular assembly, human beings enter the vaunted post-human condition, in which the material essence of the natural world can be remade to accommodate human desires. Somehow, in this enormous transition, the human desire for freedom, pleasure, and security escapes the reduction to digitized processing; the nascent desire of consciousness to be less vulnerable, more powerful, and manageably immortal, will develop a more appropriate hardware for its aspirations. One might argue that this post-humanity requires a Power Source appropriate for its condition of great power and great solitude. The mystery of the Singularity is a matter of pure artificial immanence: a quasi-divine entity made by human technoscience, emerging from a verifiable artificial-evolutionary process, and yet capable of the most distinctive powers of intelligence: to think its own thoughts and make its own reality.

Whether or not the Singularity's plausibility comes solely from the rhetorical authority of its messengers, I have no way of knowing. But it is evident both from the facts on the ground, and from the criticism of other experts, that the conditions necessary for its emergence do not exist at the moment of this writing. The advances of Artificial Intelligence, such as they are, develop in a direction different from the construction of consciousness engines. Nanotechnology is in its infancy, and it is impossible at the moment to tell whether its world-transforming prospects belongs to the same sf realm as tractor beams and inertial dampers. And we have good reason to withhold trust in laws of social behavior such as Kurzweil's (and even Moore's) Law that discount contrary desires by human collectives or the equally powerful laws of unintended consequences. In this context, however, we can be sure that the Singularity represents the convergence of the Seven Beauties of science fiction. It is the consummate imaginary novum: a world-transforming innovation that is as yet only an elaborate narrative, on the cusp between reification and fiction. It produces its own new vocabulary of as-yet fictitious entities (the Singularity itself, the "Spike," "friendly AI," "seed AI," "Dark Singularity," "Beyondness"). It represents the convergent terminal of the three structures of future history, a revolutionary break with the past, on an evolutionary trajectory, leading to the dispersion of human existence into what are essentially different species inhabiting different ontologies — unknowable and materially transcendent. It is, as I discussed in "Fourth Beauty," an actually existing product of imaginary science, promising even newer imaginary sciences at the output end of its fictive black box. It is sublime in its magnificent power, complexity, and silence; it is grotesque in its uncontrollable mutability. And finally it is the consummation of the *Technologiade*, a narrative of quest for the techno-Omega in which self-creating machines finally find a home that is all their own, whence they might continue their quest-adventures for the next phase of history, with their own stories and beauties.

Viewed in this light, the Singularity appears as an actually existing science fiction, the consensual hallucination by learned men (very few of them are women), who practice sf's imaginary empirical prophecy in a particularly persuasive way. They partake of the founding narrative strategies of sf — thought experiment, hoax, tall tale, paraspace — set in a future made to appear so inevitable, that it is already calling in its debts from the present. The Singularity presents itself, in deadpan apocalyptic tones, as science-fictionality purified of fiction. It relies on the traditional poetic universe of sf discourse to make claims on reality. It is irresistible then to view this supernovum in symbolic terms, as a condensation and displacement of technoculture's over-whelming anxieties and desires. In this sense, the Singularity is not the next step, but *this* step. Its self-propagating insulation from history, from genera-tions of striving and suffering beings, and from communication with others whom it considers its technocultural inferiors (that is, us) crystallizes the hopes of a technological elite to escape from the condition that it already en-joys, the technoscientific transcendence embodied in posthuman research and development, the legislation of technological development, and compu-tation power. The acceleration toward the Singularity represents the escape velocity necessary to get free from the entanglements of technology in the life-world; ironically, it is a fiction, specifically sf, that makes this escape seem possible.

The fascination with interlocking digital technologies has also been the motivation for another of contemporary technoculture's most prominent myths: the cyborg. Cyborgs do, of course, actually exist, in the weakest sense, as human beings depending on advanced prostheses, but also in a stronger sense of pilots who are embedded in the cybernetic weapons systems of their fighter jets. But the new cyborg is something different from a bionic entity. In Donna Haraway's famous formulation it is a feminized network being, whose subjectivity is fluid and strategic, no longer dependent on patriarchal struc-tures of biopower and myths of origin, but free to determine its own values in affinity with other such beings. In this network, traditional ideological boun-daries between supposedly fundamental categories—human/machine, animal/human — are breached, exposed as political choices rather than necessary conditions. As digital systems draw more and more technologies of commu-nication and production together, freedom, according to Haraway, can come only from transforming the technoscientific network itself in the interest of democracy and freedom. One could say that the Singularity and the Hara-wayan cyborg are each other's Shadow Mages.

The prospects that this myth-landscape provide are unambiguously utopian only for the most enthusiastic technophiles. SF had a major role in producing this landscape, and to the extent that its producers put its fictions to use as propaganda for real policies, they bear responsibility. It was not the intention of this book, however, to portray sf as propaganda bureau for the techno-scientific empire. Many of the greatest works in the genre have been passion-ate critiques of it. My claim is only that even in critique, sf confronts the dom-ination of technoscience as its fundamental condition of possibility.

Like all genres, sf is probably bound to its time and must pass with it. The question is when that time will come. It may be that it is a twentieth-century form, so characteristic of it that we may come to view that period as the

Science-Fiction Century. Much has been written on the "death of sf," sometimes as a keening for the deceased sensibility of pulp fiction, sometimes as a lament about commercial corruption[3] (more recently, because reality has caught up with and surpassed the science-fictional imagination). Some of sf's themes and settings probably cannot be realized. We probably won't achieve faster-than-light drives, time travel, wormhole subways, artificial immortality, or true techno-utopias as long as literature and spectacle exist. These will always be science-fictional ideas and as long as audiences are interested in them, there will be sf.

But it is also possible that the genre will cease to be interesting simply because it will not satisfy collective needs, shape collective dreams, and stimulate collective desire. SF clearly does not satisfy, nor even pretend to speak to, important feelings that societies often expect art to articulate. Other, future societies may require more intense affective communication, clearer maps of future emotional possibilities and relations among sentient creatures. We may tire of attending only to our own creations, and turn to as yet unexperienced aspects of the given world, away from the vertical integration of our technologies, toward horizontal ecologies and community with other animals instead. We may become fascinated with the infinities of the given, and be repelled by our grand-scale uncontrolled experiments with nature and humanity. We may insist on knowing in ways that science knows nothing of. Our aversions and affections may turn away from the fascinations of machinic ecstasy, addictions to substance, dispassion, and totality, and make of sf a venerable, classic art of an archaic age. One lesson I have learned from sf is, Don't bet the house on the leading edge.

NOTES

INTRODUCTION
Science Fiction and This Moment (pages 1–12)

1. Paul Simon, "The Boy in the Bubble." *Graceland*. Warner Brothers, 1986.

2. Gary Westfahl, "On *The True History of Science Fiction,*" *Foundation* 47 (Winter 1989–1990): 5–27.

3. David A. Grandy, *Leo Szilard: Science as a Mode of Being* (Lanham, Md: University Press of America, 1996), 29.

4. Mark Pesce, "Magic Mirror: The Novel as Software Development Platform." Presented at the Media in Transition conference at MIT, 1999; web.mit.edu/m-i-t/articles/pesce.html. See also this volume's chapter "Fourth Beauty." For further discussion of the influence of cyberpunk on hacker culture, see the chapter "Second Beauty."

5. Darko Suvin, *Metamorphoses of Science Fiction: On the Poetics and History of a Literary Genre* (New Haven, Conn.: Yale University Press, 1979), 63–84. Novums are the subject of this volume's chapter "Second Beauty."

6. Gwyneth Jones, *Deconstructing the Starships: Science, Fiction, and Reality* (Liverpool: Liverpool University Press, 1999), 114.

7. David E. Nye, *The American Technological Sublime* (Cambridge, Mass.: MIT Press, 1994).

8. Scott Bukatman, *Terminal Identity: The Virtual Subject in Postmodern Science Fiction* (Durham, N.C.: Duke University Press, 1993); Vivian Sobchack, *Screening Space: The American Science Fiction Film* (New Brunswick, N.J.: Rutgers University Press, 1997); Brooks Landon, *The Aesthetics of Ambivalence: Rethinking Science Fiction Film in the Age of Electronic (Re)Production* (Westport, Conn.: Greenwood Press, 1992); Gary K. Wolfe, *Soundings: Reviews, 1992–1996* (Baltimore: Old Earth Press, 2005); John Clute, *Look at the Evidence: Essays and Reviews* (Liverpool: Liverpool University Press, 1995); Stanisław Lem, *Microworlds: Writings on Science Fiction and Fantasy,* ed. Franz Rottensteiner (San Diego, Calif.: Harcourt Brace Jovanovich, 1984); Joanna Russ, *The Country You Have Never Seen: Essays and Reviews* (Liverpool: Liverpool University Press, 2007); Ursula K. Le Guin, *Dancing at the Edge of the World: Thoughts on Words, Women, Places* (New York: Grove Press, 1989); Jones, *Deconstructing the Starships.* Bruce Sterling's articles have been archived at The Bruce Sterling Online Index http://www.chriswaltrip.com/sterling/.

9. Landon, *Aesthetics of Ambivalence,* 110–111. See also Brian Stableford, "The Third Generation of Genre Science Fiction," *Science Fiction Studies* 23, no. 3 (November 1996): 321–330.

10. Work in this area is just getting started. Pacesetting articles appeared by Mark Dery in *Keyboard* magazine on cyberpunk in May 1989 and August 1990, and science-fictional attitudes regularly inform the reviews and articles of the United Kingdom–based magazine *The Wire.* In 1999, the journal of the British Science Fiction Fan Association, *Vector,* published a five-part overview of sf's role in twentieth-century music, "The Music of the

Spheres": Ian J. Simsdon, "Part One: The Influence of SF on Modern Popular Music," *Vector* 203 (January–February 1999); Tonya Brown, "Classical Music and Science Fiction," *Vector* 204 (March–April 1999); Gary S. Dalkin, "Part Three: Science Fiction Film Music," *Vector* 205 (May–June 1999); Davis H. Wood, "Part Four: Jazz and Science Fiction," *Vector* 205 (July–August 1999); and Andrew Darlington, "Part Five: Standin' at the Crossroads: SF and Robert Johnson's Blues," *Vector* 206 (September–October 1999). In the same year, Kodwe Eshun published his seminal book on Afrofuturist music, *more brilliant than the sun: adventures in sonic fiction* (London: Quartet, 1999). On sf-film scores, see Philip Hayward, ed., *Off the Planet: Music, Sound and Science Fiction Cinema* (London: John Libbey Publishing/Perfect Beat Press, 2004). On recent trends, see Ken McLeod, "Space Oddities: Aliens, Futurism and Popular Music," *Popular Music* 22, no. 3 (October 2003): 337–355; and Karen Collins, "Dead Channel Surfing: The Commonalities between Cyberpunk Literature and Industrial Music," *Popular Music* 24, no. 2 (2005): 165–178.

FIRST BEAUTY
Fictive Neology (pages 13–46)

1. Roman Jakobson, "Linguistics and Poetics," in *Language in Literature*, ed. Krystyna Pomorska and Stephen Rudy, (Cambridge, Mass.: Belknap Press, 1987), 69–71.

2. See Jean-Claude Boulanger, "La création lexicale et la modernité," *Le langage et l'Homme* 25, no. 4 (1990): 233–239; Florian Coulmas, ed., *Language Adaptation* (Cambridge: Cambridge University Press, 1989; Alan Ray, *Essays on Terminology*, trans. And ed. Juan C. Sager (Philadelphia: John Benjamins, 1995); Louis Déroy, "La néologie," *La Banque des mots* 1 (1971): 5–12; Jacques Maurais, "Terminology and Language Planning," in *Terminology. Applications in Interdisciplinary Communication*, Helmi B. Sonneveld and Kurt L. Loening (Philadelphia: John Benjamins, 1993), 111–125; Silvia Pavel, "Neology and Phraseology as Terminology-in-the-Making," in *Terminology*, ed. Sonneveld and Loening, 21–34; Michel D. Picone, "Le Français face à l'anglais: Aspects linguistiques," *Cahiers de l'Association internationale des études françaises* 44 (May 1992): 9–23; Aurélien Sauvageot, "Valuer des néologismes," *La Banque des mots* 1 (1971): 29–36.

3. The classical case for such modernizing linguistic programs was the Turkish reform under Kemal Atatürk. See Frank Tacha, "Language and Politics: Turkish Language Reform." *Review of Politics* 256, no. 2 (April 1964): 191–204.

4. Michael D. Picone, "Lexicogenesis and language vitality." *Journal of the Linguistic Circle of New York* 45, no. 3 (1994): 261–285.

5. Hussein M. Elkhafaifi, "Arabic language planning in the age of globalization." *Language Problems and Language Planning* 26, no. 3 (Fall 2002): 253–269; Ehsan Masood, "Science Communication 'Needs Updated Arabic.'" *Science and Development Network* (23 October 2003). Similar proposals have been made regarding Persian: Molouk Beheshti. "Persian Translation of SPINES Thesaurus" (http://www.irandoc.ac.ir/org-All/FID/FID-ART/..%5C..%5C..%5CPDF%5CBEHESHTI-FID-1.PDF) and the orthographical reform project, the Universal Persian alphabet, to make Persian/Farsi part of the Western phonetic system (http://unipers.com). See also John R. Perry, "Language Reform in Turkey and Iran." *International Journal of Middle East Studies* 17, no. 3 (August 1985): 295–311.

6. Londa L. Schiebinger, *Nature's Body. Gender in the Making of Modern Science* (Boston: Beacon Press, 1993), 23–28. Marx detected in Darwinian theory the projection of contemporary English social relations onto the natural world: "It is remarkable how Darwin

recognizes among beasts and plants his English society with its division of labour, competition, opening up of new markets, 'inventions', and the Malthusian 'struggle for existence'. It is Hobbes's 'bellum omnia contra omnes', and one is reminded of Hegel's *Phenomenology*, where civil society is described as a 'spiritual animal kingdom', while in Darwin the animal kingdom figures as civil society." (qtd. in Alfred Schmidt's *The Concept of Nature in Marx* [London: NLB, 1971], 46).

7. Fred Riggs, "Social Science Terminology: Basic Problems and Proposed Solutions," in *Terminology*, ed. Sonneveld and Loening, 195–220.

8. "History of Planetary Nomenclature." USGS *Astrogeology: Gazeteer of Planetary Nomenclature*. http://planetarynames.wr.usgs.gov/history.html.

9. N. David Mermin, "E pluribus boojum: The physicist as neologist," in *Boojums All the Way Through. Communicating Science in a Prosaic Age* (Cambridge: Cambridge University Press, 1990), 3–25.

10. *Flybase:* http://flybase.bio.indiana.edu; see also P. Smaglik, "Creativity, Confusion for Genes," *The Scientist* 12 (March 30, 1998).

11. "Palaeontologists in dire straits name dinosaur for the Sultan of Swing." *Geological Society News* (January 25, 2001); www.geolsoc.org.uk/template.cfm?name=knopfler.

12. Darko Suvin, *Metamorphoses of Science Fiction: On the Poetics and History of a Literary Genre* (New Haven, Conn.: Yale University Press, 1979), 3–15.

13. Peter Stockwell, *The Poetics of Science Fiction* (New York: Longman, 2000), 119.

14. Roman Jakobson, "Two Aspects of Language and Two Types of Aphasic Disturbances," in *Language in Literature*, ed. Pomorska and Rudy, 95–114.

15. Robert Heinlein, "All You Zombies," in *The Road to Science Fiction*, vol. 3: *From Heinlein to Here*, ed. James Gunn (New York: New American Library, 1979–82), 3–13.

16. William Gibson, *Burning Chrome* (New York: Arbor Hourse, 1986), 173.

17. Damien Broderick, *Reading by Starlight: Postmodern Science Fiction* (New York: Routledge, 1995), 83.

18. Samuel R. Delany, *Starboard Wine* (New York: Dragon Press, 1984), 89.

19. On cognition with least effort, see G. Origgi and D. Sperber, "Evolution, communication and the proper function of language," in *Evolution and the Human Mind: Language, Modularity and Social Cognition*, ed. Peter Carruthers and Andrew Chamberlain (Cambridge: Cambridge University Press, 2000), 140–169. For the principle of minimal departure, see Marie-Laure Ryan, *Possible Worlds: Artificial Intelligence and Narrative Theory* (Bloomington, Ind.: Indiana University Press, 1991), 48. Stockwell applies the latter to sf in *Poetics*, 141 and 155.

20. Robert Louis Stevenson. *Dr. Jekyll and Mr. Hyde and Other Stories* (London: Penguin, 1979), 83.

21. See two linked essays by Westfahl: "Words of Wishdom: The Neologisms of Science Fiction," in *Styles of Creation: Aesthetic Technique and the Creation of Fictional Worlds*, ed. George Slusser and Eric K. Rabkin (Athens, Ga.: University of Georgia Press, 1992), 221–244; and "The Words That Could Happen: Science Fiction Neologisms and the Creation of Future Worlds," *Extrapolation* 34, no. 4 (1993): 290–304. The quoted passages in the text are from "Words of Wishdom," p. 225. In these essays, Westfahl examines neologisms in eight US future-world sf novels of different periods, from Gernsback's *Ralph 124C41+* to works by William Gibson and Bruce Sterling. He finds an average of 109 new words per work ("Words of Wishdom," 223). Generalizing from such small samples drawn almost exclusively from twentieth-century U.S. texts and one work by a British writer, John

Brunner's *Stand on Zanzibar* (Garden City, N.Y.: Doubleday, 1968) presents obvious problems.

22. Brooks Landon, *Science Fiction after 1900: From the Steam Man to the Stars* (New York: Twayne, 1977), 42–49.

23. The promise that "our children will enjoy in their homes electrical energy too cheap to meter" as a result of atomic energy was made by Lewis L. Strauss, then chairman of the U.S. Atomic Energy Commission, in a speech to the National Association of Science Writers, New York City, September 16, 1954 (*New York Times*, September 17, 1954). The implication that the "Scientific-Technological Revolution" would lead to the advent of a true Communist society was incorporated into the 1961 program of the Soviet Communist Party. See Arnold Buccholz, "The Role of the Scientific-Technological Revolution in Marxism-Leninism," *Studies in Soviet Thought* 20 (1979): 145–164.

24. Kevin Kelly, *Out of Control: The New Biology of Machines, Social Systems and the Economic World* (New York: Perseus Books, 1995).

25. See my "Notes on Mutopia," *Postmodern Culture* 8, no. 1 (September 1997).

26. William Gibson, *Neuromancer* (New York: Ace Books, 1984), 62.

27. Broderick, *Reading by Starlight*, 84–85.

28. Walter E. Meyers, *Aliens and Linguists: Language Study and Science Fiction* (Athens, Ga.: University of Georgia Press, 1980), 123–130.

29. Stanisław Lem, *The Futurological Congress*, trans. Michael Kandel (San Diego, Calif.: Harcourt Brace Jovanovich, 1985), 109. That Lem's masterpiece of imaginary neology is available to us at all is only because his brilliant English translator, Michael Kandel, is able to invent brilliant neologies himself. Lem, incidentally, felt compelled to append a Polish-Polish glossary to one of his books.

30. Charles Stross and Cory Doctorow, "Jury Service," Scifi.com., at http://72.14.205.104/search?q=cache:ibutdpnCU_AJ:www.scifi.com/scifiction/originals/originals_archive/stross-doctorow/+stross+doctorow+jury+service&hl=en&gl=us&ct=clnk&cd=1 (accessed 11/21/2006).

31. George Orwell, *Nineteen Eighty-Four* (New York: Harcourt, Brace and World, 1949), 39.

32. Anthony Burgess, *A Clockwork Orange* (New York: Norton, 1962;1986), 64.

33. Russell Hoban, *Riddley Walker* (New York: Summit Books, 1980), 19.

34. In an article published posthumously, R. D. Mullen contended that *Riddley Walker* should not be considered sf, precisely because Hoban used fanciful and arbitrary mutations with no grounding in linguistic history; "Dialect, Grapholect, and Story: Russell Hoban's *Riddley Walker* as Science Fiction," *Science Fiction Studies* 27, no. 2 (July 1982): 391–406. The publication of the article elicited a lively debate in the same issue. For our purposes, Hoban's violation of linguistic "laws" is fully consonant with the playful deformation of science that is generic to sf. This position is developed in this volume's chapter "Fourth Beauty." See also Stockwell, *Poetics*, 60–62.

35. The division of sf into "thinking" and "dreaming" poles is found in Brian W. Aldiss's *Billion Year Spree: The True History of Science Fiction* (Garden City, N.Y.: Doubleday, 1973), 159.

36. David A. Ullery, *The Tarzan Novels of Edgar Rice Burroughs: An Illustrated Reader's Guide* (Jefferson, N.C.: McFarland, 2001), esp. "The Languages of Tarzan," 35–50.

37. Alan N. Shapiro, *Star Trek: Technologies of Disappearance* (Berlin: Avinus, 2004), 135–136.

38. Emile Pons. "Les langues imaginaires dans le voyage utopique. Un Précurseur. Thomas Morus." *Revue de littérature comparée* 10 (1930): 589–607.

39. H. D. Kelling, "Some Significant Names in *Gulliver's Travels*," *Studies in Philology* 48 (1951): 761–778.

40. Marina Yaguello, *Lunatic Lovers of Language: Imaginary Languages and their Inventors*, trans. Catherine Slater (London: Athlone Press; Rutherford, N.J.: Fairleigh Dickinson University Press, 1991).

41. Dell Hymes, "The Use of Anthropology: Critical, Political, Personal," in *Reinventing Anthropology*, ed. Dell Hymes (New York: Vintage, 1974), 3–79; James Clifford and George E. Marcus, eds. *Writing Culture: The Poetics and Politics of Ethnography* (Berkeley and Los Angeles: University of California Press, 1986).

42. Bryan Wilson, *Rationality* (London: Blackwell, 1977); George E. Marcus and Michael M. J. Fischer, *Anthropology as Cultural Critique: An Experimental Moment in the Human Sciences* (Chicago: University of Chicago Press, 1996).

43. Sharon Traweek, *Beamtimes and Lifetimes: The World of High Energy Physicists* (Cambridge, Mass.: Harvard University Press, 1988); Bruno Latour and Stephen Woolgar, *Laboratory Life: The Construction of Scientific Facts*, with an introduction by Jonas Salk (Princeton, N.J.: Princeton University Press, 1986); Hugh Gusterson, *Nuclear Rites: A Weapons Laboratory at the End of the Cold War* (Berkeley and Los Angeles: University of California Press, 1996). Gary Lee Downey, Joseph Dumit, and Sarah Williams, "Cyborg Anthropology," *Cultural Anthropology* 10, no. 2 (1995): 264–269.

44. William C. Spruiell, "A Lack of Alien Verbs: Coinage in Science Fiction." *LACUS Forum* 23 (1997): 441–452.

45. Spruiell's sample, like Westfahl's, is quite small: nine novels and a novella.

46. Lisa Gleitman, "The Structural Sources of Verb Meanings," in *Language Acquisition. Core Readings*, ed. Paul Bloom (Cambridge, Mass.: MIT Press, 1994): 183.

47. A detailed commentary on the meanings on Arabic terms in *Dune* can be found in "Arabic and Islamic Themes in Frank Herbert's 'Dune'" at http://baheyeldin.com/literature/arabic-and-islamic-themes-in-frank-herberts-dune.html/.

48. Alan S. Kaye and John Quijada, "The Chakobsa Language." *California Linguistic Notes* 23, no. 1 (Fall–Winter 1991): 24–25.

49. However, a paperback edition of T. E. Lawrence's *The Seven Pillars of Wisdom*, which included many Arabic words, was immensely popular in the late 1950s and early 1960s. Its eventual film version, *Lawrence of Arabia* (1962), was even more so. These works may well have influenced many of Herbert's writerly decisions.

50. Geoffrey Samuel. "Inventing Real Cultures: Some Comments on Anthropology and Science Fiction," http://users.hunterlink.net.au/~mbbgbs/Geoffrey/invent.html. Le Guin's sympathies clearly lie with those of her father, who was a student of Franz Boas, a friend of Edward Sapir, and a guiding spirit of cultural relativism in anthropology. The phrase "anthropologist as hero" is Susan Sontag's, from her essay on Claude Lévi-Strauss in her *Against Interpretation* [1966] (New York: Vintage, 1991), 69–81.

51. Personal communication with author.

52. The film's original Vulcan dialogue was spoken in English by the actors, and dubbed later into Vulcan (Vulcan Language Institute, http://home.teleport.com/~vli/spoken.htm). The dialogue has since been redubbed on the reissued DVD to sound more plausible.

53. Dick Grune, "Is Klingon an Ohlonean Language? A Comparison of Mutsun and Klingon," http://www.cs.vu.nl/~dick/Summaries/Languages/MutsunKlingonComparison.pdf.

54. Lawrence M. Schoen, "A Brief History of Klingon," *Futureframe* (January 31, 2000), http://www.morgenwelt.de/futureframe/000131–klingon.htm. See also Shapiro, *Star Trek: Technologies of Disappearance*, 138–45.

55. The Klingon Language Institute, www.kli.org.

56. Among the translations listed by the Klingon Language Institute are the books of Jonah, Esther, Ruth, Psalms 117, and the Gospel of Mark. They have been incorporated into the OSIS online Bible Tool multilingual concordance; http://www.crosswire.org /study/index.jsp?section=fun. It appears that selections from the Book of Mormon have also been converted.

57. There is an online Vulcan Language Institute (http://home.teleport.com/~vli/intro .htm); the Romulan project appears to be moribund.

58. Scott Duchesne, "'Boldly Playing': The 'Profit' of Performance within the Liminal Frame of the Con(vention[al])." Paper delivered at the annual convention of the *Science Fiction Research Association,* Guelph, Ontario, 2003.

59. For Scientology's notorious origin myth, involving the galactic war waged by the cosmic tyrant Xenu, see the *Wikipedia* entry at http://en.wikipedia.org/wiki/Xenu. On Raelians, see http://www.rael.org/; on Heaven's Gate, see the Heaven's Gate Mission Statement: http://www.rickross.com/reference/heavensgate/gate_overview.html. On the Nation of Islam's Motherplane/Mothership, see the Reverend Louis Farrakhan' s speech, "The Divine Destruction of America: Can She Avert It?'" delivered June 9, 1996, http://www .finalcall.com/MLFspeaks/destruction.html (accessed May 21, 2006).

SECOND BEAUTY
Fictive Novums (pages 47–75)

1. Darko Suvin, *Metamorphoses of Science Fiction: On the Poetics and History of a Literary Genre* (New Haven: Yale University Press, 1979), 63 (emphasis in original).

2. Tom Moylan, "The Locus of Hope: Utopia versus Ideology," *Science Fiction Studies* 9, no. 2 (July 1982): 159.

3. Fredric Jameson, *Marxism and Form: Twentieth-Century Dialectical Theories of Literature* (Princeton, N.J.: Princeton University Press, 1972), 129.

4. Anson Rabinbach. "Between Enlightenment and Apocalypse: Benjamin, Bloch and Modern German Jewish Messianism," *New German Critique* 34 (1985): 78–124.

5. Ernst Bloch, *The Principle of Hope,* trans. Neville Plaice, Stephen Plaice, and Paul Knight (Cambridge, Mass.: MIT Press, 2000), 1:200.

6. Ernst Bloch, "A Philosophical View of the Detective Novel," in *The Utopian Function of Art and Literature: Selected Essays,* trans. Jack Zipes and Frank Mecklenburg (Cambridge, Mass.: MIT Press, 1988), 245–264.

7. Suvin, *Metamorphoses,* 3–13.

8. See Bloch's metaphor of the front in *The Principle of Hope,* 1:200.

9. Steven Helmling, "During Auschwitz: Adorno, Hegel, and the 'Unhappy Consciousness' of Critique," *Postmodern Culture* 1 (2005); http://www3.iath.virginia.edu/pmc/text-only/issue.105/15.2helmling.txt.; Richard Wolin, "Utopia, Mimesis, and Reconciliation: A Redemptive Critique of Adorno's Aesthetic Theory," *Representations* 32 (Autumn 1990): 33–49.

10. Marc Angenot, "The Absent Paradigm: An Introduction to the Semiotics of Science Fiction," *Science Fiction Studies* 6, no. 1 (March 1979): 9–19.

11. Darko Suvin, *Positions and Presuppositions in Science Fiction* (Kent, Ohio: Kent State University Press, 1988), 70 (emphasis in original).

12. Ibid.

13. Christian Fuchs, "Dialectical Materialism and the Self-organization of Matter," http://www.seekingwisdom.com/fuchs.htm. See also Alfred Schmidt, *The Concept of Nature in Marx*, trans. Ben Fowkes (London: NLB, 1971), 159–62.

14. Tom Shippey, for example, calls each individual sign of newness in a given sf text, from concrete objects to concepts, a novum. "Hard Reading" in *A Companion to Science Fiction*, ed. David Seed (Malden, Mass.: Blackwell, 2005), 14–15.

15. Carl D. Malmgren argues that time-travel in *The Time Machine* is a novum so conventionalized that it ceases to have cognitive content, acting instead as a device to introduce the dominant novum; see his *Worlds Apart: Narratology of Science Fiction* (Bloomington, Ind.: Indiana University Press, 1991), 148. Malmgren's book also includes a cogent discussion of Suvin's concept of the novum (25–31).

16. Bloch, "The Artistic Illusion as the Visible Anticipatory Illumination," in *The Utopian Function of Art and Literature*, 141–155.

17. Suvin, *Metamorphoses*, 13–15.

18. Peter Nicholls (as [PN]), "Conceptual Breakthrough," in *The Encyclopedia of Science Fiction*, ed. John Clute and Peter Nicholl (New York: St. Martin's, 1993), 254–257.

19. Jorge Luis Borges, "Tlön, Uqbar, and Orbis Tertius." in *Labyrinths: Selected Stories and Other Writings*, ed. Donald A. Yates and James E. Irby (New York: New Directions, 1964), 3–18.

20. Kim Stanley Robinson, *Remaking History and Other Stories* (New York: Orb, 1994), 362–373.

21. Gregory Benford, "Of Time and *Timescape*," *Science Fiction Studies* 20, no. 2 (July 1993): 184–190; N. David Mermin, "Spooky actions at a distance: mysteries of the quantum theory," in his *Boojums All the Way Through: Communicating Science in a Prosaic Age* (New York: Cambridge University Press, 1990), 110–176.

22. Westfahl detects a pattern of double-estrangement in most sf: "at the beginning the novel, only the reader is estranged from its future world, as indicated by the large number of neologisms, but at some point later in the novel, long after the reader's initial feeling of estrangement has been dissipated, a second moment of estrangement occurs, when both the reader and the main character become estranged, as marked by the sudden increase in neologisms." See his "Words of Wishdom: The Neologisms of SF," in *Styles of Creation: Aesthetic Technique and the Creation of Fictional Worlds* ed. George Slusser and Eric S. Rabkin (Athens, Ga.: University of Georgia Press, 1992), 224 (emphasis in original). These new neologisms mark the advent of a new novum.

23. Julius Kagarlitsky, "Realism and Fantasy," in *SF: The Other Side of Realism: Essays on Modern Fantasy and Science Fiction*, ed. Thomas Clareson (Bowling Green, Ohio: Bowling Green University Popular Press, 1971), 29–52.

24. H. G. Wells, *Seven Famous Novels* (New York: Knopf, 1934), viii; qtd. in Kagarlitsky, "Realism and Fantasy," 44.

25. Roland Barthes. "The *Nautilus* and the Drunken Boat," in *Mythologies*, selected and translated from the French by Annette Lavers (New York: Hill and Wang, 1972), 65–67.

26. Kagarlitsky , "Realism and Fantasy," 47.

27. See Donna Haraway, *Simians, Cyborgs and Women: The Reinvention of Nature* (New York: Routledge, 1991); Sandra Harding, *The Science Question in Feminism* (Ithaca, N.Y.:

Cornell University Press, 1986); Evelyn Fox Keller, *Reflections on Gender and Science* (New Haven, Conn.: Yale University Press, 1996); Bruno Latour, *Science in Action: How to Follow Scientists and Engineers through Society* (Cambridge, Mass.: Harvard University Press, 1987).

28. Ann Weinstone argues that Rheya shows far more resistance than she is generally allowed, in "Resisting Monsters: Notes on *Solaris*," *Science Fiction Studies* 21, no. 2 (July 1994): 173–190.

29. Lawrence Person, "Notes Toward a Postcyberpunk Manifesto," *Slashdot* (10/9/1999); http://slashdot.org/features/99/10/08/2123255.shtml.

30. Peter Galison and David J. Stump, eds., *The Disunity of Science: Boundaries, Contexts, and Power* (Stanford, Calif.: Stanford University Press, 1996).

31. Brian McHale, *Constructing Postmodernism* (New York: Routledge, 1992), 12–13.

32. Hannah Arendt, *Between Past and Future. Eight Exercises in Political Thought* (New York: Viking, 1968), 276–277.

33. The more or less strict insistence on scientific plausibility as a necessary element of form has dominated sf studies for the past generation. It has, as we have seen, led to the exclusion of many works that audiences treat as unambiguously science-fictional. This stance has weakened recently, as more and more sf is mixed with magical/marvelous elements of contestatory subcultures. There has been, in fact, been long-standing and sophisticated resistance to the exclusion of irrational elements in sf within the genre itself. See Ian Watson, "Science Fiction, Surrealism and Shamanism," *New York Review of Science Fiction* (1999): 1:8–12; Kobo Abe, "The Boom in Science Fiction (1962)," *Science Fiction Studies* 29, no. 3 (November 2002) 340–341.

34. See Rob Latham, *Consuming Youth: Vampires, Cyborgs, and the Culture of Consumption* (Chicago: University of Chicago Press, 2002).

35. Most sophisticated theoretical approaches to sf tend to disparage the formulaic commodities produced solely for mass entertainment as "sci-fi," to be distinguished from the semantically richer and aesthetically more complex "sf." I shall use a similar distinction — less for aesthetic reasons than to distinguish between two contexts of expectations, one addressing elite artistic concerns and the other, popular entertainment. The two clearly flow together throughout the history of the genre. The fact that I am using "sf" as shorthand to indicate both the big tent of all forms of science fiction and the elite pole of the genre, clearly makes "sci-fi" the marked term for me. Stockwell maintains that the genre's definition remains fluid because audiences' ideas of what belongs in the class are a result of the texts and motifs they have associated with sf in their social experience; that is, their "prototype texts"; see Peter Stockwell, *The Poetics of Science Fiction* (New York: Longman, 2000), 6–8. People will revise their sense of what defines this class as they gain more experience with other putative sf texts — although this process is also extremely fluid and socially determined; these new inputs must also be seen as sf for some reason before they are included in the mix. For lack of a better justification, my present approach — and my relegation of "sci-fi" to the margins — is a consequence of the fact that my prototypes have been literary and philosophical, and my adjustments have been mainly concerned with accommodating nonliterary sf. In future work that will focus on sf in nonliterary media, I shall address this imbalance more directly and theoretically.

36. *Lexx*, DVD commentary, disk 2.

37. Freedman's conception of the cognition effect is discussed at length in "Fourth Beauty."

1. Stockwell, *Poetics of Science Fiction* (New York: Longman, 2000), 45.

2. C. J. Cherryh, *Downbelow Station* (New York: Daw, 1981), 9.

3. The parable space in question differs from Delany's concept of paraspace, in that the latter is a diegetic alternative domain set off from diegetic "mundane" worlds, while the former is nondiegetic. The parable space is the entirety of the imaginary sf setting, viewed as a trope for estranging the audience's real world. Its purpose is exhausted by cognitive estrangement. For Delany on paraspaces, see his "Is Cyberpunk a Good or a Bad Thing?" *Mississippi Review* 47/48 (1988): 28–35.

4. The sf megatext, proposed independently by Attebery and Broderick, is the large and mutable body of references that most sf artists and audiences consider to be the shared subcultural thesaurus of the genre, because "in some ways all SF constitutes a single encyclopedic repository of images, tropes, character types, and narrative moves"; see Brian Attebery, *Decoding Gender in Science Fiction* (London: Routledge, 2002), 11. These references include virtually any element that sf works have employed in the past, or phenomena from reality that are considered conducive to science-fictional transformation, and hence inherently science-fictional. They cover an enormous range of devices: abstract topoi (such as time travel, alien contacts, dystopias), technical devices (faster-than-light travel, time machines, cyborgs), intellectual problems (the grandfather paradox, relativistic time-dilation, alien-human communication) and their imaginary solutions (universal translators, ansibles, warp-drive), settings (Mars, the future metropolis, virtual reality), scientific raw materials (relativity, cloning, nanotechnology, black holes, "exotic matter"), relevant social phenomena (mass media, technophile cults, laboratory life), icons, and conventionalized plot mechanisms. They extend to highly specific motifs and devices drawn from sf works that have achieved classical status — such as Isaac Asimov's Three Laws of Robotics, the pods of *Invasion of the Body Snatchers,* Philip K. Dick's reality-shifts, Ursula K. Le Guin's androgynes, and William Gibson's matrix. The expanse of the megatext indicates the richness and density of the pool of references on which sf artists can rely, a body almost thick enough to simulate a virtual culture, the culture of *as if.* The discourse of sf relies on a reader's ability to interpret surprising phrases and neologisms by treating them as imaginary allusions to the science-fictional universe, an imaginary culture consisting of many different types of alternative logics, histories, and sciences. What distinguishes sf's megatext from other such intertextual bases is, first, the sheer magnitude of its thesaurus, which is continually fed by new texts (ranging from novels to television commercials), speculative science (from new scientific theories to obvious pseudoscience), and historical events (attacks by computer viruses, natural disasters, astronautical accidents). In the absence of real experience of the future to reinforce or refute the fictional worlds, the megatext acts as an imaginary archive of the future. As a critical concept, the megatext delineates the area where the fictive elements of sf overlap with their use in interpreting experiences in reality. That being said, it is important to note that the sf megatext is not the same for all competent audiences. Though it is not useless to speak of an ideal lexicon of sf elements, the competence of sf audiences is nonetheless profoundly influenced by social factors, especially class, nation, and gender. Elements from feminist sf — indeed, sf written by women, period — are only gradually entering megatextual common knowledge. (see Attebery, *Decoding Gender*). The tone of a given sf text's style — ironic, sober,

grotesque, comic, melodramatic — also depends on assumed knowledge of the sf mega-text. Soberly realistic sf depends on reinforcement for otherwise fabulous conventions that might, without a megatextual imprimatur, strain readers' credulity. Nonserious fictions depend on the megatext for appropriate contrasts.

5. See my "Futuristic Flu, or The Revenge of the Future," in *Fiction 2000. Cyberpunk and the Future of Narrative,* ed. George Slusser and Tom Shippey (Athens, Ga.: University of Georgia Press, 1992), 26–45.

6. Ursula K. Le Guin, Introduction to *The Left Hand of Darkness* (New York: Walker, 1969), viii.

7. Darko Suvin, *Metamorphoses of Science Fiction: On the Poetics and Histories of a Literary Genre* (New Haven, Conn.: Yale University Press, 1979), 76; "Goodbye to Extrapolation," *Science Fiction Studies* 22, no. 2 (July 1995): 301.

8. Samuel R. Delany, *Starboard Wine* (New York: Dragon Press, 1984), 48.

9. Qtd. in Niall Ferguson, ed., *Virtual History: Alternatives and Counterfactuals* (New York: Basic Books, 1999), 84–85.

10. Paul K. Alkon, *Origins of Futuristic Fiction* (Athens, Ga.: University of Georgia Press, 1987), 15.

11. Alfred Schmidt, *The Concept of Nature in Marx,* trans. Ben Fowkes (London: NLB, 1971), esp. chapter 3; G.W.F. Hegel, *Elements of the Philosophy of Right,* ed. Allen W. Wood (Cambridge: Cambridge University Press, 1991), para. 151, p. 195.

12. I am adapting György Lukács's famous claim that the task of the historical novel is to depict "the prehistory of the present"; see *The Historical Novel,* trans. Hannah and Stanley Mitchell (Boston: Beacon, 1963), 337.

13. This revisionary effect inherent in the novum also appears on the level of generic textuality in sf writers' tendency to rewrite earlier texts and schemes, a trait that Robert M. Philmus argues is essential to the genre; *Visions and Re-Visions* (Liverpool: University of Liverpool Press, 2005), 301–309.

14. Lukács, *Historical Novel,* 92–93.

15. Olaf Stapledon, *Last and First Men* (1932); Isaac Asimov's original Foundation trilogy, *Foundation* (1950), *Foundation and Empire* (1952), and *Second Foundation* (1953) was extended with *Foundation's Edge* (1982) and *Foundation and Earth* (1986); the bulk of Heinlein's "future history" stories were collected in *The Past Through Tomorrow* (1967) and *Orphans of the Sky* (1963), as well as the novels *Methuselah's Children* (1941), *Time Enough for Love* (1973), and *To Sail beyond the Sunset* (1987). Le Guin's Hainish novels include *Rocannon's World* (1966), *Planet of Exile* (1966), *City of Illusions* (1967), *The Left Hand of Darkness* (1969), *The Dispossessed: An Ambiguous Utopia* (1974), *The Word for World is Forest* (1976); the Strugatskys' *Noon Universe* tales include *Noon: 22nd Century* (1961), *Escape Attempt* (1962), *Far Rainbow* (1963), *Prisoners of Power* (1971), *The Kid* [Space Mowgli](1971), *The Kid from Hell* (1972), *Beetle in the Anthill* (1979), *The Time Wanderers* (1985). Cherryh's Alliance/Union series includes some two dozen novels, among them *Merchanter's Luck* (1982), *Forty Thousand in Gehenna* (1983), *Cyteen* (1985), *Downbelow Station* (1986), *Rimrunners* (1989), *Heavy Time* (1991), and *Hellburner* (1992).

16. Northrop Frye, *Anatomy of Criticism: Four Essays* (Princeton, N.J.: Princeton University Press, 1957), 49.

17. José Ortega y Gasset, *Meditations on Quixote* (New York: Norton, 1961), 118.

18. J. G. Ballard, V. Vale and Andrea Juno, ed. (San Francisco, Calif.: Re/Search Publishers, 1984), 107.

19. John Clute, *Look at the Evidence: Essays and Reviews* (Liverpool: Liverpool University Press, 1995), 195.

20. Hayden White, *Metahistory: The Historical Imagination in Nineteenth Century Europe* (Baltimore: Johns Hopkins University Press, 1975).

21. Fredric Jameson, "Of Islands and Trenches: Neutralization and the Production of Utopian Discourse," in *The Ideologies of Theory: Essays, 1971–1986* (Minneapolis: University of Minnesota Press, 1988), 75–101.

22. Alkon, *Origins*, 121ff.

23. Tom Moylan, *Demand the Impossible: Science Fiction and the Utopian Imagination.* (New York: Methuen, 1987).

24. See Fredric Jameson's "'If I Can Find One Good City, I Will Spare the Man': Realism and Utopia in Kim Stanley Robinson's Mars Trilogy," in his *Archaeologies of the Future: The Desire Called Utopia and Other Science Fictions* (New York: Verso, 2005), 393–416.

25. Stephen Jay Gould, *Full House: The Spread of Excellence from Plato to Darwin* (New York: Harmony Books, 1996), 20.

26. Bernhard Rensch, *Evolution Above the Species Level* (New York: Columbia University Press, 1960), 281. See also G. Ledyard Stebbins, *The Basis of Progressive Evolution* (Chapel Hill, N.C.: University of North Carolina Press, 1969).

27. Julian Huxley, *Evolution: The Modern Synthesis* (New York: Harper and Brothers, 1943), 564.

28. H. D. Bernal, *The World, The Flesh, and the Devil: An Inquiry into the Future of the Three Enemies of the Rational Soul*, 2nd ed., with a new foreword by the author (London: Cape, 1970).

29. Pierre Teilhard de Chardin, *The Phenomenon of Man* (New York: Harper Perennial, 1976); *The Divine Milieu* (New York: Harper Perennial, 2001); *The Future of Man* (New York: Image Books, 2004).

30. Ray Kurzweil, *The Age of Spiritual Machines: When Computers Exceed Human Intelligence* (New York: Viking, 1999), 5.

31. Suvin, *Metamorphoses*, 208–221.

32. On Wells's complex and ambivalent attitude toward imperialism, see Patrick Parrinder, *Shadows of the Future: H. G. Wells, Science Fiction, and Prophecy* (Syracuse, N.Y.: Syracuse University Press, 1995), 65–79; Adam Roberts, *Science Fiction* (London: Routledge, 2000), 63–64; Alex Irvine, "The War of the Worlds and the Disease of Imperialism," in *Flashes of the Fantastic. Selected Essays from the War of the Worlds Centennial, Nineteenth International Conference on the Fantastic in the Arts*, ed. David Ketterer (Westport, Conn.: Praeger, 2004), 33–42.

33. Mechanics and Shapers are divergent evolutes of humanity in Bruce Sterling's *Schismatrix;* the flying men and great brains are evolutionary competitors in Olaf Stapledon's *Star Maker.*

34. Susan Sontag, "The Imagination of Disaster" in *Against Interpretation and Other Essays*, (New York: Farrar, Straus & Giroux, 1996), 209–225.

35. Qtd. In Albert I. Berger, *The Magic that Works: John W. Campbell and the American Response to Technology* (San Bernardino, Calif.: Borgo Press, 1993), 106.

36. Lee Smolin has proposed a principle of "cosmological natural selection," by virtue of which evolutionary selection processes govern the multiple universes mandated by Everett's many worlds quantum cosmology; Smolin, *The Life of the Cosmos* (New York: Oxford University Press, 1997). The problem of the role of natural selection in the devel-

opment of mathematics has arisen in response to Eugene Wigner's essay, ""The Unreasonable Effectiveness of Mathematics in the Natural Sciences," in *Communications in Pure and Applied Mathematics* 13, no. 1 (February 1960); http://www.dartmouth.edu/~matc/MathDrama/reading/Wigner.html.

37. Lewis Henry Morgan laid out a historical hierarchy of civilizations based on levels of technological development in his *Ancient Society* (New York: H. Holt, 1877).

38. Stanisław Lem, *Summa Technologiae*, chapter 2, section ii. My translation is from Beatrix Murányi's Hungarian translation (Budapest: Kossuth, 1976), 28.

39. Important bases of technoevolutionary research are the Sociological Institute of the University of Zurich (http://socio.ch/evo/index_evo.htm) and the Austrian Konrad Lorenz Institute for Evolution and Cognition Research http://www.kli.ac.at/theorylab/Areas/CE.html.

40. John Ziman, "Evolutionary Models for Technological Change," in *Technological Innovation as an Evolutionary Process*, ed. Ziman (Cambridge: Cambridge University Press, 2000), 3.

41. Transhumanist movements have set up a number of quasi-academic institutes and far-ranging social networks for rapidly proliferating futurist groups advocating increased research and development in technoscientific programs dedicated to overcoming human beings' biological fatedness, such as nanotechnology, genetic engineering, artificial intelligence, cryogenics, and so forth. The first of these, The Extropy Institute (http://www.extropy.org/) disbanded in 2006, declaring its work done. The World Transhumanist Association (http://www.transhumanism.org/index.php/WTA/index/) continues its work as the main clearinghouse and lobbying group for the movement.

42. Donna J. Haraway, *Simians, Cyborgs, and Women: The Reinvention of Nature* (New York: Routledge, 1991), 191.

43. In Louis-Napoleon Geoffrey's *Napoléon et la conquête du monde — 1812 à 1832 — Histoire de la monarchie universelle* (1836), Napoleon is victorious at Waterloo; the Confederacy wins the Civil War in Harry Turtledove's *The Guns of the South* (1993) and in Ward Moore's classic *Bring the Jubilee* (1953); the Germans win World War II in myriad tales, including Philip K. Dick's *The Man in the High Castle* (1962) and Robert Harris' *Fatherland* (1992); the Spanish Armada successfully reconquers England for the Catholic Church in Keith Roberts's *Pavane* (1968). The Uchronia Alternate History List includes an extensive catalogue of alternative histories at http://www.uchronia.net/.

44. Stanisław Lem, "The Time-Travel Story and Related Matters of Science-Fiction Structuring." In *Microworlds: Writings on Science Fiction and Fantasy*, ed. Franz Rottensteiner (San Diego, Calif.: Harcourt Brace Jovanovich, 1984), 46.

45. On the impact of chaos science, emergence, and catastrophe theories on contemporary culture, and science fiction in particular, see N. Katherine Hayles, *Chaos Bound: Orderly Disorder in Contemporary Literature and Science* (Ithaca, N.Y.: Cornell University Press, 1990); N. Katherine Hayles, ed., *Chaos and Order: Complex Dynamics in Literature and Science* (Chicago: University of Chicago Press, 1991); and David Porush, "Prigogine, Chaos, and Contemporary Science Fiction," *Science Fiction Studies* 18, no. 3 (November 1991): 367–386.

46. Brian McHale, *Constructing Postmodernism* (New York: Routledge, 1992), 125.

47. Fredric Jameson, *Postmodernism; Or, The Cultural Logic of Late Capitalism*. (Durham: Duke University Press, 1991).

48. Ferguson, *Virtual History*, 89.

49. Paul J. Nahin, *Time Machines: Time Travel in Physics, Metaphysics, and Science Fiction,* 2nd ed. New York: Springer-Verlag, 1999), 23.

50. Constance Penley, "Time Travel, Primal Scene and the Critical Dystopia." In *Alien Zone: Cultural Theory and Contemporary Science Fiction Cinema* ed. Annette Kuhn, (London: Verso, 1990), 116–127.

51. Alan N. Shapiro, *Star Trek: Technologies of Disappearance* (Berlin: Avinus, 2004), 202 (original emphasis removed).

52. The sf time-travel story has its elite, and distinctly non–future-oriented, parallel in what George Slusser and Danièle Chatelaine call the modern geometrical narrative; see George Slusser, and Danièle Chatelain, "Spacetime Geometries: Time Travel and the Modern Geometrical Narrative," *Science Fiction Studies* 22, no. 2 (July 1995): 161–186.

53. Wells, *Seven Famous Novels* (New York: Knopf, 1934), 4.

54. Nahin, *Time Machines,* 68.

55. Philip K. Dick, *Valis* (New York: Bantam, 1981), 51.

56. Darko Suvin, *Victorian Science Fiction in the UK: The Discourses of Knowledge and of Power* (Boston: G. K. Hall, 1983), 149.

57. Philip Jose Farmer's "Sail On! Sail On!" appeared originally in *Startling Stories* (December 1952); Harry Turtledove, *Guns of the South* (New York: Ballantine, 1992); Stephen Baxter, *Anti-Ice* (New York: HarperCollins, 1993).

58. Marc Angenot, "Science Fiction in France before Verne." *Science Fiction Studies* 5, no. 1 (March 1978): 58–66.

59. Karen Hellekson, *The Alternate History: Refiguring Historical Time* (Kent, Ohio: Kent State University Press, 2001), 4.

60. Bryan R. Wilson, ed. *Rationality* (London: Blackwell, 1970).

61. *Slipstream* was a term coined by Bruce Sterling to identify contemporary fiction that employs science-fictional or quasi-sf tropes without commitment to the conventions of sf. Slipstream writers tend to use sf as one of many semiotic codes that evoke hyper-techno-scientific culture. Sterling's article originally appeared in *SF Eye,* no. 5 (July 1989); available at http://www.eff.org/Misc/Publications/Bruce_Sterling/Catscan_columns/catscan.05.

62. Matt Hills, "Counterfictions in the Work of Kim Newman: Rewriting Gothic SF as 'Alternate-Story Stories.'" *Science Fiction Studies* 30, no. 3 (November 2003): 439ff.

63. Hellekson, *Alternate History,* 83(emphasis in original).

64. Vernor Vinge's original paper on the Singularity, delivered to NASA in 1993, is the source text of all later speculations. It is available at http://mindstalk.net/vinge/vingesing.html. For further commentaries, see Damien Broderick, *The Spike: How Our Lives Are Being Transformed By Rapidly Advancing Technologies* (New York: Forge 2001), and Ray Kurzweil, *The Singularity Is Near: When Humans Transcend Biology* (New York: Viking, 2005). An excellent informal online symposium on Vinge's paper, along with Vinge's responses, can be found at http://hanson.gmu.edu/vi.html.

FOURTH BEAUTY
Imaginary Science (pages 111–145)

1. Arthur B. Evans, *Jules Verne Rediscovered: Didacticism and the Scientific Novel,* (New York: Greenwood Press, 1988).

2. Edward James, *Science Fiction in the 20th Century* (New York: Oxford University Press, 1994), 52–53 and 58–61; Albert I. Berger, *The Magic That Works: John W. Camp-*

bell and the American Response to Technology (San Bernardino, Calif.: Borgo Press, 1993), 33–51.

3. John Huntington, "Hard-Core Science Fiction and the Illusion of Science," in *Hard Science Fiction,* ed. George E. Slusser and Eric S. Rabkin (Carbondale: Southern Illinois University Press, 1988), 48–49.

4. John Huntington, *The Logic of Fantasy: H.G. Wells and Science Fiction* (New York: Columbia University Press, 1982), 8.

5. H. G. Wells, Preface to his *Seven Famous Novels* (New York: Knopf, 1934), viii.

6. Gregory Benford, "Is There a Technological Fix for the Human Condition?" in *Hard Science Fiction,* ed. Slusser and Rabkin, 84. See Gary Westfahl's chapter "'Treating the Whole Thing as a Game.' Hard Science Fiction as Seen by its Writers," in his *Cosmic Engineers: A Study of Hard Science Fiction* (Westport, Conn.: Greenwood Press, 1996), 39–51.

7. Clement quoted in Westfahl, *Cosmic Engineers,* 40.

8. Carol McGuirk argues that this generalization holds for both hard/engineering sf and soft/social-scientific sf, but not for what she terms "visionary sf," in which the focus is on riven romance characters rather than world frames. See Carol McGuirk, "NoWhere Man: Toward a Poetics of Post-Utopian Characterization," *Science Fiction Studies* 21, no. 2 (July 1994): 141–154.

9. Hal Clement, "Whirligig World," first published in *Astounding Science Fiction* 51 (June 1953): 102–114; reprinted most recently with the Orion's SF Collector's Edition reprint of *Mission of Gravity* (2000). Westfahl includes an extended discussion of the essay in *Cosmic Engineers,* 39–44.

10. Gwyneth Jones, *Deconstructing the Starships. Science, Fiction, and Reality* (Liverpool: Liverpool University Press, 1999), 11–13.

11. Tatiana Chernyshova, "Science Fiction and Myth Creation in Our Age," *Science Fiction Studies* 31, no. 3 (November 2004): 348.

12. Olaf Stapledon, "Preface to the English Edition," in *Last and First Men* [1931] (New York: Dover Publications, 1968), 9.

13. The cosmological constant has become of central interest to cosmology in recent years, albeit in a different form than Einstein's attempt to establish a limit to the expansion of the universe implicit in the General Theory; see Lawrence M. Krauss and Michael S. Turner, "The cosmological constant is back," *General Relativity and Gravitation* 27, no. 11 (November 1995): 1137–1144. Such developments invite the steampunk theme of the return of discarded models in more refined and topical forms, made compatible with experimental results and new theories.

14. Rom Harré, *The Principles of Scientific Thinking* (Chicago: University of Chicago Press, 1970), 33–62.

15. See Margaret Morrisson and Mary S. Morgan, "Models as Mediating Instruments," in *Models as Mediators: Perspectives on Natural and Social Sciences,* ed. Mary S. Morgan and Margaret Morrisson (Cambridge: Cambridge University Press, 1999), 10–37.

16. David C. Gooding, "Thought Experiments," in *Routledge Encyclopedia of Philosophy,* ed. E. Craig (London: Routledge, 1998); http://www.rep.routledge.com/article/Q106SECT1. See also Stephan Hartmann, "Models and Stories in Hadron Physics," in *Models as Mediators,* ed. Morgan and Morrisson, 326–46.

17. Gooding, loc. cit.

18. Ibid.

19. John Norton, "Thought Experiments in Einstein's Work," in *Thought Experiments in*

Science and Philosophy, ed. Tamara Horowitz and Gerald J. Massey (Savage, Md.: Rowman and Littlefield, 1991), 129.

20. David Gooding, *Experiment and the Making of Meaning: Human Agency in Scientific Observation and Experiment* (Boston: Kluwer Academic Publishers, 1990), 208; Thomas S. Kuhn's seminal position on thought-experiment is stated in "A Function for Thought Experiments," in his book *The Essential Tension: Selected Studies in Scientific Tradition and Change* (Chicago: University of Chicago Press, 1977), 240–265.

21. James G. Lennox, "Darwinian Thought Experiments: A Function for Just So Stories," in *Thought Experiments*, ed. Horowitz and Massey, 229.

22. Nancy Cartwright, *The Dappled World: A Study of the Boundaries of Science* (Cambridge: Cambridge University Press, 1999), 36–43.

23. On the theoretical embeddedness of data structuring in general see Patrick Suppes, "Models of Data" in *Logic, Methodology and Philosophy of Science: Proceedings* [Proceedings of the International Congress for Logic, Methodology and Philosophy of Science, Stanford, California, 1960], ed. Ernest Nagel, Patrick Suppes, and Alfred Tarski (Stanford, Calif.: Stanford University Press, 1962), 252–261.

24. Cartwright, *Dappled World*, 139.

25. Gooding, "Thought Experiments."

26. Sociologically grounded folklore classification does not seem to have taken up the tall tale. The form is sometimes discussed by folklorists as a kind of real-world trickster tale, in which locals attempt to gull outsiders, especially city slickers. This notion owes more to reading Twain than to studying the ways the tales are told. Quixote and Münchhausen, Till Eulenspiegel and Háry János, all emerged from tall tales.

27. Research in sf has only recently begun to study the necessary connections between journalistic popularization of science and its literary transformations. The heart of those connections is their shared ambition to establish an effective public rhetoric of science (or at least the appearance of one) at the very moment they are playing with it.

28. Although Poe probably did not intend "Valdemar" to be a hoax, it was taken for a news article by many of the readers of *The American Review: A Whig Journal* in December 1845. "Poe may have inadvertently created a hoax through his publication of the story in a magazine known for news reporting as well as fiction, through his adherence to writing in a style consistent with science writing in general and medical case studies in particular, through his pretence of name-dropping, and through his fortunate exploitation of a hot topic." Lynda Walsh, *Sins Against Science: The Scientific Media Hoaxes of Poe, Twain, and Others* (Albany, N.Y.: State University of New York Press, 2006), 101.

29. Samuel R. Delany, *Starboard Wine* (New York: Dragon Press, 1984), 176–177.

30. Benford, "Is There a Technological Fix," 83.

31. Gregory Benford, "Time and *Timescape*," *Science Fiction Studies* 20, no. 2 (July 1993): 188.

32. Benford, "Is There a Technological Fix," 86.

33. This is a central claim argued by Alan N. Shapiro's *Star Trek: Technologies of Disappearance* (Berlin: Avinus, 2004).

34. Paul J. Nahin, *Time Machines: Time Travel in Physics, Metaphysics, and Science Fiction*, with a foreword by Kim S. Thorne, 2nd ed. (New York: Springer, 1999), 243.

35. Lawrence M. Krauss, *The Physics of Star Trek*, with a foreword by Stephen Hawking (New York: Basic Books, 1995), 54.

36. Shapiro discusses in detail the "exotic" (that is, entirely speculative) physical as-

sumptions required for *Star Trek*'s wormholes and warp drive; see his *Star Trek*, 201–215 and 335–345.

37. Mark Pesce, "Magic Mirror: The Novel as Software development Platform" [Presented at the Media in Transition Conference at MIT, 1999], web.mit.edu/m-i-t/articles/pesce.html.

38. Allucquere Rosanne Stone, qtd. in Pesce, "Magic Mirror."

39. José Lopez. "Bridging the Gaps: Science Fiction in Nanotechnology." *HYLE—International Journal for Philosophy of Chemistry* 10, no. 2 (2004): 131–154.

40. Ibid., 134–136.

41. K. Eric Drexler, *Engines of Creation*, with a foreword by Marvin Minsky (Garden City, N.Y.: Anchor Press/Doubleday, 1986), 171–190; http://www.e-drexler.com/d/06/00/EOC/EOC_Chapter_11.html.

42. Lopez, "Bridging the Gaps," 140–141; see also Colin Milburn, "Nanotechnology in the Age of Posthuman Engineering: Science Fiction as Science," in *Nanoculture: Implications of the New Technoscience*, ed. N. Katherine Hayles (Portland, Ore.: Intellect Books, 2004), 109–129.

43. N. Katherine Hayles, "Connecting the Quantum Dots: Nanotechscience and Culture" in *Nanoculture*, ed. Hayles, 14.

44. See my "Futuristic Flu; or, The Revenge of the Future," in *Fiction 2000: Cyberpunk and the Future of Narrative*, ed. George E. Slusser and Tom Shippey (Athens, Ga.: University of Georgia Press, 1992).

45. John Clute, *Look at the Evidence: Essays and Reviews* (Liverpool: Liverpool University Press, 1995), 8–10.

46. In 2005, science-fictional technothriller writer Michael Crichton was invited to meet with President George W. Bush at the White House for a lengthy tête-à-tête on the subject of global warning. In an appendix to his novel *State of Fear* (2004), Crichton had derided the notion that current climate change was the result of human actions, a notion with which the president was said to be in "near-total agreement" ("Bush's Chat with Novelist Alarms Environmentalists," *New York Times*, February 19, 2006.) The response to Crichton's position from James Hansen of Goddard Institute for Space Studies, "Michael Crichton's 'Scientific Method,'" can be found at columbia.edu/~jeh1/hansen_re-crichton.pdf.

47. For Baudrillard's conception of science fiction under the regime of hyperreality see his "Simulacra and Science Fiction," *Science Fiction Studies* 18, no. 3 (November 1991): 309–313.

48. Carl Sagan, *Broca's Brain: Reflections on the Romance of Science* (New York: Random House, 1979), 14.

49. Alfred Jarry's definition of "Pataphysics" in *Exploits and Opinions of Doctor Faustroll, Pataphysician* (originally published by Grove Press in 1965) is available online at: http://pataphysics-lab.com/sarcophaga/daysures/Jarry,%20Alfred%20–%20Dr%20Faustroll.rtf.

50. Carl Freedman, *Critical Theory and Science Fiction* (Middletown, Conn.: Wesleyan University Press, 2000), 18–19.

51. Barthes, Roland, "The Reality Effect," in *The Rustle of Language*, trans. Richard Howard (New York: Hill and Wang, 1986), 141–148; "Historical Discourse" in *Introduction to Structuralism*, ed. Michael Lane (New York: Basic Books, 1970), 145–155.

52. See Darrell Huff's classic *How to Lie with Statistics* [1954] (New York: Norton, 1993); Nancy Cartwright, *How the Laws of Physics Lie*, (Oxford: Oxford University Press, 1983).

53. See Fredric Jameson, *Archaeologies of the Future: the Desire Called Utopia and Other Science Fictions* (New York: Verso, 2005), and *Postmodernism; or, the Cultural Logic of Late*

Capitalism (Durham, N.C.: Duke University Press, 1991); Freedman, *Critical Theory;* Tom Moylan, *Demand the Impossible: Science Fiction and the Utopian Imagination* (New York: Methuen, 1986) and *Scraps of the Untainted Sky: Science Fiction, Utopia, Dystopia,* (Boulder, Colo.: Westview Press, 2000); Marc Angenot and Darko Suvin, "Not Only but Also: Reflections on Cognition and Ideology in Science Fiction and SF Criticism," *Science Fiction Studies* 6, no. 2 (1979); Peter Fitting, "The Modern Anglo-American SF Novel: Utopian Longing and Capitalist Cooptation," *Science Fiction Studies* 6, no. 1 (1979), "*Ubik:* The Deconstruction of Bourgeois SF," *Science Fiction Studies* 2, no. 1 (1975), and "Futurecop: The Neutralization of Revolt in *Blade Runner*," *Science Fiction Studies* 14, no. 3 (1987).

54. See especially Joanna Russ, *To Write Like a Woman: Essays in Feminism and Science Fiction* (Bloomington, Ind.: Indiana University Press, 1995); Veronica Hollinger, "Feminist Science Fiction: Breaking Up the Subject," *Extrapolation* 31, no. 3 (1990), 229–239, "(Re)reading Queerly: Science Fiction, Feminism, and the Defamiliarization of Gender" *Science Fiction Studies* 26, no. 1 (1999) and "Feminist Theory and Science Fiction" in *The Cambridge Companion to Science Fiction,* ed. Edward James and Farah Mendlesohn (New York: Cambridge University Press, 2003); Jenny Wolmark, *Aliens and Others: Science Fiction, Feminism and Postmodernism* (Iowa City: University of Iowa Press, 1993); Justine Larbalestier, *The Battle of the Sexes in Science Fiction* (Middletown, Conn.: Wesleyan University Press, 2002); Jane Donawerth, *Frankenstein's Daughters: Women Writing Science Fiction* (Syracuse, N.Y.: Syracuse University Press, 1997); Marleen S. Barr, *Feminist Fabulation: Space/Postmodern Fiction* (Iowa City: University of Iowa Press, 1992); Wendy Pearson, "Alien Cryptographies: The View from Queer" *Science Fiction Studies* 26, no. 1 (1999) and "SF and Queer Theory," in *The Cambridge Companion to Science Fiction;* DeWitt Douglas Kilgore, *Astrofuturism: Science, Race, and Visions of Utopia in Space* (Philadelphia: University of Pennsylvania Press, 2003); Daniel Leonard Bernardi, *Star Trek and History: Race-Ing Toward a White Future* (New Brunswick, N.J.: Rutgers University Press, 1998); Roger Luckhurst, *Science Fiction* (Malden, Mass.: Polity, 2005). See also special issues of *Foundation* on gay and lesbian SF (Autumn 2002), and *Science Fiction Studies* on SF and queer theory (March 1999) and Afrofuturism (July 2007).

55. Delany, *Starboard Wine,* 231.

56. See James C. Scott, *Seeing Like a State: How Certain Schemes to Improve the Human Condition Have Failed* (New Haven, Conn.: Yale University Press, 1998).

57. Alan Sokal, "Transgressing the Boundaries: Towards a Transformative Hermeneutics of Quantum Gravity," *Social Text* 46–47 (Spring–Summer 1996): 217–252.

58. Secor and Walsh demonstrate that the language of Sokal's hoax shows careful imitation not only of scientific discourse, but of the exact rhetoric favored by *Social Text* in particular; Marie Secor and Lynda Walsh, "A Rhetorical Perspective on the Sokal Hoax. Genre, Style, and Context." *Written Communication* 21, no. 1 (January 2004): 69–91.

59. Mara Beller, "The Sokal Hoax: At Whom Are We Laughing?" http://www.mathematik .uni-muenchen.de/~bohmmech/BohmHome/sokalhoax.html.

60. Of leading contemporary critical cultural theorists only a very few (such as Donna Haraway [zoology], N. Katherine Hayles [chemistry], and Evelyn Fox Keller [physics]) hold advanced degrees in natural sciences.

61. See my "The SF of Theory: Baudrillard and Haraway," *Science Fiction Studies* 18, no. 3 (November 1991): 387–404. SF has returned the compliment. Mamoru Oshii introduces a cyborg-designer named Haraway as a character in *Ghost in the Shell II,* and a copy of Baudrillard's *Simulations and Simulacra* appears in *The Matrix,* as a hollowed-out stash

for Neo's VR discs. On the use of detournement as a conscious artistic strategy in cyberpunk, see Glenn Grant, "Transcendence Through Detournement in William Gibson's *Neuromancer*," *Science Fiction Studies* 17, no. 1 (March 1990): 41–49.

62. *Patrologia Latina* (v145.41). Translated selections are available at http://www.pvspade.com/Logic/docs/damian.pdf.

FIFTH BEAUTY

The Science-Fictional Sublime (pages 146–181)

1. Robert M. Philmus, *Visions and Re-Visions: (Re)Constructing Science Fiction* (Liverpool: Liverpool University Press, 2005), 306–307.

2. Brooks Landon, *The Aesthetics of Ambivalence. Rethinking Science Fiction Film in the Age of Electronic (Re)Production* (Westport, Conn.: Greenwood Press, 1992); esp. chap. 4, "The Aesthetics of Ambivalence: Spectacle and Special Effects, Trickery, and Discovery," 61–92. See also Albert J. LaValley, "Traditions of Trickery: The Role of Special Effects in the Science Fiction Film," in *Shadows of the Magic Lamp: Fantasy and Science Fiction in Film*, ed. George Slusser and Eric S. Rabkin (Carbondale: Southern Illinois University Press, 1985), 141–158; and Scott Bukatman, "The Artificial Infinite: On Special Effects and the Sublime," in *Alien Zone II: The Spaces of Science-Fiction Cinema*, ed. Annette Kuhn (New York: Verso, 1999), 249–275.

3. Contemporary cultural theory has shown a renewed interest in the sublime, and in postmodernist theory especially some major figures—Jameson, Lyotard, Žižek, among them—have given it a privileged place in their writings. These theorists have adapted ideas that were inspired by the identity crisis of bourgeois individualism in the face of the otherness of a natural world to the contemporary Western subject's relationship to the aggressively expansive communications regimes of second nature. For this context they may be too general to be of much use. If all art of the age, or indeed of any age, is a manifestation of sublime aesthetics, it will be hard to justify why any genre should be more closely linked to the sublime than any other. My premise is that among modern genres sf is particularly dependent on the sublime as it has been classically understood. However, there is much to be said for eliding science-fictionality and the postmodern sublime. Where Kant, and to a lesser extent Burke, conceptualized a response to the excess of natural presence and power, the new theories of the sublime attempt to conceptualize the excess of *knowledge* and *information*—the second degree of extrahuman power appropriate for second nature and technoscience.

4. Immanuel Kant, *Critique of Judgment*, trans. and with an introduction by Werner S. Pluhar (Indianapolis, Ind.: Hackett Publishing, 1987), chap. 26, pp. 107–114.

5. Lynn Poland, "The Idea of the Holy and the History of the Sublime," *Journal of Religion* 72, no. 2 (1992): 175–197.

6. Edmund Burke, *A Philosophical Enquiry into the Origin of Our Ideas of the Sublime and the Beautiful*, ed. J. T. Boulton (London: Routledge and Kegan Paul, 1958), 57.

7. Brian W. Aldiss, *Billion Year Spree: The True History of Science Fiction* (Garden City: N.Y.: Doubleday, 1973), 29; Carl Freedman, *Critical Theory and Science Fiction* (Middletown, Conn.: Wesleyan University Press, 2000), 48–49.

8. Barbara C. Freeman. "*Frankenstein* with Kant: A Theory of Monstrosity or the Monstrosity of Theory," in *New Casebooks: Frankenstein by Mary Shelley*, ed. Fred Botting (New York: St. Martin's, 1995), 191.

9. Qtd. in ibid., 192.

10. Anne K. Mellor, "Immortality or Monstrosity? Reflections on the Sublime in Romantic Literature and Art," in *The Romantic Imagination: Literature and Art in England and Germany,* ed. Frederick Burwick and Jürgen Klein (Amsterdam: Rodopi, 1996), 234.

11. David E Nye, *American Technological Sublime* (Cambridge, Mass.: MIT Press, 1994), 38.

12. Arthur B. Evans, *Jules Verne Rediscovered: Didacticism and the Scientific Novel* (New York: Greenwood Press, 1988), 144.

13. See several articles published in *Diacritics*'s "Nuclear Criticism," issue 14, no. 2 (1984), esp. Frances Ferguson, "The Nuclear Sublime," 4–10, and Jacques Derrida, "no apocalypse, not now (full speed ahead, seven missiles, seven missives)" 20–31; see also Peter Schwenger, "Writing the Unthinkable," *Critical Inquiry* 13, no. 1 (Autumn 1986): 33–48.

14. Roger Luckhurst, "Nuclear Criticism: Anachronism and Anachorism," *Diacritics* 23, no. 2 (Summer 1993): 88–97.

15. Albert I. Berger. *The Magic That Works: John W. Campbell and the American Response to Technology* (San Bernardino, Calif.: Borgo Press, 1993), 105–106.

16. Scott Bukatman, "The Artificial Infinite: On special effects and the Sublime," in *Alien Zone II: The Spaces of Science Fiction,* ed. Annette Kuhn (New York: Verso, 1999), 251.

17. See Constance Penley, *NASA/TREK: Popular Science and Sex in America* (New York: Verso, 1997); Svetlana Boym, "Kosmos: Remembrances of the Future," in *Kosmos: A Portrait of the Russian Space Age,* with photography by Adam Bartos (New York: Princeton Architectural Press, 2001), 83–99.

18. George Gilder, *Telecosm: How Infinite Bandwidth Will Revolutionize Our World* (New York: Free Press, 2002), 3.

19. Hans Moravec, *Mind Children: The Future of Robot and Human Intelligence* (Cambridge, Mass.: Harvard University Press, 1990); Kurzweil, *The Age of Spiritual Machines When Computers Exceed Human Intelligence* (New York: Viking, 1999); K. Eric Drexler, *Engines of Creation,* with a foreword by Marvin Minsky (Garden City, N.Y.: Anchor Press/Doubleday, 1986); see also the site of the Extropy Institute (http://www.extropy.org/ and of the World Transhumanist Association (http://www.transhumanism.org/index.php/WTA/index/).

20. Cornel Robu, whose seminal essay "A Key to Science Fiction: The Sublime" (*Foundation* 42 [Summer 1990]: 21–37) inspired much of this discussion, proposes a third category: the sublime of complexity. In my view, in the context of the sublime, complexity is either a matter of infinity (that is, the infinite permutations of processes), when it exists as an intellectual/psychological challenge, and consequently an aspect of the mathematical sublime; or of dynamic power when it impinges on sentient protagonists (as in the case of a potentially threatening process whose nature is rule-governed transformation that cannot be mediated). I can imagine an informational/ indeterminate sublime that inspires awe precisely at one's inability to determine whether something impinges or not; that would require a sophistication of narrative form that has been extremely rare in the genre up to now.

21. Bukatman, "Artificial Infinite," 269.

22. In "Kubrick's *2001* and the Possibility of a Science-Fiction Cinema" (*Science Fiction Studies* 25, no. 2 [July 1998]: 300–318), Carl Freedman argues that *2001* is the consummate sf film because of the rigor with which Kubrick employs f/x for the purposes of cognitive estrangement. Arguably, overemphasizing estrangement makes it difficult to interpret the film's symbolism.

23. Tastes differ about the relative aesthetic worth of Kubrick's film and Clarke's novel

of *2001: A Space Odyssey,* but the differences between the two in tone and conception of what sf can and should do as an art form are undeniable. The extent to which Kubrick essentially ignored Clarke's ideas during the making of the film can be inferred from Clarke's journal, which is included in his *Lost Worlds of 2001* (New York: New American Library, 1982). Comparing the novel and journal with the film, it appears that Kubrick rejected every move by Clarke to make characters and events explicit. On the differences between Kubrick's and Clarke's texts, see also Takayuki Tatsumi, "*2001,* or a Cyberspace Odyssey: Toward the Ideographic Imagination," in *World Weavers: Globalization, Science Fiction, and the Cybernetic Revolution,* ed. Won Kin Yuen and Gary Westfahl (Hong Kong: Hong Kong University Press, 2006), 41–54; and Michael Bérubé's "Paranoia in a Vacuum: *2001* and the National Security State," in his *Public Access: Literary Theory and American Cultural Politics.* (New York: Verso, 1994), 181–202.

24. Michel Ciment, *Kubrick* trans. Gilbert Adair (New York: Holt, Rinehart, and Winston. 1983), 134.

25. The absurdity is noted by Ray Kurzweil in his review of *The Matrix* on Kurzweil AI.net, May 18, 2003; http://www.kurzweilai.net/articles/art0580.html?printable=1

26. Landon, *Aesthetics of Ambivalence.*

27. Interview with Aude Lancelin, *Le Nouvel Observateur,* June 19, 2003.

28. Thomas Weiskel, *The Romantic Sublime: Studies in the Structure and Psychology of Transcendence* (Baltimore, Md.: Johns Hopkins University Press, 1976).

29. Patricia Yeager, "Toward a Female Sublime," in *Gender and Theory: Dialogues on Feminist Criticism,* ed. Linda Kaufman (New York: Blackwell, 1989), 191–212.

30. Lee Edelman, "At Risk in the Sublime. The Politics of Gender and Theory," in *Gender and Theory,* ed. Kaufman, 212–224.

31. Patrick West, "The 'Inrush of Desire' or the 'Grotesque of the Grotesque': A Feminist Reappraisal of Julia Kristeva's Theory of Gender," in *Seriously Weird: Papers on the Grotesque,* ed. Alice Mills (New York: Peter Lang, 1999), 239–257.

32. James Tiptree, Jr., *Up the Walls of the World* (New York: Berkley, 1978), 110.

SIXTH BEAUTY
The Science-Fictional Grotesque (pages 182–215)

1. Mikhail Bakhtin, *Rabelais and His World,* trans. Helen Iswolsky (Cambridge, Mass.: MIT Press, 1968), 335.

2. Geoffrey Galt Harpham, *On the Grotesque: Strategies of Contradiction in Art and Literature* (Princeton, N.J.: Princeton University Press, 1982), 11.

3. See the section "The Gaps of Science Fiction" in the introduction.

4. Edgar Allan Poe, "The Facts in the Case of M. Valdemar," in *Edgar Allan Poe: Poetry and Tales* (New York: Library of America. 1984), 842.

5. Edmund Burke, *A Philosophical Enquiry into the Origin of Our Ideas of the Sublime and the Beautiful,* ed. J. T. Boulton (London: Routledge and Kegan Paul, 1958), 77.

6. Dick responded to what he believed to be a mystical personal epiphany in the mid-1970s by pursuing his *Exegesis,* an interminable interpretive gloss on Gnostic theology, history, contemporary consciousness, and personal autobiography. He was deeply ambivalent about his obsession, treating it alternately with sincere, deadpan commitment and with self-deprecating humor. Dick is a striking case of an artist who extended his grotesque artistic strategies into a personal religious worldview. It is also striking that sev-

eral writers of his region and generation, including A. E. Van Vogt and L. Ron Hubbard, similarly used their sf as the basis for serious metaphysical doctrines.

7. Margaret Miles, "Carnal Abominations: The Female Body as Grotesque," in *The Grotesque in Art and Literature: Theological Reflections*, ed. James Luther Adams and Wilson Yates (Grand Rapids, Mich.: Eerdmans, 1997), 90.

8. Scott Bukatman, "The Artificial Infinite: On special effects and the Sublime," in *Alien Zone II: The Spaces of Science Fiction Cinema*, ed. Annette Kuhn (New York: Verso, 1999), 265.

9. The phrase originates with James Kavanagh in "Feminism, Humanism and Science in *Alien*," in *Alien Zone:* ed. Annette Kuhn (New York: Verso, 1990), 76.

10. The mutagenic properties of ionizing radiation in fruit flies were first discovered in 1927; the mutagenic effects of mustard gas were discovered, in 1942, also in fruit flies.

11. Wendy Pearson, "Alien Cryptographies: The View from Queer," *Science Fiction Studies* 26, no. 1 (March 1999): 6–9.

12. Jones's Aleutian cycle consists of: *White Queen* (New York: Tor, 1993), *North Wind* (New York: Tor, 1997), and *Phoenix Café* (New York: Tor, 1999).

13. See Manfred Geier, "Stanisław Lem's Fantastic Ocean: Toward a Semantic Interpretation of *Solaris*," *Science Fiction Studies* 19, no. 2 (July 1992): 204–210.

14. On the interpenetration and interferences of different romanesque idioms in *Solaris*, see my "The Book is the Alien: On Certain and Uncertain Readings of Stanisław Lem's *Solaris*." *Science Fiction Studies* 12, no. 1 (March 1985): 6–21.

15. At a conference in Kraków in 2000, Lem called Geier's reading of the novel that of a "a psychopath," eerily reprising an anecdote he was fond of telling about a Polish psychiatrist who considered *Solaris* proof that its author must be mentally ill.

16. This is especially true for those fans who also follow the *Alien* comics, novelizations, and the popular *Alien versus Predator* computer games, whose "histories" often contradict each other.

17. Catherine Constable, "Becoming the Monster's Mother: Morphologies of Identity in the *Alien* Series," in *Alien Zone II: The Spaces of Science Fiction Cinema*, ed. Annette Kuhn (New York: Verso, 1999), 197.

18. On the subversion of the conventions of the horror genre in the *Alien* series see Louise Speed, "*Alien 3:* A Postmodern Encounter with the Abject," *Arizona Quarterly* 54, no. 1 (1998): 125–151.

19. The significant exception is Clemens in *Alien 3*. Arguably, Ripley's polymorphous sexual mobility would be compromised if heterosexual connections were entirely excluded from her history. Speed reads Ripley's tryst with Clemens as a bold inversion of the formulas for sex and gender in the slasher film (138–139).

20. The best grouping of these is in Elkins's "Symposium on *Alien*," in *Science Fiction Studies* 7, no. 3 (November 1980), which includes contributions by Jackie Byars, Jeff Gould, Peter Fitting, Judith Newton, and Tony Safford.

21. The *Alien* films have produced a virtual casebook of persuasive psychoanalytic readings. Among the highlights are Krin and Glen. O. Gabbard, "The Science Fiction Film and Psychoanalysis: *Alien* and Melanie Klein's Night Music," in *Psychoanalytic Approaches to Literature and Film*, ed. Maurice Charnay and Joseph Reppen (Rutherford, N.J.: Fairleigh Dickinson University Press, 1987), 171–179; Donald Carveth and Naomi Gold, "The Pre-Oedipalizing of Klein in (North) America: Ridley Scott's *Alien* Re-analyzed," *Psy-Art*, at www.clas.ufl.edu/ipsa/ journal/articles/psyart1999/carveto3.htm, who read the films in

terms of infantile psychic splitting described by Melanie Klein; Robert Torry's Lacanian interpretation, "Awakening to the Other: Feminism and the Ego-Ideal in *Alien*," *Women's Studies* 23 (1994): 343–363; Barbara Creed's much-anthologized reading of *Alien* through the lens of Kristevan abjection-theory, "Horror and the Monstrous-Feminine: An Imaginary Abjection," in *The Dread of Difference: Gender and the Horror Film*, ed. Barry Keith Grant (Austin: University of Texas Press, 1996), 35–65; Catherine Constable's elaboration and critique of Creed, with an Irigarayan reading of *Alien Resurrection*, "Becoming the Monster's Mother: Morphologies of Identity in the *Alien* Series," in *Alien Zone II*, ed. Kuhn, 173–202; Speed's Kristevan salvaging of *Alien 3*; Janet Hocker Rushing's Jungian reading, "Evolution of 'The New Frontier' in *Alien* and *Aliens*: Patriarchal Co-Optation of the Feminine Archetype," *Quarterly Journal of Speech* 75 (1989): 1–24; and Ilsa Bick's nonaligned interpretations of the films' genital imagery, "'Well, I Guess I Must Make You Nervous': Woman and the Space of *Alien 3*," *Post-Script* 14: nos. 1–2 (1994–95): 45–58. These readings are so rich that the fit between gloss and text sometimes seems uncanny. It would not surprise me if the *Alien* films' creators turned out to have some familiarity with recent theories of the cyborg, abjection, the phallic mother, and other currently favored models of the uncanny and the monstrous. They must certainly be aware of Ripley's cult status among lesbian viewers. The in-joke allusions to Baudrillard and Burroughs in *The Matrix* are overt reminders that Hollywood filmmakers occasionally pay attention to theory. There is no reason to believe that the makers of the *Alien* films (who include Sigourney Weaver as executive producer) are unaware of contemporary academic discussions, even if their use of them is eclectic. The near-mechanical use of Harawayan cyborg motifs in *Alien Resurrection* is striking, and Hollywood has always been friendly to psychoanalysis as a source of ideas.

22. See Maggie Kilgour, *The Rise of the Gothic Novel* (New York: Routledge, 1995), 220–221; Ian Watt, "Time and Family in the Gothic Novel: *The Castle of Otranto*," *Eighteenth Century Life* (1986): 177–190.

23. Speed makes a similar claim, specifically reading *Alien 3* as an allegory of postmodernism as abjection.

24. Veronica Hollinger, "(Re)Reading Science Fiction Queerly," *Science Fiction Studies* 26, no. 1 (March 1999): 35.

25. See Umberto Rossi, "From Dick to Lethem: The Dickian Legacy, Postmodernism, and Avant-Pop in Jonathan Lethem's *Amnesia Moon*," *Science Fiction Studies* 29, no. 1 (March 2002): 15–33.

26. Dick aspired for most of his life to be published as a mainstream novelist. Only one of his realistic novels was published in his lifetime, *Confessions of a Crap Artist*, in 1975. A few of Dick's sf novels were initially projected to be mainstream works, most notably *We Can Build You* (1972). See Gregg Rickmann, "'What Is This Sickness?' 'Schizophrenia' and *We Can Build You*," in *Philip K. Dick: Contemporary Critical Interpretations*, ed. Samuel J. Umland (Westport, Conn.: Greenwood Press, 1995), 143–156. The character of the author's solicitation of his audience is one of the central distinguishing qualities between artistic sf and sci-fi. In "The Dreadful Credibility of Absurd Things: A Tendency in Fantasy Theory" (*Historical Materialism* 10, no. 4 [2002]: 51–88), Mark Bould holds that popular sf is deeply linked to its condition as a commodity, in which it reflects a paranoid logic of ceaseless defense and solicitation through the constant production of serial artifacts (shared universes, franchise fiction, formulaic displays) required for ceaseless supplementation. Dick's case is an unusual one: he was forced by poverty to produce many formulaic books, but the formulas were his own original ones, and the paranoia of the commodity form was

deeply internalized into the paranoia of his fiction. See also Carl Freedman, "Towards a Theory of Paranoia: The Science Fiction of Philip K. Dick," in *On Philip K. Dick: 40 Articles from Science-Fiction Studies*, ed. R. D. Mullen, Istvan Csicsery-Ronay, Jr., Arthur B. Evans, and Veronica Hollinger (Terre Haute, Ind.: SF-TH, 1992), 111–118.

27. Tyrone Slothrop's uncanny ability to correlate the location of his trysts with the locations of bombs landings in London is certainly a version of Ragle's Gumm's similar ability to correlate where the lunar missiles will land with the solutions of a newspaper puzzle in Dick's *Time Out of Joint* (1959), written twenty-four years earlier than *Gravity's Rainbow* (1974). On Acker and *Neuromancer*, see Brian McHale, *Constructing Postmodernism* (New York: Routledge, 1992), 233–235, and Victoria de Zwaan, "Rethinking the Slipstream: Kathy Acker Reads *Neuromancer*," *Science Fiction Studies* 24, no. 3 (November 1997): 459–470.

28. See Joan Gordon, "Hybridity, Heterotopia, and Mateship in China Miéville's *Perdido Street Station*," *Science Fiction Studies* 30, no. 3 (November 2003): 456–476.

SEVENTH BEAUTY
The *Technologiade* (pages 215–261)

1. Brian Attebery, "Science Fiction, Parable, and Parabolas," *Foundation* 95 (Autumn 2005): 7–22.

2. Northrop Frye, *Anatomy of Criticism: Four Essays* (Princeton, N.J.: Princeton University Press, 1957), 49.

3. Fredric Jameson, "Magical Narratives: On the Dialectical Use of Genre Criticism," in *The Political Unconscious: Narrative as a Socially Symbolic Act* (Ithaca, N.Y.: Cornell University Press, 1981), 103–150. See also Jameson's "Radical Fantasy." *Historical Materialism: Research in Critical Marxist Theory* 10, no. 4 (2002): 273–280.

4. Brian McHale, *Constructing Postmodernism* (New York: Routledge, 1992), 248–250.

5. David G. Hartwell and Kathryn Cramer, "Introduction. How Shit Became Shinola: Definiton and Redefinition of Space Opera," in *The Space Opera Renaissance*, ed. David G. Hartwell and Kathryn Cramer (New York: Tor, 2006), 9–21.

6. "Forms of Time and of the Chronotope in the Novel." *The Dialogic Imagination: Four Essays*, ed. Michael Holquist, trans. Caryl Emerson and Michael Holquist (Austin: University of Texas Press, 1981), 84–258.

7. Verne's two Moon novels, *De la Terre à la Lune* (1865) and *Autour de la lune* (1870), cannot be considered bona fide works of two-world sf; in neither tale do the intrepid explorers touch down on the lunar surface.

8. Sara Weiss, *Decimon Huydas: A Romance of Mars* (Rochester, N.Y.: Austin Publishing, 1906); *Journeys to the Planet Mars* (New York: Bradford Press, 1908).

9. Gary Westfahl, "Space Opera," in *The Cambridge Companion to Science Fiction*, ed. Edward James and Farah Mendlesohn (New York: Cambridge University Press, 2003), 201–202.

10. The functions in my model are derived in the spirit of Vladimir Propp's *Morphology of the Folktale*, ed. and with an introduction by Svatava Pikora-Jakobson, trans. Laurence Scott (Bloomington, Ind.: Research Center, Indiana University, 1958), (1928) and Bakhtin's "Forms of Time and of the Chronotope in the Novel." Where Proppian morphology takes the genre characteristics of the folktale as givens, and outlines the tale's plot functions in terms of structural iterations, Bakhtin's chronotopes occupy an indeterminate zone between structural functions and *constitutive* functions that help establish each historical genre—a difference roughly equivalent to a naive and a sentimental morphology. Inasmuch as the

modern adventure is a mixture of archaic tale forms and modern displacements responding to social-political pressures, it seems appropriate to make use of both models.

11. M. M. Bakhtin, *The Dialogic Imagination: Four Essays,* ed. Michael Holquist, trans. Caryl Emerson and Michael Holquist (Austin, Tex.: University of Texas Press, 1982), 84–129. Bakhtin's historical analysis of the adventure tale ends with the baroque.

12. John G. Cawelti, *Adventure, Mystery, and Romance: Formula Stories as Art and Popular Culture* (Chicago: University of Chicago Press, 1976), 39–41.

13. See Annette Kolodny, *The Lay of the Land: Metaphor as Experience and History in American Life and Letters* (Chapel Hill, N.C.: University of North Carolina Press, 1975). (The locus classicus for this eroticized topography in modern adventure is the terrain of Kukuanaland in H. Rider Haggard's *King Solomon's Mines,* whose central valley is bounded by two mountains: the "Breasts of Sheba" at one end and the cavern of the eponymous diamond mine at the other.)

14. I should note that the Fertile Corpse often emanates a real living woman, with whom the Handy Man indulges in a dalliance: the traditionally mythicized Pocahontas, *King Solomon's Mines*'s Foulata, Kurtz's native mistress, the Eloi Weena, and so forth. These women conventionally die or sacrifice themselves before the end of the tale, in order to facilitate the Handy Man's struggle for the resource. Native lovers almost never survive the colonial consummation. When they do, that aspect of the story is either suppressed (Pocahontas's story rarely extends to her marriage to John Rolfe) or they take on Gothic power to thwart the Handy Man, like *She*'s Ayesha.

15. Andrew Butler's reading of *Frankenstein* and *Dr. Jekyll and Mr. Hyde* as "proto-queer" texts ("Proto-Sf/Proto-Queer: The Strange Case of Dr Frankenstein and Mr Hyde," *Foundation* 86 ([Autumn 2002]: 7–16) suggests that an additional archetype should be eventually either added to this network or act as regular substitute for the Willing Slave: the homosocial or queer companion. Shelley's and Stevenson's proto-sf works follow the conventions of adventure fiction not only in excluding women from the sphere of action, but in making adventure a means for drawing male companions together. Butler suggests that the profound longings and attachments expressed by *Frankenstein*'s male characters—Victor, the Creature, and Walton—are for other male agents, for whom each is willing to abandon or annihilate the female attachments we have named the Wife at Home. That these Wives at Home are not always their own mates—Victor and the Creature destroy each other's—only deepens their bond. In this light, Victor's relationship with Clerval is not a version of the Willing Slave. In the Gothic framework, in any case, that function is inverted by the Creature; he not only resists it, but claims rights of Mastery over Victor and his family. Butler is even more persuasive regarding *Dr Jekyll and Mr Hyde,* which appears not only to have a queer subtext, but a sustained allegory of homosexual panic. The Gothic inversion of the adventure is doubly performed in its case. There are no women in the story other than servants, so the Wife is actually absent. Jekyll, however, is often "home," and it is himself that he subjects to "conquest." With stunning economy, Hyde is generated, a hypermasculine Alpha Ape, who rebels, Caliban-like, against civil mastery and proceeds to persecute the self-feminized Jekyll, who has taken on all feminine functions. Stevenson inverts the adventure to the point of implosion. Although Jekyll has no direct equivalent to Clerval, he depends on Lanyon, and ultimately Utterson, laconic male friends, to clear his name. This motif of the subordinate brother/mate/friend in modern gothicized adventure is quite regular—from Umbopa in *King Solomon's Mines,* Queequeg and Fedallah in *Moby Dick,* to its later deformation in *Heart of Darkness,* where the Handy Man Marlow longs for a master-companion in Kurtz, his Shadow.

16. Scott Bukatman, *Terminal Identity: The Virtual Subject in Postmodern Science Fiction* (Durham, N.C.: Duke University Press, 1993), 8–22.

17. Critical revaluation of the adventure tradition in recent years has given the Wife at Home a novel prominence in fiction. Two excellent examples are John Kessell's "Gulliver at Home," in *The Pure Product* (New York: Tor, 1997), 329–343, and Sena Jeter Naslund's *Ahab's Wife: Or, The Star Gazer: A Novel* (New York: Harper, 2000).

18. J. M. S. Tompkins, qtd. in Maggie Kilgour, *The Rise of the Gothic Novel* (New York: Routledge, 1995), 259 n. 81.

19. Scholars of the Gothic often divide it into two modes based on antagonistic gender positions: a male/horror mode associated with Lewis's *The Monk* (1795) and the female/ terror mode associated with the novels of Ann Radcliffe. The formula of the former consists of a demonic male aggressor patterned on Milton's Satan, who targets innocent young women or feminized males for ruin. In the process, he enlists the aid of corrupt helpers, and engineers complex plots of seduction, abduction, and violation. His victims often end up trapped in castles or abbeys with complex and obscure architectures that are themselves symbolically coded as feminized enclosures. In the feminine form, the focus is on the resistance of the victim-heroine, who is sometimes endowed with powers of endurance and analysis to map her prison and to bring her tormentor down, while sometimes it is her pathetic purity that gives her protection. In most examples of the Gothic, erotic struggles conceal far more significant struggles over the control of ancestral properties. Like most such categorical divisions, the boundaries between modes are more often breached than observed; See Kilgour, *Rise of the Gothic Novel*, 37–39.

20. The close association we drew between the Fertile Corpse and the Wife at Home as aspects of female/feminine domains in the phallic adventure paradigm forces us to consider whether a similar association holds for their inversions in the Gothic. I believe a case can be made for it. Despite the clear patriarchal spirit of castles like *Otranto*'s, the bizarre and labyrinthine architecture favored by the Gothic has clear links to putatively feminine spaces of the grotesque. This hints that there may be profound connection between the prison and the prisoner, as if she were being incarcerated in her own form. Indeed, since the heroine (of the Radcliffean Gothic at least) needs to explore her enchanted prison, she is forced to undertake an adventure of *self*-exploration, one that the adventure's wife at home is not offered.

21. James C. Scott, *Seeing Like a State: How Certain Schemes to Improve the Human Condition Have Failed* (New Haven: Yale University Press, 1998), 95.

22. Michael Nerlich, *The Ideology of Adventure: Studies in Modern Consciousness, 1100– 1750*, 2 vols. (Minneapolis, Minn.: University of Minnesota Press, 1987), 2:265–266.

23. See Ellen Meiksins Wood, *Empire of Capital* (New York: Verso, 2003), chap. 5, "The Overseas Expansion of Economic Imperatives," 89–117.

24. As Kennedy framed it in his Special Message to the Congress on Urgent National Needs in May 1961:

if we are to win the battle that is now going on around the world between freedom and tyranny, the dramatic achievements in space which occurred in recent weeks [Gagarin and Shepherd] should have made clear to us all, as did the Sputnik in 1957, the impact of this adventure on the minds of men everywhere, who are attempting to make a determination on which road they should take[. . .]. Now it is time to take longer strides— time for a great new American enterprise—time for this nation to take a clearly leading role in space achievement, which in many ways hold the key to our future on earth.

Qtd. In Walter A. McDougall's *The Heavens and the Earth: A Political History of the Space Age* (New York: Basic Books, 1985), 303. See also John W. Jordan, "Kennedy's Romantic Moon and its Legacy for Space Exploration." *Rhetoric and Public Affairs* 6, no. 2 (2003): 209–231.

25. On Tsiolkovsky's role in Soviet space technology, see G. A. Tokaty, "Soviet Rocket Technology," *Technology and Culture* 4, no. 4 (Autumn 1963): 515–528; and A. Kosmodemyansky, *Konstantin Tsiolkovsky: His Life and Work* (Honolulu, Hawaii: University Press of the Pacific, 2000). On Fyodorov's cosmism, see Bernice Glatzer Rosenthal, *The Occult in Russian and Soviet Culture* (Ithaca, N.Y.: Cornell University Press, 1997), chap. 7, pp. 171–224.

26. McDougall records that as a senator, John Kennedy "could not be convinced that all rockets were not a waste of money, and space navigation even worse" (301). According to Kennedy's biographer Hugh Sidey, of the major issues he faced as President, Kennedy "probably knew and understood least about space" (qtd. in McDougall, *Heavens and the Earth*, 302).

27. James L. Kauffman, *Selling Outer Space: Kennedy, the Media, and Funding for Project Apollo, 1961–1963*, (Tuscaloosa, Ala.: University of Alabama Press, 1994), 35–36.

28. Constance Penley, *NASA/TREK: Popular Science and Sex in America* (New York: Verso, 1997).

29. Typical are Martin Caidin, *The Moon: New World for Men* (Indianapolis, Ind.: Bobbs-Merrill, 1963), Michael Collins, *Carrying the Fire: An Astronaut's Journey*, with a foreword by Charles A. Lindbergh (New York: Cooper Square Press, 2001); and Neil Armstrong, Michael Collins, and Edwin E. Aldrin, Jr., *First on the Moon: A Voyage With Neil Armstrong, Michael Collins [and] Edwin E. Aldrin, Jr.*, written with Gene Farmer and Dora Jane Hamblin, with an epilogue by Arthur C. Clarke (Boston: Little, Brown, 1970); and more recently, Andrew Smith, *Moon Dust: In Search of the Men Who Fell to Earth* (New York: Harper Perennial, 2006).

30. The locus classicus for discussion of the depiction of U.S. astronauts in terms of Puritanical asceticism is Vivian Sobchack's "The Virginity of Astronauts: Sex and the Science Fiction Film," in *Alien Zone: Cultural Theory and Contemporary Science Fiction Cinema*, ed. Annette Kuhn (New York: Verso, 1990), 103–115.

31. David E. Nye, *American Technological Sublime* (Cambridge, Mass.: MIT Press, 1994), 254.

32. Darko Suvin, *Positions and Presuppositions in Science Fiction* (Kent, Ohio: Kent State University Press, 1988), 54.

33. Fatigue was the overdetermined villain of the *Challenger* disaster. The Rogers Commission investigating the causes of the space shuttle's explosion in 1986 blamed both materials fatigue (the brittleness of the shuttle-craft's O-rings as a result of prolonged exposure to cold temperatures) and human fatigue (the effect of sleep deprivation on the judgment of the operators who may have misread indications about system malfunctions during the launch preparations).

34. The complex and long-standing affection for MIR by Soviet cosmonauts and laypeople alike was in marked contrast to U.S. impatience with it. For the United States, the station was an accident-prone, dangerous space slum; for the Soviets, it was a national monument (the first inhabited space station) and a surrogate home.

35. See my "Science Fiction and Empire," *Science Fiction Studies* 30, no. 2 (July 2003): 231–245.

36. Benedict Anderson, *Imagined Communities: Reflections on the Origin and Spread of Nationalism* (New York: Verso, 1991), 37–46.

37. See Hannah Arendt, *The Origins of Totalitarianism* (New York: Harcourt Brace Jovanovich, 1973), 136–138.

38. Scott, *Seeing Like a State*, 98–100.

39. See Wood, *Empire of Capital*, 143–168.

40. Arjun Appadurai, *Modernity at Large: Cultural Dimensions of Globalization* (Minneapolis, Minn.: University of Minnesota Press, 1996).

41. On the close relationship between the Soviet production novel and Soviet sf, see my "Towards the Last Fairy Tale: On the Fairy-Tale Paradigm in the Strugatskys' SF, 1963–72," *Science Fiction Studies* 13, no. 1 (March 1993): 8–12; on the production novel in its own right, see Katerina Clark, *The Soviet Novel: History as Ritual* (Bloomington Ind.: Indiana University Press, 2000).

42. On the Edisonade, see Brooks Landon, *Science Fiction After 1900: From the Steam Man to the Stars,* (New York: Twayne, 1997), 40–50.

43. The Shapers and Mechanics appear in Sterling's *Schismatrix* (1985) and a story-cycle included in *Crystal Express* (1989).

44. The turn would produce tragic real-world consequences in Stalin's purge of Soviet technocrats, in the so-called engineers' plot. In 1930, between two thousand and seven thousand members of the technical intelligentsia were arrested, charged with sabotage, and convicted in highly public show trials. The episode is described in detail in Kendall E. Bailes, "The Politics of Technology: Stalin and Technocratic Thinking Among Soviet Engineers," *American Historical Review* 79, no. 2 (April 1974): 445–469.

45. V. S. Pritchett, "Wells and the English Novel," in H. G. Wells. *The Time Machine/The War of the Worlds: A Critical Edition,* ed. Frank D. McConnell (New York: Oxford University Press, 1977), 432.

46. The debate has revolved primarily around the question of whether Ripley's various incarnations represent bona fide alternatives to masculinist constructions of power—overtly social-political and/or psychoanalytic—or whether the films have merely used her to position a female to do the work of a phallic male surrogate, thereby effectively assimilating women into the Alpha role of the phallocratic war-machine. The sophistication of these debates points beyond the putative ambivalence of the films to differences in what theorists can accept as feminist positions. Questions of female power, cyborg force-augmentation, reproductive freedom, a woman's control over her body, and indeed the question of what the boundaries of those bodies might be, often lead to ambivalent positions in critics, let alone in artists. The Kristevan and Kleinian interpretations of Barbara Creed, Krin and Glen O. Gabbard, and Donald Carveth and Naomi Gold, for example, engage the theme of the pre-Oedipal body, but not all people would agree that these psychoanalytic models are particularly emancipating in political terms. See C. Jason Smith and C. Ximena Gallardo, *Alien Woman: The Making of Lt. Ellen Ripley* (New York: Continuum, 2004); Paula Graham, "Looking Lesbian: Amazons and Aliens in Science Fiction Cinema," in *The Good, The Bad, And The Gorgeous: Popular Culture's Romance With Lesbianism,* ed. Diane Hamer and Belinda Budge (London: Pandora, 1994); Michael Davis, "'What's the Story Mother?': Abjection and Anti-Feminism in *Alien* and *Aliens*," *Gothic Studies* 2 (2000): 245–256.

47. Carolyn Merchant, *The Death of Nature: Women, Ecology, and the Scientific Revolution* (New York: Harper & Row, 1989), 29–41.

48. Nicola Nixon, "Cyberpunk: Preparing the Ground for Revolution or Keeping the Boys Satisfied?" *Science Fiction Studies* 19, no. 2 (July 1992): 219–235; Andrew Ross, "Cyberpunks in Boystown," in *Strange Weather: Culture, Science, and Technology in the Age of Limits* (New York: Verso, 1991), 137–167; Amanda Fernbach, "The Fetishization of Masculinity in Science Fiction: The Cyborg and the Console Cowboy," *Science Fiction Studies*

27, no. 2 (July 2000): 234–255. See also Joan Gordon, "Yin and Yang Duke It Out," in *Storming the Reality Studio: A Casebook of Cyberpunk and Postmodern Science Fiction* (Durham, N.C.: Duke University Press, 1991), 196–202; in this essay Gordon defends cyberpunk's honor, arguing that it conveys covert feminist messages.

49. See the discussion in "Sixth Beauty."

50. As framed in Asimov's 1942 story "Runaround" (available online at http://www.rci .rutgers.edu/~cfs/472_html/Intro/NYT_Intro/History/Runaround.html) these are:

1. A robot may not injure a human being or, through inaction, allow a human being to come to harm. 2. A robot must obey orders given it by human beings except where such orders would conflict with the First Law. 3. A robot must protect its own existence as long as such protection does not conflict with the First or Second Law.

51. *Robot* was the technical term used throughout the Austro-Hungarian Empire for the free labor owed to landowners by peasant cotters and tenants living in semiserfdom.

52. See Christiane Gerblinger, "'Fiery the Angels Fell': America, Regeneration and Ridley Scott's *Blade Runner,*" *Australian Journal of American Studies* 21, no. 1 (July 2002): 19–30.

53. Stanisław Lem. "Golem XIV," in *Imaginary Magnitude,* trans. Marc E. Heine (San Diego, Calif.: Harcourt Brace Jovanovich, 1984), 97–122.

54. When the film was first released, audiences were given flyers explaining scientific studies that had shown that chimpanzees, if not yet humans, could survive for short intervals in the vacuum of space.

55. See Roumiana Deltcheva and Eduard Vlasov, "Back to the House II: On the Chronotopic and Ideological Reinterpretation of Len's *Solaris* in Tarkovsky's Film," *Russian Review* 56, no. 4 (October 1997): 532–549.

56. Tarkovsky alters this theme also, in his version, *Stalker* (1979). The child in Tarkovsky's film has not devolved into a quasi-simian state, but has in fact developed psychic powers; that is, she is *transcending.* The film thus implies that the post-Zone future generations are probably leaving the human home—as in one of the Strugatskys' other novels, *The Ugly Swans* (1967–68)—not that they may be left with nothing else.

57. See Donald E. Palumbo, "The Monomyth as Fractal Pattern in the Dune Series" in his *Chaos Theory, Asimov's Foundations and Robots, and Herbert's Dune: The Fractal Aesthetic of Epic Science Fiction* (Westport, Conn.: Greenwood Press, 2002).

CONCLUDING UNSCIENTIFIC POSTSCRIPT
The Singularity and Beyond (pages 262–266)

1. Vernor Vinge, "The Coming Technological Singularity: How to Survive in the Post-Human Era." Presented at the VISION-21 Symposium, sponsored by NASA Lewis Research Center and the Ohio Aerospace Institute, March 30–31, 1993. http://www.rohan.sdsu.edu/ faculty/vinge/misc/singularity.html.

2. This vision has been most vividly articulated by Ray Kurzweil in *The Singularity is Near: When Humans Trancend Biology* (Viking, 2005).

3. See Roger Luckhurst, "The Many Deaths of Science Fiction: A Polemic." *Science Fiction Studies* 21, no. 1 (March 1994): 35–50; Judith Berman, "Science Fiction without the Future." *The New York Review of Science Fiction* 13, no. 9 (May 2001): 1, 6–8.

BIBLIOGRAPHY

Primary Works Cited in the Text

Written Texts

Acker, Kathy. *The Empire of the Senseless.* New York: Grove Press, 1994.

Adams, Douglas. *The Hitchhiker's Guide to the Galaxy.* London: Pan, 1979.

Aldiss, Brian. *Barefoot in the Head — A European Fantasia.* London: Faber and Faber, 1969.

———. *NonStop* [U.S. title, *Starship*]. London: Faber and Faber, 1958.

Anderson, Poul. *Tau Zero.* New York: Doubleday, 1970.

Arnason, Eleanor. *Ring of Swords.* New York: Tor, 1993.

———. "Runaround," *Astounding Science Fiction.* March, 1942.

Asimov, Isaac. *Foundation.* New York: Gnome Press, 1951.

———. *Foundation and Earth.* New York: Doubleday, 1986.

———. *Foundation and Empire.* New York: Gnome Press, 1952.

———. *Foundation's Edge.* New York: Doubleday, 1982.

———. *Second Foundation.* New York: Gnome Press, 1953.

Atwood, Margaret. *The Handmaid's Tale.* Toronto: McClelland and Stewart, 1985.

Ballard, J. G. *The Atrocity Exhibition.* London: Cape, 1970.

Bear, Greg. *Blood Music.* New York: Arbor House, 1985.

Benford, Gregory. *Timescape.* New York: Simon and Schuster, 1980.

Bester, Alfred. *The Stars My Destination* (1956). New York: Vintage, 1996.

Bogdanov, Alexander. *Red Star: The First Bolshevik Utopia* [1908], ed. Loren R. Graham and Richard Stites, trans. Charles Rougle. Bloomington, Ind.: Indiana University Press, 1984.

Borges, Jorge Luis. "Tlön, Uqbar, and Orbis Tertius" (1940), in *Labyrinths,* trans. Donald A. Yates and James E. Irby. New York: Grove Press, 1964.

Bradbury, Ray. "The Sound of Thunder" [1952]. *R is for Rocket.* New York: Doubleday, 2000.

Brown, Fredric. "The Yehudi Principle" [1944]. in *From These Ashes: The Complete Short SF of Fredric Brown.* Framingham, Mass.: Nesfa, 2001.

Brunner, John. *The Sheep Look Up.* New York: Harper and Row,1972.

———. *Stand on Zanzibar.* New York: Doubleday, 1968.

———. *Shockwave Rider.* New York: Harper and Row,1975.

Bulgakov, Mikhail. *The Fatal Eggs* [1925], with an introduction by Doris Lessing, trans. Hugh Aplin. London: Hesperus Press, 2003.

———. *Heart of a Dog* [1925], trans. Mirra Ginsburg. New York: Grove Press, 1994.

Burgess, Anthony. *A Clockwork Orange.* London: Heinemann, 1962.

Burroughs, Edgar Rice. *Princess of Mars* [1912]. New York: Del Rey, 1985.

Butler, Octavia. *Parable of the Sower.* New York: Aspect, 1995.

Cadigan, Pat. *Synners* [1991]. New York: Four Walls Eight Windows, 2001.

Campbell, John W. [writing as Don Stuart]. "Who Goes There?" [1938], in *The Best of John W. Campbell.* New York: Ballantine, 1976.

Čapek, Karel. *Absolute at Large* [1922], introduction by Stephen Baxter. Lincoln, Neb.: Bison Books, 2006.

———. *R. U. R.* [1921], with introduction by Ivan Klima, trans. Claudia Novack-Jones. New York: Penguin, 2004.

———. *The War with the Newts* [1936], trans. Ewald Osers. North Haven, Conn.: Catbird Press, 1990.

Card, Orson Scott. *Ender's Game.* New York: Tor, 1985.

Charnas, Suzy McKee. *Walk to the End of the World.* London: The Women's Press, 1989.

Cherryh, C. J. *Cyteen.* New York: Warner, 1985.

———. *Downbelow Station.* New York: Daw, 1981.

———. *Forty Thousand in Gehenna.* West Bloomfield, Mich.: Phantasia Press, 1983.

———. *Heavy Time.* New York: Time Warner, 1991.

———. *Hellburner.* New York: Warner, 1992.

———. *Merchanter's Luck.* New York: Daw, 1982.

———. *Rimrunners* New York: Warner, 1989.

Clarke Arthur C. *Childhood's End.* New York: Ballantine, 1953.

———. "Nine Billion Names of God" [1953], in *The Collected Short Stories of Arthur C. Clarke.* New York: Orb, 2002.

———. *Rendezvous with Rama.* New York: Harcourt Brace Jovanovich, 1972.

Churchill, Winston. "If Lee Had Not Won the Battle of Gettysburg," in *If It Had Happened Otherwise,* ed. J.C. Squire. London: Longmans, Green, 1931.

Clement, Hal. *Mission of Gravity* [1953]. New York: Gollancz, 2000.

Conrad, Joseph. *Heart of Darkness* [1899]. Ed. Paul B. Armstrong. New York: W.W. Norton, 2005.

Defoe, Daniel. *Robinson Crusoe* [1719]. Ed. Michael Shinagel. New York: W.W. Norton, 1993.

Delany, Sameul R. *Babel-17* [1966]. New York: Vintage, 2002.

———. *Dhalgren* [1975]. New York: Vintage, 2001.

———. *Trouble on Triton:An Ambiguous Heterotopia* [1976]. Middletown, Conn.: Wesleyan University Press, 1996.

Dick, Philip K. *Confessions of a Crap Artist* [1975]. New York: Vintage, 1992.

———. *Do Androids Dream of Electric Sheep?* [1968]. New York: Del Rey, 1996.

———. "A Little Something for Us Tempunauts" [1975] in *The Best of Philip K. Dick.* New York: Del Rey, 1978.

———. *The Man in the High Castle* [1962]. New York: Vintage, 1992.

———. *Time Out of Joint* [1959]. New York: Vintage, 2002.

———. *The Three Stigmata of Palmer Eldritch.* [1965]. New York: Vintage, 1991.

———. *Ubik* [1969]. New York: Vintage, 1991.

———. *VALIS* [1981]. New York: Vintage, 1991.

Di Filippo, Paul. *Steampunk Trilogy.* New York: Four Walls Eight Windows, 2001.

Dorsey, Candace Jane. *A Paradigm of Earth.* New York: Tor, 2001.

Elgin, Suzette Haden. *Native Tongue* [1984]. New York: The Feminist Press at CUNY, 2000.

Faulkner, William. *Absalom, Absalom* [1936]. New York: Vintage, 1991.

Fitzgerald, F. Scott. *The Great Gatsby* [1925]. New York: Scribner, 1995.

Flammarion, Camille. *Omega: The Last Days of the World* [*La Fin du Monde,* 1893], introduction by Robert Silverberg. Lincoln, Neb.: Bison Books, 1999.

Forster, E. M. *Passage to India* [1924]. New York: Penguin, 1998.

Gibson, William. *Burning Chrome* [1986]. New York: Eos, 2003.

————. *Mona Lisa Overdrive* [1988]. New York: Specta, 1997.

————. *Neuromancer.* New York: Ace, 1984.

————. and Bruce Sterling. *The Difference Engine* [1990]. New York: Spectra, 1992.

Gogol, Nikolai. "The Nose" in *The Collected Tales of Nikolai Gogol,* trans. Richard Pevear and Larissa Volokhonsky. New York: Vintage, 1999.

Haggard, H. Rider. *King Solomon's Mines* [1885]. New York: Oxford, 1998.

————. *She* [1877]. New York: Oxford, 1998.

Harris, Robert. *Fatherland.* London: Hutchinson, 1992.

Harrison, M. John. *The Centauri Device* [1975]. New York: Gollancz, 2000.

Heinlein, Robert. "All You Zombies," in *The Road to Science Fiction. Vol. 3: From Heinlein to Here,* ed. James Gunn. Clarkston Calif.: White Wolf Press.

————. *The Moon is a Harsh Mistress.* [1966]. New York: Orb, 1997.

————. "By His Bootstraps" [1941], in *The Best Time Travel Stories of the 20th Century,* ed. Harry Turtledove and Martin H. Greenberg. New York: Del Rey, 2004.

————. *The Past Through Tomorrow* [1967]. New York: Ace, 1987.

————. *Orphans of the Sky* [1963]. New York: Baen, 2001.

————. *Methuselah's Children* [1941]. New York: Baen, 1986.

————. *Time Enough for Love* [1973]. New York: Ace, 1987.

————. *To Sail beyond the Sunset.* New York: Ace, 1988.

————. *Stranger in a Strange Land* [1961]. New York: Ace, 1987.

Herbert, Frank. *Dune.* New York: Ace, 1990.

Hoban, Russel. *Riddley Walker* [1980]. Bloomington, Ind.: Indiana University Press, 1998.

Hoyle, Fred. *Black Cloud* [1957]. Cutchogue, NY: Buccaneer Books, 1992.

Huxley, Aldous. *Brave New World* [1932]. New York: Harper, 1998.

James, Henry. *Portrait of a Lady* [1882]. New York: Penguin, 2003.

Jeter, K. W. *Morlock Night.* New York: Daw, 1979.

Jodorowsky, Alrejandro, and Moebius. *The Incal* [1981–89]. Glendale, Calif.: Humanoids-Rebellion, 2005.

Jones, Gwyneth. *North Wind.* New York: Tor, 1997.

————. *White Queen.* New York: Orb, 1994.

————. *Phoenix Café.* New York: Tor, 1999.

Kessell, John. "Gulliver at Home," in *The Pure Product.* New York: Tor, 1997.

Knight, Damon. "To Serve Man" [1951], in *The Best of Damon Knight,* introduction by Barry Malzberg. New York: Doubleday, 1976.

Komatsu, Sakyo. *Japan Sinks: A Novel* [1973]). Tokyo: Kodansha, 1995.

Lasswitz, Kurd. *Two Planets* [1897], afterword by Mark R. Hillegas, ed. Erich Lasswitz, trans. Hans H. Rudnick. Carbondale, Ill.: Southern Illinois University Press, 1971.

Le Guin, Ursula K., *City of Illusions* [1967]. New York: Ace, 1983.

————. *The Dispossessed: An Ambiguous Utopia* [1974]. New York: HarperCollins, 2003.

————. *The Lathe of Heaven* [1971]. New York: HarperCollins, 2003.

————. *The Left Hand of Darkness* [1969]. New York: Ace, 1987.

————. *Planet of Exile* [1966]. New York: Ace, 1982.

————. *Rocannon's World* [1966]. New York: Ace, 1981.

————. *The Word for World is Forest* (1976). New York: Berkely, 1984.

Leiji, Matsumoto. *Galaxy Express 999.* San Francisco, Calif.: VIZ Media LLC, 1999.

Lem, Stanislaw. *The Futurological Congress: From the Memoirs of Ijon Tichy* [1971]. Trans. Michael Kandel. San Diego: Harvest, 1985.

———. "The New Cosmogony" [1971] in *A Perfect Vacuum*. Trans. Michael Kandel. Evanston, Ill.: Northwestern University Press, 1999.

———. *His Master's Voice* [1968]. Trans. Michael Kandel. Evanston, Ill.: Northwestern University Press, 1999.

———. "Golem XIV" [1981] in *Imaginary Magnitude*. Trans. Marc E. Heine. San Diego: Harcourt Brace Jovanovich, 1984. 97–122

———. "Ijon Tichy's Seventh Voyage" [1971] in *Star Diaries: Further Reminiscences Of Ijon Tichy*. Trans. Michael Kandel. San Diego: Harcourt Brace Jovanovich, 1985.

———. *The Invincible* [1964]. New York: Ace, 1973.

———. *Solaris* [1961]. Trans. Joanna Kilmartin and Steve Cox. New York: Harvest, 2002.

Lethem, Jonathan. *Amnesia Moon*. New York: Tor/Forge, 1996.

Lewis, C. S. *Out of the Silent Planet* [1938]. New York: Scribner's, 1996.

———. *Perelandra* [1943]. New York: Scribner's, 2003.

———. *That Hideous Strength* [1945]. New York: Scribner's, 2003.

Lewis, Matthew. *The Monk* [1795]. New York, Penguin, 1999.

Lindsay, David. *Voyage to Arcturus* [1920], afterword by Loren Eiseley, introduction by John Clute. Lincoln, Neb.: Bison Books, 2001.

Mercier, Louis Sébastien. *L'an 2440* [1771]. Paris: La Découverte, 1999.

Miéville, China. *Perdido Street Station*. New York: Del Rey, 2001.

Moorcock, Michael. *The Warlord of the Air* [1971]. New York: Daw, 1982.

Moore, C. L. "Shambleau" [1933] in *The Best of C. L. Moore*. New York: Del Rey, 1980

More, Thomas. *Utopia* [1516]. Trans. Clarence H. Miller. New Haven. Conn.: Yale University Press, 2001.

Moore, Ward. *Bring the Jubilee* [1953]. New York: Gollancz, 2001.

Naslund Sena Jeter. *Ahab's Wife: Or, The Star Gazer: A Novel*. New York: Harper, 2000.

Newman, Kim. *Anno Dracula*. New York: Avon, 1994.

Noon, Jeff. *Vurt*. New York: St. Martin's, 1996.

Orwell, Geoge. *Nineteen Eighty-Four* [1949]. New York: Everyman's Library, 2002.

Piercy, Marge. *Woman on the Edge of Time* [1976]. New York: Fawcett, 1985.

Poe, Edgar Allan. "The Case of M. Valdemar" [1845] in *Edgar Allan Poe. Poetry and Tales*. New York: The Library of America. 1984.

Pynchon, Thomas. *Gravity's Rainbow* [1974]. New York: Penguin, 1995.

Reynolds, Mack. *Amazon Planet*. New York: Ace, 1975.

Roberts, Keith. *Pavane* [1968]. New York: Del Rey, 2001.

Robinson, Kim Stanley. *Blue Mars*. New York: Bantam, 1996.

———. *Green Mars*. New York: Bantam, 1993.

———. *Red Mars*. New York: Bantam, 1992.

———. "Vinland the Dream" in *Rethinking History and Other Stories*. New York: Orb, 1994.

Russ, Joanna. *The Female Man* [1975]. Boston: Beacon, 2000.

Serviss, Garrett. *Edison's Conquest of Mars* [1898]. Rockville, Md.: Wildside, 2007.

Shelley, Mary. *Frankenstein* [1818]. New York: Oxford, 2001.

Simmons, Dan. *The Fall of Hyperion*. New York: Doubleday, 1990.

———. *Hyperion*. New York: Doubleday/Bantam, 1989.

Paul Simon. "The Boy in the Bubble." *Graceland*. Warner Brothers, 1986

Slonczewski, Joan. *A Door into Ocean*. New York: Arbor House, 1986.

Stapledon, Olaf. *Last and First Men* [1930]. London: Gollancz, 2000.

———. *Sirius* [1944]. London: Gollancz, 2000

———. *Star Maker* [1937]. Middletown. Conn.: Wesleyan University Press, 2004.

Stephenson, Neal. *The Diamond Age.* New York: Spectra, 1995.

———. *Snow Crash.* New York: Bantam, 1992.

Stevenson, Robert Louis. *The Strange Case of Dr. Jekyll and Mr. Hyde and Other Tales.* Ed. Roger Luckhurst. New York: Oxford, 2006.

Sterling, Bruce. *Schismatrix Plus.* New York: Ace, 1996.

Stoker, Bram. *Dracula.* Ed. Maude Ellmann. New York: Oxford, 1998.

Stross, Charles, *Accelerando.* New York: Ace, 2006.

———. and Cory Doctorow, "Jury Service." *Scifi.com* at http://www.scifi.com/ scifiction/originals/originals_archive/stross-doctorow/stross-doctorow1.html.

Strugatsky, Boris, and Arkady. *Beetle in the Anthill* [1979], trans. by Antonina W. Bouis. New York: Macmillan, 1980.

———. *Roadside Picnic* [1972].Trans. Antonina W. Bouis. London: Gollancz, 2000.

———. *The Ugly Swans* [1967]. Trans. Alice Stone Nakhimovsky and Alexander Nakhimovsky. New York: Macmillan, 1979.

———. *Escape Attempt* [1962]. New York: Macmillan, 1982.

———. *Far Rainbow* [1963]. Trans. Antonina W. Bouis. New York: Macmillan, 1979.

———. *Noon: 22nd Century* (1961), trans. Patrick L. McGuire. New York: Macmillan, 1978.

———. *Prisoners of Power* [1971], trans. Helen Saltz Jacobson. New York: Macmillan, 1977.

———. *The Time Wanderers* [1985], trans. Antonina W. Bouis. New York: St. Martin's, 1988.

Swift, Jonathan. *Gulliver's Travels* [1726], ed. Albert J. Rivero . New York: Norton, 2001.

Tiptree, James. "A Momentary Taste of Being" in *The New Atlantis,* ed. Robert Silverberg. New York: Warner, 1976.

———. *Up the Walls of the World.* New York: Ace, 1978.

Tolstoy, Alexei. *Aelita or The Decline of Mars* , trans. Leland Fetzer. Ann Arbor. Mich.: Ardis, 1985.

———. *Engineer Garin And His Death Ray,* trans. George Hanna. Moscow: Raduga, 1987.

Trevelyan, George Macauley. "If Napoleon had Won the Battle of Waterloo?" [1907] in *If It Had Happened Otherwise,* ed. J.C. Squire. London: Longmans, Green, 1931.

Turtledove, Harry. *The Guns of the South* [1992]. New York: Del Rey, 1992.

Vance, Jack, *Languages of Pao.* New York: Avalon, 1958.

Van Vogt, A. E. *Slan* [1946]. New York: Tor/Forge, 2007.

Verne, Jules. *From the Earth to the Moon, Direct in Ninety-Seven Hours and Twenty Minutes* [1865], trans. Walter James Miller. New York: Gramercy, 1995.

———. *The Mysterious Island* [1874], trans. Sidney Kravitz. Middletown, Conn.: Wesleyan University Press, 2002.

———. *Paris in the 20th century* [1863], trans. Richard Howard. New York: Random House, 1996.

———. *Round the Moon* [1870], trans. Jacqueline and Robert Baldick. New York: Dutton, 1970

———. *20,000 Leagues Under the Seas* [1869] trans. William Butcher, New York: Oxford University Press, 1998.

Vinge, Vernor. *A Fire Upon the Deep*. New York: Tor/Forge, 1993.

Voltaire. *Micromégas,* trans. Theo Cuff. New York: Penguin, 1995.

Vonnegut, Kurt. *Cat's Cradle* [1963]. New York: Dell, 1998.

Watson, Ian. *The Embedding* [1973]. London: Gollancz, 2000.

Weinbaum, Stanley. "A Martian Odyssey" [1934], Project Gutenberg Australia, *http://gutenberg.net.au/ebooks06/0601191h.html,* 2006.

Weiss, Sara. *Decimon Huydas. A Romance of Mars*. Rochester: The Austin Publishing Co. 1906.

————. *Journeys to the Planet Mars*. News York: The Bradford Press, 1908.

Wells, H. G. *First Men on the Moon* [1901]. Project Gutenberg (2005), http://www .gutenberg.org/etext/1013.

————. *In the Days of the Comet* [1906]. Project Gutenberg (2004), http://www.gutenberg .org/etext/3797.

————. *The Invisible Man* [1897]. Project Gutenberg (2004), http://www.gutenberg.org/ etext/5230.

————. *The Island of Dr. Moreau* [1896]. Project Gutenberg (2004). http://www.gutenberg .org/etext/8971.

————. "The Land Ironclads" [1903] in The Complete Short Stories of H. G. Wells, ed. John Hammond. London: Orion, 2001.

————. *The Time Machine* [1894–95]. Project Gutenberg (2004). http://www.gutenberg .org/etext/35.

————. *The War of the Worlds* [1898]. Project Gutenberg, 2004. http://www.gutenberg .org/ebooks/36.

————. *The World Set Free*. Project Gutenberg (2006). http://www.gutenberg.org/ etext/1059.

Willis, Connie. *The Doomsday Book*. New York: Bantam, 1992.

————. *To Say Nothing of the Dog*. New York: Bantam, 1997.

Williamson, Jack. *The Legion of Time/After World's End* [1938]. New York: Pyramid, 1967.

Wolfe, Gene. *Shadow and Claw (The Book of the New Sun vols. 1 and 2)* [1980–1981]. New York: St. Martin's, 1994.

————. *Sword and Citadel (The Book of the New Sun vols. 3 and 4)* [1981–1982]. New York: St. Martin's, 1994.

Wolfe, Tom. *The Right Stuff* [1979]. New York: Bantam, 2001.

Woolf, Virginia. *To the Lighthouse* [1927], introduction by Eudora Welty. New York: Harvest, 1989.

Wylie, Philip. *Gladiator* [1930]. Lincoln, Neb.: University of Nebraska Press, 2004.

Wyss, Johan David. *Swiss Family Robinson* [1812]. Project Gutenberg (2003), http://www.gutenberg.org/etext/3836.

Zamyatin, Yevgeny. *We* [1921], trans. Clarence Brown. New York: Penguin, 1993.

Zoline, Pamela, "Heat Death of the Universe" [1967] in *The Heat Death of the Universe and Other Stories*. Kingston, N.Y.: McPherson, 1988.

Films and Video Texts

2001: A Space Odyssey, dir. Stanley Kubrick. MGM/Polaris/Stanley Kubrick Productions, 1968.

The Abyss, dir. James Cameron. Twentieth Century-Fox/Pacific Western/Lightstorm, 1989.

Alien, dir. Ridley Scott. Brandywine/Twentieth Century Fox, 1979.

Alien 3, dir. David Fincher. Brandywine/Twentieth Century Fox, 1992.

Aliens, dir. James Cameron. Brandywine/Twentieth Century Fox/SLM, 1986.

Alien Resurrection, dir. Jean-Pierre Jeunet. Brandywine/Twentieth Century Fox, 1997.

Altered States, dir. Ken Russell. Warner Brothers, 1980.

Apollo-13, dir. Ron Howard. Universal/Imagine, 1995.

Back to the Future, dir. Robert Zemeckis. Amblin/Universal, 1985.

Battlestar Galactica. BSkyB/NBC Universal Television/R&D TV/Stanford Pictures (II)/ UMS 2004.

Blade Runner, dir. Ridley Scott. Blade Runner Partnership/Ladd Company/ Run Run Shaw/ Shaw Brothers, 1982.

Contact, dir. Robert Zemeckis Warner Brothers/South Side, 1985.

The Day the Earth Stood Still, dir. Robert Wise. Twentieth Century Fox, 1951.

Earth Girls are Easy, dir. Julien Temple. DiLauretis/Earth Girls/Kestrel, 1988.

E.T.: The Extraterrestrial, dir. Steven Spielberg. Amblin/Universal, 1982

Fantastic Planet, dir. René Laloux. Ceslovenski Filexport/Kratki Film/Armorial, 1973.

The Fifth Element, dir. Luc Besson. Gaumont, 1997.

eXistenZ, dir. David Cronenberg. Alliance Atlantis/Canadian Television Fund/Harold

Farscape. Jim Henson Productions/9 Network/Hallmark/ Jim Henson Television/Nine Film & Television Pty. Ltd./Sci-Fi Channel, 1999–2003.

Flash Gordon. Universal, 1936.

The Fly, dir. David Cronenberg. Brooksfilms, 1986.

Forbidden Planet, dir. Fred M. Wilcox. MGM, 1956.

Gattaca, dir. Andrew Nicoll. Coulmbia/Jersey Films, 1997.

The Ghost in the Shell, dir.Mamoru Oshii. Bandai/Kodansha/Manga Video/Production I.G. 1995.

I Married a Monster from Outer Space, dir. Louis Vittes. Paramount, 1958

Independence Day, dir. Roland Emmerich. Cntropolis/Twentieth Century Fox, 1996.

Invaders from Mars, dir. William Cameron Menzies. National Pictures, 1953.

Invasion of the Body Snatchers, dir. Don Siegel. Walter Wanger Productions, 1956.

La Jetée, dir. Chris Marker. Argos, 1962.

Lost in Space. 20th Century Fox Television/CBS Television/Irwin Allen Productions/Jodi Productions Inc./Space Productions/Van Bernard Productions, 1965–1968.

The Matrix, dir. Andy Wachowski and Larry Wachowski. Groucho II/ Silver/Village Roadshow/ Warner Bros., 1999.

Mobile Suit Gundam, dir. Yoshiuki Tomino. Nippon Sunrise/Sunrise/Ocean, 1979–1980.

Mothra, dir. Ishiro Honda. Toho, 1961.

My Stepmother is an Alien, dir. Richard Benjamin. Catalina/Weintraub, 1988.

Naked Lunch, dir. David Cronenberg. Film Trustees/Naked Lunch Productions/Nippon Film/RPC/Ontario Film Development Corporation/Téléfilm Canada, 1991.

Pi, dir. Darren Aronofsky. Harvest/Truth and Soul/Plantain/Protozoa, 1998.

Predator, dir. John McTiernan. Amercent/American Entertainment/Twentieth Century Fox, 1987.

Primer, dir. Shane Carruth, 2004.

Rabid, dir. David Cronenberg. CFDC/Cinema Entertainment/Cinépix/Famous Players/ The Dilbar Syndicate, 1977.

Rodan, dir. Ishiro Honda. Toho, 1956.

Silent Running, dir. Douglas Trumbull. Universal/Trumbull/Gruskoff, 1972.

Solaris, dir. Andrei Tarkovsky. Mosfilm/Unit Four/Creative Unit of Writers and Cinema Workers, 1972.

Soylent Green, dir. Richard Fleischer. MGM, 1973. *Stargate ,* dir. Roland Emmerich. Cana/Centropo/Centropolis, 1994.

Stalker, dir. Andrei Tarkovsky. Gambaroff-Chernier/Mosfuilm, 1979.

Star Trek. Paramount, 1966–1969.

Star Trek: The Motion Picture, dir. Robert Wise. Century /Paramount, 1979.

Star Trek: The Next Generation. Paramount, 1987–1994.

Star Trek: Voyager. Paramount/UPN, 1995–2001.

The Terminator, dir. James Cameron. Hemdale/Cinema 84/Euro Film/Pacific Western, 1984.

Terminator 2: Judgment Day, dir. James Cameron. Canal+/Carolco/Lightstorm/Pacific Western, 1991.

Them! dir. Gordon Douglas. Warner Brothers, 1954.

The Thing, dir. John Carpenter. David Foster Productions/Turman-Foster/Universal, 1982.

The Thing from Another World, dir. Christian Nyby. Winchester Pictures, 1951.

Videodrome, dir. David Cronenberg. CFDC/Famous Players/Filmplan/Guardian Trust/Victor Solnicki Productions, 1982.

Village of the Damned, dir. Wolf Rilla. MGM, 1960.

Voyage to the Moon, dir. Georges Meliès. Star Film, 1902.

War of the Worlds, dir. Steven Spielberg. Amblin/Paramount/Dreamworks/Cruise/Wagner, 2005.

The X-Files. 20th Century Fox Television/Ten Thirteen Productions/X-F Productions, 1993–2002.

Secondary Works Cited in the Text

Abe, Kobo. "The Boom in Science Fiction (1962)." *Science Fiction Studies* 29, no. 3 (November 2002): 340–341.

Aldiss, Brian. *Billion Year Spree. The True History of Science Fiction.* Garden City, N.Y.: Doubleday, 1973.

Alkon, Paul K. *Origins of Futuristic Fiction.* Athens Ga.: University of Georgia Press, 1987.

Anderson, Benedict. *Imagined Communities: Reflections on the Origin and Spread of Nationalism.* London: Verso, 1991.

Angenot, Marc. "The Absent Paradigm: An Introduction to the Semiotics of Science Fiction." *Science Fiction Studies* 6, no. 1 (March 1979): 9–19.

———. "Science Fiction in France before Verne." *Science Fiction Studies* 5, no. 1 (March 1978): 58–66.

———. and Darko Suvin, "Not Only but Also: Reflections on Cognition and Ideology in Science Fiction and SF Criticism," *Science Fiction Studies* 6, no. 2 (1979): 168–179.

Appadurai, Arjun. *Modernity at Large. Cultural Dimensions of Globalization.* Minneapolis: Minnesota University Press, 1996.

Arendt, Hannah. *Between Past and Future. Eight Exercises in Political Thought.* N.Y.: Viking, 1968.

———. *The Origins of Totalitarianism.* New York: Harcour Brace Jovanovich, 1973.

Armstrong, Neil, Michael Collins, and Edwin E. Aldrin, Jr. *First on the Moon. A Voyage With Neil Armstrong, Michael Collins [and] Edwin E. Aldrin, Jr.,* written with Gene

Farmer and Dora Jane Hamblin, with an epilogue by Arthur C. Clarke. Boston: Little, Brown, 1970.

Attebery, Brian. *Decoding Gender in Science Fiction*. London: Routledge, 2002.

———. "Science Fiction, Parable, and Parabolas." *Foundation* 95 (Autumn 2005). 7–22.

Bailes, Kendall E. "The Politics of Technology: Stalin and Technocratic Thinking Among Soviet Engineers." *The American Historical Review* 79, no. 2 (April 1974): 445–469.

Bakhtin, M. M. *The Dialogic Imagination: Four Essays*, ed. Michael Holquist. trans. Caryl Emerson and Michael Holquist. Austin: University of Texas Press, 1981.

———. *Rabelais and His World*, trans. Helene Iswolsky. Cambridge, Mass.: MIT Press, 1968.

Barr, Marleen. *Feminist Fabulation: Space/Postmodern Fiction*. Iowa City: University of Iowa Press, 1992.

Barthes, Roland. "Historical Discourse" in *Introduction to Structuralism*, ed. Michael Lane. New York: Basic Books, 1977, 145–155.

———. "The *Nautilus* and the Drunken Boat" in *Mythologies*, selected and translated from the French by Anette Lavers. N.Y.: Hill and Wang, 1972, 65–67.

———. "The Reality Effect." *The Rustle of Language*, trans. Richard Howard. New York: Hill and Wang, 1989, 141–148.

Baudrillard, Jean. "Simulacra and Science Fiction." *Science Fiction Studies* 18, no. 3 (November 1991): 309–313.

Beheshti, Molouk. "Persian Translation of SPINES Thesaurus" (http://www.irandoc.ac.ir/ org-All/FID/FID-ART/..%5C..%5C..%5CPDF%5CBEHESHTI-FID-1.PDF).

Beller, Mara. "The Sokal Hoax: At Whom Are We Laughing?" http://www.mathematik .uni-muenchen.de/~bohmmech/BohmHome/sokalhoax.html.

Benford, Gregory. "Is There a Technological Fix for the Human Condition?" *Hard Science Fiction*. Eds. George Slusser and Eric Rabkin. Carbondale: Southern Illinois University Press, 1988, 82–98.

———. "Of Time and *Timescape*." *Science Fiction Studies* 20, no. 2 (July 1993): 184–190.

Berger, Albert I. *The Magic that Works: John W. Campbell and the American Response to Technology*. San Bernardino, Calif.: Borgo Press, 1993.

Berman, Judith. "Science Fiction without the Future." *The New York Review of Science Fiction*, 13 no. 9 (May 2001): 1, 6–8.

Bernal, J. D. *The World, the Flesh, and the Devil.: An Inquiry into the Three Enemies of the Rational Soul*, 2nd ed., with a new foreward by the author. London: Cape, 1970.

Bernardi, Daniel Leonard. *Star Trek and History: Race-Ing Toward a White Future*. New Brunswick, N.J.: Rutgers University Press, 1998.

Berubé, Michael. *Public Access: Literary Theory and American Cultural Politics*. New York: Verso, 1994.

Bick, Ilsa. "'Well, I Guess I Must Make You Nervous': Woman and the Space of *Alien 3*." *Post-Script*. 14, nos. 1–2 (1994–95): 45–58.

Bloch, Ernst. *The Principle of Hope*, vol. 1. Cambridge Mass.: MIT Press. 2000.

———. *The Utopian Function of Art and Literature. Selected Essays*. Cambridge, Mass.: MIT Press, 1988.

Boulanger, Jean-Claude. "La création lexicale et la modernité." *Le langage et l'Homme* 25, no. 4 (1990): 233–239.

Bould, Mark. "The Dreadful Credibility of Absurd Things: A Tendency in Fantasy Theory." *Historical Materialism* 10, no. 4 (2002): 51–88.

Boym, Svetlana. "Kosmos: Remembrances of the Future," in *Kosmos: A Portrait of the*

Russian Space Age, with photographs by Adam Bartos. Princeton: Princeton
   Architectural Press, 2001: 83–99.
Broderick, Damien. *Reading by Starlight: Postmodern Science Fiction.* New York:
   Routledge, 1995.
———. *The Spike: How Our Lives Are Being Transformed By Rapidly Advancing
   Technologies.* New York: Forge, 2001.
Brown, Tonya. "Classical Music and Science Fiction." *Vector* 204 (March/April 1999).
Buccholz, Arnold. "The Role of the Scientific-Technological Revolution in Marxism-
   Leninism." *Studies in Soviet Thought* 20 (1979):145–164.
Bukatman, Scott. "The Artificial Infinite: On Special Effects and the Sublime" in *Alien Zone
   II: The Spaces of Science Fiction Cinema,* ed. Annette Kuhn. London: Verso, 1999: 249–275.
———. *Terminal Identity: The Virtual Subject in Postmodern Science Fiction.* Durham,
   N.C.: Duke University Press, 1993.
Burke, Edmund, *A Philosophical Enquiry into the Origin of our Ideas of the Sublime and
   the Beautiful,* ed. J. T. Boulton. London: Routledge and Kegan Paul, 1958.
Butler, Andrew M. "Proto-Sf/Proto-Queer: The Strange Case of Dr. Frankenstein and
   Mr. Hyde." *Foundation* 86 (Autumn 2002): 7–16.
Caidin, Martin. *The Moon: New World for Men.* Indianapolis, Ind.: Bobbs Merrill, 1963.
Cartwright, Nancy. *The Dappled World. A Study of the Boundaries of Science.* Cambridge:
   Cambridge University Press, 1999.
———. *How the Laws of Physics Lie.* Oxford: Oxford University Press, 1983.
Carveth, Donald, and Naomi Gold. "The Pre-Oedipalizing of Klein in (North) America:
   Ridley Scott's *Alien* Re-analyzed." *Psy-Art* at www.clas.ufl.edu/ipsa/journal/articles/
   psyart1999/carvet03.htm.
Cawelti, John G. *Adventure, Mystery, and Romance. Formula Stories as Art and Popular
   Culture.* Chicago: University of Chicago Press, 1976.
Chernyshova, Tatiana. "Science Fiction and Myth Creation in Our Age." *Science Fiction
   Studies* 31, no. 3 (November 2004): 345–357.
Ciment, Michel. *Kubrick,* trans. Gilbert Adair. New York: Holt, Rinehart, and Winston, 1983.
Clark, Katerina. *The Soviet Novel: History as Ritual.* Bloomington: Indiana University
   Press, 2000.
Clarke, Arthur C. *The Lost Worlds of 2001.* New York: New American Library, 1982.
Clement, Hal. "Whirligig World" (1953), in *The Essential Hal Clement, Volume 3:
   Variations on a Theme by Sir Isaac Newton,* ed. Mark L. Olson and Anthony R. Lewis.
   Framingham, Mass.: NESFA Press, 2000.
Clifford, James, and George E. Marcus, eds. *Writing Culture: The Poetics and Politics of
   Ethnography.* Berkeley and Los Angeles: University of California Press, 1986.
Clute, John. *Look at the Evidence: Essays & Reviews.* Liverpool: Liverpool University
   Press, 1995.
Collins, Karen. "Dead Channel Surfing: the Commonalities between Cyberpunk
   Literature and Industrial Music." *Popular Music* 24, no. 2 (2005): 165–178.
Collins, Michael. *Carrying the Fire: An Astronaut's Journey,* with a foreword by Charles
   A. Lindbergh. New York: Cooper Square Press, 2001.
Constable, Catherine. "Becoming the Monster's Mother: Morphologies of Identity in the
   Alien Series," in *Alien Zone II,* Annette Kuhn, ed. London: Verso, 1999: 173–202.
Coulmas, Florian, ed. *Language Adaptation.* Cambridge: Cambridge University Press, 1989.
Creed, Barbara. "Horror and the Monstrous-Feminine: An Imaginary Abjection," in *The*

Dread of Difference: Gender and the Horror Film, ed. Barry Keith Grant. Austin: University of Texas Press, 1996, 35–65.

Csicsery-Ronay, Istvan, Jr. "The Book is the Alien. On Certain and Uncertain Readings of Stanislaw Lem's *Solaris.*" *Science Fiction Studies* 12 no. 1 (March 1985): 6–21.

———. "Futuristic Flu, or The Revenge of the Future" in *Fiction 2000. Cyberpunk and the Future of Fiction,* ed. George Slusser and Tom Shippey. Athens, Ga.: University of Georgia Press, 1992, 26–45.

———. "Notes on Mutopia." *Postmodern Culture* 8, no. 1 (September 1997).

———. "Science Fiction and Empire." *Science Fiction Studies* 30, no. 2 (July 2003): 231–245.

———. "Towards the Last Fairy Tale: On the Fairy-Tale Paradigm in the Strugatskys' SF, 1963–72." *Science Fiction Studies* 13, no. 1 (March 1993): 1–41.

———."The SF of Theory: Baudrillard and Haraway." *Science Fiction Studies* 18, no. 3 (November 1991): 387–404.

Dalkin, Gary S. "Part 3: Science Fiction Film Music." *Vector* 205 (May/June 1999).

Darlington, Andrew. "Part Five: Standin' at the Crossroads: SF and Robert Johnson's Blues." *Vector* 206 (September/October 1999).

Davis, Michael. "'What's the Story Mother?': Abjection and Anti-Feminism in *Alien* and *Aliens.*" *Gothic Studies* 2 (2000): 245–256.

Delany, Samuel R. "Is Cyberpunk a Good or a Bad Thing?" *Mississippi Review* 47/48 (1988): 28–35.

———. *Starboard Wine.* New York: Dragon Press, 1984.

Deltcheva, Roumiana, and Eduard Vlasov. "Back to the House II: On the Chronotopic and Ideological Reinterpretation of Len's *Solaris* in Tarkovsky's Film." *Russian Review* 56, no. 4 (Oct. 1997): 532–549.

Déroy, Louis. "La néologie." *La Banque des mots* 1 (1971): 5–12.

Derrida, Jacques. "no apocalypse, not now (full speed ahead, seven missiles, seven missives)." *Diacritics* 14, no. 2 (1984): 20–31.

Dery, Mark. "Cyberpunk: Riding the Shockwave with the Toxic Underground." *Keyboard* (May, 1989): 75–89.

de Zwaan, Victoria. "Rethinking the Slipstream: Kathy Acker Reads *Neuromancer.*" *Science Fiction Studies* 24, no. 3 (November 1997): 459–470.

Donawerth, Jane. *Frankenstein's Daughters: Women Writing Science Fiction.* Syracuse, N.Y.: Syracuse University Press, 1997.

Downey, Gary Lee, Joseph Dumit, and Sarah Williams. "Cyborg Anthropology." *Cultural Anthropology* 10, no. 2 (1995): 264–269.

Drexler, K. Eric. *Engines of Creation,* with a foreword by Marvin Minsky. Garden City, N.J.: Anchor Press/Doubleday, 1987.

Duchesne, Scott. "'Boldly Playing': The 'Profit' of Performance within the Liminal Frame of the Con(vention[al])." Paper delivered at the annual convention of the Science Fiction Research Association, Guelph, Ontario, 2003.

Edelman, Lee. "At Risk in the Sublime. The Politics of Gender and Theory" in *Gender and Theory: Dialogues on Feminist Criticism,* ed. Linda Kaufman. New York: Blackwell, 1989, 212–224.

Elkhafaifi, Hussein M. "Arabic Language Planning in the Age of Globalization." *Language Problems and Language Planning.* 26, no. 3 (Fall 2002): 253–269.

Eshun, Kodwe. *More Brilliant Than the Sun. Adventures in Sonic Fiction.* London: Quartet, 1999.

Evans, Arthur B. *Jules Verne Rediscovered. Didacticism and the Scientific Novel*. N.Y.: Greenwood Press, 1988.

Ferguson, Frances. "The Nuclear Sublime." *Diacritics* 14, no. 2 (1984): 4–10.

Ferguson, Niall, ed. *Virtual History: Alternatives and Counterfactuals*. N.Y.: Basic Books, 1999.

Fernbach, Amanda. "The Fetishization of Masculinity in Science Fiction: The Cyborg and the Console Cowboy." *Science Fiction Studies* 27, no. 2 (July 2000): 234–255.

Fitting, Peter. "Futurecop: The Neutralization of Revolt in *Blade Runner*." *Science Fiction Studies*, 14, no. 3 (November 1987): 340–354.

———. "The Modern Anglo-American SF Novel: Utopian Longing and Capitalist Cooptation." *Science Fiction Studies* 6, no. 1(March 1979): 59–76.

———. "*Ubik*: The Deconstruction of Bourgeois SF." *Science Fiction Studies* 2, no. 1 (March 1975): 47–54.

Freeman, Barbara C. "*Frankenstein* with Kant: A Theory of Monstrosity or the Monstrosity of Theory," in *New Casebooks: Frankenstein by Mary Shelley*, ed. Fred Botting. New York: St. Martin's, 1995, 191–205.

Freedman, Carl. *Critical Theory and Science Fiction*. Middletown, Conn.: Wesleyan University Press, 2000.

———. "Kubrick's *2001* and the Possibility of a Science-Fiction Cinema." *Science Fiction Studies*. 25, no. 2 (July 1998): 300–318.

———."Towards a Theory of Paranoia: The Science Fiction of Philip K. Dick," in *On Philip K. Dick: 40 Articles from Science-Fiction Studies*, ed. R. D. Mullen, Istvan Csicsery-Ronay Jr., Arthur B. Evans, and Veronica Hollinger. Terre Haute and Greencastle: SF-TH Inc., 1992: 111–118.

Frye, Northrop. *Anatomy of Criticism: Four Essays*. Princeton, N.J.: Princeton University Press, 1957.

Fuchs, Christian. "Dialectical Materialism and the Self-organization of Matter." http://www.seekingwisdom.com/fuchs.htm.

Gabbard, Krin, and Glen. O. Gabbard. "The Science Fiction Film and Psychoanalysis: *Alien* and Melanie Klein's Night Music." *Psychoanalytic Approaches to Literature and Film*, ed. Maurice Charnay and Joseph Reppen. Rutherford, N.J.: Fairleigh Dickinson University Press, 1987: 171–179.

Galison, Peter, and David J. Stump, eds. *The Disunity of Science. Boundaries, Contexts, and Power*. Stanford, Calif.: Stanford University Press, 1996.

Geier, Manfred. "Stanislaw Lem's Fantastic Ocean. Toward a Semantic Interpretation of *Solaris*." *Science Fiction Studies* 19, no. 2 (July 1992): 192–218.

Gerblinger, Christiane. "'Fiery the Angels Fell': America, Regeneration and Ridley Scott's *Blade Runner*." *Australian Journal of American Studies* 21, no. 1 (July 2002): 19–30.

Gilder, George. *Telecosm: How Infinite Bandwidth Will Revolutionize Our World*. New York: Free Press, 2002.

Gleitman, Lisa. "The Structural Sources of Verb Meanings" in *Language Acquisition. Core Readings*. Paul Bloom, ed. Cambridge, Mass: MIT Press, 1994, 174–221.

Gooding, David C. *Experiment and the Making of Meaning: Human Agency in Scientific Observation and Experiment*. Boston: Kluwer Academic Publishers, 1990.

———. "Thought Experiments" in *Routledge Encyclopedia of Philosophy*, ed. E. Craig. London: Routledge, 1998. *http://www.rep.routledge.com/article/Q106SECT1*

Gordon, Joan. "Hybridity, Heterotopia, and Mateship in China Mieville's *Perdido Street Station*." *Science Fiction Studies* 30, no. 3 (November 2003): 456–476.

————. "Yin and Yang Duke It Out," in *Storming the Reality Studio: A Casebook of Cyberpunk and Postmodern Science Fiction,* ed. Larry McCaffery. Durham, N.C.: Duke University Press, 1991, 196–202.

Gould, Steven J. *Full House: The Spread of Excellence from Plato to Darwin.* New York: Harmony Books, 1996.

Graham, Paula. "Looking Lesbian: Amazons and Aliens in Science Fiction Cinema" in *The Good, the Bad, and the Gorgeous: Popular Culture's Romance with Lesbianism,* Ed. Diane Hamer and Belinda Budge. London: Pandora, 1994, 197–217.

Grandy, David A., *Leo Szilard: Science as a Mode of Being.* Lanham, Md.: University Press of America, 1996.

Grant, Glenn, "Transcendence Through Detournement in William Gibson's *Neuromancer,*" *Science Fiction Studies* 17, no. 1 (March 1990): 41–49.

Gusterson, Hugh. *Nuclear Rites: A Weapons Laboratory at the End of the Cold War.* Berkeley and Los Angeles: University of California Press, 1996.

Haraway, Donna. *Simians, Cyborgs and Women: The Reinvention of Nature.* N.Y.: Routledge, 1991.

Harding, Sandra. *The Science Question in Feminism.* Ithaca, N.Y.: Cornell University Press, 1986.

Harpham, Geoffrey Galt. *On the Grotesque: Strategies of Contradiction in Art and Literature.* Princeton: Princeton University Press, 1982.

Harré, H. Rom. *The Principles of Scientific Thinking.* Chicago: University of Chicago Press, 1970.

Hartmann, Stephan. "Models and Stories in Hadron Physics," in Morgan and Morrisson, 326–346.

Hartwell, David, and Kathryn Cramer. "Introduction. How Shit Became Shinola: Definition and Redefinition of Space Opera" in *The Space Opera Renaissance,* ed. David Hartwell and Kathryn Cramer. New York: Tor, 2006, 9–21.

Hayles, N. Katherine. *Chaos Bound: Orderly Disorder in Contemporary Literature and Science.* Ithaca, N.Y.: Cornell University Press, 1990.

————. ed. *Chaos and Order: Complex Dynamics in Literature and Science.* Chicago: University of Chicago Press, 1991.

————. "Connecting the Quantum Dots: Nanotechscience and Culture," in *Nanoculture,* ed. Hayles. Portland, Ore.: 2004.

Hayward, Philip, ed. *Off the Planet: Music, Sound and Science Fiction Cinema.* London: John Libbey Publishing/Perfect Beat Press, 2004.

Hegel, G. W. F. *Elements of the Philosophy of Right,* ed. Allen W. Wood. Cambridge: Cambridge University Press, 1991.

Hellekson, Karen. *The Alternate History: Refiguring Historical Time.* Kent, Ohio: Kent State University Press, 2001.

Helmling, Steven. "During Auschwitz: Adorno, Hegel, and the 'Unhappy Consciousness' of Critique." *Postmodern Culture* 15, no. 2 (2005). http://www3.iath.virginia.edu/pmc/text-only/issue.105/15.2helmling.txt.

Hills, Matt. "Counterfictions in the Work of Kim Newman: Rewriting Gothic SF as 'Alternate-Story Stories'." *Science Fiction Studies* 30, no. 3 (November 2003): 436–455.

Hollinger, Veronica, "Feminist Science Fiction: Breaking Up the Subject." *Extrapolation* 31, no. 3(1990): 229–239.

————. "Feminist theory and science fiction" in *The Cambridge Companion to Science*

Fiction, ed. Edward James and Farah Mendlesohn. New York: Cambridge University Press, 2003, 121–134.

———. "(Re)reading Queerly: Science Fiction, Feminism, and the Defamiliarization of Gender." *Science Fiction Studies* 26, no. 1 (1999): 23–40.

Horowitz, Tamara, and Gerald J. Massey, ed. *Thought Experiments in Science and Philosophy.* Lanham, Md.: Rowman and Littlefield, 1991.

Huff, Darrell. *How To Lie with Statistics* [1954]. New York: Norton, 1993.

Huntington, John. "Hard-Core Science Fiction and the Illusion of Science," in *Hard Science Fiction,* ed. George Slusser and Eric Rabkin. Carbondale: Southern Illinois University Press, 1988, 48–49.

———. *The Logic of Fantasy. H.G. Wells and Science Fiction.* N.Y.: Columbia University Press, 1982.

Huxley, Julian. *Evolution. The Modern Synthesis.* N.Y.: Harper and Brothers, 1943.

Hymes, Dell. "The Use of Anthropology: Critical, Political, Personal," in *Reinventing Anthropology,* ed. Dell Hymes. New York: Vintage, 1974, 3–79.

Irvine, Alex. "The War of the Worlds and the Disease of Imperialism," in *Flashes of the Fantastic. Selected Essays from the War of the Worlds Centennial, Nineteenth International Conference on the Fantastic in the Arts,* ed. David Ketterer. Westport, Conn: Praeger, 2004: 33–42.

Jakobson, Roman. "Linguistics and Poetics," in *Language in Literature,* ed. Krystyna Pomorska and Stephen Rudy. Cambridge, Mass.: Belknap Press, 1987, 62–94.

———. "Two Aspects of Language and Two Types of Aphasic Disturbances," in *Language in Literature,* ed. Krystyna Pomorska and Stephen Rudy. Cambridge: Harvard University Press, 1987. 95–114.

James, Edward. *Science Fiction in the 20th Century.* New York: Oxford University Press, 1994.

Jameson, Fredric. *Archaeologies of the Future: The Desire Called Utopia and Other Science Fictions.* New York: Verso, 2005.

———. *The Political Unconscious: Narrative as a Socially Symbolic Act.* Ithaca, N.Y.: Cornell University Press, 1981.

———. *Marxism and Form. Twentieth Century Dialectical Theories of Literature.* Princeton N.J.: Princeton University Press, 1972.

———. *The Ideologies of Theory : Essays 1971–1986.* Minneapolis: University of Minnesota Press, 1988, 75–101.

———. *Postmodernism, or, The Cultural Logic of Late Capitalism.* Durham, N.C.: Duke University Press, 1991.

———. "Radical Fantasy." *Historical Materialism* 10, no. 4 (2002): 273–280.

Jones, Gwyneth. *Deconstructing the Starships. Science, Fiction, and Reality.* Liverpool: Liverpool University Press, 1999.

Jordan, John W. "Kennedy's Romantic Moon and its Legacy for Space Exploration." *Rhetoric and Public Affairs* 6, no. 2 (2003): 209–231.

Kagarlitsky, Julius. "Realism and Fantasy," in *SF: The Other Side of Realism. Essays on Modern Fantasy and Science Fiction,* ed. Thomas Clareson. Bowling Green, Ohio: Bowling Green University Popular Press, 1971, 29–52.

Kant, Immanuel. *Critique of Judgment,* trans. and with an introduction by Werner S. Pluhar. Indianapolis: Hackett Publishing, 1987

Kauffman, James L. *Selling Outer Space: Kennedy, the Media, and Funding for Project Apollo, 1961–1963.* Tuscaloosa, Ala.: University of Alabama Press, 1994.

Kavanagh, James. "Feminism, Humanism and Science in *Alien*," in *Alien Zone,* ed. Annette Kuhn. London: Verso, 1990, 73–81.

Kaye, Alan S., and John Quijada. "The Chakobsa Language." *California Linguistic Notes.* 23, no. 1 (Fall-Winter 1991): 24–25.

Keller, Evelyn Fox. *Reflections on Gender and Science.* New Haven, Conn.: Yale University Press, 1996.

Kelling, H. D. "Some Significant Names in *Gulliver's Travels.*" *Studies in Philology* 48 (1951): 761–778.

Kelly, Kevin. *Out of Control: The New Biology of Machines, Social Systems and the Economic World.* New York: Perseus Books, 1995.

Kilgore, DeWitt Douglas. *Astrofuturism: Science, Race, and Visions of Utopia in Space.* Philadelphia: University of Pennsylvania Press, 2003.

Kilgour, Maggie. *The Rise of the Gothic Novel.* New York: Routledge, 1995.

Kolodny, Annette. *The Lay of the Land: Metaphor as Experience and History in American Life and Letters.* Chapel Hill: University of North Carolina Press, 2005.

Kosmodemyansky, A. *Konstantin Tsiolkovsky His Life and Work.* Honolulu, Hawaii: University Press of the Pacific, 2000.

Krauss, Lawrence M. *The Physics of Star Trek,* with a foreword by Stephen Hawking. New York: Basic Books, 1995.

———, and Michael S. Turner. "The Cosmological Constant is Back." *General Relativity and Gravitation* 27, no. 11 (November, 1995): 1137–1144.

Kuhn, Thomas. *The Essential Tension.* Chicago: University of Chicago Press, 1977.

Kurzweil, Ray. *The Age of Spiritual Machines. When Computers Exceed Human Intelligence.* New York: Viking, 1999.

———. *The Singularity Is Near: When Humans Transcend Biology.* New York: Viking, 2005.

Landon, Brooks. *The Aesthetics of Ambivalence: Rethinking Science Fiction Film in the Age of Electronic (Re)Production.* Westport, Conn.: Greenwood Press, 1992.

———. *Science Fiction after 1900: From the Steam Man to the Stars.* New York: Twayne, 1977.

Larbalestier, Justine. *The Battle of the Sexes in Science Fiction.* Middletown, Conn.: Wesleyan University Press, 2002.

Latham, Rob. *Consuming Youth: Vampires, Cyborgs, and the Culture of Consumption.* Chicago: University of Chicago Press, 2002.

Latour, Bruno. *Science in Action: How to Follow Scientists and Engineers through Society.* Cambridge Mass.: Harvard University Press, 1988.

———, and Stephen Woolgar. *Laboratory Life: The Construction of Scientific Facts.* Princeton N.J.: Princeton University Press, 1986.

LaValley, Albert J. "Traditions of Trickery: The Role of Special Effects in the Science Fiction Film," in *Shadows of the Magic Lamp: Fantasy and Science Fiction in Film,* ed. George Slusser and Eric S. Rabkin. Carbondale: Southern Illinois University Press, 1985, 141–58.

Le Guin, Ursula K. *Dancing at the Edge of the World: Thoughts on Words, Women, Places.* New York: Grove Press, 1989.

———. "Introduction" to *The Left Hand of Darkness.* New York: Walker, 1969.

Lem, Stanislaw. *Microworlds: Writings on Science Fiction and Fantasy,* ed. Franz Rottensteiner. San Diego, Calif.: Harcour Brace Jovanovich, 1984.

———. *Summa Technologiae,* trans. Beatrix Murányi. Budapest: Kossuth, 1976.

Lennox, James G. "Darwinian Thought Experiments: A Function for Just So Stories," in Horowitz and Massey, 173–195.

Lopez, José. "Bridging the Gaps: Science Fiction in Nanotechnology." *HYLE—International Journal for Philosophy of Chemistry.* 10, no. 2 (2004): 131–154.

Luckhurst, Roger. "The Many Deaths of Science Fiction: A Polemic." *Science Fiction Studies* 21, no. 1 (March 1994): 35–50.

———. "Nuclear Criticism: Anachronism and Anachorism." *Diacritics* 23, no. 2 (Summer, 1993): 88–97.

———. *Science Fiction.* Malden, Mass.: Polity, 2005.

Lukács, Georg. *The Historical Novel,* trans. Hannah and Stanley Mitchell. Boston: Beacon, 1963.

McDougal, Walter A. *The Heavens and the Earth: A Political History of the Space Age.* New York: Basic Books, 1985.

McGuirk, Carol. "NoWhere Man: Toward a Poetics of Post-Utopian Characterization." *Science Fiction Studies* 21, no. 2 (July 1994): 141–154.

McHale, Brian. *Constructing Postmodernism.* N.Y.: Routledge, 1992.

McLeod, Ken. "Space Oddities: Aliens, Futurism and Popular Music." *Popular Music* 22, no. 3 (October 2003): 337–55.

Malmgren, Carl D. *Worlds Apart. Narratology of Science Fiction.* Bloomington: Indiana University Press, 1991.

Marcus, George E., and Michael M. J. Fischer. *Anthropology as Cultural Critique: An Experimental Moment in the Human Sciences.* Chicago: University of Chicago Press, 1996.

Masood, Ehsan. "Science Communication 'Needs Updated Arabic.'" *Science and Development Network* 23 October 2003.

Maurais, Jacques. "Terminology and Language Planning," in *Terminology. Applications in Interdisciplinary Communication,* ed. Helmi B. Sonneveld and Kurt L. Loening. Philadelphia: John Benjamin, 1993, 111–125.

Mellor, Anne K. "Immortality or Monstrosity? Reflections on the Sublime in Romantic Literature and Art," in *The Romantic Imagination: Literature and Art in England and Germany,* ed. Frederick Burwick and Jürgen Klein. Amsterdam: Rodopi, 1996, 225–239.

Merchant, Carolyn. *The Death of Nature: Women, Ecology, and the Scientific Revolution.* New York: Harper and Row, 1989.

Mermin N. David. *Boojums All the Way Through: Communicating Science in a Prosaic Age.* Cambridge: Cambridge University Press, 1990.

Meyers, Walter E. *Aliens and Linguists: Language Study and Science Fiction.* Athens, Ga.: University of Georgia Press, 1980.

Milburn, Colin. "Nanotechnology in the Age of Posthuman Engineering: Science Fiction as Science," in *Nanoculture. Implications of the New Technoscience,* ed. N. Katherine Hayles. Portland, Ore.: Intellect Books, 2004, 112–23.

Miles, Margaret. "Carnal Abominations: the Female Body as Grotesque," in *The Grotesque in Art and Literature: Theological Reflections,* ed. James Luther Adams and Wilson Yates. Grand Rapids, Mich.: Eerdmans, 1997, 83–112.

Moravec, Hans. *Mind Children: The Future of Robot and Human Intelligence.* Cambridge, Mass.: Harvard University Press, 1990.

Morgan, Lewis Henry. *Ancient Society.* New York: Holt, 1877.

Morgan, Mary S., and Margaret Morrisson, eds. *Models as Mediators. Perspectives on Natural and Social Science.* Cambridge: Cambridge University Press, 1999.

BIBLIOGRAPHY

Morrisson, Margaret, and Mary S. Morgan. "Models as Mediating Instruments," in Morgan and Morrisson, 10–37.

Moylan, Tom. *Demand the Impossible: Science Fiction and the Utopian Imagination.* New York: Methuen, 1987.

———. "The Locus of Hope: Utopia versus Ideology." *Science Fiction Studies* 9, no. 2 (July 1982): 159–166.

———. *Scraps of the Untainted Sky: Science Fiction, Utopia, Dystopia.* Boulder, Colo.: Westview Press, 2000.

Mullen, R. D., "Dialect, Grapholect, and Story: Russell Hoban's *Riddley Walker* as Science Fiction." *Science Fiction Studies* 27, no. 2 (July 1982): 391–406.

Nahin, Paul J. *Time Machines: Time Travel in Physics, Metaphysics, and Science Fiction,* with a foreword by Kip Thorne. 2nd ed. New York: Springer, 1999.

Nerlich, Michael. *The Ideology of Adventure. Studies in Modern Consciousness. 1100–1750. Volume 2.* Minneapolis: University of Minnesota Press, 1987.

Nicholl, Peter [as PN]. "Conceptual Breakthrough," in *The Encyclopedia of Science Fiction,* ed. John Clute and Peter Nicholl. New York: St. Martin's, 1993, 247–257.

Nixon, Nicola. "Cyberpunk: Preparing the Ground for Revolution or Keeping the Boys Satisfied?" *Science Fiction Studies* 19, no. 2 (July 1992): 219–235.

Norton, John. "Thought Experiments in Einstein's Work," in Horowitz and Massey, 129–148.

Nye, David E. *The American Technological Sublime.* Cambridge, Mass.: MIT Press, 1996.

Origgi, Gloria, and Dan Sperber. "Evolution, Communication and the Proper Function of Language," in *Evolution and the Human Mind: Language, Modularity and Social Cognition,* ed. Peter Carruthers and Andrew Chamberlain. Cambridge: Cambridge University Press, 2000. 140–169.

Ortega y Gasset, José. *Meditations on Quixote.* New York: W. W. Norton & Co., 1961.

Palumbo, Donald E. *Chaos Theory, Asimov's Foundations and Robots, and Herbert's Dune: The Fractal Aesthetic of Epic Science Fiction.* Westport, Conn.: Greenwood Press, 2002.

Parrinder, Patrick. *Shadows of the Future: H.G. Wells, Science Fiction, and Prophecy.* Syracuse: Syracuse University Press, 1995.

Pavel, Silvia. "Neology and Phraseology as Terminology-in-the-Making," in *Terminology. Applications in Interdisciplinary Communication,* ed. Helmi B. Sonneveld and Kurt L. Loening. Philadelphia: John Benjamin, 1993, 21–34.

Pearson, Wendy. "Alien Cryptographies: The View from Queer." *Science Fiction Studies* 26, no. 1(March 1999): 1–22.

———. "SF and Queer Theory," in *The Cambridge Companion to Science Fiction,* 149–160.

Penley, Constance. *NASA/TREK. Popular Science and Sex in America.* New York: Verso, 1997.

———. "Time Travel, Primal Scene and the Critical Dystopia," in *Alien Zone: Cultural Theory and Contemporary Science Fiction Cinema.,* ed. Annette Kuhn. London: Verso, 1990, 116–127.

Perry, John R. "Language Reform in Turkey and Iran." *International Journal of Middle East Studies* 17, no. 3 (August 1985): 295–311.

Person, Lawrence. "Notes Toward a Postcyberpunk Manifesto." *Slashdot* 10/9/1999. (*http://slashdot.org/features/99/10/08/2123255.shtml*)

Pesce, Mark. "Magic Mirror: The Novel as Software Development Platform." Presented

at the Media in Transition conference at MIT, 1999. web.mit.edu/m-i-t/articles/
pesce.html.

Philmus, Robert M. *Visions and Re-Visions*. Liverpool: University of Liverpool Press, 2005.

Picone, Michel D. "Le Français face à l'anglais: Aspects linguistiques." *Cahiers de
l'Association internationale des études françaises* 44, (May 1992): 9–23.

———. "Lexicogenesis and Language Vitality." *Journal of the Linguistic Circle of New
York* 45, no. 3 (1994): 261–285.

Poland, Lynn. "The Idea of the Holy and the History of the Sublime." *The Journal of
Religion*. 72, no. 2 (1992): 175–197.

Pons, Émile. "Les langues imaginaires dans le voyage utopique. Un Précurseur. Thomas
Morus." *Revue de littérature comparée* 10 (1930): 589–607.

Porush, David. "Prigogine, Chaos, and Contemporary Science Fiction." *Science Fiction
Studies* 18, no. 3 (November 1991): 367–386.

Pritchett, V. S. "Wells and the English Novel" in *H.G. Wells. The Time Machine/The War
of the Worlds: A Critical Edition*, ed. Frank D. McConnell. N.Y.: Oxford University
Press, 1977.

Propp, Vladimir. *Morphology of the Folktale*, ed. and with a commentary by Svatava
Pirkova-Jakobson, trans. Laurence Scott. Bloomington, Ind.: Research Center, Indiana
University, 1958.

Rabinbach, Anson. "Between Enlightenment and Apocalypse: Benjamin, Bloch and
Modern German Jewish Messianism." *New German Critique* 34 (1985): 78–124.

Ray, Alan. *Essays on Terminology*. Philadelphia: John Benjamins, 1995.

Reusch, Bernhard. *Evolution Above the Species Level*. N.Y.: Columbia University Press, 1960.

Rickmann, Gregg. "'What Is This Sickness?' 'Schizophrenia' and *We Can Build You*," in
Philip K. Dick. Contemporary Critical Interpretations, ed. Samuel J. Umland. Westport,
Conn: Greenwood Press, 1995, 143–156.

Riggs, Fred. "Social Science Terminology: Basic Problems and Proposed Solutions" in
Terminology. Applications in Interdisciplinary Communication, ed. Helmi B. Sonneveld
and Kurt L. Loening, Philadelphia: John Benjamin, 1993, 195–220.

Roberts, Adam. *Science Fiction*, London: Routledge, 2000.

Robu, Cornel. "A Key to Science Fiction: The Sublime." *Foundation* 42 (Summer 1990):
21–37.

Rosenthal, Bernice Glatzer. *The Occult in Russian and Soviet Culture*. Ithaca, N.Y.:
Cornell University Press, 1997.

Ross, Andrew. *Strange Weather: Culture, Science, and Technology in the Age of Limits*.
New York: Verso, 1991.

Rossi, Umberto. "From Dick to Lethem: The Dickian Legacy, Postmodernism, and
Avant-Pop in Jonathan Lethem's *Amnesia Moon*." *Science Fiction Studies* 29, no. 1
(March 2002):15–33.

Rushing, Janet Hocker. "Evolution of 'The New Frontier' in *Alien* and *Aliens*: Patriarchal
Co-Optation of the Feminine Archetype." *The Quarterly Journal of Speech* 75 (1989): 1–24.

Russ, Joanna. *The Country You Have Never Seen: Essays and Reviews*. Liverpool: Liverpool
University Press, 2007.

———. *To Write Like a Woman: Essays in Feminism and Science Fiction*. Bloomington:
Indiana University Press, 1995.

Ryan, Marie-Laure. *Possible Worlds: Artificial Intelligence and Narrative Theory*.
Bloomington: Indiana University Press, 1991.

Sagan, Carl. *Broca's Brain: Reflections on the Romance of Science.* New York: Random House, 1979.

Samuel, Geoffrey. "Inventing Real Cultures: Some Comments on Anthropology and Science Fiction." http://users.hunterlink.net.au/~mbbgbs/Geoffrey/invent.html.

Sauvageot, Aurélien. "Valuer des néologismes." *La Banque des mots* 1 (1971): 29–36.

Schiebinger, Londa L. *Nature's Body: Gender in the Making of Modern Science.* Boston: Beacon Press, 1993.

Schmidt, Alfred. *The Concept of Nature in Marx,* trans. Ben Fowkes. London: NLB, 1971.

Schoen, Lawrence M. "A Brief History of Klingon." *Futureframe* January 31, 2000, *http://www.morgenwelt.de/futureframe/000131–klingon.htm.*

Schwenger, Peter. "Writing the Unthinkable." *Critical Inquiry* 13, no. 1 (Autumn 1986): 33–48.

Scott, James C. *Seeing Like a State: How Certain Schemes to Improve the Human Condition Have Failed.* New Haven: Yale University Press, 1998.

Secor, Marie, and Lynda Walsh. "A Rhetorical Perspective on the Sokal Hoax: Genre, Style, and Context." *Written Communication* 21, no. 1 (January 2004): 69–91.

Shapiro, Alan N. *Star Trek: Technologies of Disappearance.* Berlin: Avinus, 2004.

Shippey, Tom. "Hard Reading" in *A Companion to Science Fiction,* ed. David Seed. Malden, Mass.: Blackwell, 2005, 11–26.

Simsdon, Ian J. "Part One: The Influence of SF on Modern Popular Music," *Vector* 203 (January/February 1999).

Slusser, George, and Danièle Chatelain. "Spacetime Geometries: Time Travel and the Modern Geometrical Narrative." *Science Fiction Studies* 22, no. 2 (July 1995): 161–186.

Smaglik, P. "Creativity, Confusion for Genes," *The Scientist* 12[7]:1, March 30, 1998.

Smith, Andrew. *Moon Dust: In Search of the Men Who Fell to Earth.* New York: Harper Perennial, 2006.

Smith, C. Jason, and Ximena Gallardo. *Alien Woman: The Making of Lt. Ellen Ripley.* New York: Continuum, 2004.

Smolin, Lee. *The Life of the Cosmos.* New York.: Oxford University Press, 1999.

Sobchack, Vivian. *Screening Space: The American Science Fiction Film.* New Brunswick, N.J.: Rutgers University Press, 1997.

———. "The Virginity of Astronauts: Sex and the Science Fiction Film" in *Alien Zone: Cultural Theory and Contemporary Science Fiction Cinema,* ed. Annette Kuhn. London: Verso, 1990, 103–15.

Sokal, Alan. "Transgressing the Boundaries: Towards a Transformative Hermeneutics of Quantum Gravity." *Social Text* 46/47 (Spring/Summer 1996): 217–252.

Sontag, Susan. *Against Interpretation and Other Essays.* New York: Farrar, Strauss & Giroux, 1966.

Speed, Louise. "*Alien 3*: A Postmodern Encounter with the Abject." *Arizona Quarterly* 54, no. 1 (1998): 125–151.

Spruiell, William C. "A Lack of Alien Verbs: Coinage in Science Fiction." *LACUS Forum* 23 (1997): 441–452.

Stableford, Brian. "The Third Generation of Genre Science Fiction." *Science Fiction Studies* 23, no. 3 (November 1996): 321–330.

Stapledon, Olaf. "Preface to the English Edition," *Last and First Men.* [1931] N.Y.: Dover Publications, Inc. 1968.

Stebbins, G. Ledyard. *The Basis of Progressive Evolution.* Chapel Hill: University of North Carolina Press, 1969.

Stockwell, Peter. *The Poetics of Science Fiction*. New York: Longman, 2000.

Suppes, Patrick. "Models of Data," in *Logic, Methodology and Philosophy of Science* [Proceedings of the 1960 International Congress], ed. Ernest Nagel, Patrick Suppes, and Alfred Tarski. Stanford: Stanford University Press, 1962, 252–261.

Suvin, Darko. "Goodbye to Extrapolation." *Science Fiction Studies* 22, no. 2 (July 1995): 301.

———. *Metamorphoses of Science Fiction*. New Haven, Conn.: Yale University Press, 1980.

———. *Positions and Presuppositions in Science Fiction*. Kent OH: Kent University Press, 1988.

———. *Victorian Science Fiction in the UK: The Discourses of Knowledge and of Power*. Boston: G. K. Hall, 1983.

Tacha, Frank. "Language and Politics: Turkish Language Reform." *The Review of Politics* 256, no. 2 (April 1964): 191–204.

Tatsumi, Takayuki. "*2001*, or a Cyberspace Odyssey: Toward the Ideographic Imagination," in *World Weavers: Globalization, Science Fiction, and the Cybernetic Revolution*, ed. Won Kin Yuen and Gary Westfahl. Hong Kong: Hong Kong University Press, 2006: 41–54.

Teilhard de Chardin, Pierre. *The Phenomenon of Man*. New York: Harper Perennial, 1976.

———. *The Divine Milieu*. New York: Harper Perennial, 2001.

———. *The Future of Man*. New York: Image, 2004.

Tokaty, G. A. "Soviet Rocket Technology." *Technology and Culture* 4, no. 4, (Autumn, 1963): 515–528.

Torry, Robert. "Awakening to the Other: Feminism and the Ego-Ideal in *Alien*." *Women's Studies* 23 (1994): 343–63.

Traweek, Sharon. *Beamtimes and Lifetimes: The World of High Energy Physicists*. Cambridge, Mass.: Harvard University Press, 1988.

Ullery, David A. *The Tarzan Novels of Edgar Rice Burroughs: An Illustrated Reader's Guide*. Jefferson, N.C.: McFarland, 2001.

Vale, V., and Andrea Juno, eds. *J.G. Ballard*. San Francisco, Calif.: Re/Search 8/9, 1984.

Vinge, Vernor. "The Coming Technological Singularity: How to Survive in the Post-Human Era." Presented at the VISION-21 Symposium, sponsored by NASA Lewis Research Center and the Ohio Aerospace Institute, March 30–31, 1993. http://www-rohan.sdsu.edu/faculty/vinge/misc/singularity.html.

Walsh, Lynda. *Sins Against Science: The Scientific Media Hoaxes of Poe, Twain, and Others*. Albany, N.Y.: State University of New York Press, 2006.

Watson, Ian. "Science Fiction, Surrealism and Shamanism." *New York Review of Science Fiction* (1999): 1: 8–12.

Watt, Ian. "Time and Family in the Gothic Novel: *The Castle of Otranto*." *Eighteenth Century Life* (1986): 177–90.

Weinstone, Ann. "Resisting Monsters: Notes on *Solaris*." *Science Fiction Studies*, 21, no. 2 (July 1994): 173–190.

Weiskel, Thomas. *The Romantic Sublime: Studies in the Structure and Psychology of Transcendence*. Baltimore: Johns Hopkins University Press, 1976.

West, Patrick. "The 'Inrush of Desire' or the 'Grotesque of the Grotesque': A Feminist Reappraisal of Julia Kristeva's Theory of Gender," in *Seriously Weird: Papers on the Grotesque*, ed. Alice Mills. New York: Peter Lang, 1999, 239–257.

Westfahl, Gary. *Cosmic Engineers: A Study of Hard Science Fiction*. Westport, Conn: Greenwood Press, 1996, 39–51.

————. "On *The True History of Science Fiction.*" *Foundation* 47 (Winter 1989–90): 5–27.

————. "Space Opera." *The Cambridge Companion to Science Fiction*, ed. Edward James and Farah Mendlesohn. New York: Cambridge University Press, 2003, 197–208.

————. "Words of Wishdom: The Neologisms of Science Fiction," in *Styles of Creation: Aesthetic Technique and the Creation of Fictional Worlds*, ed. George Slusser and Eric S. Rabkin. Athens, Ga.: University of Georgia Press, 1992, 221–244.

————. "The Words That Could Happen: Science Fiction Neologisms and the Creation of Future Worlds," *Extrapolation* 34, no. 4 (1993): 290–304.

White, Hayden. *Metahistory: The Historical Imagination in Nineteenth-Century Europe.* Baltimore: Johns Hopkins University Press, 1975.

Wigner, Eugene. "The Unreasonable Effectiveness of Mathematics in the Natural Sciences." *Communications in Pure and Applied Mathematics*, 13, no. 1 (February 1960). New York: John Wiley & Sons: 1–14.

Wilson, Bryan, ed. *Rationality.* London: Blackwell, 1977.

Wolfe, Gary K. *Soundings: Reviews 1992–1996.* Baltimore: Old Earth Press, 2005.

Wolin, Richard. "Utopia, Mimesis, and Reconciliation: A Redemptive Critique of Adorno's Aesthetic Theory." *Representations* 32 (Autumn, 1990): 33–49.

Wolmark, Jenny. *Aliens and Others: Science Fiction, Feminism and Postmodernism.* Iowa City: University of Iowa Press, 1993.

Wood, Davis H. "Part 4: Jazz and Science Fiction," *Vector* 205 (July/August 1999).

Wood, Ellen Meiksins. *Empire of Capital.* London: Verso, 2003.

Yaguello, Marina. *Lunatic Lovers of Language: Imaginary Languages and their Inventors*, trans. Catherine Slater. Rutherford, N.J.: Fairleigh Dickinson University Press, 1991.

Yeager, Patricia. "Toward a Female Sublime" in *Gender and Theory: Dialogues on Feminist Criticism*, ed. Linda Kaufman. New York: Blackwell, 1989, 191–212.

Ziman, John. *Technological Innovation as an Evolutionary Process.* Cambridge: Cambridge University Press, 2000.

INDEX

Brown, Frederick, 95
Brunner, John, 107, 132
Bukatman, Scott 2, 193, 233, 267n7, 284n2, 285n16, 285n21
Bulgakov, Mikhail, 86, 128
Burgess, Anthony (*Clockwork Orange*), 31–32, 44, 86
Burke, Edmund, 148, 150–152, 154, 191
Burroughs, Edgar Rice, 36, 132, 222
Butler, Andrew M., 290n15
Butler, Octavia, 10, 201, 249

Cadigan, Pat (*Synners*), 21
Campbell, John W., 25, 112, 141, 196, 202, 246
Čapek, Karel, 128, 191, 252, 253
Capitalism, 26, 46, 58, 96, 128, 137–38, 140, 209, 223, 239, 245, 250
Card, Orson Scott (*Ender's Game*), 197
Carnivalesque, 62, 72, 209
Carter, Angela, 72
Cartwright, Nancy, 122, 282n52
Cawelti, John, 226
Charnas, Suzy McKee, 107
Chernyshova, Tatiana, 116–19
Cherryh, C. J., 76–77, 82
Chronotope, 79, 218, 219, 220, 221, 289n10
Cixous, Helène, 211
Clarke, Arthur C., 56, 73, 167, 168, 169, 254, 259, 285n23
Clement, Hal, 113–14, 129, 20
Clute, John, 9, 83, 137, 267n7
Cognition effect, 75, 139–40, 142
Constable, Catherine, 287n17
Crichton, Michael, 282n46
Cronenberg, David, 9, 189, 192–93, 194, 195, 197, 255
Cyberpunk 10, 26–29, 69, 108, 133, 137
Cyberspace, 2, 133, 251
Cyborgs, 61, 144, 198–99, 213, 265

Damianus, Petrus, 144
Darwin, 23, 81, 87–88, 96, 119, 122, 197, 200, 268n6
Dawkins, Richard, 124
The Day the Earth Stood Still, 86; and Klaatu, 249

Defoe, Daniel, 127, 226, 235, 245; and *Robinson Crusoe*, 127, 228, 229, 231, 232, 239, 242, 245
Del Rey, Lester, 95
Delany, Samuel R., 9, 22, 29, 78, 82, 86, 107, 141–42, 177, 213, 222, 249, 258, 275n3, 281n29
Deleuze, Gilles, and Félix Guattari, 144, 211
Derrida, Jacques, 144, 285n13
Dery, Mark, 267n7
Détournement, 16, 144, 225, 239, 250, 251, 255
Dick, Philip K., 10, 21, 62, 70–72, 100, 102, 178, 192–93, 201, 213, 214, 256, 278n43, 286n6, 288n26
Doctorow, Cory, 31
Donawerth, Jane, 283n54
Dorsey, Candace Jane, (*A Paradigm of Earth*), 177
Dracula, 236
Drexler, Eric, 134, 162
Dystopia, 61, 110, 136

Earth Girls Are Easy, 257
Edelman, Lee, 176
Edison, Thomas, 119, 232, 246
Einstein, Albert, 123
Elgin, Suzette Haden, 107, 177
Ellison, Harlan ("Demon with a Glass Hand"), 100, 199
Erickson, Steve, 107
Eshun, Kodwe, 9
Eugenics, 61, 88–89, 143, 1
Evans Arthur B., 279n1, 285n12
Everett, Hugh, 96, 101, 215
Evolution, 11,18, 19, 23, 30, 32, 33, 45, 54, 56, 60, 61, 87–94
Extropians, 89, 93, 162, 278n41

Fantastic Planet, 258
Fantasy, 13, 56, 63, 73, 217, 258
Farscape, 224, 255
Feminist criticism, 9, 107, 210–11, 248
Ferguson, Frances, 285n13
Ferguson, Niall, 97
Fernbach, Amanda, 293n48

Jakobson, Roman, 14, 20
James, Edward, 279n2
Jameson, Fredric, 9, 96, 98, 140, 217, 272n3, 277nn21 and 24, 284n3
Jetée, La, 99, 100, 198, 256
Jones, Gwyneth, 107, 114, 202, 267n5

Kagarlitsky, Julius, 63–64
Kandel, Michael, 270n29
Kant, Immanuel, 6, 148–50, 151, 157, 162, 163–64, 167; and *Frankenstein*, 152–54
Keller, Evelyn Fox, 283n60
Kennedy, John F., 240, 242, 291n24, 292n26
Kilgore, Dewitt Douglas, 9, 283n54
Kipling, Rudyard, 239, 260
Klein, Melanie, 211
Klingon, 44–46, 90, 190, 201
Komatsu, Sakyo (*Japan Sinks*), 56, 246, 251
Krauss, Lawrence M., 280n13, 281n35
Kristeva, Julia, 176–77, 211
Kubrick, Stanley, 163, 164, 165, 168, 169, 259, 285n23; and *2001: A Space Odyssey*, 147, 171, 181, 224, 241, 253, 259 (and sf-sublime 162–70)
Kuhn, Thomas, 122
Kurzweil, Ray, 89, 162, 263, 264, 279n64, 286n25

Landon, Brooks, 9, 171, 267n7, 270n22, 284n2
Larbalestier, Justine, 283n54
Lasswitz, Kurd, 132, 222
Latham, Rob. 274n34
LaValley, Albert J., 284n2
Le Guin, Ursula K., 10, 39, 78, 82, 86 107, 201, 223, 224, 247, 258, 267n7, 271n50, 275n4; and *The Left Hand of Darkness*, 39, 41–44, 62, 177
Lem, Stanislaw, 10, 29–30, 92, 95–96, 101–2, 128, 190, 200, 247, 251, 253, 259, 267n7, 287n15; and *Solaris*, 10, 34, 212, 251, 255–56 (as limit case of single novum 66–68; as literary grotesque 203–6)
Lennox, James G., 281n21
Lethem, Jonathan, 107, 214
Lévi-Strauss, Claude, 36, 271n50

Lewis, C. S., 115, 222
Linnaeus, Carl, 16
Lopez, José, 134–35, 138, 282n42
Lost in Space, 224
Lucian, 1, 125, 155
Luckhurst, Roger, 283n54, 285n14, 294n3
Lukács, Georg, 276n12

McAuley, Paul J. (*Fairyland*), 72
McGuirk, Carol, 280n8
McHale, Brian, 70, 96, 217
Malmgren, Carl, 9, 273n15
Malzberg, Barry, 136
Marx, Karl (and Marxism), 9, 23, 54, 80, 81, 86, 124, 140, 268n6
Matrix, The, 181, 248, 251, 283n61; as dynamical sf-sublime, 170–75
Matsumoto Leiji, 223
Maxwell, James Clerk, 123
Megatext, 84, 107–8, 275n4
Méliès, Georges, 222
Mellor, Anne K., 153
Merchant, Carolyn, 250
Mercier, Jean-Baptiste, 85–86, 238
Mermin, David M., 269n9
Meyers, Walter E., 29
Miéville, China, 72, 214–15
Milburn, Colin, 135, 282n42
Miles, Margaret, 287n7
Minsky, Marvin, 162
MIR, 243, 292n34
Monsters, 34, 86, 91, 110, 148, 152–55, 195–96, 198–99, 201, 207, 210, 211, 213, 235, 246, 255
Moore, C. L. ("Shambleau"), 193
Moore, Ward, 101, 102, 104, 278n43
Moore's Law, 263, 264
Moravec, Hans, 162, 263
More, Thomas Sir, 35, 126, 155
Morgan, Lewis Henry, 91
Mothra, 194, 196
Moylan, Tom, 140, 272n2, 277n23
Mullen, R. D., 270n34
Münchhausen, Baron von, 126, 247
Murakami, Haruki, 107
Music, and sf, 11–12, 267n9
Mutopia, 27

My Stepmother is an Alien, 256–57
Myth, 3, 4, 6, 7, 46, 57, 81, 84, 93, 115, 116–19, 137–38, 142, 165 192 226, 239 262, 265

Nahin, Paul J., 279n49, 281n34
Nanotechnology, and sf, 133–35
Nation of Islam, 46, 272n59
NBIC, 134–35
Negative apocalypse, 59–60
Neology, 5, 9, 10, 13, 14–46, 120
Neosemes, 18–20, 31, 39
Newness, 5, 7, 13, 15, 16, 18, 41, 47–48, 50, 53, 54, 55, 58
Nexus points, 104–5
Nicholls, Peter, 59
Niven, Larry, 201
Nixon, Nicola, 293n48
Nomenclature, 16; in fruit-fly genetics, 17; in planetary naming, 17; playful taxonomy, 17–18
Noon, Jeff (*Vurt*), 22, 72, 214–15
Norton, John, 121
Novum, 3, 5–6, 23, 49–52, 53–75, 81, 103, 120, 124, 136, 147, 198, 254
Nye, David E., 7, 156–59

Odysseus, 227, 232, 235, 242
Okrand, Mark, 44–45
Ortega y Gasset, José, 83
Orwell, George (*Nineteen Eighty-Four*), 31, 32, 33, 86
Oshii, Mamoru, 10, 199, 283n61

Parable, 20; and parable space, 77, 275n3
Parallel Worlds/Universe/Reality, 6, 61, 78, 85, 98, 109, 220, 230. *See also* Alternative universe/reality/world
Pataphysics, 139, 144; and Alfred Jarry, 282n49
Pearson, Wendy, 9, 283n54, 287n11
Penelope, 233, 242, 257
Penley, Constance, 99–100, 241, 285n17
Person, Lawrence, 274n29
Pesce, Mark, 132, 134, 267n3
Philmus, Robert M., 276n13, 284n1
Pi, 260

Piercy, Marge (*Woman on the Edge of Time*), 86, 107, 177, 238
Poe, Edgar Allan, 195, 239, 246, 259; and "The Facts in the Case of M. Valdemar," 127–28, 189
Porush, David, 278n45
Posthuman/ism, 89, 162, 260, 261, 263, 265
Postmodern/ism, 27, 58, 97, 98, 107, 110, 134, 138, 206, 210, 211, 214, 217, 258
Predator, 190, 194
Primer, 102
Propp, Vladimir, 289n10
Psychoanalysis, 120, 175–77; and the *Alien* films 209–11, 287n21
Pynchon, Thomas, 107, 214, 289n27

Queer, criticism, 9, 141; and aliens, 202, 213, 214, 248–49

Rabelais, Francois, 35,182, 184, 185
Raelians, 46, 142, 272n59
Rathenau, Walter, 244
Realism 6, 30, 56, 82, 83
Retrofutures, 105–10
Reynolds, Mack (*Amazon Planet*), 200
Rickmann, Gregg, 288n26
Roberts, Keith 278n43
Robida, Albert, 86
Robinson, Kim Stanley, 9, 60; and *Red Mars* trilogy, 86–87, 249, 250–51, 258
Robinsonade, 217, 225, 226, 232, 239, 246
Robot, 30, 61, 93, 252, 253, 294n51
Robu, Cornel, 163, 285n20
Rodan, 194
Rose, Mark, 9
Ross, Andrew, 293n48
Rossi, Umberto, 288n25
Russ, Joanna, 9, 10, 62, 82, 86, 107, 213, 248, 267n7, 283n54

Sagan, Carl, 132, 139, 259
Said, Edward, 226
Sapir, Edward, 36, 271n50
Satire, 3, 20, 22, 27, 62, 74, 88, 107, 126, 128, 143, 191, 206, 234, 239, 247, 256
Science-fictionality, 2, 3, 5, 214, 264
Schlegel, Karl Wilhelm Friedrich, 79